Sharon Blackie

The Long Delirious Burning Blue

s
ept
em

b
er

1 3 5 7 9 10 8 6 4 2

Published in 2024 by September Publishing
First published in 2008 by Two Ravens Press

Copyright © Sharon Blackie 2008

The right of Sharon Blackie to be identified as the author of this work has
been asserted by her in accordance with the Copyright, Designs and Patents
Act 1988.

Typeset by RefineCatch Limited, www.refinecatch.com
Printed in the UK by CPI Books Ltd

MIX
Paper from
responsible sources
FSC® C171272

ISBN 9781914613463
EPUB ISBN 9781914643470

September Publishing
www.septemberpublishing.org

Dr Sharon Blackie is an award-winning writer, psychologist and mythologist. Her highly acclaimed books, courses, lectures and workshops are focused on the development of the mythic imagination, and on the relevance of myth, fairy tales and folk traditions to the personal, cultural and environmental problems we face today.

As well as writing five books of fiction and nonfiction, including the bestselling *If Women Rose Rooted*, her writing has appeared in anthologies, collections and several international media outlets – among them the *Guardian*, the *Irish Times*, the *i* and the *Scotsman*. Her books have been translated into several languages, and she has been interviewed by the BBC, US public radio and other broadcasters on her areas of expertise. Her awards include the Society of Author's Roger Deakin Award and a Creative Scotland Writer's Award.

Sharon is a Fellow of the Royal Society of Arts, and has taught and lectured at several academic institutions, Jungian organisations, retreat centres and cultural festivals around the world.

The Long Delirious Burning Blue is Sharon's first novel, emerging from a time when, in the great American south-west, she struggled to obtain a pilot's licence to overcome a fear of flying.

www.sharonblackie.net

Also by Sharon Blackie:

Fiction
Foxfire, Wolfskin and Other Stories
of Shapeshifting Women

Non-fiction
If Women Rose Rooted: A Journey from
Authenticity to Belonging
The Enchanted Life: Reclaiming the Magic
and Wisdom of the Natural World
Hagitude: Reclaiming the Second Half of Life

For David

High Flight

Oh! I have slipped the surly bonds of Earth
And danced the skies on laughter-silvered wings;
Sunward I've climbed, and joined the tumbling mirth
of sun-split clouds, — and done a hundred things
You have not dreamed of — wheeled and soared and swung
High in the sunlit silence. Hov'ring there,
I've chased the shouting wind along, and flung
My eager craft through footless halls of air...

Up, up the long, delirious, burning blue
I've topped the wind-swept heights with easy grace.
Where never lark, or even eagle flew —
And, while with silent, lifting mind I've trod
The high untrespassed sanctity of space,
Put out my hand, and touched the face of God.

John Gillespie Magee Jr

*John Gillespie Magee Jr was an officer in the Royal Canadian
Air Force who served in England during the Second World War.
He was killed in 1941.*

'The past clings to you, like a skin.'

That's what you told me, in that last letter you wrote. You remember: the one that arrived just before the news came. The news that forced me into this final pilgrimage across the ocean, from the deserts of Arizona to this water-logged land where you chose to make your home. Where you came with my father as a newly married woman, ablaze with your hopes and your dreams.

But I have my own take on skins. It's a simple one: they're there to be shed. Like the desert rattlesnake, which sheds its skin two or three times a year. To enable it to grow; to remove parasites. It's a process of renewal, you see. It rubs its nose along the ground until it pushes the skin up over its head – and then it just crawls right on out of it. And leaves it there: a ghostly, inside-out skin. There are millions of them, all over the desert.

A sea of shed skins.

It's just like your selkies, don't you see? – your mythical seal-women. Shrugging off their skin for one night each month, they become another creature entirely. Seal becomes woman; woman becomes seal.

You and your fairy stories.

The truth is that we humans are so much less efficient. We shed our skins piece by piece, flake by flake. Slowly, over time; slowly enough that we never even notice that it's happening. Did you know that we shed and re-grow the outer cells of our skin every twenty-seven days? I'm talking facts again now – did

I

you notice? I've always been more comfortable with facts. And I did some research, after that last letter you sent: by the age of seventy an average person will have lost one hundred and five pounds of skin. Seas and seas of shed skin.

'Golf Delta Charlie, cleared for takeoff.'

The voice in my ear startles me. The sounds and smells of the cockpit leap back into my consciousness; once again I'm aware of your presence beside me. You're unusually silent. Are you ready to go? I can't see your face but I can picture it clearly – that same old small smile, one thin dark eyebrow tilted in amusement. Judging me. Testing. *Come on, Cat – jump. Let's see what you're made of. Look – the other children can do it. Why can't you?* But you needn't worry, Mother – I'm really not going to lose my nerve.

'Cleared for takeoff, Golf Delta Charlie.' My voice cracks and my mouth is dry, but this time it's not from fear. I know you don't quite believe it yet, but I've mostly dealt with the fear.

A firm push of the throttle and the engine begins to roar. We're moving forward quite slowly now; we cross the line at the beginning of the runway and we are in a place of transition. But once we reach takeoff speed, throttle fully open – once I pull the yoke towards me and lift up the nose – well, then we're committed. There is no turning back: we are quite out of choices. We move on and move upwards – or we crash, and the chances are that we die.

And there it goes again: that same old flutter in my stomach as the small Cessna lifts herself gently from the runway. Yes, we're leaving the ground now – and do you see how it is? How all that's familiar – all that's known and understood – falls away there beneath as we hurl ourselves recklessly into this clear blue void. The earth recasts itself beneath us, it pitches and lists as we bank to the south and turn out of the airport traffic pattern. But it's no longer the earth that concerns us here: it's the cold crisp blue of the sky. We've transformed ourselves now:

2

we're creatures of air, and we'll swoop and we'll wheel and we'll soar.

'Golf Delta Charlie, clearing the zone en route.'

'Golf Delta Charlie, roger. Have a good flight.'

Communication ends with a decisive click. We're on our own now; we're heading out west and there's no-one out there to talk to even if we wanted to.

We were on our own for so long, you and I. *You and me against the world,* you used to sing. In the days before it became you and me against each other. And so here we are again – here, just the two of us; so very tightly strapped into the confined world of this tiny cockpit. Together again – now, when I finally get to show you that I've learned how to fly.

Such a perfect day. Do you see the firth down there below us? The water strangely becalmed after the night's wind and rain; sea in the distance merging with sky. Everything so very still. And you – you're so quiet over there; you seem quite relaxed. It's a morning worth relaxing into: on a blue-sky day like this you can see clear into forever. The mountains shimmer in the morning sun, hovering in the distance like a mirage. Currents of air rush by, tumbling around the propeller, slipping under and over the wings, constantly shifting, ever-changing. For a little while longer there's nothing to be done; nothing that will stop me from basking in the healing solitude of these high places.

You always loved planes, didn't you? Sunday afternoons watching the old war movies on TV – *The Battle of Britain*; *The Dambusters*. They were your heroes, you always said. *Pilots! Think how much courage they must have, Cat. To hover all the way up there, in those tiny, flimsy machines. Can you imagine how much courage it must take to fly like that? Taking their lives into their own hands?*

So does it make you happy now, to be flying with me? Did I finally make you happy? I never was too skilled at that. Perhaps

3

a better daughter might have succeeded, but I never could seem to do enough for you. So many ways I found to disappoint you. *For heaven's sake, Cat – smile, can't you? Oh, Cat – don't you have any emotions at all? Why won't you play, like normal children?* And sometimes I would think about the children you lost – all those babies that never were born. And find myself wondering if, somewhere among those lost children, there might have been the daughter you wanted.

I know what you're thinking – that I'm talking crazy. But you were the crazy one; I was the rock. You – ah, but you had no fear. You threw back your head and your red shoes glittered and you laughed and you swung and you danced. You danced, and it seemed that you would never stop. *You're so wooden, Cat. Relax, why can't you? Just close your eyes and let go.*

Let go. Time after time, you said it. You said it that day when you were teaching me to swim: when I slipped off the platform and gashed my face on the side of the diving board. But I wouldn't cry. Not once. Not once on the journey to the hospital; not once as the doctor put the stitches into my cheek. *Let go,* you said, your face flushed and hectic, eyes brimming with anger. *For God's sake, Cat – just let go now, and cry.*

But I knew what happened when you let go.

The past clings to you, like a skin.
The trick is to learn how to shed it.

1
Cat

'Jack – there's no way I'm getting on that plane.' We step off the moving walkway and I clutch at his left arm as if its warm, uncomplicated solidity is all that I need to keep me grounded. And to shield me from the small propeller-driven commuter plane that is just pulling up outside the gate area from which our connecting flight is due to depart. It stops and settles on the wet asphalt like an over-sized mosquito; the drone of its propellers drifts up through the open door that leads to the ramp. And then it happens. Ice-cold fingers creep around my neck and squeeze and let go, squeeze and let go, over and over.

Oh, dear God, not again.

'Honey – we don't have a choice if you want to get to Cornell in time for this meeting.' I flinch as Jack's cellphone shrieks yet again and he groans, stops, reaches into his pocket with his free hand. 'What's the matter with the plane? Wrong colour? Wrong brand?' He flashes me a quick sideways grin and glances at the screen to check the caller ID. He exhales loudly, presses something that makes the ringing stop and thrusts it back into his pocket. 'It's Tom. Doesn't your goddamn boss ever go away? He's probably trying to get hold of you. Do you have your cellphone switched off again?'

'It doesn't have proper engines. Look – it just has those propeller things.' My heart is pounding a deep bass rhythm and a grizzly bear is crushing my rib-cage in a death-grip. There's something wrong here. I know there's something wrong. I can't

5

catch my breath. I can't seem to breathe in properly, and even when I do, I can't breathe out again.

The piercing tones that signal an announcement blare out from a speaker directly over our heads. I jump. A bored female voice announces the arrival of the incoming flight from Ithaca, and all at once I'm aware of my surroundings again. Aware that we're partially blocking the exit from the moving walkway. An elderly woman edges around us with a murmured 'Excuse me', and Jack moves to the side to let a small family group pass by. A little blonde girl with big dark eyes and a purple dress catches my eye and, seeing me stare, smiles shyly; she's holding on to one of her father's hands as he clamps a cellphone to his ear with the other.

'Cat, those "propeller things" *are* proper engines. And there are two of 'em, see? Now isn't that great? One to fly with and one for spare.' He pats my arm and detaches it from his own. He strides over to a row of empty seats that faces the plate glass windows through which the offending aircraft can clearly be seen, and shrugs his overnight bag off his shoulder.

After a few moments I follow him. I don't know what frightens me most: the thought of getting on that plane, or the persistent gnawing awareness that something is seriously wrong with me. But I'm not going to think about that. Not until I get back home to Phoenix. Not until I get the results back from the doctor on Tuesday morning.

I fix my gaze on the aircraft as if I can transform it into a jet by sheer force of will. But it remains resolutely itself, small propellers protruding from the wings like switchblades all set to bore bloody holes in the sky. A door opens in its side and it spews out a clutch of passengers who stagger, dazed, into the full force of the wind that is now erupting into squally gusts, tearing through hair and penetrating coats. They clutch at the handrail as they fight their way down the steps and onto the relative safety of the asphalt. Blue-black storm clouds loom on the horizon and enormous drops of rain are just beginning to lash the windows. I try to swallow, but something is stuck in my throat. The spasms intensify, and helplessness sweeps over me like a dank grey fog. I start to shiver.

I can't do this. Please God, I can't do this.

'Come on, Jack.' My voice cracks. 'You've heard all the stories about those things. It's winter out there, Jack. It's raining, and it's cold. Don't you know that those blades can ice up in winter? And then do you know what happens? Well, I'll tell you what happens. What happens is that they get too heavy and the engine slows and the plane begins to lose altitude and eventually it crashes. That would hurt, Jack. It would hurt and then you're dead.' I'm shrill – too shrill. I try to take a deep gulp of air but something is stopping me and my breathing accelerates in a vain attempt to get more oxygen into my shaking body. I don't know what's happening to me but there's something wrong and I clench my fists tightly and grit my teeth but that only seems to make the spasms worse.

Jack takes back my arm as finally he grasps that I'm not joking. 'Cat, hon. You have way, way too vivid an imagination. Those guys up there in the cockpit, they're trained to fly those planes in all kinds of weather. That's their job. They know how to handle icy conditions. Hell, these guys fly all the time in rainstorms. This is the north-east. Normal winter weather. It's no big deal.'

Can he smell my fear? I can. The sharp, musky scent of a mouse caught in a trap, just when it realises it's out of options. Just before it dies. 'I just don't trust those things, Jack. What if something gets caught in the blades and stops them from going around? What if a blade breaks off?'

'Cat.' He rolls his eyes and sighs, running a hand through permanently dishevelled brown hair. 'Propeller blades don't just drop off.'

'Let's get on a different flight, huh? We'll tell them we missed the connection.' I lick ice-cold lips that seem to have lost all moisture. 'I can't believe Janie did this to me.' Janie is the perfect secretary; she's always very careful to check the aircraft type before she books. She knows I don't do turboprops. Why did she do this to me? I fold my arms across my chest in a vain attempt to stop myself shaking. The passengers are walking up the ramp now; some of them are even laughing and joking as they emerge through the door. A little bedraggled from their brief encounter with the elements, but seemingly none the worse for wear.

'There won't be any different flights. Most of the flights to Ithaca are turboprops. That's probably why Janie booked it.' The customary amused twinkle in Jack's rich brown eyes has been replaced by guarded perplexity. He looks so solid, standing there: so sure. Every inch the voice of reason. And it's just as well that it's Jack I'm travelling with; he's about the only person in the whole company that I trust. He's my friend. The best vice-president of research and development that Sanderson Pharmaceuticals has ever had – or so I'm told. His motto: the job comes first. You can fall to pieces all you like, but do it after you've got the job done.

So why do I feel as if I'm letting him down, as if he's judging me? Because I always get the job done, and I never fall to pieces. I don't even come close. He knows that.

This is just a blip. Just a momentary lapse.

He's watching me closely, appraising, and I can't seem to hold his gaze. I can't believe I'm doing this; I'm as bewildered as he is.

'Come on, honey. Get a grip. You know how much trouble we've had getting everyone's schedules to coincide for this meeting. Stein could be a really important expert witness; we don't want to irritate him before we've even got him signed up. And your New York lawyer buddies are flying up from

LaGuardia; they aren't going to be too happy if we mess up their flight schedules and waste their time. Hell, not at several hundred dollars an hour between them.' I've lost him again; he's rummaging in his overnight bag, extracting a battered plastic wallet overstuffed with documents. He settles himself into a seat with the wallet on his lap and glances back up at me. 'And weren't you just telling me the law department budget is about to go bust?'

He's right, of course.

I need to focus on the facts here. Facts are good. I'm a lawyer: we deal in facts. I concentrate on simply trying to breathe in and breathe out, and hold on to the fact that it took Jack a long time to persuade Joe Stein to meet with us. If it hadn't been for the fact that he and Jack shared a pharmacology lab for a while during their postdoctoral fellowships at NIMH, we'd have had no chance.

The disembarking passengers are dispersing now, drifting off into the airport. So many people, rushing from one place to the next. Everything in a state of perpetual motion. Giddiness sweeps over me but I clutch at another fact: we need Joe Stein for the trial up in Seattle. His recent work casts significant doubt on the claims that Calmate is addictive. And no matter how I feel about it, I don't really have a choice. I'm vice-president of litigation and this trial is my responsibility, and I'm supposed to be in control.

Fact: I can't possibly not get on this plane.

I attempt another deep breath and this time I succeed. My fists turn back into hands and my jaw slowly begins to unlock. Calm, Cat. Calm.

'Okay, okay. I know. But I'm still going to check with the desk before I decide I'm completely out of choices here.' I throw him what I hope is a reassuring smile before I turn away, but he doesn't look convinced.

Smart guy: neither am I.

With the disembarking passengers gone, it's quiet again here at the gate. I make my way over to the desk; a handful of people are clustered in the seats around it, reading newspapers, playing with electronic organisers. The father of the little girl is still hooked up to his cellphone, pacing up and down in front of her. She sits quietly, face grave, staring out of the window. I had a purple dress, too, when I was her age. I wonder what happened to it? I don't remember ever seeing it again after we left Scotland. After we left my father. I pass close to her; she's clutching her battered little teddy bear tightly against her stomach. I wonder what she's thinking. I wonder where her mother is.

The gate agent barely glances at me as I approach the desk. She's frowning down at the screen in front of her, thin red lips rolling from side to side as she silently chews her gum. She looks tired; dark brown bangs hang lankly against her forehead. She doesn't look as if she's having a particularly good day. You and me both, I think.

'Good morning. Can you tell me whether any of the other flights to Ithaca are on regional jets, or are they all turboprops?'

She doesn't answer; doesn't even flicker. My mouth purses and the muscles in my stomach clench violently. Am I invisible? 'Excuse me?'

'I'll be with you in just a moment, ma'am.'

She doesn't even have the courtesy to look at me. I tap my foot and drum my fingers on the grey melamine shelf below the countertop, straining just to keep breathing. What on earth is the matter with her? Is she being rude on purpose? She can't be much older than twenty. Nearly half my age. Doesn't she have any respect? Something is building up inside me and any minute now I'm going to explode. Now. Here and now. Look at me, damn you. Look at me!

Just in the nick of time she tears herself away from her keyboard. She aims an artificial smile at me but it misses and lands in the empty space just over my left shoulder. 'Can I help you?'

Swallowing. And again. Burying the monster that is erupting from my stomach. I repeat my question. 'I asked whether any of the other flights to Ithaca are on regional jets, or are all of them turboprops?'

The gate agent – Tiffany, according to the embossed plastic label above her left breast – raises a pair of over-plucked brown eyebrows. 'You want a regional jet?'

'That's right.'

A man who's just walked up behind me is yelling loudly into his cellphone. I can hardly hear myself think. I turn and glare at him but he's completely oblivious. It's the little girl's father. But where is she? Ah, there. Clinging on to the pocket of his khakis as if he might run away and leave her alone. Does he even realise she exists? She can't be any more than four or five years old. Does he even know she's there? She lets go and wanders a few paces away, her teddy trailing on the floor beside her, and he doesn't even notice. She's your *daughter*, I want to yell at him. Don't you even care?

Stop it. Right now. I clench my fists, turn back to the desk.

'You have a problem with turboprops?' Tiffany blinks: a slow, incredulous blink.

I blink back. 'That's right.'

She raises her eyes to heaven, no doubt asking the good Lord to save her from all the crazy people in the world. One part of me wants to take her by the throat and shake the smirk off her face, another to sink down onto the floor and weep. Another announcement booms out from the overhead speakers and the gate area is beginning to fill with people – I can feel them pressing in on me – and right now I need be anywhere in the world other than here.

And the spasms in my throat won't go away.

What do I have to do to make them go away?

'There's a later flight on a regional jet…' she reels off the flight number and the departure time, 'but I'm afraid it's full.' She presses her lips together in satisfaction and for a moment I hate her and the sudden force of that hatred shocks me. I try to swallow it down; force myself to shrug. Oh, well. The flight would've been too late, anyway. I guess I'm out of luck. And then she looks up at me with the kind of expression you'd expect her to reserve for an escapee from the local funny farm. 'Turboprops are quite safe, you know, ma'am.'

I flush; the scary monster grapples with the weepy child and before one or the other of them wins, I bite down hard and turn away. The large man is still bellowing into his phone even as he pushes forward into my place, almost knocking me over with the laptop case that's slung over his shoulder. He doesn't even see me.

Am I invisible?

Rage, hot, incandescent, sparks in my belly and the monster roars in triumph as I swing round to face him and somehow it happens that I'm yelling 'Excuse me!' and out of the corner of my eye I see Tiffany's head jerk up from her computer screen and swivel in my direction.

The cellphone man stops in mid-sentence and peers down at me in bewilderment. 'Gee, sorry, lady. I didn't see you there.'

'Of course you didn't see me. You weren't even looking.' Is that me shouting? 'Can't you put that damn thing away for a few minutes and just watch where you're going?'

No. Not me. I don't shout.

He stares at me, open-mouthed. There's a movement behind him and the little girl catches hold of his arm. He reaches behind him and pulls her protectively to his side, looking at me all the while as if I'm a mad axe murderer.

Perhaps I am. Perhaps the monster has always been there inside me. Watching. Waiting. Hungry.

Around us there's a sudden silence as conversations ebb and

die and the little blonde girl looks up at me with fearful brown eyes and the monster crumples and flees, wailing its sorrow into the empty air.

I know her. I've known her all my life.

Dear God, what is the matter with me? What am I doing? What am I *doing?*

'That's okay,' I mumble. I raise my hands. 'I'm sorry. I just –' I close my mouth and turn away. I want to fade, to dissolve into peaceful nothingness, just like I always used to do. I want to float up above it all where I can watch from a safe distance. But that doesn't seem to be an option now. In my shame I'm completely visible. My face is burning. I avert my eyes from all the curious faces and make a dash for the restroom. I head for an empty cubicle at the far end of the row, sink down onto the closed toilet seat and bend over, putting my head in my hands.

What the hell is the matter with me?

The little girl's frightened eyes; the look of utter bewilderment on her father's face as he drew her to his side.

What is happening to me?

I close my eyes and see myself as they must have seen me. A thin blonde-haired woman on the cusp of forty with a livid face and brown glittering eyes and an angry twisted mouth and as I watch the features thicken and coarsen and it isn't my face any more, it's my father's – so very alike, they said; you must be very proud of her – and I am that little girl – *stop your whimpering or I'll tan your hide, ye wee bundle o' shite* – I've always known her – and the voices have always been there, won't ever go away and I pull my hair until it hurts and oh, dear God, what is happening to me?

I'm losing it; I'm out of control and I can't be out of control. I can't. It's just not an option. Not here. Not now. Not ever.

Calm. I must be calm. I'm breathing rapidly – too rapidly; I'm light-headed and there's a strange tingling in my fingertips. Calm, Cat. Calm. I know how to be calm. Calm is my speciality.

The original cool, calm and collected, that's me. So very original. Trademarked. Copyrighted. I want to giggle but I'm not sure I'd be able to stop, so I breathe out and hold it and the fog in front of my eyes begins to clear and I will my heart to stop racing and I zero in on the featureless beige door in front of me and, little by little, everything starts to slow down. I focus on each one of the sounds I can hear around me – people talking and doors slamming and toilets flushing – and it's okay: everything will be fine.

Everything is fine.

I'm quite safe now.

This isn't just about flying: it can't be. I've always been a nervous flyer, but this is ridiculous. I close my eyes, try to breathe slowly. Try just to breathe. And it isn't only turboprops: I just don't like flying. Oh, I take flights – I have little choice, really. Phoenix is a long way away from anywhere, and I have to travel – it's my job. But I fly reluctantly, nervously. At every moment of the flight I am alert to the possibility of complete disaster. I am the kind of passenger that you see on every airplane if you look closely enough. The passenger who sweeps confidently on board, perfectly groomed, not a neatly bobbed blonde hair out of place, smartly dressed and complete with all the appurtenances of success: the briefcase, the latest-model cellphone, the laptop, the attentive subordinate. The passenger who sits quite still, with an expression of concentrated insouciance as the plane prepares for departure. The passenger who, nevertheless, gives herself away with little things. A slight drumming of the fingertips on her thigh as the plane waits to enter the runway. An occasional furtive glance out of the window to see what's happening, then a calculatedly casual return to whatever document she is pretending to review. Tension evident in every line of her body. A visible gritting of the teeth as the plane leaves the ground. A sudden brief clutching at the arm of the seat as the aircraft banks steeply to leave the airport's traffic pattern. The passenger who never really relaxes, never really switches off.

But I've never reacted like this before. Not like this. No. This isn't just about flying. This is something else. I don't know what it is, but whatever it is, it's starting to happen to me more and more. I rub my eyes; I can't afford to worry about that now. Right now I'm still breathing and I seem to be able to see again and the shuddering tremors have gone away. I need to pull myself together and get back out there before Jack comes looking for me. I need to get on that plane.

Next week. I'll think about it next week. I'll see Dr Rubenstein and he'll give me the results and once I know the score, I'll deal with it. Just like I always do.

I stand up straight and tall and grit my teeth and walk out of the cubicle as if I haven't a care in the world. I hum a cheerful little tune as I stand at the sink and splash cold water on my face, smiling brightly at the mirrored reflection of the woman next to me. I hold my head high as I walk back to Jack, eyes fixed straight ahead to avoid the stares of anyone who might have seen the altercation at the desk.

Jack looks at me carefully as I approach, but he shows no sign that he was aware of what happened. He smiles, a brief upward quirk of his mouth. 'No luck?'

'Nope.' I lower myself into the seat next to him and force myself to look out of the window at the plane. A couple of men in brightly coloured rain gear are loading baggage into the hold; other vehicles swarm around in a carefully choreographed dance, feeding it with fuel and loading it with trolleys.

The rain is torrential.

He nudges me with his elbow. 'You going to be okay?'

I nod; try to smile. The sympathy in his voice makes me want to cry. 'Sorry. I lost it there, for a moment.'

He laughs softly. 'Bullshit. You're the least likely person to lose it that I've never known. You're a rock.'

I wince. A rock. My mother's voice reverberates in my head. *Cat, I don't know what I'd do without you. You're all that I have. You're my life, Cat. You're my rock.* But don't they know? Even a rock can get worn down eventually. Just like in the desert, back home in Arizona. Hundreds and hundreds of square miles of rock that's simply given up the fight. Turned to sand.

Minutes pass – or maybe hours – as I stare out at the teeming rain. Finally, I'm jolted out of my reverie by another jab of Jack's elbow. 'Come on, honey – buck up. They're boarding.'

And so I pick up my bags, grit my teeth and board along with everyone else. Please God, I think. Please do not let that man and his child be sitting anywhere near me. Please do not let me have to face them again. I avoid Tiffany's eyes as she takes my boarding card, passes it through a scanner and tells me tersely to have a nice flight.

But then I'm sitting down and I can't stop the terror as the storm rages around us and the wind buffets the body of the aircraft and we stumble and rock and fall through the turbulence, and I haven't a thought for the man or his child or for Tiffany or for anything else at all except for the overwhelming need to just hold on.

Jack looks at my hands, clasped tight on the arms of my seat, white-knuckled. My jaw aches from tension. 'You know,' he says, 'I've got just the answer for that.' I snort in response and he laughs quietly. 'The perfect cure for fear of flying. Dr Walker prescribes.'

'Really?' I say through gritted teeth. 'Do tell. Half a bottle of bourbon, perhaps? Or how about a general anaesthetic?'

He grins. 'No. What you need are flying lessons.'

'Flying lessons? Oh, that's a really good idea, Jack.' I brandish my shaking hands before another sharp jolt causes me to clutch at the armrest again. 'Flying lessons? Do I look like I'd be capable of learning to fly a plane? I've never heard anything so ridiculous in my entire life. This plane is already too small for me, and it carries thirty people and has two engines – if that's what those twirling things hanging from the wings are supposed to be. You are completely insane.' There's a high-pitched whining sound and the plane lurches to one side and my whole body is damp with sweat. 'What on earth makes you imagine I'd ever in a million years manage to leave the ground in one of those tiny single-engine toy birds that people learn to fly in? I've seen them at Scottsdale airport.' I shudder. 'I'd scream. I'd have vertigo. I'd have a panic attack.'

He raises an eyebrow and his mouth twists in his trademark crooked smile. 'Honey, I've worked with you for five years now. I've watched you approach situations in the boardroom that would cause most people to quake. I've seen you calm when everyone else is stressed out of their tiny minds, and I've seen you fire up the troops when everyone is sinking into apathy, convinced we're going to lose a case. I've watched you tear a strip off someone who thinks he's your superior because you thought he wasn't taking you seriously enough, and because you do it with that oh-so cool-and-collected British charm the guy doesn't even know he's been had.' He rests a dry cool hand briefly on mine; I resist the temptation to grab hold of it. 'I think you could do pretty much anything you put your mind to, if you would just stop telling yourself all the reasons why you can't.'

I produce what I hope is a crooked smile of my own. 'Ah, but I'm only fooling. Deep down inside I'm the Cowardly Lion, all bluster and noise, searching for my lost courage. Bet you a beer I won't find the Wizard of Oz hiding inside one of those miniature airplanes, holding it out on an emerald-green platter.'

'Hey – get it right when you're quoting great American literature, or stick to quoting your own. It wasn't the Wizard who gave the Lion his courage. It was there inside him all the time. He just had to find it.' He smoothes imaginary whiskers and grins toothily.

I shake my head and turn away. Because Jack doesn't know that the problem isn't just fear: it's that I don't really believe in the possibility of flight. Well, of course I accept that it occurs: I get on board a vehicle at an airport and we travel through the air and when we arrive and I disembark, we are somewhere else. And so logic tells me that flight must exist. But believing in it is altogether a different thing. Because how does it happen? At what point do several tons of earthbound metal transform themselves into a winged creature that can soar, that can glide, that can fly? At what point does the magical metamorphosis occur? At what point does the airplane itself come to believe that it can take flight?

I spare Jack these ramblings, resume my clutching and my hyperventilating and only just manage to restrain myself from kissing the ground when we arrive at our destination. I dismiss the suggestion as just another example of his off-beat sense of humour.

I don't think of it again.

❦ ❦ ❦

We step out of the air-conditioned baggage claim area and even though we're on the lowest level, shaded, heat blasts us in the face. Good old Phoenix. I'm still dressed for Ithaca temperatures, and already the sweat is beginning to form in warm, sticky beads on my back. We're close to the end of October but the temperature is showing no significant sign of cooling down. Sometimes I wonder what I'm doing in this arid hell-hole; sometimes I find myself longing for winter. Thinking of home. Bright, breezy mornings walking along the seafront and your ears hurt and your eyes water and it's enough to blow you off your feet but damn it, you're feeling: you're alive.

But I left home a long, long time ago. I can't go back now. There's nothing to go back to.

I trot after Jack, overnight bag slung over my shoulder and black winter coat over my arm. The place is crazy with activity; frantic travellers laden with luggage jay-walk around the terminal buildings. Taxi horns blare and their drivers gesticulate wildly at driving that doesn't meet their questionable standards. Cars stop and unload in all the wrong places, their apparent aim to cause as much inconvenience to other road users as possible. Shuttle buses swarm like parasites, pulling in and out of loading bays without bothering to indicate or wait for a gap.

Narrowly avoiding a taxi bent on homicide I follow Jack across the pedestrian walkway that leads into the multistorey parking garage. It doesn't take him long to locate his car; somehow he'd managed to find a spot enviably close to the terminal. I watch as he unlocks it and slings his overnight bag into the trunk.

'Drive carefully. Don't get anything caught in those propellers, now.'

'Very funny, Jack.' I fumble in my purse for my car keys – why is it that wherever I put them they manage to escape and work their way down to the very bottom corner of the bag? – and stick my tongue out as he slides into the shiny black Lexus, reverses smoothly out of his parking space, and zooms away with a wave and a grin. As always, he leaves me smiling.

Alone again. My shoulders sag and I exhale loudly. Thank God that's over. I didn't like the journey home from Ithaca this morning much more than I liked the journey there yesterday, but at least this time the weather was calm. And more importantly, so was I. Back to normal. A momentary lapse, that's all it was yesterday. Just a blip, and now everything's fine again. Everything's still.

I trudge on up the ramp and around the corner to the place where I parked the Jeep. A sharp press of the key fob and a familiar, comforting clunk as the locks leap open. The standard-issue black overnight bag is loaded into the trunk; I peel off my navy woollen jacket and drape it over the back of the driver's seat. I've never discovered an elegant way of climbing into a Grand Cherokee wearing a skirt that stops just short of the knees; happily there's no-one close enough to see me struggle. But it's just a quick drive home from the airport – depending on the traffic on the freeway, of course – and then I'll be able to get out of this business suit and into something more civilised. Something loose, something sloppy. And then I'll shut up the mask of competence and efficiency in the closet along with the suit and slam the door and lock it tight.

And wish, just for a moment, that I could throw away the key.

I push the thought away and sink into the deep cushioned comfort of the driver's seat. One turn of the ignition and the engine purrs into life. Air-conditioning on: ah, that's better already. Not too cold, though: just a gentle, cool breeze. I pull out of the parking garage and make my way slowly through the usual Saturday madness at Phoenix Sky Harbour, curbing my impatience at the frequent stops and starts. Once I'm on the freeway I can put my foot down; I can build up speed and start to relax. The traffic's heavy, but it's moving. Heat waves dance off the burning asphalt; sunlight bounces off the hood and angles into my eyes. I can't seem to put my hands on my sunglasses. I switch on the CD player and press the 'play' button, taking my chances on whatever is loaded up. A male voice, thin, plaintive, fills the car. 'I'm gonna be a happy idiot, and settle for the legal tender ...' Jackson Browne. Nope – I don't think so. 'The Pretender' really isn't what I need to hear right now. I press another button, try the radio instead. 'I Believe I Can Fly'. With a sharp burst of laughter I switch it off again; settle for the soft hiss of molten asphalt under my tyres.

A few minutes later, I'm turning north onto Scottsdale

Road. The streets are bustling. Saturday is a day devoted to worshipping the god of conspicuous consumption all across America, and Scottsdale is no exception. The roads are packed with cars heading from one fine 'shopping experience' to another; each store neatly wrapped and blandly packaged so as not to offend, so as to resemble the rest. In downtown Scottsdale the streets are lined with pedestrians exploring tourist traps in the Old Town and the prestigious 5th Avenue stores.

Heading north; manicured concrete and emerald-green lawns dotted with pools and artificial fountains protect residents from the reality of the desert, whilst the carefully placed saguaro cacti pretend to embrace it. I've lived here for ten years now, and still I can't work out why it is that people come to live in the desert and insist on trying to make it into something that it's not. Wasting precious water to maintain grassy verges and golfing greens. Subdivisions that advertise 'lakeside living' in the heart of the desert south-west. Go figure, as Jack would say. And each year the concrete virus multiplies. It constantly reinvents itself, gobbling the desert, encroaching on the mountains, soaking up the water. This is a comfortable place to live, but lately I have become aware that something dark lurks beneath the orderly, artificial façade. Something lies in wait for me, biding its time.

I shake off the fanciful thoughts and crawl on through the traffic. Turning, finally, into a street filled with sparkling stucco-clad houses that bask self-satisfied in the shadow of Camelback Mountain. Not quite Paradise Valley, but close enough to satisfy Adam's aspirations. One more turn and then here we are: another 'custom home', the glare of its white walls so bright that it hurts. Most of the exteriors around here are painted terracotta – supposedly to blend in with the desert landscape. But not ours. Ours is different. Ours screams. The Jeep swings onto the pristine asphalt driveway – and then I see it through the still-open door of the double garage. Adam's car.

Shit.

I'd expected him to be at work. Just as he's always at work on Saturdays – because there's never any rest for a senior partner in a big-city law firm. And I'd really been counting on having that couple of hours alone. To ground myself, before he got home. My shoulders slump as I pull up next to the gleaming white BMW and force myself out and through the door that connects the garage to the kitchen.

Icy conditioned air shivers over me. Too cold. I hate it when it's too cold. He's been fiddling with the thermostat again.

Adam is standing by the refrigerator with an unopened can of caffeine-free Diet Coke in his hand, his air of weary preoccupation lightening as he catches sight of me. I soften; I should be grateful to come home to someone who is always glad to see me. He is a good man; I'm safe with Adam. Safe here.

'Hey,' I say, offering my face for a kiss as he approaches. 'You're home early. Or didn't you go in this morning?' His cool, smoothly shaved skin briefly brushes mine and the faded smell of 'Polo' lingers as he retreats back to the fridge.

Is that it? No ardent embrace? No frantic murmurings between kisses, telling me how much he missed me? No seduction, no ravishment on the central island, sweeping the bowl of fruit and white china jars filled with utensils to the floor in the unstoppable throes of his desperate passion?

'Yeah – we finished up all the trial strategy meetings sooner than we thought yesterday. Went out to dinner. Late night; those guys from the Washington office don't know when to stop.' He runs a hand through short blond hair that is greying rapidly now. Grey-blue shadows under his eyes mar the evenness of his tan. He should take time away from work. Relax a little. 'So I just went in to clear up the urgent stuff this morning and then came right back home.'

I drop my purse and my car keys on the pale, uncluttered work surface; they clatter loudly against the cold tile, crashing through the silence that is beginning to press into the room. I know his eyes are on the back of my neck. My hands grip the smooth, rounded edges of the counter. Beige. It hasn't really occurred to me before but there's no colour in this kitchen; everything is beige or cream or some tasteful, understated variation of it. Cream painted cupboards. Antique white walls. White ash veneer floors. It isn't the air-conditioning that makes me shiver this time. There's nothing out of place. And the cold air smells of nothing at all. Does anyone live here?

I close my eyes; a sudden pang of dislocation tugs at my chest. Do I really live here?

Two clicks, followed by the soft thrum of the refrigerator and the gentle hiss of the air as it swishes through the vents. The sharp crack like a rifle-shot as Adam pulls the top off his Coke.

'How was Cornell?' he asks.

'Oh, you know: it was a university. Like any other. Nothing special.' I turn around to him; fold my arms across my chest. Watch as he takes three or four small sips from the can.

'Witness work out okay?'

'Yup. All signed up.'

'Good job.' A pause. He puts his can down, walks over to me and, smiling, he reaches out to take me in his arms. That's better. Drawn to the warmth I let myself lean in towards him but then his hands touch the blouse that's hanging damp at my back and he screws up his nose and pulls away. 'You're kind of sweaty. What have you been up to?'

My whole body tenses. Sweat: a cardinal sin. Nice women aren't supposed to sweat, not even in the searing heat of the desert. I've always imagined that American women have some kind of neatness gene – something that bestows that enviable ability to look cool and well-groomed whatever the climate. Because if it's some other trick, then it's one that I've never managed to work out. I move back abruptly. Sometimes it would be nice just to be held – really held – sweat and all.

'Sorry.' Why am I apologising? 'I'll go and have a shower in a minute. It's pretty hot out there, in case you hadn't noticed.'

In contrast, Adam's navy polo shirt looks just as crisp and fresh as it would have been this morning when he first put it on, his beige chinos neatly pressed and with a perfect well-defined crease running down the centre of each leg.

'Where have you been?'

The noose tightens around my neck and I feel the muscles in my throat contract. I turn away, clamping down on the monster that so badly wants to be free. No more monsters. Not now. It's a perfectly reasonable, friendly question, Cat. Chill. 'Nowhere. I came straight home from the airport.'

'Was Jack with you?' His voice is sharper now; I can sense his body stiffen.

Where did you go, who were you with, where are you going now, will you be back soon...

I clench my fists as the weight of his need presses down on my head. I can't bear it. I'm not his first wife – I'm not Joanna. There's no need for this. 'Jack didn't need a ride today. He had his own car.'

The sound of the mailman pulling up outside breaks the tension and lets me off the hook. Adam strides off through the garage door and out to the mailbox. I reach for a glass from the cupboard above me and fill it with chilled water from the refrigerator door. I rest my forehead against the cool aluminium surface. There's no reason why I shouldn't tell him what I've been doing – I've absolutely nothing to hide. But I hate this claustrophobic feeling of having to account to someone for every minute of my day. He doesn't really deserve my irritation, but I can't seem to help it. It seems to be my normal state of mind right now.

I watch blankly as he returns, places the mail on the island in the centre of the kitchen and starts to flick through it, sifting out the usual handfuls of junk and stacking them into a neat pile. His face brightens as he opens a large brown envelope and scans the contents. He flourishes a glossy booklet at me, grinning broadly. 'Hey – look here. I sent away for some holiday brochures about Scotland.'

It takes a moment to sink in. What? 'You did what? Scotland? Why?'

He shrugs. 'I thought maybe we could make a trip next summer, get away from the heat. You know I've always wanted to go, take a look at the Old Country. Maybe do a bit of digging into my family tree. And now that your mother has moved there, it'd be great for you all to see each other again.' He catches the expression on my face and sighs. 'Cat, I know you haven't gotten along too well over the years, but hell, you can't go on like this for ever.'

Haven't gotten along too well? That doesn't *begin* to cover it. A flush blooms and spreads hot pink petals across my cheeks. I stand up straight, shoulders back. 'Don't you think we might have talked about this before you decided?' My voice comes out sharper than I'd intended.

He throws his hands up in front of him and backs off towards the door. 'Whoa. I haven't decided anything. That's not how we do things around here. All I did was to send away for some information. Don't you think you're overreacting?'

Overreacting?

He's right. I don't do this. I don't get angry; I hate conflict. He's not used to me behaving like this. I'm not used to me behaving like this.

Why am I behaving like this?

I take a deep breath and move away to the dishwasher, placing my glass carefully inside. A 'cupboard for dirty things', my mother used to call it. She would never dream of using a dishwasher. The scent of lemon air-freshener spills out as I close the door; it mingles uncomfortably with the stale smells of dried-on food and old coffee. 'I'm just not sure I want to go back to Scotland for a holiday. It's not like it's not familiar. After all, I lived there when I was a child.'

'Yes, but how long is it since you were back?'

Thirty-five years. I shake my head, firmly banishing the memories. Oh, no. I'm not going there, thank you very much. 'That's not the point. I'm just not sure I want to go and visit my mother right now, and I can't see how I can reasonably go to Scotland and not see her.'

He rests his hands on the countertop to take the weight of his upper body, and then lowers his head and sighs. 'Cat – you haven't seen her for – what must it be, three years now?' He looks up at me with weary eyes. We've been here before. 'On a business trip to London where you spent, if I recall correctly, precisely three hours in her company over dinner in the noisiest restaurant you could find, you said. So that you didn't have to work too hard at making conversation.'

'Once every three years is more than enough, Adam, thank you very much. You don't know my mother and you can't possibly understand.' Of course, my relationship – if that's the word for something so fragile – with my mother is a complete mystery to him. Adam has two older brothers and two younger sisters and they all adore each other; along with his Mom and Dad they're his best friends in the whole world. He runs back home to Atlanta to visit half a dozen times a year. And I have to admit that when I go along with him, I like the closeness that they have. Maybe I even envy it a little. But it's not something I ever had. It's not something I even understand.

'Well hell, Cat, I wish one of these days you'd explain it to me. You speak to her on the telephone once every couple of months and you come away tearing your hair out. Surely it can't be that difficult. What's the big deal? I've haven't met her once in the five years we've been together. On your annual telephone call on Christmas Day I maybe get to exchange a dozen sentences with her, if I'm lucky and get to the phone first. And I gotta tell you, she seems quite charming to me.'

I throw up my hands and turn away from him. Stare out blindly through the kitchen window. The sun beats down relentlessly on the bleached wooden deck. There's no sign of life out there: it's too damn hot.

Yes, my mother has always seemed quite charming to other people. My school friends all adored her. *Oh, Cat – you're so lucky. Your mum's so much fun. She's so young. She's so pretty. I wish my mum was like her.* Yeah, right. I sigh; I don't want to think about this. Not any time, but certainly not today. 'Let's not talk about it now, huh? You're tired and I need a shower.' I turn; dredge up a smile intended to pacify. Please leave this alone. Please just leave me alone. 'We'll think about it tomorrow.'

'Scarlett O'Hara will never be dead while you're around. Always postponing the difficult stuff.' He means only to tease, but the sharp truth of the statement slices through me and deprives me of breath. Oblivious, he strolls over to me, smiles and cups my face in a large soft hand. 'Sorry, sweetheart. I didn't mean for you to think I'm railroading you. I just thought it might be something you'd like to do – show me where you grew up, and all. It doesn't matter.' He strokes his thumb over my mouth and I watch, cornered, as a light kindles in his eyes. 'But since I'm home early, we have some time to kill. How about we go fool around for a while?'

Fool around – I hate that phrase. Sounds like something a couple of teenagers might get up to in the back seat of a car. And right now it's the last thing I want to do.

I nod with as much enthusiasm as I can muster. Buying time, I rest my forehead lightly against his shoulder.

All I want is to find a quiet room where I can be by myself, where I can lie down and close my eyes and forget about all the stuff that's going on inside my crazy muddled head. But there have been too many times lately when 'fooling around' has been the last thing I've wanted to do. And he doesn't deserve that either. I have no doubt that Adam loves me. I ought to be grateful for it. This is just a phase I'm going through. Maybe it's a phase all forty-year-olds go through. Maybe it's something I'm going to have to get used to.

He breaks away, turns me around and pushes me towards the hall, patting me smartly on the backside.

'It'd be good if you had that shower first, though.'

Sex has never been dramatic for me. Oh, it's pleasant enough, but the expected transcendental experience has never occurred. No lights, no music. No misty merging of souls. Most of the time I feel clumsy, ill at ease. I have to have the lights out; I have to hide my face. I don't seem to know how to turn myself loose. I focus; I analyse. I can't let go.

Adam applies himself to my body with admirable enthusiasm, and I do my best to respond. I touch his shoulders, caress his face. And it's the same old familiar routine. I can predict every movement, anticipate each touch. It's as if he's struggled to learn the steps – and is afraid to improvise in case he loses track of the dance. My eyes are wide open; I murmur my appreciation but inside I'm hollow. Telltale moisture gathers at the corners of my eyes; thank God he drew the blinds. I draw in a deep shuddering breath.

'That's right, come on now,' he whispers, and I don't want to hurt him; I don't want him to feel that he's failed. I turn my face away, inhale again, slowly, but the cool dry air catches in my throat and I gasp. The weight of my isolation presses down on my chest like an incubus.

I don't want this. I don't want it but I don't know how to make it stop.

I let out a series of short ragged breaths and he doesn't see – he doesn't understand I'm not shuddering with pleasure.

I'm crying.

'Good girl,' he says.

And then his breathing is coming faster now – faster and I close my eyes tightly and clench my fists and he convulses against me, fills me.

Invades me.

I want to shrug him off but he's so heavy.

'I love you,' he says.

As he lies dozing beside me I reach across my bedside table for *The Pillow Book of Sei Shonagon*. I reach for Sei Shonagon whenever I can't shut off the thoughts that crowd out sleep. There's something comforting about her lists, the trivia, her preoccupation with the small details of life. The delicate clarity of the prose sweeps clutter from the mind and lulls me to sleep.

But today the magic doesn't work. Quietly, so as not to disturb Adam, I put it back.

Then I close my eyes and make some lists of my own.

Three things that weigh heavily on the heart:

- *A robin, dead under a tree as the first warm promise of spring gently ruffles its feathers.*
- *Having to tell someone that you love them when you don't love them any more.*

I pause.

- *Watching your mother cry.*

2
Laura

The wind is strong this morning; another raw gust bites at her face and tears seep from the corners of her eyes. Tears that seem to be wrung out only by the weather these days. She's become far too desiccated for the real kind.

She stops for a moment; watches as the heron down by the lochside struggles to take off, the unpredictable flurries confounding his usual flight path. The wind is in her face as she makes her way down the steep sloping field, but she tries to focus on the welcome momentum that it will lend to her return journey. Her limbs are beginning to lose the mobility of youth. And the pain in her chest is a little sharper today. She wonders whether perhaps she should have stayed indoors, but it would be all too easy to just clothe herself in darkness and never come out again. She knows how easy it is to lose yourself. To let yourself slip away. And in an odd sort of way she's come to depend on these early morning excursions to the water's edge. The wind helps to sweep away the residues of each night's increasingly bizarre dreams.

Meg's cat makes her way through the fence from the croft next door and joins her, a black shadow dancing among the stones that litter the grass, chasing elusive phantoms that threaten and taunt. Mab: the fairy queen. Such a fitting name for so regal and dainty a creature.

Laura passes through the creaky metal gate that leads to the shore; it closes behind her with a clang. Right there ahead of her is a small rowan tree. In that place of transition, where land meets sea, it clings tenaciously to the rocks that populate the shore. As you look on it from the house you see only how solitary it stands, steadfast and unyielding: proud sentinel. And yet, as you approach it, you can see how the south-westerly winds have battered and bent it through the years. This is no Canute, holding back the tide. Tight though it holds there to the earth, its roots disappearing into small clefts in the stone, refusing to let go, still it bends and it reaches towards the sea. Firmly rooted to one element, still it yearns towards another. Always wanting what can't be had.

She hugs her thick quilted jacket around her, fighting off the insistent intrusions of the wind. The air here is never still. Even on a calm day it seethes with invisible thermals and up-draughts that carry the kestrels aloft as they whirl around invisible, shifting dance floors in the sky. And a symphony of sounds: the whistle of the wind through the cracks in the rocks; the sound of the burn as it skips down from the brae behind the house, dancing from rock to rock, building up speed and hurling itself loudly, ecstatically into the sea-loch. The gulls squealing overhead, competing for attention with the strident *to-wheep* of the oystercatchers. The sudden sharp splash as a solitary seal dives for a breakfast of fish.

This is how Laura begins each empty day. Cut adrift, ship-wrecked, she wanders aimlessly from house to loch, from loch back to house. She looks and she listens and she watches, but she never quite manages to feel a part of it. It is separate from her; it is beyond her. When it rains she roams from room to room, a bewildered shadow severed from its more solid twin. Fingering old, familiar objects in the futile hope of enlightenment. She gazes trancelike out of rain-splattered windows, waiting for the heavens to open and a hand to reach down and pluck her from this purgatory.

She fled here three months ago, to this most unlikely of sanctuaries from the sudden swift severance of retirement. And from the aching hollowness that's the only tangible residue of yet another failed relationship. Back to this wild north-west Highland shore where once upon a time she began her life as a married woman. Over forty years ago. She still doesn't understand why she felt the need to return to this of all places, at this twilight time in her life. Fleeing from a present that drips with failure; fleeing all the way back to a place that is filled with the failures of her past. Yet if she sifts out the memories of Alec and all that he did to her, she is left with echoes of simple tranquillity, of incandescent skies and heather-coated mountains and shimmering seas. A place where she might find the clarity that she needs to break through the murk that enshrouds her. She could hide away here, never need to emerge till she found a way forward. And if no way forward could be found? Well then. This would be a good place to fade away.

And right now it seems that fading away is the most likely option. She has never been so alone in all her life. It isn't in Laura's nature to be alone; she's always needed company. And more than anything else, she's needed a man. Someone to validate her; someone to make her real. Someone to take care of her. But then, let's face it: which of them ever did that?

Joe, perhaps. She closes her eyes against another sharp stab of pain. A pair of blue eyes, a warm crinkly smile. The scent of machine oil and sawdust and the warm hardness of his body against hers. Urgent, seeking. Even at sixty, their lovemaking had the intensity that she'd always craved: the drama, and the passion.

She flinches from the memory. All too new, too raw. Joe had made a pretty good stab at it – at taking care of her. They'd been together for a full five years before he just walked out, a year ago now. Saying she was too needy, too emotional. It was exhausting, he'd said, just being with her. There was a big bottomless pit inside her that no-one could fill. Lord knew, he'd tried and he'd tried but after five long years he was all worn out with it because whatever he gave her, it was never enough. Maybe she should think about trying to fill the hole herself, he'd said, rather than looking for other people to fill it for her. Who was she, anyway? A bag full of stories and fantasies. Was there anything real inside there at all?

Laura had no answer for him then; she has no answer now.

When the barrenness of each day threatens to engulf her, she goes next door to visit Meg. When the weather is fine, Laura will find her out in her herb garden, engaged in vigorous conversation with her plants. Learning from them, Meg assures her with a twinkle in her jet-black eyes: listening to their stories. If it's raining she'll find her sitting in her rocking chair by the ageing Rayburn, eyes half-closed, smiling softly to herself, maybe humming an old tune she learned in the islands when she was young.

Wherever Laura finds her, it is Meg's way to smile and nod and then to stay in silence for a while. At some point she'll turn, and continue a conversation that Laura didn't even know they'd been having. Alert and agile as Meg is, it seems sometimes to Laura that her mind has begun to wander ahead of her in the journey to that dim Celtic Otherworld that she talks about so often when she sits by the fire and tells her stories.

For Meg, too, is a storyteller.

ᚴ ᚴ ᚴ

'A fine day.' Meg removes from the soil hands that bear the faded brown badges of age. 'The elements are kind to us today, so.'

Laura shrugs wearily. She can't seem to shake off the lassitude this morning. Not even the crisp, almost effervescent clarity of the autumn air can pull her around. 'They've been fairly kind ever since I moved here. Haven't seen too much of the infamous west coast drizzle.'

'Ach, but today it's particularly important that it's fine.' Meg turns to her, eyes glinting merrily at the blankness on Laura's face. 'You don't know why, then?'

Laura shakes her head.

'Well, now. What date is it today?'

She has to think hard. The days blur here: she no longer has cause to care what day of the week it is, let alone what date. But then it comes to her, something half-heard on the radio as she brewed the first bleary pot of early morning tea. 'October the thirty-first. Halloween.'

'Aye. Samhain eve, they used to call it, in the old days. And tomorrow is the first day of winter.' Meg wipes her hands on her old green quilted waistcoat and sits back on her heels. Laura wonders how she stays so supple. Her own limbs, a good ten years younger, began to seize up years ago. 'They say that the weather at Samhain shows us the pattern of the winter to come.'

'Well, let's hope it's true. I spent a good few winters up here forty years ago, and every one of them filled with rain and wind.' Or so it seems to her, looking back on it now. Strange how little encouragement the memories need these days, after so many years of refusal. 'Plenty of snow, too.'

'Now that would be the work of the Cailleach.'

'The what?'

'The Cailleach. The Old Woman. An old hag with blue skin and boar tusks who brings winter to the land. Every year she's born again at Samhain.'

'More of your stories.' Laura tries, but she can scrape up only the slightest spectre of a smile. Once upon a time, she thinks, she could have done better than that. No matter how she was feeling, she could always produce a smile. A smile that covered a thousand small sadnesses; a smile that could convince – even dazzle. Ah, but then once upon a time she had energy and hope.

34

Once upon a time.

'And every one of them true.' Meg's face crinkles like a brown paper bag as she grins up, mischief gleaming in her eyes. 'It's the Cailleach who strides across the mountains, whipping up the winter storms and causing it to snow. She rules over the season. Aye, and it's a harsh rule that she brings. One that lasts till the beginning of February, when she's reborn as Brighid, the spring maiden.' She raises an eyebrow as Laura shakes her head. 'Do you not know all this, then?'

'I've never heard it before.'

'Aye, well. Nobody knows the old ways any more, and people have forgotten the old tales. And more's the pity, for they taught us to respect the land and the seasons.' Her eyes fix on Laura's face, sweep like searchlights over the chalky pallor of her skin, the dark smudges under her eyes, the lethargy that permeates every pore of her body. Laura looks away. She knows all too well what Meg sees: the vision of hopelessness that lies in wait for her in every reflective surface whose snare she fails to avoid. 'In the old days, winter was seen as a time for reflection: for tying up loose ends.'

Laura tries to laugh, but it doesn't quite come off. She hates this grey, dull person that she's become. Hates this old woman – this stranger who's beginning to invade her, wrapping her cold winter tendrils around her heart. 'I've all the time in the world for reflection, but I'm not so sure about the loose ends. They don't seem to lend themselves to being tied up so neatly.'

'Maybe not.' Meg shrugs and turns away. 'But it used to be said, all the same, that winter was a time for turning inwards. And not so long ago, before radio and the television came along, it was also a time for stories. The storytelling season would begin again, and folk would gather in the houses of the storytellers and pass away the long nights.' She nods slowly, looking out across the loch to the sea, eyes scanning the far bright horizon where blue sky melts seamlessly into the water. 'Aye, this is the time of year for stories.'

Laura shivers as a random gust of chill north-westerly wind hits her full in the face. 'Stories.' She shakes her head. 'I think I've lost my faith in stories.'

Sacrilege. Stories have always been such an important part of her life. And over the past twenty years she's even made something of a living from them – supplementing her meagre librarian's income by writing stories for children. Fairy tales, mostly.

But now the stories have deserted her. They have retired from her just as it seems that she is supposed, gracefully, to retire from them – and indeed from life itself – at this grand old age of sixty-one years. All done and dusted. Move over now, dear, and let the younger ones have a go. And now all that stretches before her is a never-ending sea of monochromatic, empty days. Days filled only with the past: filled with 'used to be', with 'used to do' ...

She realises that she is pulling out small fistfuls of the grass that she's sitting on, and stops, momentarily embarrassed. Meg doesn't condone plant abuse.

She watches as Meg bends back over the earth, small fork in hand, uprooting the last weak weeds of the season. They are in the section of garden that is mostly reserved for herbs. It's populated by all of the usual culprits: mint, sage, rosemary and chives. A few varieties of thyme, curly and flat-headed parsley. Something that smells like marjoram. But there are many more plants that Laura doesn't recognise at all; Meg grows herbs for medicinal as well as culinary purposes.

Mab darts across the lawn to join them. She loves this game; she pounces and picks the weeds out of the battered wooden trug as fast as Meg tosses them in, pitching them into the air and batting them lightly with a delicate black paw.

'Stories don't seem to work out quite so neatly in real life, do

36

they?' Laura breaks into the silence – a sharp, discordant note. 'And then they just end. Because you get to this point in your life when you're supposed to have finished with your story. All of it behind you, now. Nothing to do except just sit and wait to die.' She sounds bitter, she knows, but right now any attempt at levity seems to come across as false. She hates this too. She's never been a bitter person, though sometimes she thinks that she ought to have been. There have been more than enough knocks and bruises in her life to justify a little bitterness, that's for sure. Though she supposes that she should be grateful to have come this far. After all, she never really expected to make it to forty.

'Well, of course, you can do that if you like. It seems a wee bit of a waste to me, though.' Meg, on the other hand, wraps up even her disapproval in a smile, and you feel nothing but the warmth of it.

'So what's the alternative?'

The question is casual enough, but Meg throws her a sharp sideways glance from under snow-white brows. 'To keep living up to the point where you die, lassie. It's as simple as that. You don't accept anyone else's ending to that story of yours. You keep on writing it, in whatever way you want.'

'Even when you lost the thread of it a long, long time ago?'

'Especially when you've lost the thread of it.' Meg's voice is firm and sure. How do you get to be so sure? Laura wonders. How do you get to be so ... comfortable in your skin? 'And maybe that's part of what winter is for. A time to rest, to let the story find you again.'

Laura shakes her head; it seems to her that some stories are best buried deep. 'I'm not sure I want the story to find me. It hasn't exactly been a great one so far.'

'Oh, aye?'

She shifts uncomfortably on the cool grass. 'Well, you know. Miserable childhood. Worse marriage. Hopeless at

37

relationships. Pretty bad as a mother. Wrote a few nice fairy tales for children, but not much more than that to show for my life except a series of bad choices. I haven't exactly excelled at any of it.'

Meg moves the trug to one side and settles back down on the lawn with her legs stretched out in front of her and her arms behind her back. Dark green woollen socks peek out from a pair of brown tweed trousers that have seen better days; her feet are tucked firmly into green rubber shoes. Never one to miss an opportunity, Mab springs onto her lap, does a couple of circuits, and after a few false starts settles down in precisely the position that she began. Meg looks away down the loch to the mountains, a faraway expression in her eyes.

Laura sits in silence, running a hand over the blunt-cut, thickly knit blades of grass. She wonders if Meg has lost the thread, if she's away in one of her daydreams again, when suddenly she says, 'Why don't you write it down?'

'What?'

'Your story. You're a writer. Write your own story. Maybe it'll help you to make sense of it all. Write it down, and you'll see the pattern.'

Laura rubs eyes that ache from lack of sleep. 'Ah, Meg. If only it could be that easy.'

Meg looks up at her sharply. 'Maybe it *is* that easy. Maybe it's just yourself that's making it complicated.'

Laura flushes and looks down again. Her mind skits away; she doesn't want to hear this. Doesn't want solutions. She is too filled with failure. And she is safe in this failing place – almost comfortable. It's a place that she knows all too well. 'It's all irrelevant, anyway. I can't write stories any more.'

'And why not?'

'Writer's block, I suppose.'

Meg snorts. 'No such thing, lassie. It's all in your mind.'

Laura bristles. 'Whether it's in my mind or not, it's very real.

I haven't been able to write anything for over a year now. The stories just don't come to me.'

Meg laughs: a clear, tinkling sound. That's what I've lost, Laura thinks. That's what's missing. I can't seem to laugh at myself any more. 'Don't they, now. And have you gone out looking for them?'

'Oh yes, I've tried.' And she has tried. She really has. 'I've sat for hours with a pen in my hand, thinking and thinking, but nothing happens. I've tried all the old tricks, but still nothing comes.'

But there are other things, now, that come instead. Ghosts. Memories. Memories that she hasn't allowed for years. And how thickly they flood in, filling this sudden shocking void in her mind.

Meg examines her for a few moments, cocking her head to one side in a sharp, bird-like motion. Then she turns away.

Laura shivers.

Meg moves Mab to one side. The cat looks up at her disdainfully and swishes an affronted tail in Laura's direction before stalking off to settle down on an old wooden bench behind them. Meg kneels again and continues her work in silence, easing the weeds so gently from the soil that Laura suspects they don't even know they've been uprooted until they're dead.

'You should come to the storytelling circle.'

'What storytelling circle?'

'We meet in the village hall. Just a small group of us. Mostly women. Saturday nights, at seven-thirty. We tell stories. Any stories. New and old.' Meg puts her fork on top of the weeds in the overflowing trug and stretches, placing a hand at the small of her back. She grimaces. 'I think that's enough weeding for one day, don't you?' Slowly, she hauls herself to her feet. 'Perhaps it'll help get you started again.'

Laura shakes her head. She doesn't go out these days. A

weekly trip into the village for provisions is the most that she's ventured away from the house since she moved in. She supposes that she ought to get out a bit more, but the days are so short now and it's so cold. And besides, she really doesn't feel like it at all. It's too difficult, meeting new people. It's all too much effort. It's so much easier just to light the fire and spend the day staring into the flicker of the flames. So much easier just to sit, and let the memories carry her away. Though she wonders where it is that she thinks they're going to carry her: right now she seems to be going nowhere, fast.

'I don't think so, Meg. But thanks.' She grits her teeth against the pain in her legs and back, and lifts herself off the chilly earth. She staggers slightly as she stands.

'You'll be doing me a favour, if you come this week.'

'A favour? How's that?'

'I'll be needing a lift into the village. Mairi usually brings me with her, but she has a wedding to go to on Saturday.'

Laura sighs. She can't possibly refuse Meg. Meg has never asked anything of her, and already she's given her so much. Companionship. Friendship, even – and Laura doesn't make friends easily. Not to mention the steady flow of eggs and herbs and vegetables from her garden. She shrugs. 'All right. Just this once.'

Meg's face lights up. 'Ach, you'll love it. Just you wait and see.' She puts her hands on her hips and nods in the direction of the house. 'So will we have a cup of tea?'

❦ ❦ ❦

'Now – who has a story they'd like to tell?' A few nervous titters greet Meg's question; around the circle a dozen heads duck down and are shaken softly from side to side. Meg smiles. 'Well then. I'm going to have to start, I suppose. To get you all warmed up.'

Ah, that's what they want, Laura thinks, as the soft sigh of a collective settling slips through the room. A rustle and a creak as each of the women leans back in her chair and relaxes. Odd that there should be only women. Storytelling used to be the men's territory, surely, in the old days? Or was that only for the more formal occasions? But there are women here of all ages, and each one of them has her eyes fixed on Meg as if she holds the entire wisdom of the world in her grasp.

And perhaps she does, Laura thinks. Perhaps she does.

Meg looks at Laura and winks. She's dressed up tonight, the usual combination of ancient tweed and corduroy swapped for a black woollen skirt and a surprisingly fashionable lavender crew-neck sweater. And a pair of proper shoes over thin black tights. Laura smiles to see them; she would have bet her last penny that Meg simply didn't possess such a thing as a pair of tights. Though Meg, she should have remembered, is always full of surprises.

'I'm going to tell you a Welsh tale tonight. For a change. I heard it told by a Welsh storyteller at a gathering a good many years ago now, when I still used to travel and perform. And Welsh it may be, but nevertheless it's a part of our Celtic tradition. It's the story of Rhiannon.'

Ah. Laura nods, and relaxes. Rhiannon. Here's a story that she knows.

Meg sits back in her chair and clasps her hands on her lap. She closes her eyes and tilts back her head. Almost as if she's conjuring up spirits. And this would be a good atmosphere for a spirit or two. Although the room is bare and shabby, the light from two small lamps on the tables at either side softens and warms. But the corners remain shadowed. The faces around the circle are attentive, expectant; there is absolute silence as Meg opens her mouth to begin.

'Here's how it was, then. Rhiannon was the daughter of the lord of the Underworld, and she was married to Pwyll, one of the kings of Wales. How that came to be in itself is a grand story, but one for another time.'

Her eyes open; flit briefly from face to face to be sure that she has everyone's attention. This is the first time that Laura has heard Meg tell stories in a formal setting, and she is surprised by the crisp clarity of her voice. And the tone is really quite different. It's almost as if she's acting. But then that's what Meg is, after all: she's a performer. A professional storyteller.

'Now theirs was a happy marriage: they loved each other deeply. But the people of Dyfed mistrusted Rhiannon; she wasn't one of them. She was alien to them, an outsider. So they began to complain when Rhiannon remained childless after two years of marriage. "What did Pwyll expect?" they muttered to each other. And, "That's what you get when you marry a princess of the Underworld." So you can imagine the king and queen's joy and relief when finally Rhiannon fell pregnant in their third year of marriage. She gave birth to a baby boy on May Eve.

'But that same night, her baby boy was stolen by a former suitor as she lay asleep in her bed. Well, now: in the morning Rhiannon's six nurses awoke and, looking around them, they saw that the baby was gone. They panicked. They feared being punished because they too had fallen asleep and failed to keep watch. Or even worse – they feared that suspicion would fall upon them. So this was their solution: they killed a litter of puppies, and smeared their blood on Rhiannon's face and hands. They threw the small bones about her bed to make it look as if she had eaten her own child. After all, she was a stranger, a princess of the Underworld. No-one in Dyfed would be surprised by such a deed.

'Shortly afterwards, Rhiannon awoke. She called out for her baby, but the baby was gone. She looked for her nurses, and saw nothing but fear and horror in their eyes. Didn't she remember what had happened, they asked? Didn't she remember killing the boy? Didn't she remember eating him? Rhiannon, of course, knew full well that she hadn't killed her child. But the more the nurses clasped fearful hands to their mouths, and the more they shuddered, the less certain she became. And then she looked around the bed and she saw the blood and the bones, and she began to doubt herself. And the more they pressed their version of the story upon her, the more she came to believe that she had indeed killed and eaten her own child.'

Meg pauses – whether for breath or for dramatic effect, Laura doesn't know. But she raises an eyebrow as Meg catches her eye, because this isn't the version of Rhiannon's story that she knows. This isn't the story that is usually told. But Meg just smiles, and continues with the tale.

'Now Pwyll knew Rhiannon well, and he loved her. And at first he was reluctant to condemn her; he was determined that she should remain his wife. But his counsellors and wise men had never trusted their Queen. After all, wasn't she a stranger to them? And wasn't she a princess of the Underworld? So they whispered into his ear for a full day and a night. They told stories against her, and as the hours passed by Pwyll, too, began to believe those stories. And it seemed that he had no choice but to punish her.

'The punishment they chose was this: that for seven long years she should stand at the mounting block in the castle courtyard. She should stop all strangers, all visitors to the court, and she should tell them the story of her wicked deed. Then she should offer to carry them into the great hall on her back.'

Once again Meg pauses; once again she looks around the circle of rapt faces. The full force of her gleaming black eyes comes to rest on Laura. Laura shifts in her chair, strangely uneasy. 'And so for many, many years Rhiannon told that story against herself. She told it to every stranger that passed through the land. Because that was the burden that she bore: the burden of someone else's story. That story had entered into her, and

43

she believed it. And so it took possession of her, and for many, many years she lived by its punishment. Cast out from the court, and cut off from her husband and from all that she loved.'

Laura frowns, confused; Meg has changed the story. Or maybe what Meg heard at her storyteller's gathering wasn't the true story. The proper story. Because in that version of the story – the one that is written down – Rhiannon never doubts herself. And Pwyll never doubts her, either.

She listens carefully as Meg continues. 'Now in the meantime, on the very same night that Rhiannon's son was stolen, a neighbouring king had found a baby boy in the stables of his castle, lying next to a newly born colt. He raised the child as his own, and the boy grew tall and strong and had an uncommon love of horses. Well, one day it happened that the king heard the strange story of Rhiannon's punishment, and of her missing son. It came to him then that the child he had raised bore a strong resemblance to Pwyll, King of Dyfed. And so he travelled to Pwyll's court, and it was clear to everyone that looked on the boy that this must indeed be the king's son. So Rhiannon's child was restored to her, and she was released from her punishment. And she remembered then the person she had been, and the burden of the false stories fell away from her.'

Meg is quiet; silence reigns in the room. No-one wants to break the spell. Then, one by one, the women around the circle begin to react. Someone laughs softly, another stretches; the young red-haired woman next to Laura rubs her hands in apparent delight.

'That was a good one, Meggie,' someone says and the others nod and murmur their agreement.

'Aye, I've not heard that one before.'

Meg laughs and leans forward. 'Ach, it was only a warm-up. For the next course.' She looks from face to face, smiling gently. 'Now, who'll go next?'

For a moment it seems that no-one else will volunteer, but then from across the circle a large white-haired woman of around Meg's age raises her hand. 'All right, Meggie. I'll take my turn. You'll remember that my grandfather, like yours, was a fisherman. Well, there was a story he would tell me when I was a child – a story about the Blue Men of the Minch. It went something like this…'

Laura drives home slowly in the dark, ever watchful in case a deer should run out from the woods and onto the road in front of them. She remembers how it is during these cold, dark months. How the deer begin to come down from the hills to the warmer ground and the sweeter vegetation. How the forecourt of the local garage is littered with cars that have suffered the consequences of close encounters with them in the dark.

'So? Did you enjoy yourself tonight?' Meg's disembodied voice by her side breaks into her concentration, carrying the clear traces of a smile.

Laura is reluctant to admit it, but finds herself smiling in return.

'I did.'

Meg claps her hands together like a delighted child. 'Of course you did. You love stories. That love isn't going to go away just because you think you can't make them up any more.'

'So it seems.'

'And what did you think of the stories, now?'

'Most of them were new to me. Somewhere along the way I seem to have missed out on Scottish stories. And I thought I knew all about fairy tales.'

'Aye, well they've never been as well known as some of the others. When people think of fairy tales now, they think of Grimm. Or Hans Christian Andersen. Stories from other lands. Rarely do they think of our own.'

Something small and dark scuttles across the road and into the woods. A pine marten? Or just a cat? Laura hunches over the steering wheel; her night vision doesn't seem to be as good as it once was. But then that's what happens when you grow old; just one more sign of the inevitable decline. 'That was an interesting story that you told tonight – talking about stories from other lands.'

'Rhiannon? Aye. One of my favourites.'

Laura glances across at her, but she can't make out Meg's expression in the too-faint glow from the dashboard lights. As she looks back through the windscreen the headlights catch the pale golden gleam of a pair of eyes suspended well above the road. She slows down. A stag and two hinds stand there on the verge, perfectly motionless, grey as ghosts against the shadowy backdrop of trees. She holds her breath until they're safely past. 'But it wasn't the version of the Rhiannon story that I've read. The original. You know – from *The Mabinogion.*'

She can feel Meg's gaze on her, though she doesn't dare lift her eyes from the road again. There are too many twists and turns, too many woods, too many deer. And her reactions are oddly slow; it seems to be taking a surprisingly long time to translate what she's seeing into a meaningful picture.

'Aye, I know the original, all right. But tonight I changed the story a wee bit.'

'You changed the story?' That seems like cheating to Laura. 'Why would you do that? The story is the story.'

'Is it? And how do you think those old folk tales – those old myths and legends – came to be?'

Laura shrugs. 'I've never really thought about it.'

'Think about it, then, lassie. Let's say they were told first of all in one way. With one plot, and one ending. But then, like all stories, they began to change in the telling. Isn't that the way of it? As the years went by, the storytellers would change the stories – make them more relevant for the times. For the audience that was hearing them. Morals changed, and ideas changed, and societies changed – and so the stories changed too. And at various times over the years, people wrote the stories down. But all they were doing was capturing the state of the story at that time. Like taking snapshots, do you see?'

Meg's voice is light, animated. Filled with all the fire and enthusiasm that Laura seems to have lost. But where did it go, she wonders? Where did she lose it?

'And so which of those versions is the real story?' Meg asks, with a flourish of her right hand. 'The one that began it or the one that ended it? Or one of the versions of the story in between? Which teller told it true?'

'I understand what you're saying. But it just seems strange, somehow. Changing an existing story that's been written down as part of a whole series of myths – it feels sort of like changing history. I don't know.'

'Then look at the stories about King Arthur. Every Celtic country has its own version. In Wales he was Welsh. In Cornwall he was Cornish. In Brittany he was French. And each of the stories varies. Not just the names and places, but the details of the legend, too. Which one of them is the right story?'

Laura is silent.

Meg's voice is fierce. 'Listen, lassie: I've been a storyteller all my life. I've told the same stories over and over again. But here's what I've discovered – here's the beauty of stories. Stories are like life. At any point in the tale you can interrupt yourself. You can say: no, I don't like the way this story is going. Maybe you can't go back and change what's happened up until now, but you can think about where the story went astray. You can learn from that. And then you can tell the next section in a different way. And next time you can tell the whole story in a different way. And then eventually you've transformed the story into something new, something better. You've seen it with different eyes.' Laura feels rather than sees her shrug. 'It's not always easy, but it's always possible.'

In the safe cover of darkness, Laura shakes her head.

Right now, so little seems possible.

3
Cat

'It's just not possible, Cat.' Janie tosses her newly dyed champagne-coloured head and waves the pile of pink message-slips at me before throwing them back down on her desk. 'There are only so many hours in the day.'

'I don't do "not possible", Janie. Nothing's impossible.'

Janie folds her arms, sits back in her chair and scowls. Scarlet lipstick bleeds from her mouth into the cracks around her mouth and clashes violently with the burnt orange of her top. 'Yes it is. I'll tell you one thing that's not possible, and that's to be in two or three places at once. There's only one of you to go around. And you're spreading yourself way too thin.'

I perch on the edge of the filing cabinet near her desk and rub my eyes. Were Monday mornings always this bad, or is it only recently that I've begun to dread them so? I had to force myself into the office this morning; must've sat there in the car for a good five minutes or more, staring out across the parking lot and wishing the building away. Just another mirage: blink and it's gone. And Paul Simon on the radio in the background: 'Still Crazy After All These Years'.

Ah, but I was never allowed to be the crazy one, was I?

I'm not sure I even know how.

Come on, Cat – what are you frightened of? Just close your eyes and jump. The water's warm, and it's fun!

Loosen up, Cat. Mummy's going to teach you to do the twist. No, don't just stand there – God, you're so wooden. Swivel your hips – let yourself go, why can't you?

49

'There has to be a way to fit Sherri in. Run it all by me again.'

Janie sighs, reaches for the message slips and shuffles through them one more time. 'Jeff wants to talk to you about the trial team for the Seattle case; I've booked him in at one-thirty. Neil wants to talk to you about Henshaw and Finch; apparently he's not happy with some of their work on the Anderson case. He's down for two. John is coming up at two-thirty: he wants you to take a look through some of the old marketing materials for Calmate. Says they're likely to be an issue in Seattle.' She squints at something she's scribbled on one of the pink slips, holds it a few feet away, then shakes her head and reaches for her over-sized glasses. 'The good Lord knows – my eyes are getting worse every day.' She places them on her nose and glances up at me with a wry twist of her mouth. 'Sixty-two and my eyes are shot to hell. Can you believe it? Jeez, I hate getting old.' She focuses back in on the words in front of her. 'At three you have a conference call with the Seattle trial team. Then at four you have a meeting with Tom; he has some ideas he'd like to share with you –' she looks up and smirks '– about the opening statement for Seattle.'

I groan. My boss is constitutionally incapable of leaving us alone to just get on with our jobs. I'll be lucky to be through by six – it's going to be a long, long day.

Janie slaps the messages back down on her desk and peers up at me over the top of her glasses. 'Bottom line: you just don't have the time to see Sherri today.'

I grit my teeth against a sudden sharp desire to howl. 'She needs to see me.'

'You don't have the time. You have a pile of e-mails a mile long and your in-tray is two feet high. And besides – you already spent two hours with her last Wednesday on the exact same subject.'

'She's struggling, Janie. She's just had a baby and the baby keeps getting sick. Her husband doesn't lift a finger, she's falling behind in her work because of all the time she's taking off to look after the baby and Tom is just looking for an excuse to fire her.' My voice is high-pitched and tinged with desperation.

Ah, no. This won't do. This won't do at all.

Janie's face softens and she sighs again, loudly. 'Bless your heart, Cat, but you can't do her job for her. You're not responsible for everyone's problems, you know?'

I clench my fists. I need to get a grip. Such a little thing. Such a little thing, so why does it seem like the end of the world? 'I'm not trying to do her job for her; I'm just trying to help her find a way through this. It's not her fault the baby is sick. What's she supposed to do? I don't see why we can't cut her some slack for a few months until it all settles down. She's a good lawyer. She's just going through a rough patch.'

Janie's voice is soft, but firm. 'Okay – but not today. I'll tell her you'll see her tomorrow.'

I don't want to give in. There seems to be too much at stake. 'There's no time at all this morning?'

'You have the department heads' meeting.'

The *coup de grace*. I let my head fall back and exhale loudly. 'I know,' she says, 'I know. Your least favourite meeting in the whole wide world. It's at ten, in the boardroom. I put the papers in a plastic wallet on your desk.'

'Thanks.' I should walk away now, but there's a part of me that still won't let go. That's never known how to let go. 'But if it's not till ten, maybe I can fit Sherri in beforehand.'

She slams her hands flat on the desk in exasperation. 'Right. Sure you can. But if you do that, when are you going to check your voicemail and answer your e-mails and talk to whoever feels like popping his head round your office door and saying hi – because you don't do "turning people away" either – and when are you going to find the time to even pee, goddamn it?'

In spite of myself I laugh, and for a brief, blissful moment the tension is gone. Good old Janie. Wonderful cheerful Janie, the perfect secretary. Everybody's mom. And just as fiercely protective. Along with Jack, she's about the only thing that keeps me sane some days.

Some days.

'And if you try to even suggest that you see her over lunch, I'm going to resign. Okay?'

'Okay. You win. Sorry. Let's leave it till tomorrow.'

'That's better.' With a flourish, she throws the message-slips into her trash can. 'Not that tomorrow's a whole lot better, but we have a little more room for manoeuvre.' She tilts her head to one side and looks me up and down. 'You look tired. Cup of coffee?'

I put a hand out to restrain her as she swings her chair around to get up. 'I'll get it. You want a cup too?'

She grins, and her face crinkles into the hundred little lines that she says are her penance for a life in the sun. 'Sure. I just started a pot; it should be ready by now.'

The coffee smells good and fresh, and thankfully she's made it strong. The blinds in my office are down to protect me from the early morning glare, but I have a sudden yearning to see the sky. I pull at a cord and sunlight floods into the room. Across the way in the R&D building the lights are on in Jack's office: another early bird. It feels good to know he's there.

I turn away from the window and my eye falls on the in-tray at the corner of my desk. Janie wasn't exaggerating. Wearily I make my way over, sit down, and turn on my computer. The red message light is flashing on my telephone; while I wait for the computer to load itself up I dial into voicemail. There are ten new messages since I last checked at the airport on Saturday morning. Seven of them are from Tom. By the time I get to number five the hands are clutching at my throat again and my breathing is shallow and rapid.

It's only seven forty-five in the morning.

'Catriona, are you with us?' Tom's voice cuts sharply into my reverie. Shit. There I go again. He doesn't sound amused. Tom isn't accustomed to being ignored and has no patience at all with inattention. Normally we get along pretty well, though we're not exactly kindred spirits. Sometimes he scares the hell out of me. There's something about Tom that is vaguely inhuman: sort of like a male corporate version of a Stepford Wife. Though distinctly more sinister.

I look around; twenty pairs of eyes are fixed on me with varying degrees of amusement. The silence is absolute. 'Sorry, Tom. Just that Monday morning feeling. Guess I haven't had enough coffee yet.'

He looks at me as if I'm from another planet; Tom doesn't permit himself lapses in concentration and can't understand why anyone else would have them either. Across the imposing cherry-wood boardroom table, Jack winks and pushes the thermos jug in my direction. The corner of my mouth twitches in response, and I help myself to another cup of coffee. The black leather chair squeaks as I try to settle back into a position that's comfortable.

God, I hate these meetings.

Tom drums his fingers lightly on the table. Mike Smith, seated next to him at the top of the table, sits up straight and clears his throat. 'Okay, guys: I think everyone's here, so let's get started.' Mike is the Senior VP for Human Resources and Corporate Affairs; pretty harmless as corporate executives go, but a bit too wishy-washy for my liking. Not someone you can rely on to stick his neck out for an employee in trouble, and far too closely attached to the rule book. And to Tom: he follows slavishly wherever Tom leads. They came up through the ranks together, twenty-five years of steady progression. All the way to the top.

'Tom and I have asked heads of function to come along to this meeting to debate a number of important new initiatives that the Corporate Affairs department has been working on for a few months now. The first of these exciting developments that I'd like to focus on is the drafting of our corporate mission statement.'

I let my eyes drift around the table; my fellow department heads are looking at Mike with expressions that range from the enthusiastic to the vacant. Jack looks distinctly nonplussed; I badly want to yawn, and loudly, but I know that Tom, like the night, has a thousand eyes.

'Now, you've all had a chance to take a look at the statement, and some of you have already fed back comments to me.' Mike beams at Lorena, Vice President of Human Resources and the only other woman around a table of men. She has the advantage for Sanderson of being Hispanic as well as female, thus providing the company with a rare opportunity to check off two boxes on their diversity policy at the same time. Mike's gratitude for this heaven-sent blessing at such a senior level knows no bounds; Lorena is the light of his life. I fight back an urge to roll my eyes; Jack's knowing smirk across the table doesn't help at all.

Mike carries on in his dreary monotone; I suppress another yawn. I'm already bored out of my mind and we haven't even begun. I can't seem to concentrate this morning; my thoughts are all over the place. Everywhere but here, in this boardroom, surrounded by earnest, fresh-faced and largely well-meaning executives discussing aimless initiatives that detract from the real business of keeping the company afloat. Not that keeping the company afloat seems nearly as important to me as it once did.

I'm getting old, and jaded.

The air-conditioning is positively arctic; I pull my light linen jacket more closely around my body. From time to time, snatches of corporate cliché flit in and out of my head, tossed back and forth between Mike and Tom with dazzling frequency. 'We need to get all of our ducks in a row here… Make sure we're all singing from the same hymn book… Make sure everyone sees the big picture… We all need to walk the talk on this mission statement…'

The new corporate mission statement. I can hardly bear the thought of it. What do we need a *mission statement* for? Don't we already know what it is that we're supposed to be doing? It landed on my desk about a week ago, a paragraph laden with words and phrases that didn't seem to have any meaning at all, and filled to the brim with glowing examples of the very best in business jargon. Tom and Mike are completely united in their love of the latest catch-phrases. If you can go into solution mode rather than come up with a possible answer, they'll be happy. If you can ramp up the enthusiasm to go forward covering all your (level) bases while delineating the building blocks necessary to nail internal barriers to the wall and keep the train on the tracks, they'll be positively ecstatic. After all, it's a no-brainer, isn't it?

I pushed the mission statement to one side, murmuring imprecations against time-wasting Corporate Affairs initiatives, and I haven't looked at it again since.

So maybe I'd better listen now.

I sit up straight and do my best to look attentive as Mike prepares to read it aloud. He clears his throat noisily before beginning.

'Our mission as a subsidiary organisation of one of the leading global providers of pharmaceutical healthcare is to create, produce and market quality and innovative health solutions to meet the medical requirements of our customers. Our corporate ethos incorporates both the prevention and treatment of diseases, aiming to enhance the health and quality of life of our consumer base. In so doing we are committed to embedding the principles of corporate responsibility and to the process of engaging in dialogue with stakeholders. Sustainable development is one of our key business principles.'

Oh, for God's sake.

Tightness in my chest. Stomach muscles clenching.

Easy, Cat. Take it easy.

I take a deep breath, look up. Mike is grinning proudly around the room as if he's just written the Bible. Everyone else is nodding wisely.

Come on, guys. Can't you see this is bullshit?

'Excuse me, Mike – can I ask a question?'

'Sure, Cat.' He looks gratified.

'What does all this mean?' Swallow. Take it easy now. Smile.

He blinks and tilts his head to one side. 'Sorry?'

I indicate the piece of paper on the table in front of me. 'Look – maybe I'm missing something here, but I really don't see the point of this. It doesn't say anything at all.'

'Sorry?'

Am I the only person that thinks this is nonsense? Or just the only person who cares enough to open her mouth? What is the matter with everyone?

Swallow it down. Calm. You know how to do this. You've done it a thousand times. Sweet reason. Smile.

'To begin with: it takes two long and tortuous, not terribly literate and largely jargon-laden sentences to tell people what they already know – that we're a pharmaceutical company that makes drugs to cure or prevent illnesses.' I look up at Mike and raise an eyebrow. 'Well, no shit.'

Out of the corner of my eye, I see Jack slump down into his chair and bury his chin in his open-necked shirt. I ignore him. 'Then there's a whole bunch of stuff about stakeholders and sustainable development and corporate ethos – whatever that is – and corporate responsibility and embedding this and engaging on dialogue about that… But what does it mean?' I look around the table. Blank faces. 'What's it for? It's not telling anybody anything in the least bit novel or meaningful about who we are or how we do business.'

Tom's voice slashes through the silence. 'Of course it is. For one thing it's telling them we're committed to dialogue on the major issues facing our business.' I turn my head; his eyes are a stony grey. Flint.

Now would be a really good time to shut up.

'Layperson's translation: it's telling them that we'll happily sit down and have a nice little chat with anyone who might be interested in us and what we do, if they'd like us to at all, ever. Terrific. How very neighbourly of us. There's just one problem: it isn't true.' It's clear from the set of Tom's jaw that I'm not providing the kind of 'debate' he and Mike had in mind. 'We don't talk to anyone who wants to talk to us. The Corporate Affairs department spends an inordinate amount of time avoiding uncomfortable "dialogue" with precisely the "stakeholders" that this statement is meant to reassure.' I turn from Tom to Owen, Vice President of Corporate Affairs. He looks away. 'How many journalists have you brushed off in the last week who wanted to have a cosy little chat about the issues surrounding chronic use of Calmate?'

'Come on, Cat.' Owen says, with a sideways glance at Tom. 'You know we don't talk about matters that are the subject of litigation.'

'Which rules out pretty much everything we do, doesn't it? So who is it that we're really saying we'll talk to? And what about?'

Tom's face is rigid, his mouth set in a thin white line. Mike glances over at him nervously and leaps in to try to help. 'To stakeholders. About issues facing the business.'

This is going round in circles. I toss the mission statement on the table in exasperation. 'I'm sorry, Mike – I don't mean to be difficult here –' I ignore Jack's choking cough '– but I just don't get it. We're going to all this effort to produce this statement and we're all going to sit around this table and agonise over a form of words, and then we're going to proudly proclaim it to the world as if it's saying something dramatic. But all it says here is hey – we're a pharmaceutical company, in case you couldn't figure it out from our company name, and if you want to talk to us about anything, we'll be happy to talk back to you. Excuse me if I don't find any of that particularly earth-shattering.'

I have a reputation for speaking my mind, but something in Tom's eyes is telling me I've gone way too far this time.

'Catriona.' His voice is cold as ice. 'I absolutely take your concerns on board, but I think you're over-simplifying things.'

Over-simplifying? The monster is awake again, springing into life and taking hold of my throat. Over-simplifying? 'I don't think I am, Tom. I'm sorry.' I pick up the paper again. My hands seem to be shaking. 'Here's another bit: "We're committed to embedding the principles of corporate responsibility…" What on earth does that mean? Embedding? Embedding them in what?'

Once again Mike steps into the breach. 'In what we do. It means that – well, it means … it means that we're committed to being a responsible company.'

'As though we have a choice not to be? As though it's something to applaud?' Most of the other occupants of the room are looking down at the table and each one of them appears to be holding his breath. Lorena is staring fixedly at me with an expression of utter perplexity on her face. Mike looks as if he'd quite like to weep; Tom grins fiercely like the face of death. Jack is covering his face with one hand and peering out at me from between two fingers.

Unfortunately, I'm on a roll; I can't seem to find the 'off' switch.

'And besides – why should people believe it just because we say so? What are we going to do to be responsible? Isn't that what we should be talking about? Because that just might be interesting to people. It certainly would be interesting to me.'

Tom places both hands flat on the table in front of him. He leans forward slightly. I hadn't noticed before, but his head is far too big for the rest of his body. It sits on his narrow shoulders like a boulder perched on the edge of a cliff, just waiting to fall off. 'If you check your calendar I think you'll find that Mike has called another meeting next week to talk about the development of our corporate responsibility programme. I'm sure you'll be taking that opportunity to entertain us with more of your views. But if you have nothing more constructive to say on the matter at hand I'd like to move on.' He glances around the table, his voice deceptively mild. 'Does anyone else have any comments on the mission statement?'

A heavy silence follows. I seem to have nicely quashed any possibility of rational debate. And I don't even feel better for it. My heart is pounding in my chest and invisible hands still claw at my throat. Steady, now. I take a large gulp of lukewarm coffee but I don't seem able to swallow properly and anyway it's really not what I need right now: the caffeine molecules that are already in my system are whizzing round my brain like a troop of whirling dervishes, making me see spots. I cough explosively and avoid Jack's concerned eyes.

'Okay, guys. If no-one else has any major philosophical problems with the mission statement, let's all agree to adopt it in principle and return any specific – and preferably constructive – comments to Mike by e-mail. Any dissenters?' A pair of cold grey eyes fixes on me but it's perfectly obvious I'd be wasting my breath. And right now I don't seem to have too much breath to waste. I shrug. Everyone else nods or murmurs their assent. They know better than to mess with Tom when he has his sights fixed on something. 'No? Good. Then let's move on. Mike?'

'Well, that was subtle.' He's leaning against the door frame, arms folded loosely at his waist and amusement dancing in his eyes.

'Go away, Jack.' I turn back to the computer screen that I've been staring at blankly for the past several minutes.

'I am going away – I have to leave for Tucson in thirty minutes, then tomorrow I'm off to New York.'

My spirits sink even further. Jack's the only person I can really talk to in this place. And I can always count on him to make me laugh when I begin to lose perspective – it's impossible to take yourself too seriously when Jack's around.

'So what was that all about?' He saunters into the office and throws himself down into the black leather chair in front of my desk. He crosses his legs and clasps his hands behind his head, rocking backwards and forwards.

I swivel round to face him. 'Come on, Jack. You know it was bullshit. Every last word of it.'

'Of course it was bullshit. Most of what Corporate Affairs do is bullshit. But it's the kind of bullshit you're not going to change.'

'I just can't bear the – the inanity of it.'

'Sure it's inane. But it's only a mission statement. It doesn't make the least bit of difference to anything of any consequence.' He sits forward, rests his arms on his knees and jiggles his right foot up and down. 'And if you can get yourself past it, chances are you'll be left alone to get on with your proper job.'

'Whatever that is.' The sigh that escapes my throat is loud and comically tragic in tone; it even surprises me.

He raises a dark, bushy eyebrow. 'Oh, my. It's more serious than I thought. Having an existential crisis, are we? Or did you just get out of bed on the wrong side this morning?'

I force a smile. Shake my head to try to dispel the gloom. Mustn't be so melodramatic – get over it, Cat. 'Never mind. Just having a bad morning.'

'Another one?' His eyes are sharp, questioning.

I choose not to answer the question. 'I can't believe you just sat through it all and didn't say a word.'

'I know which battles to fight, sweetheart. And so do you when you're thinking straight.'

Thinking straight? Is that what it is? Is that what's happening to me – am I losing the ability to think straight? Maybe that's what happens when you turn forty: the beginning of a slow, inevitable decline into senility. Adam would probably blame it on hormones. But somehow neither explanation rings true. A persistent little devil jumping up and down and waving its arms in a corner of my mind is telling me that this whole problem is arising because I'm only just beginning to think straight.

And I don't want to even think about the possible implications of that.

'And the trouble is,' he continues blandly, 'that when you pick a battle, advisable or not, you sure do go all out to fight it.'

Yes, I sure do. Which is odd, really, because I can't seem to do the same thing at home. But at work a Cat emerges who I can almost admire. A Cat valued by all of her colleagues, and respected. A Cat who doesn't doubt; who knows and accepts her own worth and competence. A Cat who bears no traces of the cautious propitiatory twin that dominates the rest of her life.

But then it's so much easier to be passionate when it's on behalf of someone else, or over a matter of principle, isn't it?

'Earth to Cat?'

I start. 'What?'

He's frowning; poor Jack. I'm normally so much more stable than this. 'Are you okay?' he asks. 'Really?'

'Yes.' I brush off his concern with a hastily manufactured smile. 'But I'm not so sure about everyone else. Did you see poor Mike's face?'

He grins. 'He'll be down in the labs knocking back the tranquilliser samples later on, you just see.'

'Maybe we could get him to slip a few to Tom. Because somehow I suspect I'm going to suffer for my outburst.'

'If I get back from New York and find your severed head adorning one of the security gateposts I'll know you've really pissed him off.'

As always, he's succeeded in making me laugh. 'Get out of here.'

He pulls a face as he hauls himself to his feet and stretches. 'That's the trouble with you Brits. So cold, so dismissive.'

'Away with you. I'll see you later in the week – when will you be back?'

'I'm not back in the office till next Monday. So I guess I won't see you till the party on Saturday.'

For a moment my mind is a blank, but then it hits me. Oh, God. The party. My fortieth birthday party. I shudder. 'Thoughtful of you to remind me about that. For a few blissful hours I'd almost forgotten.'

'There's no escape from the heavy hand of Time ...'

'Run along now, Jack, like a good boy.'

He leaves with a wave and a lopsided grin.

I rest my elbows on the desk and place my head in my hands.

🐾 🐾 🐾

The waiting room is cool and painted in soothing shades of peach and magnolia; the inoffensively beige carpet is plush underfoot. Tastefully bland copies of pastoral landscapes lurk contentedly in lamp-lit corners. The kind of music that is often described as 'ambient' is playing softly in the background; magazines like *Town and Country* and *Golfing Today* sit cheerfully on cherry-wood side tables like promises of glossier days to come.

There are only two other people waiting. A grey-haired man in a navy blue suit and pristine white shirt beats a staccato rhythm on his crossed knee with long smooth fingers. Every couple of minutes he takes his cellphone out of his pocket and looks at it accusingly, unable to believe that no-one is finding it necessary to call him. A perfectly made-up middle-aged woman stares blankly into space, her face frozen into immobility. At the slightest sound, she jumps.

There is something about the certainty of mortal illness that lends a strange lucidity to the world around you. Each one of your senses is on full alert, responding energetically to small things that normally would pass you by. In the ten-minute period that I am kept waiting, each individual second parades itself before me like a carnival float, full of colour and music and life. 'Look at me,' it shouts. 'Aren't I grand? Just look at me and enjoy me while you can.' Laughter drifts out through the open window of the reception area; the sun slips through the horizontal bands of the blinds and paints the floor with glowing stripes.

The grey-haired man throws a disgruntled glare in my direction when eventually I am called: he clearly thinks that these people have no sense of priority. I smile at him serenely and float across the wide expanse of carpet and on down the corridor to Dr Rubenstein's office – our 'family doctor', though I've never had occasion to consult him for anything other than a minor throat infection. I place my hand on the doorknob and all at once the vivid space that surrounds me dissolves back into grey.

And all I can feel is my heart pounding rapidly in my chest and a quiver starting up in the muscles of my legs.

Dr Rubenstein smiles at me cheerfully as I enter the cool, bare office. His small, slightly rotund body is dwarfed by the enormous wooden desk in front of him. He waves me in. 'Come in, come in. Have a seat over here, Ms Munro.'

I can't seem to produce any kind of a sound. I manage a brief grimace masquerading as a smile as I perch on the edge of a vinyl-clad chair by the side of his desk. I fix my eyes on his face, carefully monitoring every expression, trying to work out just how bad the news might be.

He peers at me over a pair of round, metal-rimmed spectacles that sit snugly on a small bump halfway down his nose. 'Well, I've received all of your results now, from the cardiovascular and respiratory specialists.' He clears his throat noisily and shuffles rapidly through the pieces of paper in his hands.

Here it comes, I think. Here it comes.

'The good news is that they can't find anything physically wrong with you.'

It takes a moment for it to sink in.

I stare at him, blankly. 'Nothing at all?'

'Nothing at all. Strong as a horse, by the looks of things. ECG perfectly normal, lung function above average, throat and chest X-rays clear. Everything else – blood tests, urine tests – all show results well within the normal ranges. You're in pretty good shape.'

I close my eyes for a moment and allow myself, finally, to exhale. 'Well. Obviously that's good news.'

Good news doesn't even begin to cover it. I have been so sure that my body was harbouring some rare, fatal disease. Something to explain the hot, suffocating feeling that closes in on me at random intervals in unpredictable places, the sudden inexplicable hammering of my heart and those strange dizzy spells when people dissolve into mist and the room spins wildly around me. 'But then how do you explain the symptoms I've been having?'

'Well, in a case like yours, the first thing we have to do is rule out physical causes.' He shifts a little in his seat and rustles the papers loudly. 'When we've done that, we're left with psychological causes.'

I blink. 'I'm sorry?'

He takes off his spectacles and places them on the desk. 'What I'm saying, Ms Munro, is that your symptoms are psychosomatic.'

Psychosomatic? 'You mean I'm imagining them?'

'No, no, no. I'm sure they're very real. Otherwise you wouldn't have come to me, would you? No, no. Of course not. What I'm saying is that they're psychological in origin.'

I frown; I can't seem to process what he's saying. 'I'm sorry. I'm just not following you. Psychological?'

He smiles gently. 'I believe that you're suffering from symptoms of anxiety. Panic disorder, to be precise.'

'Panic disorder?' My brain is a fug. I don't seem to be able to do anything other than parrot back his words.

'That's right. The kind of symptoms that you described to me – feeling of constriction in your throat, palpitations and tightness in the chest, hyperventilation, dizziness – all of these are symptoms of anxiety. Once we've ruled out physical causes, that's the diagnosis that we're left with.' I stare at him, speechless. 'So what I'd like to do next is refer you to a psychiatrist.'

My head jerks back. 'A psychiatrist? You've got to be kidding.' A psychiatrist? He's telling me I need to see a psychiatrist? He can't be serious. I'm supposed to be the stable one in the family.

No, no, no. This can't be happening.

He sighs and runs a hand through thick, curly grey hair. 'A psychiatrist will be able to treat you for panic, you see. Chances are he'll put you on antidepressants…'

'Antidepressants?' My voice is shrill now; the spasms are building once again in my throat. My hand flies up and rests there protectively. 'Absolutely not. I'm not depressed.'

'I didn't say you were depressed, Ms Munro, but antidepressants are the treatment of choice for panic disorders. He'll also very likely want to talk to you about things like relaxation and breathing exercises. All of this will help you bring it under control.'

Fire burns in my cheeks. This can't be happening to me. Not to me. I clench my jaw, lift my chin. This isn't happening. 'I have no intention of taking any kind of medication that messes with my synapses. I work for a pharmaceutical company; I know about these things.'

'Then when you see the psychiatrist – his name is Dr Benson – I suggest you make your feelings known to him and I'm sure he'll take them into account and maybe concentrate on the more psychological therapies.'

'No. No way.' I shake my head, laugh shakily and pick up my purse from the floor. I have to get out of here. I have to get out. 'I'm sorry – I'm not going to be seeing any psychiatrist. I'll sort this out for myself.' Just like I've always done.

'Ms Munro…' he hesitates. I pause, not wanting to be rude. I look down; fix my eyes on the floor. The carpet is an unpleasant shade of dark brownish red. The colour of old blood. Please, I beg him silently. Please leave it alone. I don't want this to be real.

'Obviously, I can't force you to seek treatment. But I can't recommend it strongly enough. Anxiety and panic disorders may not be life-threatening, but they can seriously interfere with your quality of life. Right now your condition is manageable, though clearly very uncomfortable. But if it gets any worse – if you start to have full-blown panic attacks – things could be very different. Life could become very difficult.'

I keep my eyes down and shake my head vigorously.

He sighs and sits back in his chair. 'Okay, then. I'll leave it up to you. This has obviously been a shock to you. But I want you to go home and think about it very, very carefully. Read this, and then look up anxiety and panic disorders on the internet.' He reaches over to a shelf behind him and selects a booklet that he holds out to me. 'There are some websites listed

66

here that might be helpful.' I take it without even looking at it and stuff it into my purse. 'Do a bit of research, and then if you decide you want to go ahead with treatment, just call the office and let them know. Then I'll send a referral letter to Dr Benson as soon as I can.'

I nod and stand up, my mouth tight and my cheeks still flaming. All I want to do is get the hell out of this office and away from the mortification that is burning its way through my body. This can't be happening.

'You know, Ms Munro –' his voice brings me to a halt again just as I reach the door. I turn back reluctantly to face him. 'I'm a general practitioner – I'm no expert in anxiety disorders. But I've come to notice something over the years I've been in practice. Often it's the most unlikely people who develop panic disorders. The people who always seem to be perfectly in control. The ones who always look like they're coping.' He shrugs. 'It's got to come out somehow, you see. You can hold it in all you like – you can hold it in for years and years – but sooner or later, something's got to give. It may not seem that way to you right now, but you're one of the lucky ones. Your body's giving you a wake-up call, and if you take my advice you'll listen to it before you find yourself back in this office in a few years, in need of chemotherapy or heart bypass surgery.' He smiles faintly as I flinch, and waves a hand in the direction of the door. 'End of lecture. Go home. Take some time to think it through properly.'

Blindly, I make my way back out through the waiting room, hurl myself into the elevator and stumble out into the parking lot. A stray spasm clutches at my throat and tears of frustration rise in my eyes. Anxiety disorder. I blink them furiously away. This can't be happening. Not to me.

Not to me.

I sit in the car with the engine and the air-con running for an indeterminate period of time, my head thrown back against the headrest, eyes tightly shut against the incessant glare of the sun. *Panic attacks. Psychiatrist. Psychosomatic...* The words spin round and round in my head, dancing on the rubble that used to be the solid foundation of my world. This can't be happening to me but it is – it *is* happening and it's getting worse and I have to do something, I have to, because I can't go on like this, I just can't.

I take a deep, shuddering breath. It's okay, Cat. It's okay. You'll deal with it, just like you always do.

But I'm not dealing with it. Look at me. Just look at me.

Something has to change.

I open my eyes and sit up straight. I'm not going to see any psychiatrist. I'm not going to take any pills. Antidepressants, for God's sake!

No, no pills. But then what?

The sun is blinding; I reach down into the compartment between the seats and extract my sunglasses.

I'm not going to give up. I'm going to beat it.

I place the glasses on my nose. Anxiety? Panic? Just two more words for fear.

And I'm so very tired of being afraid.

'Cat's a little Scaredy-Cat! Cat's a little Scaredy-Cat!' The voices rise and fill the far corner of the grey concrete playground where we always spend our dinner breaks when it's not raining.

I lift my chin. 'No, I'm not. I'm not scared. I just don't want to play, that's all.' I mustn't let them think that I'm bothered by what they say: that I'm frightened. But I can't play handstands. I can't take off my glasses, and if I keep them on I might break them. Then Mummy would be cross, and we don't have very much money since we left Daddy, and so we wouldn't be able to afford a new pair and what would happen to me then?

They giggle and nudge each other but thankfully this time they decide to leave me alone and get on with their game. As always I stand apart, watching the others whoop and laugh as they see who can achieve the most fluent, the most elegant handstand. Sniggering at each other behind their hands as their skirts fly back down over their faces and their regulation waist-high navy blue knickers are exposed for the world to see.

'Come on, Four Eyes!' Mandy is the ring-leader, the meanest of all the girls. When we're in class sometimes she sits next to me and pretends she likes me so that she can see my answers when we do tests, but at playtimes and dinner times she teases me and calls me names. Janice says she's just bluffing and I'm taller than she is anyway and I shouldn't be frightened of her, but Janice doesn't wear glasses. And Janice can do handstands. 'Come on, Scaredy-Cat! Everybody else can do handstands. Why can't you?'

When I don't answer she starts to chant 'Four Eyes, Four Eyes' and the other girls clap their hands and join in. I clench my fists and turn and walk away without saying any of the answers that are in my head. 'Because if I take off my glasses I can't see properly. Because if I keep my glasses on I might break them.

'Because I might fall.'

When I arrive back at work, the cubicle outside my office is empty: Janie is out at lunch. I slip into my office and close the door behind me, leaving the light off so that no-one will know I've returned. I switch on my computer, access the internet and search under 'Flight training, Phoenix'.

Ten minutes later, I pick up the telephone.

≰ ≰ ≰

'I'm Jesse.' He smiles, a one-sided upward tilt of his lips and a crinkle of pale blue eyes: an unexpected contrast against the tanned skin. 'I'm going to be your flight instructor this afternoon.' A large warm hand clasps mine in a firm grip.

'Hi.' I swallow. An army of particularly active frogs seems to have taken up residence inside my stomach. 'Catriona Munro. But most people call me Cat.'

He tilts his head to one side. 'You're Scottish?'

'I was born there, yes. But I was raised in England.' My voice cracks. Heat rises up in my cheeks; I clear my throat. 'I'm surprised you know the difference,' I say, fighting to keep my voice light and steady. 'Not many Americans can tell.'

Someone brushes past me with a murmured apology; the small reception area is bustling. A couple of young guys dressed in shorts and tee-shirts stroll past carrying headphones and clipboards. They look so focused, so purposeful. A couple more sit chatting in chairs in a corner, and two older men are having a lively conversation with the pretty young brunette behind the reception desk. Cheerful voices, laughter. Everyone seems so normal. So relaxed.

'My grandfather – on my father's side – was Scottish,' he says. 'He made sure I got it straight. Moved from one set of mountains to another – left the Highlands and ended up in Montana.' I risk a quick glance up at him and the eyes crinkle again. How old? My age? Younger? Difficult to say. No visible grey, but then it never shows anyway in hair that colour: wet sand on a warm sunny beach. But he's not too young, thank God. Old enough to entrust with my life.

My life? Dear God. I can't believe I'm doing this. I fold my arms around my waist and focus on holding myself together.

'So. You're booked in for an introductory flight.'

'That's right.' I smile as brightly as I can and glance away. I'm afraid to look into his eyes: afraid of what he'll see in mine. Afraid that he'll discover I'm a fraud and turn me away. That he'll refuse to let me fly.

What will become of me then?

'Ever flown before?'

'Only commercially. I've never had a flying lesson before, if that's what you mean.' Through the plate glass window behind him I see half a dozen small planes. All in a line. Neat and white, noses thrust forward, presenting themselves for inspection. I don't want to look at them, but I can't seem to help myself. Their wings are tied with ropes to metal rings set in the concrete. Are they so very insubstantial, then, that they need to be tied down?

Like toy planes. With toy engines and toy wings.

A knotted rope tightens around my neck and digs into the small hollow at the base of my throat.

Stop it. I'm going to do this. I'm not going to chicken out now.

Oh, hell.

I take a long, shuddering breath and exhale loudly. Bracing myself, I look up into his face. 'I guess I'd better come clean. I'm scared of flying.'

Thick straight eyebrows flicker upwards for a moment and then settle back down again. His lips twitch up to one side. Is he laughing at me? 'Okay. Well, let's just see how we go, shall we? We're only going to be in the air for half an hour or so.'

'All right.' I clench my hands into fists; they're sweaty. What is he seeing? A forty-year-old woman filled with fear? Pale and perspiring, abject terror lurking in the depths of her dark brown eyes? What a waste of time, he must be thinking. Poor frightened little mouse. *Scaredy-Cat, scaredy-Cat!* I flush and turn away – shrink a little, inside.

'And if at any point it gets too much for you and you want to come back down, just holler. Okay?'

My chin flies up. 'It won't get too much for me.'

He shrugs, the half-smile still firmly in place. 'Whatever.'

Ah, who am I trying to kid? No doubt he's already dismissed me – already decided I'm going to fail. But I'm not going to let

71

him be right. I'm going to see this through. I just have to make it through this one lesson, just to show myself that I can. And then I don't ever have to do it again.

Fly. Just this one time.

He leans back against the reception desk and rests his hands in the pockets of his khaki-coloured chinos. The loose white shirt is neatly pressed; sleeves rolled up. No uniform here; I like that. A little less formal. A little less intimidating. I'm already quite intimidated enough.

'All we're going to do today is take off, go out into the desert a little way, stay up there for twenty, thirty minutes and then come right back in to land. While we're doing that I'm going to be talking you through the very basic elements of flying a plane.' His voice is brisk, business-like. 'I'm not going to go into a whole lot of detail today; all the theory comes later, if you decide you want to continue. This is just to give you a feel for what it's all about.' His eyes flicker over me, appraising. Instinctively, I stand up straighter. 'You ready?'

I nod, hoping that I look more certain than I feel. The receptionist follows him with her eyes as he passes behind the desk, reaches down under it and picks up a couple of sets of headphones, a small metal clipboard and a set of keys. His movements are unrushed, fluid. Uncluttered. He looks competent enough. Competent enough to entrust with my life?

He turns around, catches me watching him. Smiles slightly. 'I have around five thousand flying hours. Several hundred as an instructor. I fly training aircraft out of this airport three, sometimes four days a week.' He nods. 'You'll be okay.'

I blush and look away. Am I really so transparent?

'Let's go.' He strides off across the reception area and I fall into step behind him. We pass through a doorway that leads on out to the line of aircraft I spotted from inside. Swallowing convulsively, I follow him down to the end of the row. He comes to a halt in front of a small white aircraft with a royal blue stripe running along the length of it. A pair of ridiculously flimsy wings is attached to the top of its body. A single propeller consisting of two thin metal blades is perched on the end of its conical nose. The whole contraption is just a few inches taller than I am.

Tiny droplets of sweat burst out through the skin on my brow. Hastily, I rub them away.

I can't believe I'm doing this.

He brushes a hand lightly over the edge of the wing. Soft as a caress. 'This is the aircraft we're going to be flying in today. She's a Cessna 152, call sign Four Tango Two November Romeo.' He points to a group of large black letters and numbers near the tail. 'Most of the time we shorten it right down to Two November Romeo.' He leans up against the door; the whole plane rocks under his weight. Dear God. It can't possibly be so insubstantial. Not if we're going to fly in it. How can it possibly be so insubstantial? 'If you don't know your aviation alphabet yet, don't worry: you're not going to be working the radio this time. Just remember Two November Romeo, and then you'll know when Air Traffic Control is talking to us.' He pauses, and I tear my eyes away from what looks like a very fine crack in the place where the wing joins the fuselage. Once again, that slight smile. 'Come over here and look at her properly.'

Reluctantly, I approach the plane. He steps to one side and opens the door; heat bursts out from the cockpit and smacks me in the face. He throws the headphones onto the nearest seat. It's covered in cracked red vinyl and looks as if it's seen better days. How old is this airplane, anyway?

'As you'll see, she has two seats and she's dual control. One set of controls for the pilot, one for the co-pilot. Both sets operate all of the time. You get to sit in the pilot's seat, but I always have instant access to the controls if anything doesn't go quite according to plan.' Blue light twinkles in his eyes, but I don't find it comforting. The knotted noose tightens around my neck as I peer into the tiny, cramped space.

In there? We're supposed to fit two people in there?

'The first thing we have to do, before we even think about flying her, is a pre-flight inspection. To check that she's safe to fly.' I close my eyes. I don't even want to imagine that there's a possibility that she isn't. 'I'm going to run through it myself this time; it's more important right now that you get a feel for flying. But you need to follow along with what I'm doing; see how she's put together. Here's a copy of the checklist.' He pulls a couple of laminated cards out of a pocket in the airplane door and hands one to me. If he notices that my hands are trembling as I reach out to take it, he doesn't comment. 'I'll explain what I'm doing real quick; if you decide to go ahead with lessons, then of course we'll need to get into all of this in more detail.'

I follow him obediently around the aircraft as he pokes and prods and tests and inspects, but everything he shows me is a blur. I'm aware of his voice, light and low in the background, but I can't seem to focus on anything at all. My attention flits from place to place, hovering like a butterfly frightened to land. The steady strength of his hands as he runs them over the plane, testing and manipulating; the sweaty plastic feel of the checklist in my fingers. The dry, throbbing heat that radiates off the asphalt, and the shiny white body of the airplane itself, so bright that it hurts your eyes.

People really fly in these tiny things? In the air – all the way up there?

I can't believe I'm doing this.

The instrument panel is crammed full of knobs and switches and dials and a bewildering assortment of displays. It might as well be the space shuttle for all the sense that I can make of it. The vinyl seat burns through the thin khaki cotton of my pants and there's so little room – he's so very close to me – the

74

bulk of his shoulder extending into my space and his arm warm and solid against mine. But there's nowhere to go to, nowhere to retreat, and the seat belt and shoulder strap are pinning me down...

Calm, Cat. Calm. Breathe. Deep and slow. Good long pause between breaths. Shoulders down, forehead smooth. Unclench those stomach muscles. Relax, relax, relax. I recite the mantra to myself – the relaxation sequence rapidly memorised from the book of stress reduction exercises that I found in Barnes and Noble on Wednesday night – but I just can't seem to make it work.

And still he talks on. Can it really be this complicated? Are we ever going to fly? Part of me hopes not – hopes we'll come across a hitch, hopes we'll run out of time. And part of me just wants to get it over and done with, because this anxious anticipation is driving me insane.

A sharp jolt of electricity courses through my body as he leans out of his door and suddenly yells 'Clear prop!' He flicks a few switches, pulls a few knobs; he turns the key in the ignition. There's a shuddering roar as the engine catches and my heart starts a wild pounding in my chest – then the propeller is turning and my head is spinning and the entire aircraft trembles in its eagerness to get going, like a dog held back on a leash. He gestures that I should put on my headphones; I adjust them to fit and his voice, soft and low, slips into my head.

'Is the headset working? Can you hear me okay?'

Mouth dry, I nod.

'No, you need to speak. When we're flying I'll be looking at the panel or out of the windows, not at you.'

He sounds amused. I clear my throat. 'Sorry,' I say. 'I can hear you.'

And it all feels so strange now – as if I'm trapped inside a bubble. The world outside is muted and blurred, as if it's shrunk right down to this miniature cockpit – his voice inside my head and my voice inside his. Just the two of us, side by side, and the straining delight of the plane.

'Okay,' he says, 'so here we go. First thing we need to do is get airport information – which runway is active, what the wind speed is and what direction it's coming from; all the things that we need to know before we take off. We get that from the Automated Terminal Information Service, or ATIS...'

I can't believe I'm doing this.

You steer the plane with your feet, he says. Yes, the rudder is on the tail but you use the rudder pedals to turn the nose. Just put your hands in your lap, he says, as I frantically grapple with the wheel. The control wheel only works in the air. You put your left foot down to turn to the left; put your right foot down to go to the right. It couldn't be easier. No, those are the brakes, at the top of the pedals. Just use the rudder – that's the section below. Keep trying, he says, but it's next to impossible – we're completely out of control. We're weaving all over – all over the taxiway. Put your hands in your lap, he says – just use the pedals. You'll soon get the hang of it.

Dear God, if it's this hard on the ground, how hard is it going to be in the air?

He stirs beside me. 'You okay?'

I jerk my head. Up and down. Speech is a step too far. The runway sweeps away to our left like a sinister grey highway to hell. What am I doing here? More than anything else in the whole wide world I want not to do this. How would it be if I turned round to face him, if I asked him to just turn back? I could say I was sorry; it was all a big mistake. I shouldn't have come here. I shouldn't have believed I could ever do this. What made me believe I could ever do this?

Oh, it's a waste of time, isn't it? You'll never learn to swim: you just can't let go. How did I ever manage to give birth to someone so timid? Forget it, Cat. Let's just forget it, shall we?

'We'll be taking off soon. You okay with that?'

I clench my jaw, turn my head and I look at him properly for the first time. His is not a conventionally handsome face: the nose is maybe a little too long, the cheekbones a little too high. A strong face with a thin, sensitive mouth that twitches up at the side again now as he waits for me to finish my inspection. But it isn't his face that grabs your attention, that reels you in: it's his eyes. Light and clear and when you look into them you can't get a fix. Like the feeling you get when you tilt your head back and stare right up at the sky. Dizzy sky, stretching into the distance like a clear blue road to infinity.

A bead of sweat tickles its way down the length of my face. Ah, look at me here – I'm an utter wreck. I just can't do it. I should never have believed I could do it. What was I thinking, to imagine I could do it? I open my mouth to say no.

'Yes.'

He smiles. I turn away, perplexed.

'Good,' he says. 'That's good. So now I'm going to call for permission from the tower, switching to frequency 133.1. Keep listening; keep your hands on the yoke and just watch and feel what I do.'

I stare blindly out of the windscreen as he presses the red 'talk' button on the control wheel. What in the name of God am I doing?

'Chandler Tower, Cessna Four Tango Two November Romeo ready on Four Left, departing south-east.'

A pause and a crackle, and then: 'Cessna Two November Romeo, taxi into position and hold.'

'Position and hold,' he says. 'Two November Romeo.'

He pushes in a small black knob; the engine rumbles and we move forward. We turn. We turn, and we take our position on this strip of asphalt that marks the boundary between scorching earth and the relentlessly blue Arizona sky. My hands clutch, white-knuckled, at the control wheel. They're so small beside his. Tanned hands and arms, with a light scattering of fair hairs catching the sunlight. Large hands, brown, with long fingers, bony knuckles and short neatly clipped nails. Hands that are resting lightly on the wheel; hands poised and ready to take these controls, to propel us into the sky.

A knife slices into my chest.

This isn't happening; I can't be doing this. Part of me splits off and watches, interested, from a safe distance. *Where are you, Cat? Where do you go to all the time?* An aircraft lands on the runway to our right; I watch it with detached curiosity because it has nothing to do with me. I'm perfectly calm. Why wouldn't I be? This isn't really happening. This isn't me; I'm not the kind of person who willingly puts her life at risk. I don't take risks at all. No-one would believe this was me.

A sudden sharp pang of loneliness; that old familiar feeling of isolation. No-one knows that I'm here today. No-one is watching, nobody waiting; I have left no traces. If I should fall from the sky, no-one would believe it was me. *Cat?* they would say. *You've got to be joking. Cat wouldn't do that – she'd be too afraid. That's not our Cat,* they'd say. *It must be someone else with the same name.* I left work at three o'clock, without explanation. Janie looked at me oddly; it isn't like me to drift away on Friday afternoons in search of an early start to the weekend. But I couldn't tell Janie I was taking a flying lesson; she'd think I was crazy. It took her three months to stop talking about JFK Junior's fatal accident last year. And Adam? What could I possibly have told Adam? It was hard enough telling him what Dr Rubenstein had said. He looked at me in total perplexity. 'Panic attacks?' he said. 'But I don't understand. What have you got to panic about?'

Jack? I could have told Jack, of course. After all, this was his idea. But Jack is away. And besides, I wanted to wait before telling Jack. Because what if it all goes horribly wrong? What if I pitch a full-blown panic attack in the air? I wouldn't want to go back to Jack with a story of failure.

I don't want to go to anyone with a story of failure.

I don't do failure.

'Two November Romeo, cleared for takeoff.'

The voice in my ear startles, piercing the cocoon of unreality in which I've wrapped myself. Moth-like, fear unfurls its wings and takes flight. I shake my head but no-one is watching. He pushes in the throttle; the engine roars and the airplane shudders. Slowly, so slowly, we cross the white line at the beginning of the runway but we're picking up speed now and suspended, powerless, eyes fixed ahead of me, I watch as the runway sweeps on past us in a pale grey blur.

'Rotate,' he says steadily, 'pull back. We're approaching fifty knots.' The control wheel slips towards me and the nose is lifting and we're straining upwards and surely we're not going to make it but then oh, dear God, we're off the ground.

Reality reasserts itself like a slap in the face and I'm slick with sweat, horrified to the core of my bones.

I cannot believe that I'm doing this. We are rising now, rising and I'm trying not to look as the earth slips away beneath me and a chasm opens up in the place where my stomach should be. Eyes fixed to the instrument panel as though, if I turn away, the airplane will dissolve around us, leaving no other choice than free-fall through the unforgiving desert sky. Holding the wheel in a death-grip, knowing for certain that if I let go or even loosen my hold we'll plummet to the ground. I am holding us aloft by sheer force of will, risking an occasional glance at the horizon to be certain that our wings are level. But then we're turning and isn't the nose too high? – and the wings are dipping and I know we're going to fall, to slide, to just slip down in a beautiful graceful dive, because how can it be possible that the air supports us so, how do we dare presume?

And then we're level again and he takes his hands off his wheel. He turns to me and smiles, blue Montana skies shining out of his eyes, all space and distance and glory. 'Hey,' he says. 'You're flying.'

Time is suspended as we twist and turn, back and forth between the cold blue clarity of the sky and the blinding glare of the desert sun. The smell of the cockpit: vinyl seats, hot plastic, dusty electrics, the faint acrid whiff of combustion. The constant droning vibration of the engine, the rhythmic thrumming of the propeller. Sweat breaking out of every pore and running down my skin in small rivulets. The sun fragmenting through a web of small scratches on the Perspex windscreen, a kaleidoscope of orange and blue light. A lone cloud on the western horizon, floating in the haze like a mirage. And all the while I grip and I clutch, my movements tense and jerky and uncoordinated.

He has picked up on the fear that seems to have taken complete possession of me: I couldn't think to hide it from him in this small space. And so he requires little of me, restricting himself to short explanations, to simple manoeuvres – minor altitude changes and shallow turns. I can't seem to speak; I don't take very much in. I am surrounded by sky, by light that dazzles and bewilders. Nothing here is solid.

I don't know what to do, here in this place. I don't know how to be. Each time the wings dip, I lean in the opposite direction, trying to balance it out. As if my small weight is all it would take to just tip us over and cast us on down into the flat, burning landscape below. 'No,' he says, 'go with it. Go with the turn. Let the wings go – that's what they're built for. Let her wheel – let her swing, a little. She's built for this. Just let her fly.'

Dear God, I'm flying. I can hardly breathe and my chest is so tight I can hear every beat of my heart pounding hard against it. My stomach is in knots and blood throbs at my temples but I'm flying. Do you hear me, all of you voices? Do you hear me, Mother? I may be paralysed with fear and I may be dizzy with vertigo and part of me may want more than anything else in the world to be back on solid ground – but just this one time I'm doing it. Just this one time, I'm flying.

'Ready to go back down?'

I am so relieved that without thinking about it I turn my head and look at him for the first time since we took off. I am mildly surprised to find that the plane manages to keep itself in the sky quite nicely without me supervising it. All I can do is nod. He's completely relaxed, quite unfazed by my fear, by my lack of response.

'Okay, then. First of all we have to find our way back to the airport. Do you have any idea where that is?'

'Somewhere down there, I imagine.' My voice cracks as I nod vaguely in the direction of the ground.

He has the grace to laugh and out of the corner of my eye I see him shake his head. Lord alone knows what he's thinking.

'Okay, then let's just head down thataway, shall we? My controls.'

With relief I loosen my vice-like hold on the wheel and place my shaking hands in my lap. The airplane is all his and he's more than welcome to it: I am quite happy to relinquish the responsibility for keeping us safe. But still something in me can't just relax and let him take over. Compulsively, my eyes move in turn from the instrument panel – where I check the altimeter reading, just as he's shown me how to do; to the windscreen – where I check that the propeller is still turning; to the window on my left – where I make sure we're still the right way up. This is all so very unlikely; I can't quite seem to come to grips with what I'm doing here. And then without warning he pulls the throttle back and the sound of the engine falls off a little and my heart skips several beats and I clutch at the seat, feeling every muscle in my body tense in shock.

'It's okay, it's okay,' he murmurs softly – crooning, almost, in the kind of tone I could imagine he might use to gentle a frightened bird. 'If we want to descend, one of the things we have to do is to reduce thrust – that's the power that the engine produces...' I catch snatches of his explanation between the rhythmic waves of panic as I wait for the aircraft to settle into a new attitude. '...We also need to slow down, to reduce our airspeed – so we're going to lift the nose a little...'

I shake my head and close my eyes; I hardly dare look. Can't possibly be a good idea. How can we descend if the nose is pointing upwards?

'...And generally we need to be at an altitude of around a thousand feet above ground level when we enter an airport traffic pattern...'

I try to follow what he's saying but still can't seem to process all this information; my attention wanders as he makes the radio calls. The pressure of the headphones around my ears is beginning to hurt and I shift them around on my head, looking for a more comfortable spot. I don't find one.

'Can you see the airport now?' The airport? I scan the horizon and the ground around us but I don't understand the patterns and the distances; I can't make out anything remotely resembling an airport. I don't even know where to begin to look. 'Right there, see it? Around five miles out at twelve o'clock.' He points. I stare in the direction of his finger. What direction is that, anyway? East? North? I have no idea. There's nothing much there. Just flat, featureless desert in one direction. A handful of surprisingly green cultivated fields in the other. And right out ahead of us, a whole slew of housing developments in various stages of construction. 'Right there. Just look out in the direction that I'm pointing. See?' I bend my head in towards him and follow his line of sight. Look again. 'We're too far out to see the runways clearly yet, but can you see the control tower?' The tower? It was white and round, that's all I can remember. So I look for something white and round. Scanning; sun behind and to the left of us now, the horizon ahead of us obscured in a typical polluted valley haze. Is that...? Yes. A tiny white blob protruding from the ground.

'I see it.'

'That's good. It always helps to know where to bring the plane down.'

I manage a grin.

'When you're down here in the practice area – what we call the Greenfields – here's how you find the airport. You keep Interstate 10 – look down there below you – to the west, and the San Tan Mountains over there to the east.' I look down, out of the window by my side and the grin fades; I'd forgotten how high we were. 'Then you'll see the tower right ahead. You aim the plane in that general direction, until you get close enough to see the field and make out the runways and enter the traffic pattern. Which is what we're going to do now...'

We're coming so close now, but still I can't relax. I turn my eyes forward, and focus on the flat space of the airport – follow the runways obsessively with my eyes, afraid to look away in case they disappear on me. He points out another aircraft – down there, just below us; we're to follow it in. I'm only half-listening to the voices that crackle through my headphones.

For a moment we seem to be flying away again – flying right past the airport. I crane my head around, look back at the runway – then the magic words seep into my consciousness: 'Two November Romeo, cleared to land...'

And we're turning back so sharply now but we're too close to the ground and the nose is so low and surely this isn't right? – and I clutch at the wheel and I want to pull it back but he says,

'It's okay, Cat,' and we're levelling off – and then there it is: the runway. Right there ahead of us, there through the windscreen, so close now, so very close and we're floating on down, we seem to be floating... The main gear touch down very softly. The front wheel follows, a few moments later. A perfect landing.

We're on the ground.

I let out a breath that sounds almost like a sob.

'There you go,' he says quietly, as he works his feet on the brake pedals and rudder and we swing off the runway. 'There you go, now.'

We pause for a while as he talks on the radio yet again and then pulls onto the taxiway with its completely impenetrable signs and markings. In a minute or two we arrive back where we started all those aeons ago. He parks the airplane right where we found it, pulls out the throttle, cuts the mixture and turns off the ignition.

Entranced, I watch the propeller winding down, finally coming to a halt. The silence is startling. He opens his door to get out, but I find that I am incapable of movement. I don't seem to have the use of my legs, and my hands are shaking as I unbuckle the seat belt. Overcome with vertigo, I close my eyes. My black tee-shirt clings wetly to my body. The door opens beside me, and wordlessly he lifts me from the plane. The ground feels strangely insubstantial beneath my feet.

'You okay?' he asks me as I tentatively let go of him, reacquaint myself with concrete, with buildings, with the earth.

I take a deep breath and find that I am smiling as I exhale. Before I can falter or think or change my mind I open my mouth and the words fly out. 'When can I have another lesson?'

He laughs abruptly. He looks confused, disconcerted. 'Why are you doing this?'

Why am I doing this?

The smile fades and I clench my jaw so he will not see the sudden, rare threat of tears.

84

Why am I doing this?

Listen, I want to say to him: Listen. Have you ever woken up in the morning, stepped out of your house and noticed that the ground all around you has shifted? In some subtle, sinister way that you can't quite define? You see the cracks in the driveway and you know it's not just the heat of the desert sun that's caused them. Something is shifting, you think. Something is giving way, and you have no idea at all how to stop it, how to wrest back control. You plug the cracks with concrete, sand over the joins but the next morning there they are again. They smile darkly at your rising fear.

Why am I doing this?

Listen, I want to say to him: I don't know. All I know is that right now it feels as if my life somehow depends on it. That if I don't find a way to fly free of it, the earth will rise up and swallow me, snatching me down, down into the underworld, never to emerge, never to escape. And I'm no Persephone; there's no Demeter to rescue me from the clutches of the dark god. I will need wings to fly from this sunless place.

But of course I do not say this. I look into his eyes and the steady firmness of his gaze defeats me. He doesn't look like he's ever had a day's doubt in his life. I smile wryly; I become myself again. 'Congenital insanity?' I suggest. 'Midlife crisis?'

Gently, he shakes his head, looks at me intently, eyes narrowed, measuring, assessing. I raise my chin and return the gaze as steadily as I am able. I need to do this more badly than I can put into words, and something in him seems able to grasp the need even if the understanding of it eludes him. Because eventually, he shrugs. 'All right,' he says. 'All right. You got yourself a flying instructor.'

I walk across the burning concrete and out to the parking lot with a spring in my step and what is undoubtedly an utterly inane grin on my face. Clutched tightly against my chest is the tangible evidence of my initiation into the world of flight. 'Jeppesen Pilot Logbook', it proudly declares in the bottom right-hand corner of the hard black cover.

Pilot.

The Jeep has been baking slowly in the afternoon sun; I unlock the driver's door, bracing myself for the rush of hot air that hits me in the face. A tangle of sweaty blonde hair falls in a clump over my eyes and I run a hand through it, wishing I'd had the good sense to tie it back. I start the engine and perch on the edge of the driver's seat with my legs sticking out of the car. The air-con will need to blow a little cooler before I can bear to get in properly and close the door.

I open up the logbook and run my hand reverently over the first page and the first entry. It shows the date, the aircraft type and identification number, and then the route of flight. In the column that's headed 'remarks and endorsements' he has written in clear, tiny print: 'Discovery flight: pre-flight, run-up, takeoff.' There are more numbers in the next columns: I have achieved precisely one takeoff, one landing and 0.6 hours of flight in the 'single engine land' aircraft category. Around thirty-five minutes. How odd to see it so simply, so clearly defined, that hazy interval when time stalled and hung and merged with space and light and sound. And then his signature: Jesse J. Gordon, followed by a long number that presumably represents some kind of flight instructor identifier.

Jesse. A good Montana name. It suits him.

The car is cooler now; I swing around and close the door. The traffic is already building as I head out onto the highway and drive north to Scottsdale: the Friday evening rush hour getting into full swing. It's going to take me forever to get home. But I can't seem to bring myself to care. For once, as I drive, I am not burdened by the increasingly obvious truth that every aspect of my carefully constructed life seems to be falling apart. I am not thinking of what to do about Adam. I am not thinking about the daily and ever more nonsensical grind of life as a corporate lawyer. I do not care about who to be or where to live or what to do with the rest of my life. In my mind, I am flying.

Now that the fear has passed, only elation remains. Every few minutes the enormity of what I've done washes over me and a wild burst of laughter escapes my lips. I clench my fist and press the knuckles hard against my mouth to curb the deliciously mounting delirium. I have just taken a flying lesson. I have just taken the first step on the road to becoming a pilot. I plan to fly a plane. I plan to fly… I have just left the ground in a thirty-year-old two-seater tin can with a couple of flimsy wings attached and an engine that looks no more complex than that of the average lawnmower. Two slender strips of metal have propelled me into the sky as they spin and hum and weave their giddy dance through the warm sparse molecules of desert air. Into the sky where, against all odds, I have managed to remain. I have placed my hands on the control wheel and I have pressed my feet on the rudder pedals and I have caused us to wheel and to swoop and to soar and I have not fallen out of the sky. The gods did not strike me down for my hubris; my wings did not melt and cast me down into the glistening, shifting sea of sand below.

I giggle again at the uncharacteristic burst of excess. But I cannot believe that I've done this. I certainly can't believe that I'm planning to do it again. None of it makes any sense. This isn't how I am. I am not a brave person.

I reach up and adjust my sunglasses. I don't have to wear spectacles any more – not since I was thirteen – but just the slightest touch of the sunglasses on my nose brings it all back. Back then, if I removed my glasses, I would see two of everything. The world would dissolve into duplicates and doppelgangers and I could never be sure which was real and which the mirror image. And by then my life was quite uncertain enough. So I clung to my glasses. They set me apart from the unshrinking souls, the children who had faith that they would not fall. The children who knew that even if they did, there would always be someone there to pick them up, dust them down, and set them on their feet again.

I was not one of those brave children.

I look up; a small plane is circling around above me like a large buzzing insect. I have been there. Up there, with them. I cling to my elation; I won't let it seep away into fear. I won't think of intangibles. I slow, and crane to see up into the sky again. And beyond, higher up in the deepening blue, white vapour trails from the jets passing overhead. Lines as straight as runways.

I like straight lines. Straight lines have a certainty. Like rules; like the law. I've never been one for leaps of faith. That's why I chose to study law: I liked the idea of rules, all laid out for you. There may always be room for interpretation, but the lines are drawn and the structure is clear. You know exactly where you stand with the law. The law is solid; the law is a rock. Or so it seemed, once, to a shaky eighteen-year-old filling in the university application forms that would open up a whole new world of choices.

And I so badly needed to find a world that was solid.

The telephone begins to ring just as I close the back door behind me. I throw my bag on the floor and reach for the receiver.

'Hello?'

'Cat, darling. Glad I caught you. How are you?'

I groan inwardly; this is the last thing I need right now. I glance at the clock: almost six. 'Hello, Mother. What are you doing calling me so late? It must be the middle of the night there.'

'Not really – just one o'clock in the morning. I couldn't sleep.'

'Right.' I hunch my shoulders and hug my arms around my

chest and close my eyes tightly. I want to sigh; I want to put the telephone down. I want to scream at her: I don't want to know. I don't want to bear the weight of your problems. Not any more.

But of course, I don't do that. 'How are you?' I ask.

'I'm fine.'

No, you're not. I can hear it in your voice. The slight tremor, the false cheeriness. Do you think I don't know by now when you're faking it? But I don't want to know. Please, not now. Not tonight. I just don't want to know.

'I just called to wish you a happy birthday. For tomorrow. I know you'll probably be busy on your birthday –' Ah, here it comes, now – the tragedy queen act – too busy to talk to your poor old mother '– and as it happens, for once I'm going to be out myself.'

Well, that's a new one. She never goes out – not any more. Not since she moved back there. Back to that place. I can tell that she wants me to ask where she's going, but the perverse child that lives inside me still chooses to refuse her. 'Oh,' I say. 'Right. Well, thanks.' There's a pause, and the undercurrent of her hurt feelings is palpable even across so many miles. As ever, guilt swamps me. But isn't that always the pattern? Refusal, followed by guilt. Time after time. Time without end.

Come on, Cat. Be nice. I sigh. 'So is everything all right?'

I switch off as she launches into one of her monologues about what she's been doing. As usual, there's really not much of it: just the usual bland anecdotes about a neighbour called Meg. She's trying to weave one of her stories for me. The story of a fulfilled, busy life. But there's something in her voice. She's not happy. She thinks I can't tell, but I can read her all too well. All those years, listening for every altered tone of her voice. Watchful. Careful. Treading on eggshells. I don't play those games any more. If she wants to tell me something, she will.

But I wish she wouldn't. God help me, I wish she wouldn't.

'…and so I'm going to her storytelling circle tomorrow.' There's a pause. 'Cat. Are you still there?'

'Yes. Yes, I'm still here.'

Another pause. During which it becomes apparent that I've failed her again. Because her voice, when it comes, is cold and tight. 'So. How are you?'

Me? Well, it only took ten minutes for her to ask this time. 'I'm fine.'

'What have you been doing?'

The perverse child leaps out with a desire to shock. 'I've just come back from a flying lesson.'

Pause. 'A what?'

'A flying lesson.'

Pause. 'You've had a flying lesson?'

'Yes. Isn't that great?'

'You've got to be joking,' she says.

My stomach contracts and my jaw clenches and I hug my arms more tightly over my chest. 'Why?'

'You know perfectly well why. Because you're afraid of flying.'

'Exactly. That's exactly why I'm doing it.'

'Cat, are you crazy?'

Crazy? Oh, no. I wasn't the one who was ever allowed to be crazy, remember? You did enough crazy for the two of us.

Well, maybe it's my turn to be crazy now.

She's still talking. '…I can't believe you'd do that. Think of how dangerous it is.'

And I want to yell at her: *Don't you think I've thought of that? Don't you think I know? I've spent all of my life counting up risks. Isn't it about time I stopped?* But of course I don't say that, either. I wouldn't expect her to understand. Whyever would she want to start understanding now?

I fish for a fact in her stream of emotion. 'It isn't that dangerous.'

'Of course it's dangerous. What if the engine fails?'

'Then you glide down to a suitable landing spot.' I want to laugh at myself: the voice of reason, when not so very long ago these very questions were buzzing around in my own panicked brain.

'I really wish you weren't doing it, Cat. What am I supposed to think, thousands of miles away? How am I supposed to sleep for worrying about you?'

And that is all it takes: here comes the monster, rising again. Burning an acid hole through my stomach – seeking release. 'This isn't about you. It's about me. Why is it always about you and how you feel and what it's going to do to you? What about me? What about the fact that I've just been diagnosed with panic attacks? What about that?'

I stop. Shaking. What am I doing? I never lose my temper with my mother. She's the only one who's allowed to lose her temper. Not me. Never me. If I get angry, then I'm just like my father. That's what she always used to say.

I don't do anger.

Silence. 'Panic attacks?'

I hear the fear in her voice. I sigh; the monster slinks back into his pit. 'It's okay. It's nothing, really.' The instinct to protect her is just too strong. 'I'm fine. Just a bit of anxiety. I had a sort of panic attack just before getting onto a plane. Someone suggested that maybe if I learned to fly I'd be able to overcome the fear. It seemed like a silly idea at the time, but somehow it took hold of me.'

I can feel her trying to assimilate it. Trying to decide what to say. Because I never admit to weakness. Not to anyone, but especially not to her. But listen, I want to say to her – *listen*. This fear is different. This is a fear that I *can* talk about. Because this is a fear that I'm dealing with. *Dealing with*. Can you believe it? I'm learning to fly!

'And how was it?'

'It was fine.' The scepticism in her voice defeats me and I so badly want this conversation to be over. 'Listen, I'll keep you posted, okay? I'm going to have another lesson in a week's time. But right now I have to run. I just got in and Adam will be home any minute and I'm all hot and sweaty and I need to get changed.'

'All right.'

I hate to leave it like this; she sounds hurt. Guilt presses in on me and as hard as I try I can't push it away. But then guilt and I are old friends. I can't seem to let it go.

Midnight; once again I lie in bed, sleepless. Every inch of me is aware of Adam's sleeping bulk beside me. His regular, deep breathing fills the room and presses in on me, weighing me down. I try every trick I know to switch off the thoughts that crowd my mind. I count sheep; I walk down imaginary steps; I visualise myself on a calm, sunny desert island beach.

Nothing works.

Eventually I fall into a fitful sleep. I dream that I am alone in a hot-air balloon, which hovers quietly in a sun-spangled meadow filled with cowslip and poppies and surrounded by aspens that whisper in the breeze. The wind tugs at the balloon and it begins, very gently, to rise up from the ground. I look up at the sky and want so badly to be up there, high above it all in that light, uncluttered place. But something is stopping the balloon from rising further. I look down from the basket and I see my mother, holding on to the ropes. She won't let me go; she needs me to stay with her. I hesitate; she looks angry, and reminds me that I'm afraid of heights.

Silently, I climb down from the balloon.

4

Laura

She won't let go. What does it take to make her let go? Laura tosses fitfully in her sleep. It's hot outside, and Cat wants to go down to the beach. But Laura is trying to teach her to dance. Standing there, so solemn, tortoise-shell spectacles dwarfing her little face. Purple dress, red shoes. No, the red shoes are Laura's. Cat doesn't have any shoes. Freedom, lightness, curly black hair whirling wildly around her; Chubby Checker spinning on the turntable. 'Come here, little Cat – I'm going to teach you to do the twist!' Reaching out, laughing; taking hold of her hands – she pulls away. 'Leave me alone,' she says. Always too cautious; always afraid. But Laura – ah, Laura has no fear. Throwing back her head and her red shoes glittering and laughing and swinging and dancing. She dances, and it seems that she never will stop. 'You're so wooden, Cat. Relax, why can't you? Just close your eyes and go with the music. Let go.'

'Let go,' she says as she holds Cat in her arms, blood pouring down her cheek where the stone has gashed her face. The swing dancing backwards and forwards on the tarmac behind them. Wouldn't cry, not once on the journey to the hospital on the bus, not once as the doctor put the stitches in her cheek. Jaw clenched, eyes glittering. 'Let go,' Laura says, her face flushed and hectic, eyes brimming with anger. 'For God's sake, Cat, just let go now, and cry.'

But Cat knows what happens when you let go.

Laura doesn't want this dream.

She throws off the sweat-soaked floral sheets, sits up

and turns on the lamp at her bedside. Time has become her adversary over these past months, and the clock does nothing to dispel this notion. It is three o'clock in the morning. How long has she been lying here, tossing and turning in that strange liminal state between sleep and wakefulness? She's never been particularly good at sleep, but the bleak inevitability of this routine is beginning to fill her with dread. Each night when she goes to bed she knows what will happen: her head will touch the pillow, and as if in response to some pre-arranged signal, the memories will take flight. Voices and faces that can't be banished, no matter how hard she tries. And when eventually she hovers on the brink of a restless sleep they ambush her, annexing her dreams.

She's never had this problem before. She's always been so good at banishing the voices, at suppressing the past. After all, she spent years cultivating such wonderfully effective methods of flight. First it was the fairy tales, then it was the whisky, and finally it was the writing. And now? Now she doesn't have anything. Not any more. Nowhere to run, no means of escape.

The seemingly ever-present need to pee drives her out of bed and into the chilly air of the bathroom: another of the manifold joys of beginning to grow old. She splashes some tepid water on her face, carefully avoiding the mirror. It would be pointless to go back to bed right now – she'll never sleep. So she creeps down to the kitchen, where the dark green Rayburn continues to throw out its comforting heat. She drapes herself over it stiffly, allowing the warmth to permeate the burgundy fleece of her dressing gown, to seep into her aching bones. She has been plagued by arthritis for two decades now. She's not sure that this cold, damp climate will help, but then she's never been able to deal with hot places. Alec once said that surely there must be some wild Celtic gene somewhere in her ancestry that made her long for windswept hilltops and rainy beaches.

But then Alec was a pretty wild Celt himself.

She shakes away that most persistent ghost, takes out a pan and heats up some milk, adding a teaspoon of honey to the mug. Cups her stiff hands around it, inhaling the warm, sweet smell – redolent of drowsy bees in honeycombed hives on sun-drenched summer afternoons. When eventually she does go back to bed she'll probably be up for the rest of the night running to the bathroom, but right now that seems a small price to pay for the simple pleasure and comfort of it.

She sits at the much-scrubbed table and watches the kitchen come to life in the soft glow of the cast iron lamp on the dresser – she's always hated the glare of overhead lights. The room wraps itself around her: the thick terracotta-painted stone walls, the pine units that have served their time – they'll need replacing one of these days but right now, with shadows creeping around them like caresses and the old waxed wood glowing in the lamplight, they are a vital part of the living organism that is this room. She can feel safe here, even with the wind whining mournfully around the house and the rain pounding at the windows, thinking of all the storms that this house has seen and survived. She loves storms. There has always been something in a storm that appeals to her: the thrill of it, the wildness, the passion.

Those days are long gone. Vanished, along with everything else that she has loved and depended on. The loss of her stories is an ache in her chest that will not go away. Whatever else she might have lost in her life, she always had her stories. There was a room clearly set aside for them in her mind – a place to which she could retreat when real life was too much to bear. All too often, it seems to her now. She could simply withdraw into her head and visualise the glittering production of her latest fantasy blockbuster. Fantasies in which, of course, she played the starring role. Tales filled with jewelled palaces, fiery dragons and handsome princes who rescued fair maidens with ivory skin and ebony hair. The stories never changed much over time, except that maybe the princes grew a little older – a little more distinguished. And when she grew older and began to write the stories down, that in itself was an act of redemption. A fugitive glimpse of possible salvation.

So perhaps it's not surprising that this loss can materialise as physical pain: a dart, sharp and twisting, that takes her unawares and drives out the breath from her lungs. And nor is it surprising that she finds herself returning to Meg's words about stories, as she sips the last remaining dregs of the warm fragrant milk. 'Write it down, and you'll see the pattern,' she murmurs. And yet she cannot imagine how it might be possible to begin. Where would she start? How to make sense of it all?

But perhaps writing something – anything at all – will help her to break this block, will lure back the words that have fled from her. And perhaps she can exorcise these ghosts, these memories. Remove them from her head, capture them with bold strokes of black ink, imprison them between the lines on the crisp white paper pages of her notebook.

Perhaps she can write them down.

The wind hurls raindrops against the shaky wooden window frame that also has seen better days and slowly, slowly, the idea begins to form.

Once upon a time there was a little girl born to a mother and father who lived in a land on the north-eastern shores of the country that lies to the south of here.

No, this isn't where her story starts. Not really; not properly. Because everybody is born, so where's the story in that? Yet the sentence is telling enough, in its way. There was a mother and there was also a father. There was the sea and the shore, and both of these may matter by the end. But there are so many possible beginnings here, and each one bears the potential within it to start a different story. Which of those beginnings should she pick for this one, for this story that so badly wants to be told?

The little girl's parents were ageing and tired; they already had three daughters and had not expected to have more. Theirs was a poor village, its riches restricted to the beauty of the sea, the sweep of the silvery sands and the chattering wildlife of the dunes. And yet on either side of them there began to spring up huge towers, guarded by fiery dragons that spewed smoke and acrid fumes into the sky, clouding the clear blue horizons. Just as the little girl was born, war broke out and her father was sent to fight in a distant land. She did not know him until the war ended, six years later. When he returned home he found that much had changed in his country. Fearing that his children would go hungry, the father was forced to leave the little house by the sea each morning before the sun rose, to go to work in one of the frightening towers. The work was hard and dirty, the hours long. As a result he became angry and bitter, and turned his face from his wife and his children. Soon he began to seek solace in dark, frothy ale and the company of other men who had also known war. But the ale changed him ...

Yes. She puts her pen down for a moment, rubs her eyes and rests her head gently in her hands. This was the point where it all began.

The memory comes back to her unbidden, vivid, in need of release. Clenching her jaw, she picks up the pen and continues to write.

Laura hid behind the settee, biting her nails, trying to pretend she was somewhere else. A bright, fairy-tale land peopled by golden princesses and glittering mermaids. It wasn't working. The shouting was too loud.

There was often shouting on Sunday afternoons, when her dad

97

got back from the Traveller's Rest. He went there every Sunday at twelve and came home when they closed, at two o'clock. They always had to wait for their dinner until he came back. She didn't really know what kind of place the Traveller's Rest was or why it made him shout. She only knew that it was that big red-brick building on the corner where the men went. The women didn't go there – not if they were respectable anyway, her mam said. When Dad came back he always smelled funny. Cigarette smoke and beer, Mam said. That's what the men did in the Traveller's Rest – drank and smoked and told tall tales. Laura liked the idea of tall tales: she loved stories. She wondered what made a tale tall, but when she asked Mam just laughed, and she didn't dare to ask her dad. Little girls should be seen and not heard, her dad said. And if she and May and Alice and Florence were lucky and very, very careful, he would neither see them nor hear them on Sunday afternoons.

Dad didn't know she was there now, and if he found out he'd take the belt to her for sure. She'd been sitting curled up in the corner behind the settee, away in one of her daydreams, as Aunt Lizzie always said. Letting her dinner go down. May and Alice and Florence were playing out on the green with the two new lasses across the road, but they never asked Laura to go with them. She was the youngest, and so she was ignored most of the time anyway – especially by Dad. It was almost as if he'd forgotten he had a fourth daughter. That was because she'd been born just as he was going away to war. Laura was the cause of the war, Aunt Lizzie said; maybe that's why Dad didn't like her. There were five whole years between Laura and May, which was a long time. Laura was six now; she'd been six last June. She'd heard Mam tell Aunt Lizzie that she and Dad had thought there'd be no more, but that Dad probably would have liked a son. Back then Laura had felt sorry for Dad because she wasn't a boy. But now she didn't feel anything for him at all. She didn't know who this man was, this tall stranger who came back from the war six months ago. They called him her dad but she didn't know him, didn't like him, and who did he think he was to shout like that at her mam?

Dad's voice got louder and louder – on and on he shouted, on and on. She squeezed her eyes tight shut; she was trying not to listen to what he was saying. Trying to shut it out. He never made any sense when he was shouting, anyway: he just seemed to shout about anything that came into his head. The dinner had been too cold or it hadn't been properly cooked or Mam hadn't laughed loudly enough at one of his jokes. Mam never answered him back when he shouted – but then she never said anything very much to anyone, ever.

More shouting, and then Mam began to cry. Laura hated it when Mam cried. She cried softly, almost silently. Eyes wide open, water pouring out of her eyes and running down her soft white cheeks into her mouth. Every now and again she'd take a short gasping breath. Just like she was doing now. Laura hugged herself tightly around her middle. She had a tummy ache. She wanted to burp but she didn't dare because Dad would hear her. She wanted to go to the toilet as well.

And then suddenly the shouting stopped. Laura breathed out silently; waited for Dad to shuffle from the room like he usually did when he was all shouted out – because then he would go up to bed for a lie down. Sleep it off, Mam said. He would come down again at tea-time with his face and eyes all pale and puffy and he wouldn't say anything to anyone all night.

But he wasn't going anywhere right now. There was a sharp crack – Laura jumped – followed by a short silence followed by a sob from Mam. 'Don't, Jimmy,' Mam said. And then there was another crack. Mam cried out again. What was he doing? Was he hitting her? The knot in Laura's stomach tightened even more. She'd seen him give Mam a quick slap on the face before if she'd said something he didn't like, and sometimes he would whack Laura or one of the other girls on the behind if he thought they were cheeking him or if they moved too slowly or hesitated before doing what he said. But it had never happened like this before. Not on a Sunday afternoon.

Crack. Another sharp pain stabbed through her stomach. What was happening? What was he doing to Mam? 'No, Jimmy, no,' Mam said, over and over, but Dad didn't stop. *Crack, crack, crack.* And with every crack, Dad grunted and Mam sobbed. Laura was going to be sick, and her heart was beating so loudly that she was sure Dad would hear it. She wanted to run and she wanted to get help but if she moved he would see her and catch her and he would beat her too. She put her hands over her eyes and rocked backwards and forwards. She was just a little girl; she didn't know what to do. What was she supposed to do? Another *crack* – louder this time – and another, but now there were no more sounds from Mam. 'Bitch,' she heard him say. 'Frigid bitch.' Still no sounds from Mam – just Dad's heavy breathing and one more crack and then nothing more at all. Just silence. Laura opened her eyes. The silence was more frightening than the sound of the cracks. Why wasn't Mam saying anything? Why wasn't she moving? Maybe he'd really hurt her badly. Maybe she was dead.

As quietly as she could, Laura crept out from her hiding place behind the settee. Mam was on the floor, curled up, hands over her face, and Dad was standing over her with his fists clenched and his face red and ugly and sweat pouring down his cheeks and running down his neck into the tatty white collar of his shirt. Then he aimed a kick at Mam's stomach and she cried out again and brought her knees up to her chest and something inside Laura snapped and she ran all the way out from behind the settee and over to the fire and she picked up the poker and ran over to Dad and hit him behind the knees, hardly registering the thick black streak left by the coal dust on his Sunday best grey flannel trousers. Without even thinking about what she was doing, acting purely on instinct, she stepped around him as he whirled towards her and she positioned herself between him and Mam. She raised the poker in both hands till it was level with her waist. Holding it like the bats that you used in rounders. 'You leave my mam alone,' she shouted at him, voice shrill and shaking. 'You just leave her alone.'

Dad looked at her in astonishment. Something flickered in his eyes and he took a step forward and for a moment Laura knew that he was going to kill them both. But he stopped, breathing heavily. And then wordlessly he turned and shambled out of the door and she heard the heavy sound of his footsteps climbing up the stairs. When the bedroom door closed behind him, she dropped the poker and clasped her hands together over her stomach. She was definitely going to be sick. She couldn't believe what she'd just done. Beginning to shake, wanting to cry now, she turned to Mam. But Mam was looking at her through eyes that were already red and swelling as if she'd never seen her before in her life. As if ... all of a sudden she'd become someone else. Someone ... different. Someone a little bit scary.

Startled, tearful, Laura stared back. And then she remembered what Aunt Lizzie had said last week. 'You want to watch that bairn,' she'd said to Mam, pointing a long bony finger at Laura, her eyes and mouth screwed up in that spiteful way that she had. 'There's summat not right about that one. Why's she so different from the other lasses? Either you've been down the coalhole with the dustman, or she's a changeling.' Aunt Lizzie had nodded wisely and jabbed her finger again for emphasis. 'Aye, you mark my words. That's what she is: she's a changeling.'

Laura hadn't known what a changeling was, but from the sour expression on Aunt Lizzie's face it seemed like it wasn't a good thing to be. She looked at Mam, but Mam was blushing. 'Ee, our Lizzie – don't say that to the bairn,' she said quietly. 'She takes after our side, instead of Jimmy's family like the other three. That's why she's got dark hair when they're all blonde. That's all it is.'

But as always, Aunt Lizzie raised her voice again and Mam shut up. 'They're the spit out of their father's mouth, there's no denying. But that one – I don't know who she looks like. Nobody I know, anyhow. And she was a sickly baby an' all.' Aunt Lizzie shook her head in displeasure. She opened her mouth to say more, but then Uncle Billy walked in and she closed it again. The only time Aunt Lizzie ever stopped being mean was when Uncle Billy was around. Laura didn't know why she should be mean to her and Mam; after all, they'd all lived with her and Uncle Billy during the war, right up until it ended and Dad had come home. They'd all lived together so that Uncle Billy could take care of them. He'd been too old to go to war, so they'd made him an air raid warden instead. They gave him a whistle and a shiny metal badge. He let Laura blow the whistle sometimes. Laura loved Uncle Billy more than anyone else in the world. He had thick grey hair and laughing blue eyes and he always dressed like a gentleman, Mam said. Even though he only worked as a watchman at the steelworks.

And it was because of Uncle Billy that Laura packed her pyjamas in an Atkinson and Shire brown paper carrier bag the next morning, and announced to her bruised and shaken mother that she was going to Uncle Billy's for her holidays.

Except that she never came home.

Laura is awakened from a deep slumber by the insistent sound of Meg's cockerel, Ronnie, proclaiming his masculinity to the world. For a moment she doesn't know where she is, but then the kitchen slowly begins to take shape around her as she blinks to focus her tired, bleary eyes. Her shoulders and neck ache as she lifts her head from the table and flinches; mornings are always the worst, for the pain. The last thing she remembers is thinking she'd just rest her head on her arms for a moment before going back to bed. She looks at the clock: six-thirty. She hasn't slept for long, but if she goes back to bed now there's no chance that she'll sleep. It's going to be a long, long day. She places her hands back on the table to heave herself up, and the one eye that seems to be functioning fixes on the notebook that lays open right there in front of her, the pages covered in a familiar sloping black scrawl.

The story.

She closes her eyes again and remembers how easily, last night, the process of starting to write had cut through the clutter of memories and offered up this place to begin. A classic place to begin, just like in all the best stories. Something is profoundly wrong with our heroine's world, and she is called upon to save it. She begins, of course, in the way that all the best story-book heroes do: she leaves home. She packs her belongings in a red spotted handkerchief and ties the handkerchief to a stick. She slings the stick over her shoulder and sets out on a Great Adventure. Never mind that our heroine is only six years old.

Six years old. Ten years ago Laura asked her father, as he died a slow suffocating death from lung cancer, why they had let her go. Why had they let her just walk away, and go off to live with Uncle Billy and Aunt Lizzie? Why did they never fetch her back home again?

They had made their peace by then, Laura and her father, but they had never managed to become friends. He simply looked at her through eyes fogged with painkillers, and he shook his head. 'You knew your own mind,' he said. 'You knew what you wanted and it was always the same – once you made your mind up, nothing was going to stop you. You made your decision, and we respected it.'

'Dad,' she said to him, 'Dad. I was six years old.'

'Aye,' he said. 'Aye. You were six years old, and you wanted none of me. You only wanted your Uncle Billy. He'd been a father to you all through the war – ever since you could remember. And he was a good one, as far as I could tell. Better than me, anyroad. The other three grew up with me, for better or for worse, but you grew up with him. That was your home, down the lane there with Billy, and yes – even with Lizzie, may the wicked old bitch rot in hell.' He smiled grimly. He had hated Aunt Lizzie as much as she had hated him, and Laura had never once heard her say a good word about her father.

'You were a fighter, lass. And stubborn with it. Took after me, though you'll not thank me for saying so. If we'd have brought you back you'd have gone right back there again. And anyway, your mam thought you'd be better off with them.' A flicker of pain crossed his face. 'At the time, I thought she was right.'

Rising stiffly, she crosses the kitchen and puts the kettle on for tea. As she reaches for the tea caddy her attention is caught by a postcard from Cat, propped up against the wall. That is how they deal with each other now, Laura and her daughter – hastily scribbled postcards that wing their way across a gulf of several thousand miles. A stilted telephone call every few weeks, and at Christmas and birthdays. Each encounter like walking on a path strewn with jagged pieces of broken glass.

And now Cat's learning to fly. Laura isn't sure what she feels about that. At one level, she's delighted. Admiring, even. But at another level, it scares the hell out of her. Because this just isn't like Cat. Cat doesn't do things like that. Things that are risky. Dangerous. She's not at all like me, Laura thinks. Cat was always such a cautious child. Not at all physical. She didn't like sports, hated P.E. at school. She didn't learn to ride a bicycle till she was ten years old, and she only learned to swim around the same age. Painfully slowly. Laura can see her so vividly. Always so tall for her age, and slender. Dark brown eyes a startling contrast against the pale blonde hair. Spectacles firmly planted on her nose, face carefully free from expression. She never really knew what Cat was thinking, what she was feeling. Cat hid it all so well. She simply stood aloof, looking as if she really didn't give a damn about anyone else and what they might think of her. How did she learn to hide so well, so young? And what was it that she hid?

That's what really worries her. What is Cat hiding now? Because Cat has never done anything like this before. Laura said as much to Meg last night, sitting in the drowsy warmth of her living room, sipping from a big mug of hot tea.

'And Cat is how old, now?' Meg asked.

'Just turned forty.'

Meg grinned at her. 'Forty. And still you're surprised by this flying business?' Laura frowned; she wasn't sure what Meg meant. 'Come on now, lassie. Think about it. That's what turning forty is for. Forty is for midlife madnesses, for doing all of the wild things you've always wanted to do but never dared, for turning your back on everything that's safe and familiar. Don't you remember what you were like at forty?'

At forty? Oh, yes. Laura remembered what she was like at forty.

She whipped her head away. Mustn't tell. The shame of it, the guilt… She filed the clamouring memories, carefully, back in the farthest reaches of the filing cabinet where they belong. This is a place she does not go.

'Cat's not like me.' She hesitated. 'It's just – she's always had her feet firmly planted on the ground, eyes fixed straight ahead of her. She doesn't take any risks.' Not without very clearly weighing the odds of success and calculating the price of failure, Laura thought. No, she's not at all like me.

'Well then, we're back to stories again. Cat is forty years old, and it may be that the story of her life has been a story about caution. So she's changing that story now. And why not?'

'I don't know. I don't know what she's thinking. She said –' Laura hesitated. 'She said she'd been having some problems. Something about a panic attack. I didn't dare to ask her any more about it. She hates it when I ask her things. I just don't know how to talk to her any more. Sometimes I wonder if I ever did.'

'And is that how you intend it to go on?' Meg asked, black eyes piercing, challenging. 'Or do you plan to do something about it?'

Ah Meg, Laura thought. So much that you don't know.

'These aren't things that I can control. It's always been this way. There's nothing I can do to make Cat think differently of me.'

'Isn't there?'

Laura laughed shortly; it wasn't a pleasant sound. There I go again, she thought. Bitter. 'How could I?'

'Well, lassie, maybe you should think of something. Before it's too late.'

Too late? But it was too late a long time ago. Maybe it's always been too late.

The postcard presents a vivid view of the desert: red rocks, orange earth and unremittingly blue sky. Laura shudders. She can't imagine why anyone would want to live in such a place. But then she never understood why Cat went to America at all, though sometimes she has wondered if it wasn't to get away from her. If she were here Cat would roll her eyes at that, and tell Laura that she always thinks that everything is about her. But then she never understood me either, Laura thinks, though of course she always thought she did. She had it all worked out by the time she walked out at eighteen and went to university at the far end of the country – as far away from Laura as she could get. Bad mother, good daughter. Perpetrator, victim. The very simplest of stories, the most basic of plots. But no plot is ever really that simple: Laura doesn't need Meg to remind her of that. Because even the perpetrators have their story. And Laura's is a story that Cat doesn't even begin to know. Because she just walked away. She left, just like everyone else did. Laura bites down on a bitter mouthful of self-pity. Cat doesn't know Laura's story. She thinks she does. But she doesn't. No-one knows.

Laura's eyes flicker back to the notebook that sits on the table. And on into the corner, where her long-neglected laptop computer peeks out from under a pile of magazines. And it comes to her finally that this, at least, may be something she can change. If she wants Cat to know her story – really know it –

she can share that story with Cat. Tell Cat her story. The pieces of the story that matter, at least.

Well, Laura thinks. Well. After all, what have I got to lose?

She walks to the front door and opens it wide to taste the early morning air. The sun is just beginning to rise; the tangy sea-smell of the loch insinuates itself into her head. The sheep bleat their early morning greetings; a stag roars loudly on the hill behind the house. The rain and wind of the night have disappeared; all is still and calm. A mist is lifting from the surface of the loch.

5
Cat

My face is suspended, ghost-like, in the water-misted bathroom mirror. I look better in soft focus, there's no doubt about that.

Forty years old, and that's supposed to be a cause for celebration. The last thing I want is a fuss, but Adam insisted. 'You're only forty once,' he declared (with no apparent sense of irony), 'and so we should have a party. We had one for my fiftieth last year, remember, and it was fantastic.' Actually, I hated every moment of it, just as I hate all parties. Last year, with all its Millennium-fuelled hype, was a party-pooper's nightmare. But Adam adores parties. And for his sake I try: I do my best to smile in all the right places and exchange meaningless words with all the right people. He loves me; I suppose I owe him that much.

Fresh out of the shower, my hair is clean, soft and shiny, my legs are carefully shaved, and my body is doused in something cool and sweet-smelling. I am all of the things that are expected of a middle-class suburban woman on a Saturday night in Scottsdale.

I have no idea how I came to be such a person.

The face, strangely insubstantial, fades away from the mirror as I back up to the edge of the bathtub. I sit down and close my eyes. Breathe slowly, deeply. Clench the muscles in the throat and jaw – hold them tight for a count of five – and then let them relax. Again. And again.

That's better. Slowly, slowly, the spasms fade away.

I have a programme now – a routine. It makes sense to me at last, that awful sensation in my throat. As if something's stuck there. As if I literally can't swallow what's going on. According to Dr Lindy Brubaker, author of the imaginatively entitled *Relaxation Handbook*, the spasms in my throat are due to contractions of the muscles. They're chronically tense – and I just need to teach them how to relax again. And then everything is supposed to be just fine.

But it isn't fine. It's never going to be fine. Because, whether my muscles are chronically tense or chronically relaxed, I have no idea how I came to be this person.

I stand abruptly and walk over to the counter, pick up a pot of moisturiser and start to rub it into my face. It's really not a bad face for a forty-year-old: still pretty enough and no major wrinkles to speak of yet. Adam says it's because I grew up in such a damp, dewy climate. Added to the fact that I've never managed to have children. *Managed to have*, he says, as if it was something I always wanted to do, and failed at. But I never wanted children. I've done childhood once already; once was more than enough. I don't want to do it again, even by proxy. Anyway: perhaps Adam is right, and that's why I don't have wrinkles. Or perhaps it's just that I've never really experienced much in the way of highs and lows. Such a calm life. Such a calm Cat. Never really screwed up my face in passion, never really contorted it in anger. Never put myself into positions where I might run the risk of experiencing either deep hurt or soaring delight. Never took those risks. Never let go.

It's just as Nate said, all those years ago. *For God's sake, Cat – we can't even have a good row about this. It's like shouting at a brick wall. Why won't you ever shout back? Why won't you ever get mad?* But if I'd told you why, Nate, the chances are that you'd have pitied me. And people who allow themselves to be pitied are lacking in pride. Lacking in strength. And because I always had to be strong. Because if I wasn't strong, who else was going to be strong for me? *Do you love me, Cat? Really love me? Sometimes it's like making love to a wooden post. I don't know, half the time, whether you've even come or not. Why won't you let me see your face? Why can't you let go?* Because if I'd let go, Nate, you'd have seen who I really was; you'd have known everything. You'd have known how different I was. You'd have seen the shame and the guilt and all of those dark hidden places inside me and then you wouldn't have loved me. Couldn't possibly have loved me. But I loved you, Nate, all those years ago. And never really found a way to let you know. Never could say the words, never could force them between the bars of that iron-clad cage where I locked up my heart.

Lord above – forty years old and I'm finally turning into my mother. Melodramatic. Get a grip, now. Nate was so long ago. Long-ago, long-lost.

I don't know whether it's longing or sadness, this dull ache at the base of my throat, this hollow sinking sensation deep in my stomach. These voices from a past that has never really loosened its grip on me, never let me go. I'm forty, now. Forty, and look at me. Look at my life. I had such dreams, when I was eighteen. Dreams of escape, to be sure – escape from that dreary town, from that dreary life, from everything that held me back. And characteristically, I had it all planned out. All perfectly mapped. In a straight line, of course – no deviations allowed. In four years' time, I would graduate as a solicitor. I would work for a charity – Amnesty, probably – specialising in human rights. I'd be most likely to find that kind of work in London, so chances were that I'd end up living in a poky little flat in some bleak and built-up back street: that kind of law doesn't pay too well. But I wouldn't care about that. I'd have a cat and I'd go to concerts and for long walks in the park with men who would love me from a distance. Always from a distance. Because I wouldn't love them, and I certainly wouldn't need them. I wouldn't let them in. I wouldn't be like my mother, lurching from man to unsuitable man in a desperate search for self-definition. I'd always know who I was and I wouldn't need any man to tell me. I'd languish in safe and peaceful solitude. Distant and inviolable, how they would love me: Catriona, *la princesse lointaine*.

I played that role all too well.

So how the hell did I end up here? In this beige marble-tiled ensuite bathroom with its slippery ice-cold floors and its fluffy white towels and all the individuality of a mass-produced hotel room?

Adam is whistling loudly in the dressing room next door; it sounds vaguely like 'Scotland the Brave'. Muffled by the walls between us, still the sound lingers, dogged and insistent inside my head. Breaking into the silence – and this house is so often filled with silence. Adam doesn't like music much. Ruins his concentration, he says. And he only ever listens to classical music – he hates anything with words. When we first moved in together I'd play my music when he was away. Sneak on a little Joni Mitchell; maybe even some recent Bowie. But somehow the urge has faded over the years that we've been together. Somehow it seems wrong. Like playing rock and roll in a church, bringing an alien religion into God's house.

There weren't any jobs going at Amnesty at the time that I graduated. Nor in any related organisation I could find. So I took a position at Sanderson Pharmaceuticals – just while I was waiting for a proper job to come along. I thought it would be good experience. Just for a while. I never intended to make it my life's work. But the problem with corporate life is that once you're in, it's all so very easy. Oh, it's not just the money; I've never really cared much about money. But it's all so comfortable, so safe. You have a clearly prescribed set of responsibilities outlined in a clearly prescribed job description, and if you do your job properly you can progress on upwards at a nice steady pace. In a nice straight line.

I did just fine at Sanderson's head office. The people I worked with were friendly enough. I had my London flat, but it was right in the heart of Pimlico. At weekends I haunted the Tate Gallery, entranced by the Pre-Raphaelites. Paintings of solitary, dreamy women. Oh, and there were men, too. Just as I'd imagined, each one nicely in his place. And as soon as they ran the risk of stepping a little too close, I'd move on to the next. All so easy, all so comfortable.

But then, for some crazy reason, my mother decided to move to London. At around the same time I was offered a job in the US division of the company, and six thousand miles seemed like just about enough of a distance to put between us.

So: Phoenix, Arizona. It was all so comfortable here, too. Then along came Adam, safe and unchallenging, and it was so easy just to slide into a relationship. To move in with him. The time slips away, safe and comfortable and easy. You have a nice car and there are plenty of places to park it; you're earning large sums of money which you don't spend because your partner already owns a house and there's no mortgage... And then, before you know it, you're forty years old and having panic attacks.

And there don't seem to be any straight lines any more. Just circles.

I reach for a silk robe and head out of the ensuite, back into the master bedroom. Birthday cards are lined up on top of the light oak dresser that contains my underwear. There aren't very many. There's a card from Adam, sporting a photograph of a piece of modern sculpture against a stark white background. 'To Cat, with love from Adam', it says inside. There's a card with a painting of a tabby cat from Janie. A large black one with an enormous '40' on the front, signed by all the members of the law department. There's a small card with a fluffy bunny from my Auntie May – the only one of my mother's sisters who still bothers to remember my birthday. But then why should they? I never remember theirs. Somewhere in the world I have eight cousins. I know their names, but I don't know their lives. I don't know whether they're married or even whether they still live in the same old town. I haven't seen any of them since I was eighteen years old. At the back there's a large card from my mother: a vase of blue and white Impressionist-style flowers and 'To a Wonderful Daughter on her Fortieth Birthday' in fine italic script across the top. And next to it, one from my father. I'm surprised he remembered; he forgets at least two years out of every three. A photograph of Edinburgh castle and inside, 'To Catriona from Dad, Annie and family'.

It was probably Annie who remembered to send it.

You never talk about your father either, Adam says.

No. No, I don't.

I select a set of beige lace underwear from the top drawer of the chest. I live in the shadow of the underwear police: I'm a slave to the notion that someone will turn up on the doorstep one day, flash a badge and an ID card and demand to check that I'm wearing matching underwear. Adam would never know, though: the silk and lace is quite wasted on him. He never undresses me these days. But then I don't remember that he ever did. We undress ourselves in a business-like fashion, carefully folding or hanging our clothes; we get into bed naked and then we get on with doing whatever it is we're there to do. But something peculiar and unexpected seems to be happening to me, these days. More and more I find myself subject to strange longings that take possession of me at odd hours of the day and night. I yearn to be undressed, to be seduced, to be ravished.

I turn away and laugh quietly at myself. In the unlikely event that I'd find myself in a situation where anyone tried, I'd be more than likely to run a mile. Because it's so much simpler this way. Quieter.

Safer.

*

We drive to the golf club in silence; Adam seems preoccupied and I'm tired and more than a little spacey. My feet are uncomfortable in the black strappy sandals: the heels are a good deal higher than those I usually wear. I'm trying to enter into the spirit of things – trying to make him happy – by wearing something more glamorous than I'd normally be comfortable in. The jade green silk is one of his favourites. Sometimes I think my most successful role in this relationship is as fashion accessory: my blonde head matching his; my British accent the perfect foil for his Georgia drawl. But something about the fitted bodice of the dress is constricting my breathing. Every few breaths I find myself gulping for air like a fish hooked and tossed in a basket to die.

The clubhouse windows glow with soft peachy light; as we drive into the parking lot I can see the people clustering inside. Already I feel them beginning to press on me. I follow Adam across the asphalt in a daze; he holds the door open for me and I walk reluctantly into the room. I can't imagine who all these people are. I don't have this many friends and I don't even recognise some of the faces. The spasms begin to take hold of my throat again and I have difficulty swallowing the saliva that is welling up in my mouth. My heart pounds hollowly in my chest; my stomach muscles brace themselves for a punch that never comes. I feel sick; I want to weep.

I am so very tired of feeling like this.

Someone – one of Adam's work colleagues, I think – catches sight of us and shouts; as he gets their attention, the room quietens down for a moment before everyone claps and begins to sing 'Happy Birthday'. I struggle to fix a rigid smile on my face and try to ignore the now familiar feeling of my body spiralling out of control, the fight-flight response gone crazy.

I clasp Adam's hand for reassurance but, oblivious, he pushes me forward into the crowd. All of my instincts are telling me to turn around and hot-foot it out of there; every cell in my body is screaming for escape. I talk to myself sharply, tell myself that this is ridiculous.

I don't seem to be listening. Blindly scanning the crowd, I'm relieved to spot a familiar face – Ginny. Thank God. I launch myself at her full-tilt and she catches me and holds me at arm's length, laughing.

'Hey, girl. You looked kinda like a deer caught in the headlights there, for a minute.'

I shudder. 'More like a rabbit.'

'Drew, honey, go and get Cat a drink, will you? Adam's been waylaid by the Warners. A good stiff gin and tonic is what she needs, by the looks of things.' She puts an arm through mine and draws me away from the crowd. I follow her to the back of the room where it's quieter, recovering myself sufficiently to nod and smile at people that we pass, accepting either their congratulations or their joking condolences.

'Who are all these people? I don't believe I've ever seen some of them before in my life.'

'Sure you have. Though there are a whole lot of lawyers here from Regan Dinsdale – Adam must've sent out a general invitation to the whole firm. Drew's been pointing some of them out to me, though I know most of them by now. See that short guy over there – the one with the woman several inches taller than him, in the red dress? That's Hoffman – their star performer. It's not often you see him socialising. Arrogant little shit, if you ask me, but unfortunately they don't.' She laughs and squeezes my arm, ginger hair glinting and flickering in the soft light. 'Then there's another whole crowd who are members of the club – you've probably exchanged a few odd words with them at the bar on Saturday evenings.'

'Well, you know Adam. He doesn't need to know people too well before he decides they're his best friends.' Not like me. I don't make friends easily. I never have – especially women friends. But Ginny's different: she didn't give me a choice. She swept me up and took me firmly in hand when Adam and I first started seeing each other, because Ginny's husband Drew is Adam's closest friend and like him is a partner at Regan Dinsdale. I wouldn't say that Ginny and I are close – we mostly just see each other when Adam and Drew are present – but she's a lot of fun. And the only one of the four of us who isn't a lawyer: she works as a PR manager for a local utilities company. Or a 'corporate communications adviser', as they call it now. On the theory that the more syllables a title has, the more it must be worth.

Drew brings us our drinks, pats me on the back and swiftly heads off again to track down Adam. I take a large gulp of the ice-cold gin and tonic, tasting the tanginess of the lime, feeling the fizz slip down and settle comfortably in my queasy stomach. I don't much like strong alcohol; in fact, I hardly touch it at all except for the occasional glass of wine with a meal, but right now this seems to be exactly what I need.

'Better?' Ginny is watching me carefully.

'Much.' I exhale slowly, trying to relax my stomach muscles as I do so. 'I don't know what came over me.' I know exactly what came over me, but I'm damned if I'm going to admit it to anyone.

'You haven't been yourself lately. You've been kind of distracted, to say the least. And a little low.'

I shrug. 'It's nothing. Just a few off-days. Isn't that what's supposed to happen when you reach forty? Midlife crisis, and all that? It'll be hot flushes next.' My poor attempt at levity doesn't fool her for a minute; she raises a shrewd eyebrow.

'Come on, honey. You can't dupe me that easily. You may be the queen of cool but every now and again even you can let the cracks show.'

Cracks? She doesn't know the half of it. I shake my head; turn away. She rests her hand lightly on my arm. 'Listen – we can't talk properly here; too many people. Let's get together for lunch soon; we haven't done that for ages. I'll call you and we'll make a date. Some Saturday. We can make an afternoon of it. Maybe take in the mall.'

'That'd be good.'

She squeezes my shoulder and glances round the room, carefully assessing the choices that are open to us. 'Well, girlfriend, I guess we'd better do the social thing – you don't get to avoid that at your own party. Anyone here at all that you want to talk to? How about Andy Garfield? His wife is kind of sweet …'

After an hour of wandering around the room exchanging vague pleasantries I am feeling no less disconnected from my surroundings. There are too many people in this room, and yet my sense of isolation is profound. This always happens to me at parties; it's one of the reasons why I dread them so. This is how it happens: you look at the people milling around you, laughing and chatting, and all at once you are gripped by a strange feeling of hollowness that begins in your stomach and travels up through your chest and into your head. It's hard to describe the sensation; in a way it's just like one of those dreams where you're looking for your house, but every street that you turn into has been transformed into some place that you've never seen before. Just like in those dreams, nothing here makes sense. You have no idea what you're doing in this strange place with these strange people. You walk among them like a hungry ghost, sound and vision freeze-framing as you pass. Nothing is tangible. *This is not my world,* you think. *I do not belong here. I am not one of these people.*

Sometimes I wonder if people can sense it – if isolation is an odour that you give off. I don't know what to say to these people, and they know it. What can we talk about, after all? Work? Well, they're mostly lawyers, so that wouldn't be too hard. Boring as hell, but it's always an easy option. Golf? I hate the game with a passion. How their kids are doing at school? A little hard to join in when you've none of your own. There's no-one here who's going to talk to me about poetry. 'Hey,' I could say. 'Have you seen the latest Mary Oliver collection?' They'd think I was talking about a fashion show at the mall.

I am at the point of desperation when I see that Jack has finally arrived, Melissa by his side. I wave frantically to catch his eye; he makes his way over to me and kisses me on the cheek. 'Hey, birthday girl.'

'Hey, yourself. And not so much of the girl any more, I'm afraid.'

'Now don't give me any of that bullshit. You know perfectly well that you don't look forty, and self-pity is boring, so quit.'

It doesn't take much exposure to Jack to make me smile; that's one of the reasons I love working with him. Scientists may not be renowned for their sense of humour, but then Jack isn't your average scientist in any way that I can see. He isn't your average corporate executive either: he has an endearing and sadly uncommon tendency to tell it like it is.

'So how about a different type of bullshit? You're looking terribly smooth tonight.' The beige suit sets off his dark hair and he doesn't look quite as dishevelled as he normally manages to do. Jack is a good-looking guy but he never looks comfortable in a suit. There's always something a little ... unfinished about him.

He rolls his eyes and aims a sideways nod in the direction of his wife. 'She refused to come out unless I let her dress me properly.'

I turn to her – svelte and perfectly groomed as always, not a hair out of place, heavily but elegantly made up. 'Melissa. How are you doing?'

'I'm doing just fine, thanks. And happy birthday: we've put a little gift for you on the table back there with all the others.' She smiles coolly; Melissa is always polite but she keeps her distance. She doesn't really approve of me, though she tries hard for Jack's sake. She thinks I should be married off and safely ensconced at home with a bunch of kids by now, not out in the workplace taking a senior job from men who surely must deserve it more. She clearly thinks I only made VP litigation because of positive discrimination. And the feeling is fairly mutual; to me she is lacking in warmth and humour – the complete antithesis of Jack. She tugs at Jack's arm. 'Jack, honey, I'm just going to say hi to Neil and Kathy; I'll catch up with you later.' She pauses and turns back to me as if realising that something else may be required of her before she takes her leave of the hostess. 'Looks all set to be a great party.'

I try to smile but I suspect it's more of a grimace. 'Yeah – great.' I guess I don't sound too convincing; Jack looks at me sharply as Melissa raises a neatly plucked eyebrow and turns away.

'What's up?'

'Oh, nothing. Just a dose of the "Feeling Forty Blues", maybe.'

He puts his arm around my shoulder and leads me towards the large room next door where people are dancing. 'Come and dance with me. I'll remind you what it was like to be young and fancy-free. And besides – it'll save me from having to smile at people I don't really want to talk to.'

'I know the feeling. And you'd better watch out – Tom Frankel is around, somewhere.'

His hazel eyes widen, darken. 'Jesus. Whatever made you invite Tom?'

'I didn't. Adam did.'

'Ah.' His face says it all.

The '70s music conspires to place us firmly in the past; it also brings back way too many memories. Memories of teenage years – first kisses, first loves. Memories of my mother – her darkest days. I am so tired of all these memories, but hard as I try, I can't seem to shake off the past. It's not that I choose to dwell on it – and I certainly don't wallow in self-pity. I've seen what self-pity can do. More than anything else in the world, I'd like to let it all go. Shrug it off. But the past seems in some way always to have had possession of me, and I'm so very heavy with carrying the burden of it.

I catch sight of Adam in the doorway, frowning over at us as Jack holds me loosely in his arms, humming along to the music. Irritated, I turn my head away and smile back up at Jack.

'Guess what I did yesterday?'

'I don't know, honey. What did you do yesterday?'

'I had a flying lesson.'

He stops in his tracks and steps on my right foot. I yelp.

'Oh, God, I'm sorry. You did what?'

'I had a flying lesson, dammit. Isn't that what you told me to do? Well, I did as I was told. I had a flying lesson.' I peer down at my foot and grimace. 'Jack, I think you've broken my big toe.'

'You had a flying lesson.' The expression of disbelief on his face slowly transforms into one of delight. All of a sudden he whoops and lifts me off my feet, swinging me round in a circle before letting me back down again.

I laugh and feel several hundred pounds of gloom melt away from me. 'Jack, stop it! Everyone's looking at us.'

'I could care less. You had a flying lesson?' I nod. 'Really?' I nod. He throws his head back and laughs out loud. 'Well, good for you, kid. I mean it. I'm real proud of you.'

'Then you'll probably be even prouder if I tell you that I've booked another one.'

'No shit?'

'No shit. Though you wouldn't have been particularly proud if you'd seen me yesterday. The instructor had to lift me out of the plane at the end of it – I was completely paralysed with fright.'

He rolls his eyes. 'Now why am I not surprised? But hey – it'll get easier over time. There's no need to rush it. You'll do it – I know you will.'

I shrug. 'I don't know, Jack. It's a long way from here to going up solo, let alone passing the test. We'll see how far I can go; right now it'll be a big deal if I can just get up there and back down again without going to pieces.'

'If you leave the arms of the seat intact next time we have to get on a turboprop I'll count it a success.' I stick my tongue out at him; he winks. 'So where did you go – Scottsdale airport?'

'No – Chandler. It's close to work, at least.'

'You planning to take time off to fly?'

'Maybe once, during the week. In the early morning or late afternoon. And then I thought I'd take a second lesson on Saturdays or Sundays.'

'Would've been easier to go to Scottsdale.'

'Maybe. But it's pretty flat around Chandler airport. Not so many houses. I had some crazy idea that if we crashed it'd be safer to do it in the desert.'

'You sure *are* crazy. Have you seen what's in that desert? Rocks, boulders, giant cacti, trees, bushes…'

'Yes, thank you, Jack. I don't always have to be logical, you know.'

'I'm going to be a good boy and hush my mouth on that one.'

I punch him softly in the stomach and he grins. 'How was the instructor?'

'Very patient, very calm, very quiet. Interesting. From Montana. Jesse. I think he thought I was mad – last thing he expected was for me to book another lesson.'

'Not mad – crazy.'

'Huh?'

'One of these days I'm going to teach you to speak the

121

language properly. If you say "mad" over here it means "angry". You mean "crazy".'

I roll my eyes. 'Americans. After ten years I still can't understand you.'

'You got that back to front as well – we're the ones who can't understand you.'

I laugh delightedly and grant him this round. This is an ongoing argument, but an affectionate one. When I first came to America I found myself completely confounded by what I'd rashly assumed was a language that we all shared. Boilers became furnaces, cutlery became flatware and taps became faucets. You don't say 'sorry' when you bump into someone: you say 'excuse me'. Maybe I just never watched enough American TV shows when I was young, but in almost every aspect of daily life I found myself floundering, struggling to make myself understood. From the very beginning Jack found great delight in teasingly pointing out my frequent errors, but in reality he was a huge help. He'd spent plenty of time in the UK over the years and was one of the few colleagues I found who actually knew what I was talking about. He became my translator, and very soon became my friend.

'Frighteningly young, those instructors, aren't they?'

'This one isn't, though it's difficult to tell for sure how old he is. Late thirties, or could be forty, I guess.'

'You're lucky. When I took lessons years ago the instructor had hardly turned twenty. Frightened the hell out of me.'

A hand comes to rest firmly on my back, and I turn my head to see Adam standing there with a taut smile on his face. 'Hey, Jack – do you mind if I cut in here a moment, buddy? Something I want to ask Cat.'

Jack smiles wryly, winks at me and steps back. 'Sure. She's all yours.' As he walks away he calls back over his shoulder, 'You can tell me more about it on Monday.'

'More about what?' Adam asks as he takes Jack's place and puts his hands on my waist.

'Why did you do that?' I am stiff in his arms.

'Do what?'

'Cut in on us like that?'

He tightens his lips and looks away. 'Cat, I don't know what's gotten into you lately. You're acting kinda – hormonal, or something.'

'Hormonal? Goddamn it, Adam, don't patronise me.'

'I'm not patronising you, Cat. I just don't understand you sometimes, that's all. You're not normally this emotional.'

No, I'm not. I don't do emotional. Because I have had my fill of other people's emotions. Because my mother was the queen of emotion; how could I ever compete with that? Adam is right: I'm not normally this emotional. I sigh and run a weary hand through my hair. 'I don't feel like dancing any more. I don't suppose we can go home?'

'You bet we can't go home – it's only ten o'clock, and it's supposed to be your party, after all. You haven't even opened your gifts yet.'

'Oh, please don't tell me I'm supposed to do that in front of everyone.' He looks doubtful and I shake my head, exhausted by the very idea of it. 'No way, Adam. I can't do that. You know that's not my scene. I'd be completely mortified. I'm just going to take them home, open them tomorrow and write a whole bunch of "thank you" notes instead.'

'Whatever you want, sweetheart.' The attempt to placate me only increases my irritation.

'Well, let's go and sit down for a moment, shall we? I'm tired. It feels like it's been a long day.' I turn away from him abruptly and make my way through the remaining dancers. Once we're inside the other room, I stop and look back at him. 'So what was it you wanted to talk to me about?'

'What?'

'You said you wanted to ask me something. Just now. That's why you sent Jack away, remember.'

'Oh. Well, perhaps this isn't the time.'

'Then you won't mind if I go and talk to my friends again, will you?' I know I'm behaving childishly but I can't seem to help myself. I always try my best to be the way he wants me to be, but tonight I just can't seem to find the 'sweetness and light' switch.

'Cat.' He hesitates. 'Let's just step outside a minute, shall we?' He places a hand on my back and gently leads me towards the door.

I don't have the energy to resist him, and think that maybe the cool night air will perk me up. It's not really cold but I find myself shivering; I should have brought a wrap. Adam takes his jacket off and gently places it around my shoulders. I'm enveloped in the smell of him and for a moment I want nothing more than to shrug it off, along with all other traces of the loving web that he has wrapped safely around me. I turn and look south towards downtown Phoenix; the city lights mask the stars with a lurid orange glow. I wait for him to speak.

'Cat – I know we've talked about this before. But not for a while, now. And now that you're forty and all…' Visibly he stumbles, searching for the right words. A gift that normally doesn't fail him: a talent that always stands him in good stead in a courtroom. 'Oh, hell. What I'm trying to say is, isn't it about time we got married?'

My heart sinks; I should have known that this was coming. 'Adam.' I don't know where to start. Once again I am swamped with guilt for my irritability. I don't want to hurt his feelings; he is a good man. A caring man. It's not his fault that I seem to be going through some kind of crisis right now. He's done nothing to contribute to it. But I just can't… 'There's no need for us to get married. We've been living together just fine without it.'

'That's beside the point. People who love each other get married. Especially when they've been living together as long as we have. Especially when they know it works.'

Such a clever man, in so many ways. Such a good lawyer. And yet – so much that he misses in our relationship. Or maybe just chooses to ignore – I don't know. Sometimes I wonder whether he really sees me at all. I take a deep breath and continue to develop my argument against the motion. 'And besides – you've been married. I can't see why you'd be so keen to go and do it again.'

'Joanna and I were divorced seven years ago. I'd hardly be rushing into it, would I?'

'If it wasn't so great first time around, why would you want to go and do it all again?'

'It was great first time around. We were married for fifteen years. We had the kids. We just – grew apart, that's all. She found someone else. That can happen sometimes. It doesn't mean to say it'd have to happen again.'

I shake my head blindly. 'I can't do marriage, Adam. It's all too messy when it doesn't work.' I remember all too well how messy it can be. I lived with the broken pieces of a messy marriage all through my childhood.

'It's messy when it doesn't work whether you're married or not. Being married doesn't make any difference at all.'

'So why bother?'

He sighs. 'It just doesn't seem right, living together all these years and not getting married. That's not what people our age do.'

'Adam, I really don't give a shit what other people of our age do.' I restrain myself from reminding him that, actually, I'm ten years younger. 'And absolutely the last reason for anyone to get married is because that's what's expected of them.'

He carries on as if I haven't spoken. 'And apart from anything else, it'd show commitment. Every time I see you with Jack Walker I wonder about your commitment, Cat – I really do.'

This is absolutely the wrong tack to take: my temper flares. I grit my teeth. It's been a hard enough evening already; I won't let this develop into a row. I don't do rows. 'For heaven's sake, Adam. Jack and I are friends. We work together all the time; we spend a good deal of time in each other's company. We travel together. So yes – I'm immensely thankful that we do get along so well. But there's absolutely nothing else between us. He and Melissa are perfectly happily married.'

'I've seen the way he looks at you.'

I pass a weary hand over my forehead. 'Oh, God. Just leave it, will you? This is such an unoriginal conversation. Exactly the kind of conversation that married people have. Which is one of many reasons why I don't want to get married.' I sigh. 'I'm sorry, Adam. It's not about you: it's about me.' It's about everything I've ever experienced of other people's marriages. 'I just don't want to get married. To anyone. Ever. I'm quite comfortable with the way things are.'

'That's the whole problem, isn't it, Cat? You're comfortable. You're safe. How about taking a risk every now and again?'

I want to laugh. Risk? As always when it comes to our relationship, he's completely missed the point. Marrying Adam wouldn't be a risk: it'd be the safest thing I could do. Just look at him: respected, successful lawyer. Partner in a big-city law firm. Ten years older than me, perfectly pleasant kids from a previous marriage all grown up now, civil ex-wife, plenty of money, nice house. He's handsome enough in a smooth, clean-cut way and in good physical shape; he's easy-going and caring. And he loves me more than I love him. There's 'safe' for you.

But still the dig hurts.

'Comfortable? Safe? Do you want to know what I did yesterday afternoon?' He looks confused: good. 'I had a flying lesson.'

His expression is a picture. 'You had a flying lesson?'

'Yup.'

'What the hell'd you go and do that for? You could get yourself killed, or something. Besides, you're scared out of your wits in small planes.'

Why am I surprised? That's exactly what I thought he'd say. And the precise reason why I didn't tell him what I was going to do. And yet being right provides no satisfaction this time: he flattens me, defeats me. I close up like a clam.

He opens his mouth to continue the conversation, but I hold my hand up to stop him. 'No, Adam. That's enough now. I really don't want to talk about this any more. Not any of it. I'm tired. I don't want to argue with you; I really appreciate you asking me to marry you, but the answer is no. I'm sorry. All I want to do right now is to get this party over with and to go home. So let's put our happy faces on and go in there and smile for the people.'

I hand him back his jacket, turn abruptly and stride away. I don't look to see if he's following. I open the door and the noise and the warmth and the lights assault my senses. Amidst the crowd I see a hand waving towards me, a voice calling my name. I unclench my jaw and dredge up my best social smile. It feels like the hardest thing I've ever done. Every part of my body wants to run; to throw off my high heels and simply take flight.

᠎᠎᠎ᕔ ᕔ ᕔ

'You came back.' His smile is mostly in his eyes and a small upturn in one corner of his mouth. I remember that much at least from the last lesson, though all that I've retained of it is a vaguely dreamlike sequence of images, bereft of structure or meaning.

'Did you think I wouldn't?'

'I figured the odds were fifty-fifty. Depending on what kind of dreams you had last Friday night.'

I laugh out loud. 'They were pretty weird. Hot-air balloons came into it, I seem to remember.'

'Could have been worse. I had you down for 747s falling out of the sky, sky-dives with parachutes failing to open. Maybe a flaming space shuttle or two.' Thank heavens he has a sense of humour – I'm probably going to need that before we're through. But then so, I suspect, is he.

'Jesse!' The pretty young brunette at the desk waves a beautifully manicured red-nailed hand at us to signal her need. I curl mine reflexively into fists to hide the ragged bitten ends. Once she has his attention she flicks a stray curl back from her face and smiles winningly. 'Before you go up, could you just let me know what days you're going to be working next week? We've had a bunch of people call for lessons and I don't have you down on the schedule.'

'Sure.' He turns back to me. 'Excuse me for a moment, will you?' I nod, and watch as she leans over the counter towards him, all sparkling eyes and flashing white teeth, one hand playing with a lock of her hair, twisting it around her finger. I try not to roll my eyes. Do people really do that in real life? How obvious can you get? But then I've never had the knack of this kind of flirting, though it's another of those skills that American women seem to absorb so effortlessly as toddlers. 'How to Twist an Adoring Daddy Round Your Little Finger in Five Easy Lessons'. Well – there you have it, I guess. I seriously missed out in the Daddy department. I'm much more likely to shift my eyes away, straighten up and withdraw. I give out all the wrong signals. I don't know what to do with my hands, how to hold my body.

She's watching him closely as he marks up the chart. Of course, I can see why; there's no doubt at all that he's cute. Tall, not heavily muscled but looks like he works out a little.

Looks pretty good in those jeans. I give my head a quick shake, bring myself up short. Careful, Cat. Let's not get distracted here – and above all, let's not be a cliché. Though I can't help but be amused that he's not rising to her bait; he's quiet and professional, leaning away slightly as they bend their heads down over the weekly planning chart, gently withdrawing his hand as she lays hers on top to emphasise something she's saying to him.

Finally she allows him to end the conversation. He turns around again and looks me over for a moment with that cool, assessing glance, back straight, legs apart and arms folded over his pale blue shirt. I fight a mischievous urge to salute. The brunette is still watching every move that he makes, but he seems quite oblivious. Just for a moment her eyes meet mine; she flushes and turns away, back to her charts. Sympathy wells up unexpectedly; I know how it feels to be out in the cold.

'So,' he says abruptly, 'here's what happens now. If you're going to do this for real, you'll need to start taking some theory as well as the flying. There's a written exam you'll need to pass before you can enter for the flight exam. You have to learn about aerodynamics, aircraft systems and engines, weight and balance, weather, flight planning, navigation, the Federal Aviation Regulations...' Fortunately I've already done my research; this isn't such a shock as he might be imagining. I've always loved to study, and this is all so different from anything I've ever done before. So if he'd been thinking it might put me off, he's wrong. 'Also, you'll need to go and get a medical certificate from a doctor who specialises in aviation issues. It's nothing too complicated at this level: mostly just a general health check and an eye test. But we'll talk about all that when we come back down.'

He looks out of the window and lifts his head up to the sky. Blue sky, crystal clear, full of promise. A small smile steals into the corners of his mouth, softening the harshness of his features. When he turns back his eyes are already quite lost in the distance. 'Let's go fly.'

Clutching the ignition keys, documentation and headphones, I follow him out onto the asphalt where the aircraft waits patiently for us, gleaming and spotless in the early morning sun. The numbers and letters painted on the side show that it's the same airplane that we flew last time. But this time I'm focused; this time she's real. This time I will learn. I watch and listen carefully as he leads me through the pre-flight inspection, showing me what to look for as we tick off item after item on the detailed checklist. If I'm going to trust that she can fly and carry me safely with her, I need to know what she's made of. I need to understand her limits in order to better negotiate my own.

I run my hands slowly over the fuselage as we check for flaws and for loose rivets. She feels smooth and cool in the weak sunshine; a very fine layer of dry dust particles skims away as I sweep my fingers firmly over the metal. Tentatively, I examine the wings and the ailerons; I stroke the tail and the rudder, checking as instructed for smooth movement in the elevator. We examine the legs and feet – I'm gently informed that they're actually called 'struts' and 'gear' – scrutinise the tyres and check the brakes for leaks. Static source, pitot tube, stall warning device ... navigation lights, beacon, radio and navigation antennae ... each one is explained to me, each one ticked off on the pre-flight checklist. So much to remember, so many technical terms to learn.

I lean up against the nose while, following Jesse's instructions, I check that the engine cowling is secure. The airplane rocks a little against my weight; I shudder at her fragility. I pass my hands with particular care over the propeller blades, checking for chinks, for anything that might weaken the structure and cause them to fracture. We take fuel samples from a drain under each wing, straining the pale blue liquid into a transparent tube to see if there's water or anything else that shouldn't be there. We climb up onto the gear struts to open the fuel caps on top of the wings and we check the fuel quantity; I bend all the way over and inhale the sharp heady scent of AVGAS. We check on the oil; I poke my nose into the engine door opening as I replace the dipstick and my nostrils fill with the acrid engine odour of burnt oil, spent fuel, old friction. I want to know this plane, Two November Romeo; I want to know how she smells, how she breathes, what makes her mechanical heart beat. My life is in her hands.

I catch myself caressing the gleaming cone-shaped spinner in front of the propeller as if I were stroking a horse's nose. Reluctantly, I pull my hands away and turn back to Jesse. He's watching me, hands on lean hips and legs slightly apart, smiling that enigmatic crinkly little smile.

'What?' It comes out more defensively than I'd intended. 'What did I do wrong?'

He raises an eyebrow, shakes his head. 'Nothing. Nothing at all. It was exactly right. To be a good pilot you need to know your airplane. Get a feel for her. Maybe it sounds a little crazy, but it's kind of like building up a relationship – a trust.' His mouth twitches up at one corner. 'And I'm sure she appreciates all the attention. Come on, let's get inside and away. It's a perfect morning for flying.'

Before starting the engine we take another run through the instrument panel. It still looks like the space shuttle to me, but to my surprise I remember the basic instruments pretty well. I'm not so sure about the radio and communications set-up, but for now he doesn't seem too worried. 'I'll cover the radio today; you just listen to what's going on. We'll go through all that properly during the next lesson. Today I just want you to get more comfortable with being in the air. I'll talk you through takeoff in a bit more detail and then I want you to just fly.

However you want to do it. Straight and level, a bit of climbing and descending, a few gentle turns. Nothing more than that. Sound okay?'

'Sounds perfect.' The band across my chest loosens a little: it's exactly what I need. Time to get to know how it is to fly in this tiny plane; time to get a feel for her controls; time to learn how to relax. I'm very much aware of him crammed into the tight space beside me: the faint desert scent of sagebrush, and the solid warmth of his left arm and shoulder resting against mine. We run slowly through the pre-takeoff checks as he explains to me exactly what we're doing and why. I listen; I memorise.

We climb slowly at first, and this is the test: if the engine fails now, in this first couple of minutes, we cannot turn back to the airport and safety. We are too low. We would have to take our chances, find somewhere to land in the small wedge of ground just ahead of us. Hope to find some of it free of obstructions, empty and clear. I am rigid with tension; a heavy drumbeat resounds through my chest and my breathing is shallow and rapid. But this time I am determined; in spite of my fear I watch and I see.

The world shifts and tilts and my stomach somersaults as we bank sharply and turn to south-east to head out over the desert. Smoothly and steadily, we continue to climb. I risk a brief glance down, but what I see there below me is no longer the earth that I know. It deconstructs itself into two-dimensional patterns that I cannot interpret: a patchwork in fabrics of orange and green. Quilting lines cross it in straight lines and curves, the stitching uneven and puckered. Then once more we turn; I scan from another angle, but still it eludes my grasp.

The San Tan Mountains lie before us, and to our east, the misty haze of more mountains stretching into the distance. Jesse's voice, always soft, in my ear: 'If you're heading south-east you need to stay this side of Florence and away from the Military Operations Areas. There are a lot of them out in the desert, and so you need to be really clear about where you are on the sectional chart if you don't want to run into a fighter jet flying towards you at five hundred miles an hour. But we'll talk about navigation another time. Right now, if we keep west of the San Tans then we can relax. I'll keep an eye on where we are; you just concentrate on flying the plane.'

A few minutes later we level off. 'Okay – your controls. Just try to keep us straight and level, follow this same heading south, and stay at four thousand feet.'

It all sounds so simple. I take a deep breath and try to relax as he removes his hands from the wheel and rests them casually on his thighs. He's close enough to reach it in an instant if anything should go wrong, but I am very much aware that I am the only one of us who's flying this plane.

'Oh – and how about you release your stranglehold on the yoke?'

I laugh abruptly and shake my head. Whatever else I might be able to do, I can't seem to do that.

'Here: take your hands away for a moment: my controls. Now watch me.' He places his hands on the control wheel and then removes them again; I swallow convulsively. I twitch; I am desperate to reach out and take hold. He places an index finger on each side of the wheel and holds them there lightly. 'See? She's really a pretty stable machine. All you need is the lightest of touches and you can feel how responsive she is. She wants to fly. It's what she was built for. She wants to stay in the air. Hell, wouldn't you?' I recognise, now, the tone of voice that accompanies the quirky smile. 'Okay – now you try it. I'll keep my hands here, just an inch away, so you don't need to worry. I've got you covered.'

I place one finger on each side of the wheel, checking

nervously to see where Jesse's hands are in relation to his controls. They're close enough.

'Now press down a little with your left finger and push up with your right. See how she responds.' Gently, she begins to bank to the left. 'That's good. Now straighten her up.' I reverse my movements and we're level again. 'See? That's good. Now you can put your hands back, but keep your touch just as light as it was then. Your controls, but I'll be watching, now.'

Just as I'm beginning to feel comfortable, the plane shudders for a moment and the nose falls slightly. I let out a little yelp and clutch clumsily at the control wheel, pulling it towards me to bring up the nose. Immediately, Jesse reaches out and pushes the wheel back down again. 'It's okay. Just a spot of turbulence. The airplane will right herself: don't fight it or you'll just make things worse. Keep your hands light and keep the nose pointing right ahead. And whatever you do, don't ever pull the nose up towards you like that: you run the risk of stalling the plane. Not a good idea unless you're ready to try aerobatics already. We'll talk about stalls in a couple of lessons; don't worry about it for now.'

'Sorry.' My face flames; defeat settles, heavy and familiar, in my stomach.

'Hey – no problem – you're not supposed to know everything yet. There's a lot to take in, and a lot of it runs against your natural instincts. Don't worry about it – that's what I'm here for.'

I take a deep breath and grit my teeth. He's right, of course. I'm going to make mistakes. People make mistakes when they're learning new things. There's nothing wrong with mistakes. I don't always have to be perfect at everything that I do. I have no-one to please here but myself. No-one else's expectations to meet, no-one's needs to fulfil. This is all just for me. I can allow myself to be human and fallible, just this once.

Slowly, the litany takes hold. I begin to believe myself, to ease up a little. After all, I know about turbulence: I've read about it in the airline magazines. Just like little bumps on a road, they say. Nothing to worry about; aircraft are built to withstand all kinds of structural stress. But they're talking about heavy airliners: 747s and Airbuses and MD-11s. I'm in a little two-seater Cessna that probably weighs less than my car. But Jesse is oozing calm beside me, and I tell myself that if there was a problem he'd know.

'Even at this time of year, and this early in the morning when the air is cooler, we're going to run into a little turbulence from time to time. It's worse in the summer when the heat down there is ferocious; flying in the afternoons is like driving over a rocky beach. But by the time summer comes around you'll be an old hand.'

'Somehow I can't imagine that.'

'I've had nervous students before. Everyone's nervous at first. It wears off as you get a better sense of what's going on around you. Once you start to develop some kind of sense of control. That's why I want you to take it slowly for the first few lessons.'

'Have you ever had anyone as nervous as me?'

He hesitates; I hear the smile in his voice. 'Well, no. Not exactly.'

'There you are. I rest my case.'

'Ah. A lawyer, then.'

'Sorry.' It's an automatic response. Nobody loves a lawyer. Not in this country, anyway.

'Could be worse. I taught a psychiatrist once; psychoanalysed his way through every lesson. "Ah – now I'm feeling a little nervous as we descend. Very interesting. Since I've never actually fallen any great distance myself, this is clearly an example of an *atavistic* fear of falling – something fundamental in the design of the mammalian limbic system. Inherited memories, perhaps, or indeed a tapping into the collective unconscious..."'

I laugh and feel the muscles in my legs and shoulders begin to loosen up. 'He must've made an impact – you remember it very well.'

'Guy reminded me of a psychology professor I had once in college. And the terminology sticks with you.'

'Did he get his license?'

'No. He was way too uptight. Not nervous, but he couldn't let go enough to really get a feel for the plane. You can analyse too much; sometimes you have to just go with your gut.'

'And is that why you gave up the psychology? Because it teaches you to analyse too much?'

It takes him a moment to answer. 'Partly.'

I sense a story; I'd be curious if I wasn't concentrating so heavily on keeping the plane in the air. Not that it seems to need much help. The air is smooth and still again now; we're flying straight and level and beautifully on course, and little by little my breathing slows and deepens as I acclimatise myself to the sounds and the motion of the airplane. I am vaguely aware that there is an earth and a landscape below, but I don't want to think about that now. My sole focus is on the boundless unchanging immensity of the empty sky that surrounds me. The summer monsoon clouds are long gone; all that remains is the colour blue. I am surrounded by blue; bathed in it. Perfect, pure cerulean blue. This is no weak watercolour wash – it is a sea of saturated pigment that leaps off the canvas and launches itself into your cortex. Not a variation in tint or in shade. Blue seeps into every pore of my skin as I familiarise myself with this strange new element. I can feel it; I can almost taste it. Ripe lime with a bouquet of ozone, tangy on the tongue and cool on the skin. I am a creature of cold blue air; I am immunising myself against the earth and all that would weigh me down.

'You look very thoughtful. What do you see?'

'What?'

'What do you see out there?' He nods his head towards the windshield.

I shake my head, slowly. 'I don't know that I was focusing on something that I can see. You seem to use different senses up here. Senses I wasn't really aware of having. How do you sense immensity?'

'Good question. How are you sensing it?'

Lord. I struggle to find words. 'I suppose ... as something very ... pure, very simple. Something that doesn't judge, or have any expectations about you: that cuts through all the bullshit. That just is.' I laugh at myself. Must be the lack of oxygen, or something. I don't normally babble like this. 'That sounds crazy. I don't really know what I'm trying to say; I can't grasp hold of it properly to explain it. As if there's a mystery out there, if only I could catch a glimpse.'

'A mystery.' Again, I hear the smile. 'You know, the Native Americans call the sky "Grandfather" and the earth "Grandmother". Earth and sky: a perfect balance. Male and female energies, mother and father. But the boundary line where those energies come together is what they call the "Great Mystery". The boundary between heaven and earth.'

'Sounds like you've made quite a study of it.'

'My maternal grandfather was a Crow Indian; I grew up near the Crow reservation, in Montana. And so what do you see – or feel – when you look down?'

'I'm trying my best not to do that. Looking down makes me frightened of falling. Besides, it's not the earth that I want – it's the sky.'

'Ah – not a good idea. You can't have Grandfather Sky without Grandmother Earth. Without the protection of the sky, the earth would shatter. Without the grounding of the earth, the sky would collapse. And on a less mythological note, you need to look down to be able to navigate. How are you going to know where you are?'

137

'That's the trouble, really. It's when I look down that the problems begin. That I wonder what the hell I'm doing, so far up here above it all. Because it's the ground that causes all the problems, isn't it? It's the ground that'll break us if we crash.'

Out of the corner of my eye I see him shake his head. 'You can't have one without the other.' His voice is deep, soft – I have to strain to hear him through the headphones. 'It isn't just about being in the air and keeping yourself there, it's about your relationship to the ground. You never leave it behind, see – not even up here. Whether the surface of the earth below you is hot or cold determines what kind of air you get to fly through – that's why you get turbulence over a hot dry desert. And think about mountain waves.' He shrugs. 'Well, you'll get to study all that when we look at meteorology. Flying is about how you leave the ground, where you are in relation to it. And how you can safely approach it again. Because we can't stay up here, can we? Sooner or later, all of us have got to come to terms with the ground – and come back down.'

It is an idea that, oddly, I do not relish. When the time comes I hand him the controls with reluctance, a strange sadness seeping into me as he brings us smoothly in to land. It's not as if I've lost the fear: it's still there, vivid and consuming, albeit more manageable this time around. I just don't want to lose the clarity, the focus, the intensity of concentration that seems to define this experience. Because, as we turn the sharp, low corner onto final approach and the runway looms ahead of us, suddenly I see what this is all about.

Everything is so simple up there. Just you, and the sky, and the will to survive. Everything comes down to this: you balance on a knife-edge, but it's a clear, clean cut and what bleeds away is doubt.

Once the airplane is safely stowed, we head back to the reception area and upstairs into a room that runs the length of the building and that clearly is used for lessons. Four metal tables with wooden chairs on either side occupy one side of the room; along the other side, next to windows that look out over the airport, are half a dozen cubicles that seem to serve as offices for the instructors. Except for us, it's empty.

Jesse strolls down to the end of the room and gestures towards a chair at the farthest of the tables. 'Have a seat.' The wall next to the table is covered with navigation charts and a variety of diagrams and photographs. He throws his flight bag beside a metal desk occupying the corner cubicle. 'Want a cup of coffee?'

'Yes please. Just black.'

He heads back downstairs and returns a minute or two later with a couple of cardboard cups filled with a weak brown liquid that smells old. I wrinkle my nose. I should've known better: outside of Starbucks and a few other 'boutique' chains, most American coffee could pass for peat-flavoured water.

'So how long have you been doing this?' I ask. I'm curious about him. I can't place him – what he's doing here. He obviously has a lot of flight hours, but from what he said last week, most of them aren't instructing hours. And the other instructors are so much younger.

He puts his coffee on the table and lowers himself into a seat that looks like it was constructed for someone half his size. 'Teaching flying? Oh, not long – getting on for a year. I used to be an airline pilot, but I gave it up. Couple of years ago now.'

'You're kidding.'

He shrugs, leans his elbows on the table and holds my gaze as he speaks. He has a way of making you feel as if he's really talking to you. Not just talking: he listens, too. It's disconcerting, but on balance I like it. 'It wasn't the same, somehow, in the big planes. You don't feel like you're really flying – it's kind of like the difference between riding a motorcycle and driving a heavy truck. Too big, too clumsy. Took all of the magic out of it, for me. And you have no choices: you fly precisely the route you're told to fly, exactly when you're told. I've never been too good at that.' He smiles wryly. 'It beats a lot of jobs, there's no question. But for me, flying has always been about all kinds of freedom. And doing it like that – well, it was starting to interfere with my love of it.'

'And you hated the uniform.'

He laughs. 'Yeah, let's just say I'm not really a uniform kind of guy.'

He's right; somehow I can't picture it. He's not typical airline pilot material; everything about him is loose and easy. From the way he looks – the silky fair hair that's much longer than regulation, to the way he dresses – bare ankles peeking out of white sneakers below comfortably faded jeans. And the way he moves – the easy shrug, limbs unrestricted and fluid.

'I stuck it for ten years and then decided that wasn't what I wanted to be when I grew up after all.'

'Wow.' I take a sip of the coffee and grimace: it tastes as bad as it smells. 'Bit of a change. I can't imagine you make anything like enough to live on as an instructor. Not in comparison with an airline job.'

'No. But I saved some, over the years. Always figured that as long as I owned the roof over my head, I could get by. There's no amount of money in the world that's worth your freedom, right? I'm doing what I love: teaching people to fly.'

'But you don't instruct full-time?'

'No. I like variety. Every now and again I'll do a charter flight. Sometimes in a jet, to keep my hours up. As long as I don't have to wear a uniform.' He laughs softly. 'Promised myself I'd never do that again. Then in my spare time I'm working on my masterpiece. Which will, of course, make my fortune.' His eyes crinkle again as he sips the steaming coffee.

'Your masterpiece?'

'My Great American Novel. You know. The one we all think we can write?'

'Ah.' Somehow I'm not surprised by all this; he doesn't talk like an airline pilot any more than he looks like one. Whatever they talk like. Which is a stupid thing to think, really. What I mean is that I suppose he talks like a writer. I can *imagine* him being a writer.

What rubbish I'm thinking.

'My mother's a writer.' It slips out, thoughtlessly. Why on earth did I volunteer that?

'Really?'

'Well – not novels so much as children's stories. Fairy stories really, I guess. They're not published over here, just in the UK, so you wouldn't have come across them.' I rush the words, wanting to move on, to change the subject.

'That must've been great when you were a kid.'

'What?'

'Having a writer for a mother. It must've been great. All those stories.'

'She didn't start writing her own stories till I left home.'

My voice comes out more abruptly than I intend; I sit back and clasp my hands tightly in front of me. I look down at the table. I feel his eyes on me. Gently, he puts his coffee cup back on the table.

'Well, maybe we'd better get on with the lesson; I've another student in half an hour. What we're going to cover today is some of the theory behind flight, and some basic aerodynamics…' His voice fades gently into the background of my mind. As always she's waiting there, waiting to take control.

'Come and sit down next to me, Cat. I'm going to tell you a story.' She gestures extravagantly towards me and then pats the sofa beside her.

More than anything I want to run away, to go and hide in

my room all by myself. I don't want to sit next to her. I don't want to hear another one of her stories. I want her to leave me alone.

Reluctantly, I go over and perch on the edge of the sofa, as far away as I can get. I look down at my hands; begin picking at my bitten nails.

'No, no, little Kitty-Cat. C'mon now. Come right over here. Give Mummy a cuddle.' She takes hold of my arm, too tight, and jerks me towards her. I lose my balance and fall on my side, and she giggles and puts her hand over her mouth. 'Oops-a-daisy!' I pull myself up, and edge closer to her. I try not to inhale as she puts an arm around me; she smells of sweat, of stale whisky and cigarettes.

'Once upon a time,' she begins, and then stops, a puzzled frown settling on her face. I sneak a glance up at her; she has bags and dark blue shadows under her eyes and her complexion looks like old uncooked pastry. I bite the inside of my cheek. I want my beautiful mummy back – the one with laughing eyes and shiny red lips and neat, curly brown hair. I don't want this impostor who comes to stay with us from time to time – who takes over her body and twists her mind and turns her into someone else. 'Well, now. I've forgotten which story I was going to tell you.' She thinks for a moment, breathing heavily, and then her face brightens. 'Oh yes. That was it.' She giggles girlishly. 'What a silly mummy I am. Once upon a time, there was a little girl who had no mummy, and she didn't have any shoes either. So she collected some scraps of cloth and made herself a pair of red shoes. You've no idea how much she loved those shoes ...'

I've heard the story before, of course. It's one of her favourites. 'The Red Shoes'. And as always, when she gets to the part where the little girl is forbidden to wear her shoes and they're taken from her, she starts to snivel. At the point that the little girl steals them back but is cursed so that she'll have to

*wear the dancing shoes forever – until she dies of weariness –
she begins to cry. By the time she reaches the end and the little
girl begs the man to chop off her feet and cripple her to get rid
of the shoes, she can hardly get the words out for sobbing.*

*Dread settles deep into my stomach. I feel her thin body
shuddering next to me. A stray sob slips from her mouth. 'God,
Cat. It's such a sad story, isn't it?' She sniffs; rubs her right
hand across her nose. 'Can you imagine what she must have
felt like, that little girl? She had to ask them to cut off her own
feet to keep from dancing.' The tears flow freely; thin colourless
snot escapes from her nostrils and settles in the corners of her
mouth. 'Because she couldn't stop the dancing, you see. She
couldn't stop it.' She takes her arm away from me and hugs
herself, rocking backwards and forwards, sniffing noisily. 'See
– although it was fun at first, fun to be able to dance away like
that, she couldn't control it. Couldn't stop.' She reaches for a
paper handkerchief and blows her nose.*

*I flinch. I don't understand why she keeps on about this
same story. I hate it. I hate all her stories. I hate this constant
outpouring of emotion – it tears at me, batters me. But I daren't
move; if I try to leave she'll only get mad and that'll be even
worse. I hold myself tightly, all of my muscles tense and ready
for flight.*

*'What's the matter with you, anyway? Don't you think it's
sad?' She turns around, frowning; puts a hand on my shoulder,
gives me a little shake. 'No, you don't get sad, do you? You
never cry. Not Cat. You never show your emotions. But that's
'cause you don't have any emotions, do you?' She pulls her
hand away, turns from me, mouth twisting in disgust. 'You're
just like your father. Image of him. Right here in my house. I
don't know what I did to deserve you both. Hard, the pair of
you. Hard as nails.' She looks at me again, brown eyes filled
with hatred. 'Get out of my sight. Just get out of my sight, why
don't you. You're not my daughter. You're his. All his.'*

Upstairs in my room I lie on my bed, trembling. I become nothing; I lose myself. From time to time I hear a crash downstairs; at every noise I flinch.

6

Laura

The sharp crack of a branch snapping and crashing to the ground startles Laura. She glances briefly out of the window at the driving rain and gusting wind, and then retreats to the safety of the fire. Retreat. That's the story of her life these days.

Once upon a time there was an old, old woman who lived in a small cottage by the sea. With every day that passed she grew older but not very much wiser. Once upon a time the old woman had been young but she had never been carefree. On the contrary: she was a walking receptacle for cares. All the cares of the world sought her out and poured themselves into her, filling her up and displacing the reality of her so there was nothing left inside her but emptiness. And as the days and the months and the years went by she became increasingly transparent and more and more hollow. But she fashioned herself a special dress to hide the transparency and to cover the emptiness. A special dress and a pair of red shoes ...

Another gust, and the front window rattles in its rotting sashes. So much for Meg's predictions about the winter weather based on the crisp blue skies at Halloween: it's been raining solidly for ten days. Laura shifts restlessly in the chair but, finding no relief from the sharp pains shooting up and down her back, hauls herself heavily to her feet. A stab of pain in her chest as she stands. Oh, for God's sake, she thinks. I'm sixty-one years old, not eighty-one. And if I'm not careful I really am going to become old before my time.

Just like Aunt Lizzie. Another old woman who lived in a cottage by the sea. The parallel makes her smile, but it isn't a comfortable smile.

Once upon a time there was a little girl who lived with a wicked old witch in a small cottage by the sea. The little girl was filled with cares, and because the cares had eaten their way inside her she had become hollow and transparent. The witch was her aunt, and the little girl had gone to live with her because her mother and father hadn't wanted her. But the witch was angry and bitter and filled with spite. She hated the little girl and did everything that she could to make her unhappy. But there was an uncle too, and the little girl loved him dearly. He was the only person in her life who loved her in return. But although sometimes he protected her from the witch, he was often away at work and the witch took those opportunities to cast her wicked spells on the child.

Hard as she tries, Laura can't push it away. The story is there, possessing her. Just as it's always done. Gnawing at her, chewing out little pieces of her and spitting them onto the ground where they evaporate as soon as they're exposed to the light. Piece after piece of her, gone. Vanished, until there's hardly anything left. Just like Joe said. But there's a part of Laura that's a fighter still: a hard stone core that won't give in, that will only be dragged down so far before it awakens, comes back to itself. The part that pulled itself back up out of the pit by the bloody shreds of its fingertips all those years ago. The part that hasn't ever allowed itself to just lay down and die, no matter how restful an option that might have seemed to be.

It's that part of Laura that rises now.

Laura was going to a funeral. She'd never been to a funeral before, but this one was important because it was one of her school friends that was dead. Like Laura, Elsie was only eleven, but she'd died of a busted kidney, so Mrs Scrimshaw had told them. Laura didn't know how a kidney got busted, or why that would kill you, but the shocking discovery that your body could fail you so young and that you could die from it was festering away slowly in her mind. She'd never really thought about it much, but she'd always supposed that you only died if you were old, or if you were run over by a bus or got killed in the war. You could die having children, too – she knew that, though she hadn't quite worked out how it happened. Because Laura's great-grandmother had died having her Uncle Johnnie, so Aunt Lizzie said. But it hadn't occurred to her up until now that your body could break, all by itself, with no warning at all.

She was a bit apprehensive about the funeral; she didn't like the idea of Elsie lying there dead in the open coffin for everyone to see – red hair spreading out on the pillow like dried blood, and her long freckled limbs rigid and cold. But you had to pay your respects, Aunt Lizzie said – that's just the way it was, and that was that. Elsie hadn't been Laura's closest friend or anything, but every Tuesday night after school they would ride on their bikes together over to the new swimming pool at Seaton Carew to do their lifesaving classes. Laura had liked Elsie; she wasn't spiteful and didn't call you names like some of the other girls. She'd cried for ages when Mrs Scrimshaw said that Elsie had died, but when she'd come home from school Aunt Lizzie had just told her to stop her caterwauling and get the pan out for the cabbage.

Little girls didn't wear black to go to funerals, Aunt Lizzie said, but Laura had to wear her best frock. To show her respect. It was very important to show your respect for the dead. Laura didn't know why it was so important if they were dead anyway, because why would they care what you wore down here if they were already up there in Heaven with Jesus? But if she asked Aunt Lizzie why, she'd only get shouted at. So she dressed carefully in front of the wardrobe mirror in her new primrose yellow dress with its crisp white collar, in clean white socks and her Sunday best black leather shoes.

She was going to meet some other school friends – Margaret and Josie and Nan – at the seat at the corner of the road and they were all going to walk to church together. Uncle Billy would probably be at the seat, so if she hurried up and got there early she might be allowed to sit there with him for a few minutes. If the other men weren't there, that was. Laura's dad always met his friends in the Traveller's Rest, but Uncle Billy and his cronies met up at the seat. They sat and watched the world go by, Aunt Lizzie said, gossiping like a bunch of old biddies. But when Laura used to go down there at dinnertimes to take him his bait, she found that they mostly were silent. They sat all in a row with their wooden walking sticks between their legs, hands folded together and resting on the crudely carved handles, flat-capped heads turning from side to side as a bus or a lorry rumbled past. Nodding courteously to any passer-by. Every now and again one of them would pass a comment to the others, but mostly they just sat there quietly, smoking their pipes.

Laura tied her curly dark hair back in a ponytail and hurried down the stairs to tell Aunt Lizzie that she was ready to go. But she slowed down as she walked into the room; she remembered that Aunt Lizzie hadn't been in a very good mood all morning, and if she found any fault with Laura she might do something to make her late, just out of spite.

She was sitting in her usual chair by the big square table in the middle of the front room, chewing at her finger nails and shaking her head as she muttered to herself. The customary grey hairnet clung to her head like a spider's web. It toned with soft wavy hair that had been newly washed that morning, keeping it carefully in place so that it dried without sticking out at the back and sides. She was wearing a faded floral cotton pinafore dress over her short-sleeved summer frock; it was only on Sundays that Aunt Lizzie would take the pinny off, or on the very rare occasions that she went out somewhere. Laura sighed as she heard the angry mumbling. She had no idea what put Aunt Lizzie in her bad moods. Some days she was fine and she would even tell Laura funny stories – though usually they were funny at someone else's expense. Other times she would wake up angry and stay that way all day. She changed like the weather, Uncle Billy said. He said not to mind her but Laura didn't think he really knew what she could be like. Because when Uncle Billy was around everyone was nicer, even Aunt Lizzie.

The smell of baking wafted in through the open door that led to the small dark kitchen: raisin scones, sausage rolls, teacakes and fatty busters. Laura hoped there would be some for her tea. When Uncle Billy was home they would steal the bite-sized sausage rolls off the rack while they were still warm from the oven and Aunt Lizzie wasn't looking. 'What's the good of me making stuff and you just eating it,' she would squawk at them once she noticed they were missing, hands on her soft, wide hips and small black eyes flashing daggers through the air. Uncle Billy would look at Laura and roll his eyes. 'What's the good of you making stuff and us *not* eating it, now, Lizzie,' he'd say, smiling his warm twinkly smile at her – the one that made even Aunt Lizzie's mouth twitch up at the corners.

'I'm going now, Aunt Lizzie,' Laura said quietly. 'Is there anything you need me to do before I go?'

'Well, that would be friggin' stupid, wouldn't it, now you're all dressed? If I asked you to fetch me a cone of sea-coal out of the coalhouse you'd only mucky up your best frock.' She glanced away from Laura with her best long-suffering expression and shook her head. 'It's all right. You go out. I'll do it myself. Never mind my poor old back.'

Laura immediately felt guilty but Aunt Lizzie was right: she couldn't get her dress dirty now. But before Laura could slip away Aunt Lizzie turned around and sniffed loudly, looking her up and down. Laura's stomach fluttered as she stood still for the inspection. She bit her lower lip.

'Didn't clean your shoes, then?'

'Yes I did, Aunt Lizzie. I did them before I got dressed.'

'I didn't see you.'

'You were in the kitchen, Aunt Lizzie. I did do them, honestly I did.'

'Doesn't look to me like you did. Look at the cut of them. You get that shoe polish out again and make sure you do them properly this time. You're not going out of this house looking like a tramp.'

Laura's heart sank but she knew it was pointless to argue. She might miss the chance to sit with Uncle Billy now, but she still had a few minutes to spare. If she was quick, she shouldn't be late. She ran to the cupboard by the fire and pulled out the black woollen bag of shoe cleaning things. She slipped off her shoes and without thinking put them on the table while she fumbled for the flat round tin of Cherry Blossom and pushed off the lid.

Aunt Lizzie's high-pitched screech cut through her like a knife. 'Don't put your shoes on the table, you half-soaked little get, you! Don't you know that's seven years of bad luck?'

Startled, Laura dropped the tin of polish and watched helplessly as the inevitable happened. It brushed against her skirt on its way down, leaving a long black smudge on the primrose yellow cotton before it rolled onto the floor and settled upside down under the table.

'What's the matter with you, you daft little bugger? How can you be so bloody stupid?'

Laura was frozen, horrified.

Aunt Lizzie folded her arms under her ample bosom and pursed her lips in satisfaction. 'Well, that's that, then. You can't go now, can you, with your frock like that?'

'Of course I can. There are other dresses that I can wear. If I run up now and change there'll still be time.'

'Don't you talk back to me – I said you can't go now, you dirty little midden. Didn't you hear me?'

Laura felt the tears well up and the lump form at her throat but she wouldn't cry; she wouldn't give Aunt Lizzie the pleasure of it. She swallowed hard. Her voice was soft, placating. 'Aunt Lizzie, I can't not go. Everyone else from school will be there, and Elsie was my friend. What will they think if I don't go?'

'Well, you should've thought of that before you spread shoe

polish all over your best frock, shouldn't you? How are you going to get that out? Ruined, it is. What do you think – that we're made of money? Ruining your best frock like that.'

Laura didn't know what to do; she couldn't believe Aunt Lizzie really meant it. Surely she couldn't mean it?

'You get up them stairs and stay in your room for the rest of the day. That'll teach you. And there'll be no tea for you tonight. You just stay out of my sight. You're not worth the time I put into you, you're not. Useless little get. No wonder your mam and dad didn't want you. And what thanks do I get for taking you in? None at all. Ungrateful little bugger. Get away with you now and get out of my sight.'

Laura spent the rest of the day lying on the high wooden bed in her bedroom at the back of the house, staring at the overblown cabbage roses on the fading wallpaper. She wouldn't cry. She refused to cry. Just before tea-time she heard the sound of Uncle Billy's return – Aunt Lizzie's voice, raised and defensive; Uncle Billy's, low and soothing. A few minutes later she heard his footsteps, slow and heavy on the carpeted stairs. The door opened and it was only then that she let the tears gush out, hot and salty, tickling her cheeks as they spilled down her face. Uncle Billy sat on the bed and took Laura's cold hands in his; when she'd cried herself out he passed her a clean, pressed white handkerchief out of the breast pocket of his jacket. It smelled of the cherry pipe tobacco that he smoked. She inhaled the familiar comforting scent of it, blew her nose and wiped her eyes, and sat up.

Uncle Billy smiled faintly. 'Come on then, my lass. Let's go out to the garden and see to the animals. Then it'll be time for tea.'

She sniffed noisily and a final stray sob hiccoughed from her mouth. 'I'm not allowed any tea.'

'I think you'll find that you are, pet. Just mind you stay quiet, now. Don't speak unless you're spoken to. She'll come out of it. You know what she's like.'

Laura knew what she was like, but she didn't think that Uncle

Billy did. And more than anything else she wanted to protect him from the knowledge.

She crept behind him down the stairs, slipping straight out of the front door, round the back of the house and into the garden. They passed the old brick air raid shelter that she remembered so vividly from the years of the war. It shared a dividing wall with next door's shelter, and there was a sort of a window in the wall – well, just a hole, really, with a raggedy old curtain over it that you could draw back to give you privacy. But little Frankie Bates from next door used to reach through the hole and pull on Laura's pigtails when she sat on her mam's lap in the old wooden chair next to the wall.

Uncle Billy had wanted to turn the shelter into a coal house now that the war was over and it didn't look like there'd be another any time soon. But Aunt Lizzie wouldn't hear of it. You wouldn't catch her running in and out of the house in the wind and rain just for a couple of shovels full of coal. Uncle Billy had asked whether she'd rather have the coal man keep on carting dust all through the house when he dumped it in the cupboard in the corner of the kitchen, but Aunt Lizzie said she'd lived with that ever since they moved in and she didn't see why she should stop now and what was the matter with him anyway – was he saying she didn't clean up properly? So Uncle Billy had given up – he knew when to let her have her way. For the sake of a quiet life, he would say.

Uncle Billy clucked quietly as he walked, and soon enough Matilda emerged out from under the bushes with Jimmy Muck waddling noisily behind. Laura didn't know why they only had one hen and one duck, but they seem happy enough together and the sight of the two mismatched creatures plodding around the garden, one behind the other, always made her smile. Laura found an egg that Matilda had laid in her favourite spot under the raspberry bush, and Uncle Billy put down a tin bowl of left-over mashed-up vegetables by their ramshackle wooden hut at the far end of the garden. Wallflowers self-seeded in riotous yellow splendour all around it; Laura closed her eyes and inhaled the sweet unforgettable scent that in years to come would always transport her back to this place and time. Bindweed grew up the back garden wall ('grandmother, grandmother, pop out of bed', Aunt Lizzie called it) and there was a neat square vegetable patch where Uncle Billy grew cabbages, cauliflowers, carrots and a few tatties. Laura liked to sit in the vegetable patch in the summer, picking the small green caterpillars off the cabbage plants, sniffing the sweet earthy smell of them before she'd throw them across to Jimmy Muck, who would quack gratefully on the lawn. She felt safe here in this garden – safe here out of the house and away from Aunt Lizzie's critical gaze.

The rest of the weekend passed quietly and without incident. Aunt Lizzie was mostly silent and Laura crept round the house, heavy with dread at the thought of facing her school friends on Monday morning. She was as late as she could manage to be but Mrs Mason finally rang the bell and she couldn't put off going into the classroom any longer. She walked through the door and the din faded away as, one by one, each of the other girls turned to look at her. Hesitantly, she began an apologetic smile but every last one of them tightened their lips and turned away. It would be a week before any of them would even look her in the eye, two before anyone would talk to her again. Margaret and Josie and Nan didn't want to walk back from school with her any more; she trailed home behind them like an unwanted puppy. She had no chance to explain: no-one would listen. They wouldn't even acknowledge her presence.

Only Uncle Billy seemed to understand. He didn't say much, but when he came in from work on Monday night and saw her face, he rested his hand on her shoulder and pressed it gently. 'Good lass,' he said. 'You're a good lass, and don't you forget it.' But Laura knew that she wasn't good at all, not really. Aunt Lizzie said so, and Aunt Lizzie saw things that other people didn't. Nothing got past Aunt Lizzie; you couldn't fool her.

❦ ❦ ❦

Down by the lochside in the expectant stillness of this early
evening, the landscape seems re-cast in silver. Coarse shingle
gleams wetly in several shades of grey; jagged rock juts into
the water like polished gunmetal. Tree limbs fallen during last
winter's storms lie stranded on the shore like the ribcages of
beached whales. Autumn is over now; the leaves are all fallen,
the trees bare as skeletons. A buzzard circles overhead, its
questing shadow reflected in the quick-silvered stillness of the
loch.

Laura has become so very aware of the elements on this
remote and rocky Highland shore. You live with them and you
work with them and they forge you and they shape you. You
join them, Meg says, in the age-old dance around the wheel of
the year. Meg says that everyone has their element: the element
to which they are drawn, to which they are bound. And she
has no doubt that Laura's is water. And perhaps it is true,
Laura thinks; there is a pull that is almost gravitational, and
a sense of loss when she is away from it. She was born by the
sea and she grew up by the sea. And here she is now by the
sea again, surrounded by water in all its forms. The chattering
burns that tear their swift way down to the shore, and mark
out the boundaries from field to field. The 'broom' or drizzly
rain that lasts sometimes for days, that brings a misty softness
to the land and blurs the transition from sea to sky. And above
all, the sea loch that dominates the landscape, reinventing and
transforming itself from season to season, from day to day,
from morning to evening. Changing with the weather and the
light. It has always seemed to Laura that shorelines are magical
places: anything can happen here in this borderland between
water and earth – this fluid border that shifts with the tides, in
perpetual motion and flow.

The tangy salt smell of seaweed fills her nostrils; she takes a last deep breath of it and turns back to the rusty farm gate that leads to the field and beyond that to the house. Startled, she steps back. Meg stands quiet and still as an apparition among the trees at the edge of the shallow trickling burn; she is wreathed in shadows like the Washer at the Ford.

But it isn't the ivory shroud of some soon-to-be-dead soul that Meg holds in her hand: it's a crumpled white plastic carrier bag. 'Tide's still out,' she says, 'though it's on the turn.'

Laura nods, smiling at her over-active imagination.

'And plenty of seaweed left behind.' Meg steps out of the shadows, shakes out the carrier bag with fingers that poke haphazardly out of woollen gloves frayed with wear. 'Which is what I'm after. A wee bagful to set to soaking for a while. Makes a good feed for the indoor plants at this time of year. Sees them through the winter.' The old gate creaks on salt-corroded hinges as she pushes it open and steps through. 'Years ago we used to carry it up the fields in baskets on our backs, to fertilise the potato patch.'

'Slippery work.'

'Aye, it was that. Heavy work, too, when it was wet.' She points to the shingle down below. 'See how it forms a kind of a barrier there, stretched out along the beach? That place beyond the seaweed, down to the water there, we used to call it the "Black Shore".'

'There's something special about it, then?'

'Aye, right enough. It's a place where you're protected from evil spirits. See now, they can't cross boundaries or thresholds. And the Black Shore is an in-between place. The threshold between water and land. So you're safe.'

'I like that idea.' There are so few places in this world that are safe.

'At places like this you can cross into the Otherworld – or Fairyland, as they call it in some of the stories. Watery places

– seashores, rivers, lochs. All of them thresholds between one world and another. Places where all the old Celtic mysteries occur.'

Laura looks out at the glassy surface of the loch. Silence surrounds them, the breathless air pregnant with nightfall. 'I could believe in any mystery on an evening like this.'

'Aye.' Abruptly and with surprising agility Meg begins to pick her way down the rock-strewn grassy bank to the shore. Shrugging, Laura follows. She has nothing better to do; she may as well stay and chat for a while. Taking care not to turn her ankle on the slick uneven pebbles, she follows Meg across the beach. The seaweed changes colour as they approach from undifferentiated darkness to rich brown and orange and all the shades in between. Multi-coloured slicks of water gleam on its surface like spilled oil.

Meg stands for a while, looking out across the loch to the hills beyond. 'In the islands they say that the hills were made by giant women who fell asleep, and they slept for so long that they turned to stone.' Laura follows her line of sight and just for a moment in the dim light of evening it seems that she can make out a craggy grey face in profile, the soft swell of a belly, a long stretch of undulating green thigh and the gentle bulge of a kneecap. Meg shakes her head and turns to Laura with a smile. 'But enough of all that nonsense. How's it going now, your writing?'

Laura blinks; Meg's conversations never quite begin where you expect them to.

And what can she say? She's not used to talking about these times in her life. She's not even used to thinking about them. And she doesn't know Meg that well – not really. Does she trust her? Has she ever really trusted other women? A vision of Aunt Lizzie at Meg's age swims before her, mouth set thin and hard, eyes like small pieces of sea-coal in a face lined with discontent.

But Meg isn't Aunt Lizzie. Meg is the furthest from Aunt Lizzie that it's possible to be.

Laura takes a deep breath. Jump, she thinks. You always used to be so good at jumping. Wasn't that what you always wanted Cat to do? *Jump, Cat – for heaven's sake, just get it over with and jump!* Well, take a dose of your own medicine, and remember how to jump now. But make it a calculated leap into the unknown, for once. Something chosen. Not just something that you do to stop yourself thinking.

'It's not easy,' she says, and watches as Meg bends down and swiftly, efficiently tears away a small piece of rusty red seaweed and thrusts it into her carrier bag. 'They're not good memories, most of them. And so much that I'd forgotten; so much that I haven't thought about for years. Haven't let myself think about.'

'Aye, well now, looking back is always hard.'

'You're not kidding.' She laughs, a little too loudly. Then remembers that she means to do this differently. Honestly. This time she means to feel it – to really feel it and to see for herself what that feels like. And it strikes her: how many times in her life can she say that she's honestly let herself feel what was real in that moment? Dear God, how many times has she faked it, covered it up with false laughter or a witty retort? And Cat, seeing through it every time. *You're always such a hypocrite, Mother. Always putting on an act, always putting on a face. Can't you just be real, for once?* And pushing away the desire to scream back at her, *But I don't know how to be real. I don't know what the real me is. Is there such a thing? Does anyone possess such a thing? Do you? Am I real, Cat? Am I? If I hold on to you, will you make me real?*

And Joe: *Is there anything real inside you at all, Laura? Any little thing at all?*

Swallows. Stutters. Pushes back the image of the hollow woman that hovers in front of her, taunting. There *is* something in me, she tells herself. I am real. I will make myself real. Write myself real.

'You – I suppose – well, you see things differently when you choose to look back like this. When you write things down. See them more objectively, perhaps. My Aunt Lizzie, for example...' She hesitates, flushing, but Meg has paused and is watching her closely with a gentle smile. 'Well, she was a hard woman. Wicked, I always thought. I lived with her, you see, when I was growing up. Made my life a misery in some ways. For such a lot of years, I hated her. Blamed her for so many of the problems that I had, later on. And I was frightened of her, too – even when I grew up. She was the classic wicked old witch in the wood. And yet sometimes when I look back at her now, at the character that she seems to be playing in this story that I'm writing, all I can see is a sad and a bitter old woman.'

Meg shakes a small mauve-tinted whelk shell from the clump of seaweed that she's holding and says, 'There wasn't much in the way of affection, then?'

'Not with Aunt Lizzie. She never could accept affection any more than she could give it. She butted you away, bustled off, busied herself with something. Each night before I went to bed I would go up to her to say good-night and kiss her on the cheek. And each night she would turn her face away. But I never stopped trying. "Good-night, Aunt Lizzie," I'd say. "See you in the morning." "Aye, if I'm still here," she'd answer. Every night, the same answer.' And watching Meg carefully place the whelk into a small pool of water, thinks: if only there'd been someone like Meg in my life, instead of Aunt Lizzie. What might I have become then? Would anything really have changed?

Meg's carrier bag is full now; she throws it down on the beach and slowly hauls herself to her feet.

'Didn't I hear somewhere that you could eat seaweed?' Laura asks, taking refuge for a moment in a change of subject.

Meg picks up her carrier bag, pulls out a small piece of the rusty red seaweed inside and flourishes it at Laura. 'Dulse. We used to eat it boiled, with our dinner. Or in a nice broth, with a smattering of oatmeal.'

'I'd rather eat these.' Laura reaches down and picks a brown-grey shell from between the damp pebbles. 'Winkles. We used to pick them on the beach when I was a child. Take a bag of them home, and boil them up for supper.'

Meg grins and pulls another carrier bag out of the pocket of her heavy, over-sized tweed coat. 'Help yourself, so.'

'No, no. But thanks anyway.'

'Whyever not? They're there for the taking. Good fresh food. Clean. Maybe you need a little taste of the sea. Do you good, lassie.'

Laura laughs and takes the bag from Meg's open hand. 'You're right. Why not? And maybe the taste of them will bring back the good memories hidden amongst the bad.' And there *were* good memories, she thinks. After all, there was always Uncle Billy.

She bends down and reaches for another winkle lying among the seaweed. A sudden sharp pain in her back: no, this won't do. Squats down on her heels, legs apart. That's better. She's not entirely convinced she'll be able to get back up again, but she'll worry about that when the time comes.

'She was a strange one, Aunt Lizzie,' Laura says. 'So strong in some ways; so frightened in others. At the slightest hint of a thunderstorm she would crawl under the table in the front room and hide there, pulling the tablecloth down around her, wailing and crying. You had to put away all the knives and cover the mirrors so the lightning wouldn't reflect and bounce around the room. You had to open the back and front doors so it could get out again if it struck.' She smiles at the memory, and thinks what a wonder it is that she herself loves storms. 'It's as if – as if she lived her whole life in fear of death. You know?'

Meg nods, and squats down beside her and begins to pick a handful of winkles of her own.

'She wrapped herself in so many weird and wonderful superstitions to ward it off, and you wouldn't believe her terror if the rules were broken. Shoes mustn't be put on the table; umbrellas mustn't be opened in the house; knives mustn't be laid across each other … Her whole life was filled up with rituals that you had to follow, rules that you had to obey. To prevent something terrible from happening.' She frowns. 'What was it that she thought was going to happen? I never did understand that. But when I look back on her now – see her as a character in these pieces of story that I'm writing – I can't help but wonder what it was that made her so bitter, so unloving. How could she treat a child like that? Had she always been the same, or did something happen to make her that way?'

Meg nods. 'You're wondering what her story was.'

'Yes. I suppose I am.'

'And do you know?'

'Not really.' Aunt Lizzie's story? She hasn't ever really thought about it. Too wrapped up in her own story to think about others. See it from Aunt Lizzie's perspective? See the world from anyone else's perspective at all? Joe, again: *You're so wrapped up in your own world and your own idea of how it is and how it all affects you that there's nothing can get through it. I certainly can't. Do you ever look at it from my point of view? Think about what it does to me when you insist all the time that I'm putting you down or don't love you enough?* And she'd stared back at him, puzzled. Hadn't really known what he was talking about. Hadn't cared to know; it was all too difficult. She'd think about it some other time, maybe.

They work for a while in a silence shattered only by the raucous shriek of a heron breaking free from the cover of the shrubby willows behind them as it launches itself over the loch. Laura peers into the carrier bag. 'I think that'll be enough for now,' she says. 'There's a good plateful there, with a little salt and vinegar for taste.'

She presses down on a lichen-spotted stone for leverage and pushes herself to her feet with a long, drawn-out groan. Meg is already up and heading over to a large flat rock that juts out of the bank behind them. She sits down; Laura follows and lowers herself onto the rock beside her. The sharp tang of salt air and the distant cry of seagulls and she is back there again, on the sands with Uncle Billy. Peering into the stillness of stagnant rock-pools, looking for hidden treasure; Aunt Lizzie waiting till they came back home for their tea.

She shifts on the hard rock, the cold of it seeping through her jeans and into the soft lumpy flesh of her buttocks. Once upon a time she had a figure to die for. Who cast the spell that transformed her into this blurred, faded creature? Where did all her sharp edges go? She hoists herself up, pulls at the bottom of her heavy waxed jacket, and sits back down on it.

Aunt Lizzie's story. What was Aunt Lizzie's story?

'Aunt Lizzie never spoke much about her life. Not until she was very old, and a bit more mellow. Not all that much more mellow, though – they threatened to turf her out of the rest home where she lived for the last few years of her life if she didn't moderate her language. Apparently she was shocking the other residents – even the men.' She smiles ruefully. 'She lived to be ninety-two. "Only the good die young," she would say.'

Meg laughs. 'I'll bear that in mind, now.'

Another solitary heron stands motionless in the shallows, perfectly balanced on one spindly leg and staring out across the water with an air of weighty preoccupation. Such a different beach, Laura thinks, as colour and light slowly ebb away into the creeping twilight. No soft sand here, no sweeping dunes. A harder beach, built for storms. A granite beach, toughened with shadow.

'I suppose we know more about Aunt Lizzie now than we

did while we were growing up, because my sister May has been looking back into the family history. She sent me a pile of papers just before I moved up here. Copies of birth certificates, that kind of thing. I read them, but I didn't really think about them very much: I was too busy trying to organise the move.' Or maybe she just didn't want to think about them. She sighs. 'We always knew that Aunt Lizzie had been the oldest of thirteen children. But most of them died young, of one thing or another; only four of them made it through to adulthood. My grandmother died giving birth to the last of them. That was my mother. So it was Aunt Lizzie who had the responsibility of bringing them all up. She always said that my grandfather was a waster – drank away most of what he earned, and never lifted a hand to help her with the children.'

Laura pauses, but Meg is still watching, still listening. 'She only married when the last of them was old enough to go out to work, and she was in her late twenties. She was a cockle-gatherer by then, cut quite a handsome figure on the sands. That was one of the ways she made the money to keep them all fed. She even had her photograph printed in the local newspaper, standing barefoot on the beach with her hair tied up in a scarf and her skirts up around her knees. "A notable cockle-gatherer", the caption ran. She cut the photograph out and had it in a frame on the mantelpiece in the front room. I especially remember it because she was smiling in it, and Aunt Lizzie didn't smile often.' Except when she was laughing at someone else's expense, she thinks.

'So, anyway – her husband-to-be swept her off her feet, married her and then a few years later ran off with a showgirl, so she always said. And that was all she would tell us about her marriage. Except that he was a no-good lying cheating bastard, of course. She didn't mince her words, didn't Aunt Lizzie. Eventually she met my Uncle Billy – I never did know how – and moved in with him. She never managed to get a divorce and so they never got married. Which I suppose was scandalous at the time, though no-one would have dared say as much to Aunt Lizzie. Not to her face, at least.'

Laura shivers; her hands are growing cold. The sun is well down now and the slightest hint of a chill breeze is beginning to feather the grey wings of water that are creeping back slowly, inexorably towards the rocks. 'But what May – my sister – found out, what we didn't know, what Aunt Lizzie never spoke about, was that she'd had four children. And not one of them survived. Her first three were stillborn – one after the other. All boys. And then her fourth lived for two days; she called him Edward. One dead child for every year that she lived with her husband. And then nothing.'

Meg nods sadly. 'So many children lost, in those days. And such a low rate of survival for those that did manage to get themselves born.'

'She'd spent the best part of her teenage years and early twenties bringing up her brothers and sisters. Then two-thirds of them died, and all of her own children. Every last one. So I suppose it's not surprising, really. The way she was. How could she be expected to love someone else's child? Why shouldn't she be angry? Why shouldn't she fear death?'

Aunt Lizzie standing on the doorstep, waiting for her to come home from work in the dark. Angry if she was more than half an hour later than usual, shouting about all the dreadful things that might happen to her on the way home. Pacing up and down from the house to the front gate and back if Uncle Billy didn't come home on time for his tea. Screeching at him, calling him all the names under the sun when eventually he did show. Did he understand, though? Did he see, where Laura failed to? Is that why he'd just smile, touch her gently on the cheek, tell her not to worry? 'It's all right now, Lizzie,' he'd say. 'There's no harm done. I'm home now.' And muttering to herself, shaking her head, Aunt Lizzie would turn away and turn her trembling hands to the business of pouring him a cup of tea.

'It's strange, really. I hadn't thought of it like that before.' That's because you never let yourself think about it, she tells herself, angry now. Because you never really wanted to know, did you? Because you'd already decided what the story was. Already made up your mind. 'I don't know why it should matter, that I should understand why she acted the way she did. Maybe it's because I can tell myself that it might not have been anything to do with me. That it might not have been my fault. My lack.' Angrily, she blinks away the tears that threaten: she's done enough weeping in her lifetime. Wallowed in enough self-pity. She won't burden Meg with it.

Meg keeps the silence. Laura shivers again, pulling her jacket closer around her. After a while, Meg leans forward and touches Laura's hand. 'It'll be dark soon enough, now; we'd better be walking back up the field. Along with all our treasures.' She smiles gently as she rustles the two carrier bags at their feet. 'Will you come away in and have a cup of tea?'

It's dark by the time Laura steps out of Meg's house; the nights are drawing in so quickly now. But the moon is still full though it's on the wane, spilling otherworldly light onto the grass. The air is crisp, exhilarating; a tawny owl hoots from across the loch and a stag bellows triumphantly on the braes behind. She casts a slim, spectral moon-shadow on the field; she raises her arms and gives the shadow wings.

7

Cat

The wind whistles around us, softly buffeting the wings of the plane. The engine purrs loudly in the background; calm, anonymous voices come and go through the headphones. The sounds slip one by one into my awareness like instruments tuning up for a recital. Gradually the tension loosens its grip on my body as I begin to concentrate, searching for a pattern. But even the vibration of the engine isn't a constant sound – it pulsates. Strange that I hadn't noticed it before – thrumming, surging waves that ebb and flow. Like a rhythm section, constantly present in the background of your mind. And without the engine there would be no flight – no beat, no basis, no foundation for the music. The shrill whistle of the wind like a flute; its low moans like strings. Percussion-like bursts of static, and the crackle of voices on the radio ...

'Enjoying yourself?' Jolted out of my reverie I see Jesse sitting back in his seat, arms loosely folded, watching me closely. His mouth is curled up at one corner. 'You actually have a smile on your face.'

'I *am* enjoying myself. Would you believe it?' I'm not entirely sure I believe it myself, but there have been moments in the past couple of lessons when I've felt almost comfortable up here.

'Don't get too cosy. Now we're going to cover stalls.' Out of the corner of my eye I see him watching me. Waiting for my reaction.

'Oh.' The smile fades. 'How are we going to do that?'

'We're going to do some.'

'Stalls?'

'Right.'

I pause. 'We're going to stall the plane?'

'Right.'

No, no, no. 'Please tell me you're kidding.'

'I'm not kidding.'

Oh, dear God. I remove a hand from the wheel and place it around the base of my throat. 'That really can't be a good idea. Can it?' I clench my hand into a fist, loosen it again and put the hand back on the yoke. Stop being so pathetic, Cat. Get a grip.

'Sure it is. If we don't practise stalls, how are you going to know what to do if it happens for real? How are you going to recognise the first signs of a stall when you're coming in to land, for example, so you can stop it before it gets dangerous?'

Dangerous. My chest begins to close up around the bottom two-thirds of my lungs. I want to get out. 'So remind me just what is it that makes a stall dangerous?'

He looks out at the sky as he talks, eyes flicking from side to side, always scanning for traffic. 'A stall means you're stopping the plane from flying, right? You remember all that aerodynamic theory we went through, about how the air molecules curve and flow over and under the wing and create the lift that makes the plane fly?'

'Yes.' My voice breaks. Shit. I clear my throat.

'Well, a stall happens when you don't have lift any more. You put the wing in a position where the air molecules can't flow across it – they kind of burble and skid off. And so the plane stops flying.'

'And what happens when the plane stops flying?'

He turns to look at me, a glimmer of irony in his eyes. 'If you don't do anything to correct the situation? The nose drops, the plane falls off to one side, and it spins. It falls.'

I try to keep the tone light but my mouth is as dry as a river bed in June and my voice just as riddled with cracks. 'And you'd like to practise this, right? Making the plane fall out of the sky.'

'We're not going to fall out of the sky. What we're going to practise is correcting the developing situation. So we don't ever get to that stage where we fall out of the sky. If you recognise the signs early enough, recovery is easy.'

'Easy.' I lick my parched lips. Right.

'Sure. In three simple steps. Which I'm going to show you. Right now.'

His voice is so confident, matter-of-fact, and I want to believe him – I really want to believe him. But all my hard-won ease has evaporated; I am rigid with tension. I shouldn't be surprised; it's not as if I didn't know that there were plenty more hurdles to be overcome in this flying game. But it's been such a pleasure for the last three or four lessons, taking it slowly, getting comfortable with the basic flight manoeuvres. And now here I am again, right back where I started. Three thousand feet above the ground, and nothing to support us but cold blue sky. I risk a small sideways glance out of the window; nothing down below but burning sand and a few saguaro cacti holding up their arms as if they might try to catch us when we fall.

A sudden wave of vertigo turns my stomach upside down. What in God's name am I doing, all the way up here? And my vision is blurring and my hands are beginning to tremble and I can't lose it now ... Stop it, Cat. Stop it.

I can't do this. I want to get out.

Briefly, he rests a hand on mine. The touch is unexpected: cool and dry. 'Look – I know this is scary. I want to show you that it really isn't scary at all if you know how to recognise the first signs of a stall and if recovering becomes instinctive. But for a reaction to become instinctive, you have to practise it, right?'

I shrug, but I can't speak. My tongue seems to be glued to the roof of my mouth.

'Cat. You're quite safe, you know. Even in the worst possible scenario, if the aircraft spins, we can recover from that too. We have more than enough altitude to do that safely. All instructors have to do spin training before they qualify, and I've done aerobatics training too.'

My stomach lurches again at the very idea of it. 'I don't have to do spins, though? To get my license?'

'No.' Another small quirk of the lips. 'Not intentionally, anyway. And it's my job to see that you don't do it accidentally, either. Which brings me back to stalls.' He reaches out and places his hands on the wheel. 'My controls. Here's what's going to happen. We're going to start with power-off stalls; they're a bit gentler. You don't have to do anything right now, just sit and watch. Okay?'

Oh, dear God. But look at him: he's so calm; hands so strong and relaxed on the controls. It's all in a day's work to him; no big deal. Right now I'd rather be anywhere in the world than here, but I'm not going to go to pieces in front of this man. Not if I can help it. It's bad enough that he even knows I'm afraid.

And I trust him. Don't I? Already, I'm beginning to trust him. Warm and solid beside me; sky in his eyes and the smell of fresh sage and sharp desert air, he knows what he's doing. He'll pull us through.

'Okay.' It comes out as not much more than a croak.

'Right. Here goes. Let's imagine we're coming in to land. That's where stalls can be most dangerous – especially when you're turning from base leg to final approach. When you're about to land, power is low, right? And so is airspeed. So if you don't get the whole landing set-up right you have the perfect recipe for a stall. And if you plan to stall that close to the ground, you'd better know how to recognise it before it happens and recover from it pretty sharply. Because you're too close to the ground to recover from a spin. You need altitude to recover from a spin; three thousand feet of altitude isn't a bad idea. So that's what we're doing with power-off stalls: we're mimicking the kind of problem that can arise on landing. Are you with me?'

Staring sightlessly, straight ahead out of the windscreen, I nod. I'm never going to look at landing in the same way again.

'Right. The first thing I'm going to do here is pull the throttle out so that the engine is just ticking over.' The engine noise falls to a soft, steady purr; the unfamiliar silence settles around us like a blanket of freezing snow. 'Now in a few moments I'm going to create the stall by pulling the wheel towards me, very slowly, very gently. The nose will rise and the airspeed will drop off quite rapidly. You'll feel a slight shuddering or buffeting around the nose: that's your first sign of a stall. Then if I keep pulling back the nose will drop sharply and at the same time one of the wings will fall off to the side. There's no way of knowing which one ahead of time. As soon as the nose drops I'm going to reduce the angle of attack by pushing the control wheel forward.' Bewildered, I frown. 'Yes, I know that's counter-intuitive, but it works. This whole problem has arisen in part because the nose is too high. So we need to get the nose down again. Get the airspeed up. Now: if the wing drops off to the left, I'll apply right rudder to correct it. If it drops off to the right, I'll apply left rudder. Then push the power full on again, and slowly begin to lift the nose and reduce the power back to where you want it. Got it?'

A small vertical convulsion passes for a nod but I haven't got it at all and my hands clutch the edge of my seat, slippery on the dark red vinyl. I watch as he begins to lift the nose – please stop, I want to say to him but I can't seem to open my mouth against the horror that's clamping my jaw tightly shut.

There is a slight shudder and the nose begins to vibrate.

'Now the control wheel is beginning to lose its responsiveness – it feels mushy. Nothing much happens if I turn it. See how the airspeed indicator is in the white zone?' Suddenly, the stall warning horn shrieks and the nose falls abruptly and yaws to the left, the left wing drops away and all I can see is the laughing brown earth below, waiting to break me. I slam my eyes tight shut and clench my jaw against the sudden urge to cry out. He thrusts the yoke forward, foot slams on the rudder, and the engine roars as he pushes the throttle all the way in.

And as suddenly as it happened, everything is all right again. Everything is stable, the nose begins to rise as he gently pulls back on the control wheel, and we begin the steady climb back up to our previous altitude. By the time we've levelled off I have begun to breathe again, but there's a sharp pain in the left side of my chest and all of the heat has seeped away from my body. I'm cold and clammy with sweat.

He gestures towards my control wheel. 'Now I want you to try it.'

'You've got to be joking.'

His voice is gentle, but firm. 'You can't fly a plane if you don't know how to recover from a stall. It's dangerous.'

I shake my head. 'Jesse ...' He waits, silent.

Come on, Cat – jump. Let's see what you're made of. Look – the other children can do it. Why can't you?

Why won't you leave me alone? Everywhere I go, your voice in the back of my mind, egging me on to failure.

Come on, scaredy-Cat! What are you frightened of? Jump, why don't you?

Stop it!

The echo of the words resounds through my head. Round and around, fainter and fainter, till finally it fades away. For a moment I fear that I've shouted out loud, but the continuing silence from the seat to my right argues against it.

Scaredy-Cat!

Ah, no. No, I can't do this. It's bad enough trusting him to do it; it's another thing entirely to do it myself. What if I press the wrong rudder pedal? And what if I press the correct rudder pedal but I don't do it quickly enough? What if we spin?

No, no.

Scaredy-Cat!

No. The stakes are too high.

Fear gives way to despair. So maybe this is it. Maybe this is where I fail. I always knew there would be a limit – right from the very beginning. I always expected to fail. But I thought that perhaps it would come when the time came to fly solo; I didn't expect to reach it this soon.

'I'll keep my hands on the controls with you,' he says. 'I won't let anything happen.' I turn to him; the sun is shining right into his eyes. It doesn't seem to bother him at all. I've never seen him in sunglasses; sometimes it seems there's no aspect of the sky that is alien to him. He is a spirit of the air: a sylph. 'Cat. I won't let you fall.'

He won't let me fall. Time slowly freezes and the world tilts on its axis and over-balances. He won't let me fall.

And there you are again, black eyes filled with frustration, voice sharp inside my head. *Get a grip, Cat! Just get on with it, can't you? What are you afraid of? Jump!*

Why are you doing this to me why do I let you do this…

Do you remember when you tried once to teach me to swim? You had medals for life-saving: a wall of certificates to attest to your courage and success. You wanted me so badly to follow in your footsteps. *The first thing you do is to learn how to float. And then you'll be able to swim.* But I couldn't float, could I? I was always so afraid. If I let go of my hold I would fall through the water – slip down, insubstantial, and sink to the bottom like a displaced stone. *Just breathe now,* you told me. *Just breathe, just relax. There's really nothing to it: it feels just like flying. I'm here, little Cat. I won't let you fall.*

But I knew perfectly well that no human could fly. And even with your arms thin but strong underneath me, I was far too

171

afraid to try. Because how could I be sure that you'd be there to catch me?

How could I know that you wouldn't let go?

I let out a shaky breath. 'I'm sorry,' I tell him. 'I can't.'

I'm so very high up here, and the water seems such a long way down. I can hear your voice there below me, urging me on. Come on, Cat, get it over with – just jump. *But I don't want to jump. If I jump I just know it – I'll crash and I'll break myself on the hard flat surface of that glittering blue pool. The bouncy little diving board down below for once looks like a haven – I'm way, way above it here. Ten steps I had to climb to reach the first platform, and there are ten more up to the highest stage of all. Ice-cold fingers creep around my neck and squeeze and let go, squeeze and let go, over and over again. I can't do this. I don't want to do this. The world begins to dissolve around me as my breathing quickens and my eyes lose their focus.* Oh, for God's sake, Cat – what's the matter with you? Are you going to stay up there all day? *Your voice startles me and I sway a little.* Cat? *I close my eyes for a moment – ah, that's better. No more cold hard water, just a soft blissful darkness.* Cat! What are you doing, Cat? *And then I feel it – slipping away, everything slipping away as I sway and I tumble and I feel myself falling but it's such a blissful feeling and so very easy to let yourself go… And for a moment – just for one blissful moment – it feels as if I'm flying.*

Then something crashes into the side of my face.

And the last thing I see is a beautiful red jellyfish swimming away from my head, swimming out into the water, growing, expanding and it's so very pretty…

'It's okay.'

I turn away from the kindness in Jesse's eyes.

No. It's not okay. Nothing's changed.

Nothing's really changed.

Still the same old Cat.

We tie down the plane in silence. From time to time Jesse glances over at me, but a cannonball seems to have lodged itself in my chest. I look down at the asphalt, reposition my flight bag – anything rather than meet his eyes. I hang back, slinking a few paces behind him as he strides across the tie-down area to the Falcon Wings building. We're almost there when a small dark-haired young woman near a plane across the way smiles and waves at him. He stops; waves back. 'You go on in,' he says, eyes flicking briefly behind him. 'I'll be with you in a minute.'

I watch him stride across to her, and envy her the smile on his face as he bends down to kiss her cheek. The sun beats down heavily on the back of my neck; I turn away abruptly and head for the coolness of the building. Christina lifts her head from the weekly flight planner as I walk in, and tilts it to one side as she sees my expression. 'Oh, my. Not a good lesson today?'

'Stalls.' With a heavy sigh, I shrug my flight bag off my shoulder and onto a chair by the window.

'Oh, everybody hates stalls. Don't worry; you'll soon get used to them. Everybody does. And you know you're in safe hands with Jesse – he's the most popular instructor we have.' Her eyes flick over to the glass door, come to rest on Jesse and his companion. Hungry eyes, a little sad. He's too old for you, sweetheart, I want to say – but of course I don't. And in any case, that's the way it is now, isn't it? No self-respecting forty-year-old all-American male wants to be seen with anyone over the age of twenty-five. And the girl out by the plane can't be much more than that.

I turn and watch them too. He has his back to the window, blocking my view of her, but as he shifts a little to the side I catch a glimpse of flying fingers. Sign language? Confused, I turn back to Christina. 'Is she – can't she hear?'

'Sandy? No, she's deaf.' Her voice is soft, a little dreamy.

'And she's taking flying lessons?'

'She already has her license.'

Already has her license? But surely... 'How can she do that? How can she fly if she can't hear?'

She glances across at me briefly, but she clearly can't bear to look away from him for long. I follow her gaze; he's strolling slowly back across the asphalt, face turned up to the sky as always and fingers tucked loosely into the pockets of his jeans. 'Well, there are restrictions, of course,' she says finally. 'She can't fly into controlled airspace or into an airport with a control tower – any place where you have to communicate with ATC. But she likes the experience of doing that, and so every now and again she asks Jesse to go up with her. He handles the radio ops, she handles the flying.'

'But if there's no ATC requirement, she can fly solo?'

'Sure.' Christina sits up straight and smiles brightly as Jesse walks through the door.

'Sorry,' he says to me. 'My next flying partner.' I hand him my logbook and hover there, fidgeting, as he sinks into a chair and fishes for a pen in the pocket of his shirt.

I just can't imagine how it would be, not to be able to hear the sound of the engine. Not to know if it was still turning over, not to know if it was misfiring. Maybe you can tell by the vibration, or something. And I can't imagine how frightening it would be, not to be able to listen out for other traffic around you. How isolated you'd feel. How cut off you'd be, with no-one to call for help if anything went wrong.

'Did you teach her to fly?' I burst out finally, as he balances the logbook on a knee and begins to fill in the day's entry. 'How does it work, if she can't hear? How can you explain to her what's going on, what she's doing wrong?'

He looks up at me with a question in his eyes that I choose not to answer. I look away, over his shoulder and out to the plane where she – Sandy – still stands, patiently waiting. She's so small, so petite. I can't imagine her in charge of a plane. Alone, without hearing, and in charge of a plane. How must that feel?

'It took her far longer to learn,' he says, finally. 'You can imagine – she could only watch me carry out manoeuvres, she couldn't hear me explain them as I was doing them. During certain manoeuvres you need both your hands to fly: you can't use sign language. So I'd have to explain it all ahead of time. And it took longer to explain how to correct things that were going wrong. It wasn't impossible – just different. Slower.'

'Wasn't she scared?'

'Because she couldn't hear?'

I nod; risk a glance back down at him. His eyes are fixed firmly on mine. I look away again; I don't like to be so transparent. I don't know him nearly well enough to be so transparent.

I don't know anyone well enough to be so transparent.

'People who can't hear are used to the silence, Cat. They're used to coping with it. For those who are deaf from birth, that's all they know. They find ways to compensate. They have to be extra vigilant. But yeah – it takes some courage. There's no question that she's brave.'

A sharp pain slices through my stomach. He closes the logbook and hands it back to me. I hide my face as I carefully put the logbook back inside the front pocket of my flight bag. 'Where did you learn sign language?' I ask him, breaking into the pregnant silence with a too-bright smile.

'My younger sister, Ellie Mae, was born deaf.'

'Is she a pilot too?'

'No. Ellie Mae has her feet firmly planted on the ground.' He smiles. 'But then one of us had to have. And her husband and her kids make sure of that.'

And you, I want to ask him. What about you? Don't you have a wife and a parcel of kids to keep you grounded too?

He follows me with his eyes as I throw the flight bag over my shoulder. 'See you Saturday morning as usual?'

I hesitate. 'No. I have something else on, on Saturday.' I look away. 'Sometime next week. I'll call.'

Out of the corner of my eyes I see him nod. He doesn't say a word.

But the expression in his eyes as I turn at the door to say goodbye says it instead.

❦ ❦ ❦

I recognise the handwriting, of course, on the large brown envelope that lies face up on the kitchen worktop. I recognise it as soon as I place my car keys in the basket beside it and stand there, still and watchful; waiting for something, I don't quite know what. Out of the corner of my eye I see Adam, poking his head round the door from the hall. Dimly I register the rare occurrence that he's home from work earlier than I am.

'Hey,' he says.

I tear my eyes away from the letter and give him a distracted smile. 'Hi.' I turn back to the counter-top; it's still there.

'What's up?' He slips behind me and takes the briefcase from my clenched fist, putting it down on the floor. His arms slide around my waist, head nuzzling the soft, yielding place where shoulder meets neck. Frozen, I can't seem to relax into his embrace. She has intruded into a place where she shouldn't be, and bizarrely I don't know how to act.

'Cat?' Adam turns me around to face him, his voice filled with concern. 'What's the matter?'

'There's a letter.'

'Yeah, I guess. It's this amazing thing called mail. Maybe you all don't have it in England. See, people write stuff to other people. Called letters. Then they put the letters in a mailbox and – '

'It's from my mother.'

'Yeah, I know. I saw the postmark. Aren't you going to open it?'

Open it? Such a definitive act. Almost an invitation. If I open the letter I'll free her. She'll slip out, slip into my life again, like a genie from a jar. Taking form and substance before me, beckoning me once again to hurl myself in anger and defiance and break myself on the sharp rocky shards of her solidity.

He'll never understand how it is between us. Though that's as much my fault as his; I've never been able to bring myself to really talk to anyone about my mother. Not properly. Not the whole story. I allow myself to unfreeze a little, lean against him. Breathing in a whiff of warm deodorant and the scent of stale office air. A sudden longing to be outside takes hold of me, but it's already dark. And besides – where would I go? This isn't a neighbourhood designed for walking. If you want to walk, first you have to get in the car. Go figure.

'Want some hot tea?' Tea is something of a mystery to Adam; he doesn't quite get it. He's an Atlanta boy, raised on Coke. Or iced tea, perhaps – liberally laced with sugar. But at some time in his formative years he must have been exposed to Jane Austen: he has the unshakeable idea that hot tea is something that British people drink to prevent the onset of a fit of the vapours. I can't help but smile.

'No tea. Don't worry. It's probably nothing. It's always a bit of a shock to see her handwriting; I wasn't expecting to hear from her. And it looks awfully large.'

'I can't see why you're so surprised. It's not like you never get mail from her. Cards, or whatever.'

He's right, of course. But somehow, this looks more threatening. The envelope is large: it contains something that I can't predict. I get nervous when I can't predict my mother. And

I have a peculiar sense that whatever is inside, I don't want to know.

I pull away from him. I need to get out of these clothes, shower away the stultifying residues of the day. Shower away the failure. The letter can wait. 'I'll open it after dinner.'

'Always postponing the inevitable. Why don't you just get it over with?'

Right on schedule, irritation flares. 'Adam, I'm perfectly capable of deciding when to open my own letters, thank you very much.'

He flushes, turns on his heel and strides past me, out of the room. I rest my hands on the shiny tiled work surface, lower my head and groan.

Above me in the master suite the shower pounds furiously against the floor and the smooth cold walls of the marble-tiled enclosure. Wearily, I walk to the refrigerator to find something to cook for dinner.

Dinner is cautious, careful. We stick to safe subjects: his work day, and mine. A glass of chilled Sauvignon Blanc makes him mellow; the monkfish is tender and the salad leaves crisp. Relief creeps over me; everything is as it should be.

Once the dishwasher is loaded, he heads into the small study that leads off the great room to work on a witness disclosure.

The envelope lurks on the worktop. Untouched.

It's pointless to put it off any longer; I pick it up and take it upstairs to the smallest of our three bedrooms, which serves as my study. As I close the door behind me, the vice around my chest begins to loosen and my shoulders sag. This is the only place in the house that feels like mine: my sanctuary. The rest of the house is very much Adam's. Before I moved in with him I'd lived quite simply in a two-bedroom condo in Mesa. Adam had already been in the house for a couple of years – ever since his divorce – and had more than enough furniture for our needs. I sold most of the stuff that I owned; in any case, it wouldn't have fitted in with the minimalist elegance of the style he prefers. Boxy cream sofas and glass-topped coffee tables. Sleek steel lamps and plain beige rugs.

This room is different. I haven't dared touch the walls, of course; like every other wall in the house they are the standard contractor's shade of creamy magnolia or antique white. But in here I've surrounded myself with colourful items collected from my travels. Almost all of it business travel, but sometimes I managed to slip away from the five-star hotels and the air-conditioned meeting rooms. Toured the countryside or the cities; explored the markets. Like the market in Guatemala, at Chichicastenango – where I picked up the vividly embroidered pink and turquoise runner that lies across the chest of drawers, and the bright woven square that I've thrown over the back of the armchair by the window. If I close my eyes and lay my hand on those textiles I can still see the riotous colours of traditional clothing; I can still hear the sound of firecrackers and the cries of the hawkers and the musicians parading with their pipes and drums. I can still smell the *copal* incense in the churches where people would shake out their rugs and sit on the floor with their eyes closed, telling God about their day. As if they were just having a conversation with an old friend.

And in Bali, where I rummaged through a rack in the back room of a rickety wooden shack and found the pair of three-foot-high carved wooden temple figures that hang on the wall on either side of the window. The only windows that have curtains, not blinds. Adam doesn't like curtains – they collect dust, he says.

Sometimes I dream of colour.

I sit in the blue and red kilim-covered armchair by the window, and before I can change my mind, I open the envelope.

Her handwriting hasn't changed: a bit shakier, maybe, but still the same old mother.

Dear Cat,

Strange things can happen to people when they retire, I'm told. So much changes. And as you know, I retired from my 'proper job' a year or so ago. But when you write stories, there's not supposed to be a set age for retirement. Unfortunately, my brain seems to have decided otherwise and I've been suffering from writer's block for months now. So I'm following the advice of my neighbour Meg – the storyteller. I'm writing some of my own story. Not the whole thing – just pieces of the puzzle. Odd memories; events that seem to have been significant, now that I look back on them. Growing older is supposed to lead to new perspectives on your life, so they say, and for me perhaps it's about time. I've never had very much of that.

So, attached is the beginning of my attempt at perspective. It occurred to me that you might be interested. If you're not, let me know and I won't bother you with future extracts.

I'm sorry if I gave you the impression that I wasn't pleased to hear about the flying lessons. It was just the shock. So VERY unexpected! And of course, I worry about you. I always will. You're all that I have. But I do admire what you're doing. Really. And I'd like to know more.

With much love,

M.

You're all that I have. My throat clenches again; the weight settles back down on top of my head.

Attached to the letter with a paper-clip are a few pages of typescript. I sigh. I know exactly what to expect: more self-justification, more emotional outpourings. Haven't I heard enough of your stories over the years?

Steeling myself, I begin to read.

It seems as if a long time passes before I put the few pages of manuscript on the floor beside me, lean back in the chair, and close my eyes.

You know, I have always maintained that you and I are unalike. *I'm nothing like my mother.* I say it with a kind of pride. You would probably agree. Physically, for sure, I am nothing like you. I have my father's blonde hair and dark brown eyes, and my father's slender build and height. You are as voluble as I am silent; as emotional as I am calm. I have always believed that you are weak where I am strong. Wasn't I the one, even as a child, who held it all together? Yes, the differences between you and I have given me nothing but comfort over the years.

And yet.

A brown-haired child, just six years old, walks over to a fireplace and in an improbable act of bravery or maybe just plain desperation, picks up a poker – intervenes to stop her father from hitting her mother. An unlikely heroine, you have to admit. But then: another fireplace, twenty years later, and her four-year-old daughter follows in her mother's footsteps.

It's as vivid as if it was yesterday.

I am four years old and my daddy is angry again. He's going to hurt my mummy. He does that when he's angry. He crosses to the fireplace where she is standing. But she doesn't turn away; she doesn't say anything. Why doesn't she do something? Why doesn't she run away? But Daddy is tall and very strong and he's standing between Mummy and the door. Mummy just looks at him – looks him right in the eye. His mouth gets tight and his chin juts out and his face is red.

My stomach starts to hurt and that big bass drum is beating loudly inside my chest again. My eyes are blurring and I'm seeing double again and I shake my head and blink. Then Daddy raises his hand and makes it into a fist and he mustn't do this, he mustn't – he mustn't hurt my mummy – and without thinking about what I'm doing I run between them and I shout. 'No!' I yell at him, and I take hold of him by the knees because I can't reach up any further than that and my daddy has very long legs. 'You leave my mummy alone!'

And he stops. He looks down at me and for a moment I see something hard and shiny in his eyes and for the first time I understand that he could hurt me too. But he won't. I don't know why, but I know that he won't. And so I stare right back at him, my small hands clasping his knee-caps, and slowly I begin to push. 'You' – I push – 'leave' – I push – 'my mummy' – I push – 'alone.' One last shove and I'm out of breath now and my arms are tired but when I look behind him I see that he has backed up all the way to the front door. His mouth is open. He looks over to my mummy and then back down at me. And then something funny happens to his face and it starts to crumple up but before I can ask him if he's all right he turns around and opens the front door and then he goes away. It closes behind him, very quietly.

I turn round to Mummy, who stands watching me with her eyes wide and her hands over her mouth. I walk over to her and wrap my arms around her legs. She's safe. Everything's fine; I'll take care of her. 'It's all right, Mummy,' I tell her. 'Daddy's gone now. Shall we have a cup of tea?'

'Come to bed, Cat. It's late.'

'I'm okay. I want to stay up for a while.'

'You'll be exhausted in the morning.'

'I'll be fine.'

'Are you brooding about your mother again?'

'I'm not brooding about anything. I'm just not tired right now, and I want to stay up for a while.'

'If you come to bed, we could fool around a little. That'd help you sleep.'

A pause. 'I really just want to stay up for a while.'

'You never want to make out any more. Is there something wrong?'

'Nothing's wrong. I've just had a lot of things on my mind.'

'Maybe you should go and see Dr Rubenstein again. Maybe you should go and see that guy he wanted you to see, after all.'

'You mean the psychiatrist?'

'Well, hon – you seem a little out of sorts right now. Maybe he could help you.'

'I'm not crazy, Adam.'

'I didn't say you were crazy, hon – '

'Just because I don't want to have sex with you all the time doesn't mean I'm crazy.'

'All the time? Jesus, Cat, I can't remember the last time we had sex.'

'Get out, Adam. Get out of here and just leave me alone for a while, okay?'

🐾 🐾 🐾

'Hey, Cat. How's the flying going?'

A beat. 'Oh, I've been a bit busy this last week. Haven't had a chance, really.'

'Not thinking of giving it up, are you?'

A nonchalant shrug. 'Oh, I don't know, Jack. I've made my point, after all. Proven to myself that I can get into a small plane, maybe even fly it a little. What would be the point in carrying on just for the sake of it?'

A pause.

'Don't look at me like that, Jack. I never said I was going to

183

go all the way with this. So if I got my license, what difference would that make, after all? It's not like I'm going to fly for a living, or anything.'

'Sure, hon. Sure thing.' Another pause. 'You got that report on SP 32534?'

💥 💥 💥

'Not flying this morning then, Cat?'

'Morning, Tom. No, not this morning.'

'Given it up already, have you?'

'No. No, I haven't. Just having a break this week; I've a lot going on.'

'Seemed to me like a crazy thing to do, anyway. Never saw the point in it, myself. Just sitting up there, looking back down. Now if you got time on your hands and you want to take up a really interesting hobby, you ought to think about taking up golf...'

💥 💥 💥

It's been a long week. I haven't flown for eight days now, and although I've tried hard not to think about it, a hollow sense of loss has coloured every hour of every day. Eyes tired and heart cold and bleak as a mid-winter forest, I press the 'off' button on my laptop. Shiver a little as I reach into the corner of my desk and turn off the lamp. I should have switched the air-con to the heat setting; I can get away with that when Adam is away.

The telephone rings just as I reach the door. I stick my hand out into the brightly lit landing and peer at my watch: nine-thirty. Adam, probably – calling from Florida. I return to the desk, fumble for the phone in the half-light.

'Hello?'

'Hi, sweetheart. How you doing?'

I detect it immediately: the smallest of slurs in his voice. Automatically, I tense.

'Fine. How about you?'

'Great weather in Tampa. But missing you.'

'Have a good dinner?'

'Fantastic. Took the trial team out to a steak-house down by the waterfront.'

'Good wine?' God, I sound waspish. Cut him some slack, Cat. He's not your mother.

'I'm a little tipsy, I guess. Great bottle of Chateauneuf du Pape.'

He pronounces it 'doo Paype'; for some reason I find it immensely irritating. I close my eyes and wish he'd go away. I don't know what to say to him when he's been drinking and I'm stone-cold sober. It's not his fault, I know. It's just not something I can do.

'You're kinda quiet tonight. You okay?'

Come on, Cat. This is Adam. This is the man you live with. He's been away all week and he'll be gone for another couple of weeks at least – for as long as the trial lasts. And you're supposed to be missing him. I sigh; lower myself back into the chair at my desk. 'I'm fine. Just a bit of a crazy day at work.'

'Tell Uncle Adam all about it.' I hear what sounds like a bed creak under his weight, and I picture him settling down onto it. Kicking off his shoes, crossing his feet at the ankles. Loosening his tie, unbuttoning his shirt cuffs. Free hand rubbing away the grey shadows under his eyes. Weary.

'Oh – there was a meeting. Department heads, you know. They're talking about cutting jobs.'

'Well, times are tough out there, hon. It happens.' He yawns.

Thank you for that insight, I think, but bite my tongue. 'It's not just that they're cutting the jobs; it's all the bullshit that goes along with it. "Restructuring to give better customer value", they're trying to call it.' I close my eyes; see Mike reading from yet another impenetrable document: *We need to have an empowered workforce ... decentralised ... reorganising and de-layering to better anticipate and meet the needs of our customers ... adding value by increasing synergies...*

'So what's wrong with that?'

'What's wrong with that is that our customers really couldn't care less about our corporate structure. This isn't about customers; it's about cutting jobs to save money and increase profits.'

'Sanderson is a business, Cat. It's their job to make profits.'

'I'm aware of that, thank you, Adam. That isn't what I meant. I meant why can't we just say so – just be honest about it, instead of couching it in all this gobbledy-gook? Trying to obfuscate the issue.' A perplexed silence emanates from the other end of the line. He just doesn't get it. Doesn't anybody else get it? Anybody at all? 'Never mind,' I say. 'It doesn't matter.'

'Sure it matters, if it upset you.' He has his soothing voice switched on now. His 'humour the madwoman, it's only hormonal' voice. 'So, how many jobs are they talking about cutting?'

'Probably a hundred or so.'

He whistles.

'Including some in R&D.'

A beat. 'And what did Jack think of that?'

Maybe I'm imagining it, but isn't there the slightest trace of glee in his voice? 'He didn't think anything of it,' I say irritably. 'He wasn't there.'

'They're doing it behind his back?'

'I don't know. Bob Finkelman was there. You know, his deputy. I don't trust that guy at all.'

'Why?'

'He's always trying to undermine Jack.'

That much had been clear at the meeting. Bob in Jack's place, lurking around the head of the table with an expression of profound self-importance on his round, chubby face. 'Jack away?' I asked, trying to smile, trying to be nice.

'Yeah – more meetings down in Tucson.'

'At the University?'

'Right. A bit of damage limitation.'

I didn't much like the smirk on Bob's face. 'Damage limitation' in corporate-speak usually translates as 'someone has fucked up and we need to hide the truth'. And Bob, unlike Jack, is an expert at corporate-speak.

Damage limitation. I remembered the phrase later in the meeting, when Tom delivered the bombshell that some of the proposed job losses were likely to be in R&D. And then he turned to Bob. 'Bob, did you get a chance to discuss the proposals with Jack, since he couldn't make this meeting?'

'Yes, but only briefly. I'm afraid he's not very happy with them. Personally, I can see that they make sense, but Jack...' He shrugged in apparent helplessness and smiled with what he obviously hoped would pass for rueful sincerity. It didn't. 'Well, you know Jack.' Son of a bitch, I thought. You sneaky little son of a bitch.

Tom frowned. 'Well, Jack's going to have to be realistic for once. None of us likes the idea of cut-backs in our own area. But it's about time we took a good look at R&D budgets and resourcing. I'm just not comfortable with some of the research efforts we're funding – especially those outside the company. Seems to me that some of that stuff coming out of U of A down in Tucson is pretty questionable. Those guys are saying SP 32534 is sedative.'

I saw at once why he was rattled, of course. SP 32534 is one of our most exciting drugs in development. It falls under the company's programme to produce an anti-anxiety drug that doesn't sedate people at the same time – which represents one of the holy grails of modern psychiatric drug development. It's one that the board is watching very closely indeed: it would be a real coup for Sanderson if it came through the testing programme with all of its initial promise still intact.

'And they're saying it based on repeats of experiments we've already carried out internally,' he continued. 'Experiments carried out by Bob's group – in which we found no sedation. Right, Bob?'

How interesting, I thought. How interesting that Jack felt the need to replicate those experiments outside the company.

Bob nodded wisely. 'I agree, Tom. I think there are a lot of areas where we could do the work just as well in-house and have more control over it.'

More control over it? 'Excuse me,' I interrupted. Twenty heads swivelled in my direction in gleeful anticipation of another showdown. Maybe I do have a death wish, after all.

Tom looked up and sighed. 'Catriona?'

'The whole point of doing research externally as well as internally is to gain credibility. As a safety check. And, sometimes, as a quality check.' I looked pointedly at Bob, who flushed and glanced away. 'That research is the foundation of our entire business. I can't see how it would be wise to cut down on it.'

Tom turned the full force of his flinty eyes on me. 'I've been a bit concerned about the quality of some of the work that Jack's been commissioning recently.' Bob nodded sagely, courage boosted by Tom's support. Smug little shit – how dared he, while Jack wasn't here to defend himself? 'Perhaps if funds aren't flowing so freely there'll be more consideration given to spending them wisely.'

My temper flared. 'With respect, Tom, I'm not sure it's appropriate to talk about this without Jack being present to defend his decisions. I'm sure Bob is doing his best to fill in here' – I threw a smile at Bob that matched his own in sincerity – 'but Jack is head of R&D and we certainly shouldn't agree to cuts without him being here to express his views and have a say in the process.'

Tom leaned forward and slowly placed his hands flat on the table. He kept his eyes fixed on his hands, and for a few moments said nothing at all. The tension in the room was palpable. I could see that I was going to suffer for this, but somehow I couldn't seem to find it in my heart to care.

Eventually, Tom raised his head from the table. He smiled – a deceptively mild smile. He looked around the room; he didn't meet my eyes. 'Of course he'll have a say in the process; I was simply pointing out some of the issues. We've a long way to go before we finalise any of the details relating to these cuts.' I allowed myself to exhale as he turned his attention back to the written proposals in front of him. 'Now. Does anyone else have a comment on R&D, or shall we move on to marketing?'

I sat back in my squeaky clean black leather chair and I watched. I watched as Bob smiled knowingly and nodded at everything that Tom said. I looked at the faces around the table: smug faces, and self-satisfied. Faces that bore the comfortable traces of lives that were turning out exactly as they expected. I watched and I listened and my chest was hollow and my head was heavy and I wanted, very badly, to weep.

'Hon?'

Suddenly I realise that a silence has been building on the other end of the line and that Adam has said something that I haven't responded to. 'Sorry,' I say. 'Sorry. I didn't hear you.'

'I said, I don't see why you're letting all this get to you all of a sudden.'

'It's not all of a sudden, Adam. I've been feeling like that for a long while. It's a build-up, and like all build-ups, it *builds up* – that's what build-ups do, you see – to a stage where you just can't bear it any more. Sometimes I don't know what I'm doing there – it all seems so pointless. All the bullshit, all the jargon. All the dirty corporate politics.'

'Well, hon, that's business for you. That's just the way it is these days. No point in getting all hot and bothered about it.'

He sounds sleepy; probably the wine. I grit my teeth; try not to snap. 'Never mind,' I say. 'Let's not talk about it, hey?'

'It's just a stage you're going through. Everyone gets frustrated with their job, sometimes. We all go through these stages.'

The platitude angers me. 'Do we? Did you?'

He pauses. 'Well, no. Not really. You know me: always wanted to be a lawyer, still love it. Can't imagine doing anything else.' Yes, I know Adam. Happily filling in his time-sheet at the end of every day, every ten-minute period fully accounted for and charged out to some client or other. Working Saturdays, playing golf with the other senior partners on a Sunday afternoon. Hardly taking a day's vacation except on public holidays. That's Adam's life. That's Adam. And how lovely to be so certain: so completely immune to self-doubt. The irony, of course, is that that was one of the things that attracted me to him when we first met. He seemed so simple, so straightforward – what you saw was one hundred percent of what you got. There isn't an ounce of hypocrisy in Adam.

'Cat, hon. I worry about you. You seem so uptight lately.' He sighs sleepily and yawns again. 'When are you going to get back to normal?'

Normal? I laugh abruptly. Where's that? I want to ask him. Where is this place called *Normal*? And who lives there? Do you? And is that living, what you do? What any of you do? A sudden flash of anger. 'Maybe we can talk about it when you're sober.'

There's a clearly audible silence on the other end of the line and I let my head fall against the back of the chair and I close my eyes. 'I'm sorry, Adam. I'm sorry. I'm just really tired. It doesn't matter.' The silence lingers, heavy with hurt. 'Look, let's just call it a night. I'm going to have a bath before I go to bed. See you tomorrow?'

'Sure,' he says, and just for a moment I wish he'd fight back. I wish he'd argue; I wish for something to break. Because then I'd know whether it was possible to put it back together again. 'Sure. I'll be back home in time for dinner. We'll have a day, a day and a bit before I've got to turn back around and fly out again.' He pauses. 'Love you.'

'You too,' I lie.

I put the telephone down in its cradle and guilt immediately sets in. I completely overreacted – I know that all too well. It's not as if he's in the habit of getting drunk; he's not actually a big drinker at all.

But the reaction is instinctive, ingrained.

I know. I know as soon as I come back from school and find her at home. It's way too early; she shouldn't be back for another hour and a half.

A hard, cold stone sinks into the pit of my stomach.

'Mum?' I call quietly. But the stone disintegrates and a small spark of hope takes its place as I walk through to the kitchen and see her there, busy at the counter-top. She's on her feet and there is a pile of potatoes ready to be peeled in front of her. She's cooking; she must be okay.

'Hi, darling.' She turns and smiles brightly. Too brightly. The spark dies; another stone rolls into position. 'Good day?'

I nod. I watch closely. She hasn't spoken enough words yet; I still can't tell. 'Why are you home early?'

'I didn't feel well.' She fumbles with a pan lid; it clatters loudly on the stainless steel draining board and she swears. My ears prick up and my mind is focused, concentrated; every sense alert for a sign. I look around the kitchen, scanning for a glass. Nothing.

Maybe she really didn't feel well. Maybe she'll just take an aspirin and go to bed early and wake up in the morning and everything will be all right. Just like a normal Saturday morning. And we can go into town, maybe. Do some window shopping. Or go for a walk along the beach. Like normal people do.

'Good day at school?'

She's already asked me that. 'It was okay.' I walk over to her casually, smelling, assessing. She turns and smiles at me, leans back against the sink. 'What lessons did you have today?'

'The usual. History. Maths. English.'

'English. Your favourite. What book are you studying?' The smile is still too bright, too careful – as if it might slip if she doesn't hold on to it tightly – and her eyes ... don't they have the beginning of the Look?

Because that's how I think about it: the Look. The look that her eyes get when she's been drinking. Unfocused; glittery. Strangely hollow. But it's more than just her eyes. Her whole face undergoes a slight shift. It loosens, somehow; the mouth slips a little, to one side.

I am an expert in the detection of the Look. I am always alert, always watching for it. But the Look is just one part of a much more sophisticated system. Throw in just a few spoken words and I can assess her accurately on a six-point rating scale:

1. Sober.
2. Happy; a little dizzy. Speech slurring just a little. Eyes slightly out of focus.
3. Sentences garbled, halfway there. Face slack, lips red and moist.
4. Nonsense sounds; eyes blinking slowly.
5. Lips move but no sound; eyes completely unfocused; skin grey: about to pass out.
6. Comatose.

That's what happens on the way up. But on the way back down, the number two stage changes. Happy becomes angry: pursed lips, vicious tongue. Number two lasts for a long time. The only thing that gets me through the down phase is the knowledge that soon she'll be sober again. That soon, for just a short while, I'll be able to relax.

Right now I'd say she's somewhere between number one and number two. 'George Eliot,' I say. 'We're studying Silas Marner.'

She grimaces. 'Depressing.'

I like it, I want to say. But I don't want to argue with her. She hates it when I don't like the things that she likes. 'What are we going to do tomorrow?'

Her eyes cloud over and she shrugs vaguely. 'Oh, well. I hadn't thought about that. I'll have to see how I'm feeling.'

I persist, even though by now I already know it's no use. I already know what we'll be doing tomorrow. 'I thought we could go into town.'

'What for? What would be the point of that? You know we can't afford to buy anything.' Her voice is sharp and high; her mouth tenses.

'Not to buy anything. Just to look. Just to go out for a bit. Together.'

'Well, I don't see the point in that.' She turns back to the sink, mouth twisting, movements spasmodic and tightly controlled. 'I don't see why you want to go to the shops all the time. You know we don't have any money.'

'I know that. I wasn't asking...' Oh, but that isn't fair. I know we don't have much money. I never ask her for anything; she knows that.

'You only do it to make me feel guilty. It's not my fault. I do what I can.'

The stone in the pit of my stomach sprouts teeth and I want to suggest that if she didn't drink all the time she'd have a better

chance of holding down a job and we might have more money
– but I bite my tongue.

I'm not allowed to get angry. She's the only one who's
allowed to get angry.

'Go and get changed out of your uniform.'

I close the kitchen door and wait. I hear a cupboard door
close; hear the familiar clink of bottle against glass. Wearily, I
turn away.

I close the study door behind me but it's not so easy to close the
door on the memories, or her voice in my head. It takes me by
surprise, sometimes: the anger, the monster. It creeps up on me;
it weighs heavily on me; it won't let me go.

᠅ ᠅ ᠅

'I'm not crazy, Ginny.'

'I didn't say you were, hon. It's just – well, I'm worried
about you. We all are. Adam is.'

A waiter sweeps up to the table, refills our glasses of iced
tea, and just as quickly dashes away again. Olivetti's is buzzing,
just as it always is on Saturday lunchtimes. Filled with impatient
people who just want to eat and be on their way again. It used
to be that fast food was a novelty, a choice; now it's become
an institution. The people here have no time for contemplation.
No-one sits here over a leisurely glass of wine or cup of coffee,
watching the world drift by, contemplating their existence.
They lurch from one experience to another, afraid to stop,
afraid to slow down… What do they think is going to catch up
with them?

Ginny shakes her ginger curls. 'I declare, I don't know
what's gotten into you. You seem so – *jumpy*, lately. Adam
thinks you're having a midlife crisis or something.'

'Does he?' I take another half-hearted bite of my goat's

cheese and grilled vegetable panini, wondering just how it is that she's so well-informed about what Adam thinks of me. Wondering what he's telling people. And how many people he's telling. 'Well, then. Maybe I am.'

'People do all kinds of crazy things when they hit forty, Cat.'

'Yeah, I know. But have you ever thought that maybe it's not crazy at all, but really makes sense? That it's because they begin to develop a sense of their own mortality? Start to question, start to wonder why they're just chugging along, doing the same old thing, day in and day out? Is it so crazy, to reevaluate what you're doing with your life?'

'And is that what you're doing?' She picks delicately at her Caesar salad. With low-fat dressing on the side, no croutons and just a sprinkling of cheese. Ginny takes very few chances with her figure and her health.

'I guess I am. And you know what? From where I sit my life looks pretty arid.'

She laughs and puts her fork down. 'Come on, Cat. Look at you. What have you got to have a crisis about? You're forty, sure, but you're a young forty. You're slim, you're healthy, you're attractive; you still have that enviable English rose complexion even after ten years in the desert. You've risen pretty close to the top of the ladder at Sanderson; you earn a mint. You live in a nice house in one of the most sought-after suburbs of Phoenix. You're living with a guy who's just as successful, who's warm and kind and absolutely adores you. What's the matter with you?'

What's the matter with me? She has a point. This is the American Dream, after all, isn't it? This is what we're all striving for, what we all want to be?

I sigh. 'I don't know, Ginny. I don't know what the matter with me is. All I know is that right now this nice comfortable *safe* life doesn't seem to be what I want.'

'Are you sure you're quite well?' Her voice is careful; her

eyes skit away from mine. Down to her salad, where she picks out a stray crouton with a delicate moue of distaste.

'What's that supposed to mean?'

'Drew said…' She has the grace to hesitate. 'Adam told him you had some kind of … psychological problem. I don't know … anxiety, or panic, or some such thing. You don't think maybe that could be a part of it?'

The hastily swallowed panini settles in the pit of my stomach like a stone. How dare he? How dare he go around discussing me like that? 'I had a few issues with anxiety.' I put the remainder of the sandwich down and push the plate away. 'It's nothing. I have a bunch of relaxation exercises and breathing exercises to do. It's under control.'

She raises a sceptical eyebrow. 'And do you think that you're in control?'

'No. I feel as if everything is about to break apart. But I don't feel that way because I have panic attacks. I have panic attacks because I feel that way.'

She blinks. 'I don't get it.'

Join the club, I think. Nobody gets it. I'm not even sure I really get it myself. 'What does it matter, anyway? I'm still here; I'm still functioning. Every now and again I feel as if someone is taking hold of me by the throat and shaking me, but I'm still functioning. I'm not crazy.' How dare he even suggest it? How dare she?

'I know you're not, hon. It's just that Adam – '

'Adam has no right to be discussing me like this.'

Her voice is soothing now, concerned. 'Of course he does. Drew is his closest friend. You know how they are; they tell each other everything.'

'And then Drew tells you.' And then suddenly I get it. 'Did Adam ask Drew to ask you to talk to me?'

Like most redheads, Ginny finds it impossible to control her propensity to blush.

'He did. The son of a bitch.' I pull the napkin off my lap and throw it onto the table.

'Cat. It's only because he's worried about you.'

'No, Ginny. It's not. It's because I'm not conforming any more to what he expects of me.' I clench my fists; unclench them again. Sit back in my chair; get a grip on my breathing. Slow it down. Ginny watches me from across the table as if I'm a fuse that might blow at any minute. The idea is so ludicrous – so uncharacteristic – that it almost makes me laugh. Can I really be this person? This person that has to be watched and cajoled? This person that won't just climb back into her box and close the lid on her frustration? This person who is beginning to feel that maybe – just maybe – she has the right to a little honest anger every now and again?

The part of me that isn't totally horrified watches with a slight smile. And says, almost conversationally, 'You know – I'm really not too sure, most of the time, whether Adam and I are really suited to each other or not.' Adam Fraser III. The *third*, for God's sake: I'm living with a man who calls himself by a number. A number that announces proudly to the world: this is who I am; this is where I come from. Oh, it says: you can count on me. You can count on me to be just like my father and just like his father before him. I know my predestined place in the world; I agree to be bound by it.

No surprises.

Safe.

And I have always chosen the safe paths in my life. But sometimes in my dreams I walk rockier roads.

'Come on, Cat – he adores you.'

'I know.' I reach for the iced tea; take a long, cooling swallow. 'But he makes me feel … claustrophobic.'

'I know he asked you to marry him.'

'Jesus. We really don't have any secrets, do we?'

'Hey, girl –' she reaches out and places a warm, dry hand on my arm '– you don't have to worry about keeping secrets from me. I'm on your side.'

Are you? I wonder, as I look at her face. With its pale brown eyes that seem so earnest; the little-girl freckles across the bridge of her nose. Are you really? Is any woman ever really on the side of another woman? I don't really know you at all. What do I really know about you? What do you know about me?

Just the surface, that's all. Just the surface.

'Then you know I said no.'

'Why, Cat?'

Because I don't love him any more, I want to say.

But I don't. I don't because if I do it'll get straight back to Drew. And I don't because if I say it out loud it'll make it real and I'll have to do something about it. And that won't be safe and comfortable at all. No, siree.

The fledgling rebel creeps back into her shell. I shrug. 'We're fine as we are. We just don't need to get married. I don't want to get married. Not to Adam, not to anyone.'

She pauses. 'Cat. Is there someone else?'

Oh, for God's sake. 'Now you really are beginning to sound like Adam. He's convinced there's something going on between me and Jack.'

'Well, hon. You can't really blame him. You do seem pretty close.'

'Sure we're close. It's called being friends. Jack is the only person I can talk to about all the bullshit at Sanderson. The only one who even has a clue what I'm talking about.'

'He's an attractive guy.'

'The world is full of attractive guys. That doesn't mean that I'm fucking them all.' She sits back in her chair abruptly. Nice American ladies don't talk like that. Sometimes I forget myself. Forget who I'm supposed to be.

'What about this flight instructor of yours?'

'Jesse?' I blink. Jesse? Her words hit me somewhere in the vicinity of my solar plexus.

Jesse?

I shake my head vigorously. 'No way. He's my flying instructor, for God's sake. There's probably some law against it in this crazy country. Not that I'd be thinking about it, even if there wasn't. There isn't anyone else. Not Jack, not Jesse, not anyone.'

Jesse? All of a sudden I seem to have lost my focus.

'Look, Ginny – can we change the subject? Please? Everything's just fine. Tell me something interesting. Tell me about your week.'

And she goes along with it. Relieved, probably, to get the conversation back on its usual even keel. I listen to her tales of poor corporate communications, and I tell her a funny story about Tom. I listen to her plans for a family Christmas, and I tell her that Adam and I will be going to his family in Atlanta for a couple of days. I listen and I talk and I nod and I smile and all the while I swallow down on the loneliness that clumps up inside my stomach like piles of damp sawdust.

The telephone rings; I pick it up cautiously, praying that it won't be someone who wants to speak to Mum. I'd leave it to ring but it would only wake her up, and if she sleeps straight through for a few hours more she might wake up sober. And then it'll all be over. For now, at least. I'll be able to relax again, and to sleep.

'Hi, Cat, it's Janice.'

'Oh, hi, Janice. What's happening?'

'We're going to the youth club tonight; there's a table tennis competition going on. Brian and Paul will probably be there. I just wondered if you were coming.'

My heart sinks. 'I can't tonight. Mum's not well and I have to look after her.'

There's a pause on the other end of the line. 'What, again?'

It's clear that she doesn't believe me; she thinks I'm making excuses because I don't want to go. When the truth is that right at this minute I want to go more than anything else in the world. To be anywhere, other than here.

It's just not fair. I wish I could tell her the truth, but how can I? What could I possibly say? 'Sorry, but I can't come out tonight because my mum's a drunk and I have to stay home to make sure she doesn't kill herself or set fire to the house, like she almost did last weekend.' That would be just great. That would go down really well.

'Oh, well.' She's angry; I can hear it in her voice. It's happened too often over the past few months. Or worse: I've said I'd go somewhere with her and then not been able to go. Let her down. 'I suppose we'll see you at school on Monday then. Bye.'

'Bye.' I put the phone down and curl up into a ball by the side of the bureau in the chilly hall.

Mum's not well. I'm so very tired of saying that phrase. So tired of not being able to tell the truth. But there's no-one that I could tell it to. Who could I possibly tell? Who would understand? And, more important than that – who could I possibly want to share the shame with? And the guilt? Because if they really knew what went on – if they really, really knew me – how could they do anything other than despise me?

But it's so hard. Everywhere I go it seems that I'm the only one who isn't a part of it all. Sometimes at school I can feel them watching me, whispering. As if they sense that there is something different about me. Something that I'm hiding. Something strange that explains why it is that I can never invite them home.

Something that sets me apart.

🐾 🐾 🐾

Another extract came today. Another brown envelope, and Adam eyeing me carefully as he hands me the mail. But this time I'm not afraid of it; I smile politely as I take it from his hands. I don't say anything about lunch with Ginny; I don't say anything about betrayal. With a curiosity that surprises me I just slip right on up to my study and I close the door and tear open the envelope and once again I begin to read.

Aunt Lizzie. Oh, she was a difficult woman, was Aunt Lizzie. Brittle and bad-tempered, for sure – but I never saw her behave like that. Wicked? Well, maybe she was. I never took her all that seriously. She made us laugh, though, didn't she, you and I? Years later, looking back. Wit as sharp as a razor shell and a loud, toothless cackle to go along with it. Such strange ways of describing things: it took me years to figure out why she called the outside toilet the Twilight Zone.

Aunt Lizzie standing by the window, peering out from behind the curtains with a running commentary on all the neighbours. 'He's had that jacket since it was a top coat,' she'd say about poor feckless Lennie next door. And his bleached-blonde daughter Karen, pregnant and unmarried at eighteen: 'There she goes, the dirty little who-er, carrying all before her. That's what comes of being a barmaid, you mark my words. Aye, there's many a slip 'twixt cup and lip.'

Wicked? Well then, maybe she was that as well. I saw the spite in her, and the meanness. I suppose I should be surprised that, all those years later, you left me alone with her too. Didn't you worry that she'd be the same with me? But you really didn't have much choice at the time, did you? You had to go to work, and her house was right opposite my school. Where else would I go? What else could you do?

But Aunt Lizzie was different with me. She fed me and looked after me and most of the time she left me alone. I was never afraid of Aunt Lizzie. Maybe by the time I came along she'd mellowed; the big bad witch become nothing more than a frightened old woman. Because she was frightened, you know. Especially after Uncle Billy died. Hour after hour rocking backwards and forwards at the old wooden table in the front room. Chewing the ends of her fingers, gums bared, groaning and muttering, damp at the corners of her eyes.

School holidays at Aunt Lizzie's house. Summer days in the cabbage patch, lime green caterpillars crawling up my legs and an Enid Blyton book glued to the ends of my arms. *The Adventures of Binkle and Flip*; a *Brer Rabbit* story or two. Running errands to the betting shop: 'Sixpence each way on Lester Piggott, and don't you go telling your mam.' A quarter of best butter and a packet of 99 tea from the Co-op, and if she was feeling flush, a savoury pattie and chips for our tea. With a paper pot of mushy peas on the side.

Aunt Lizzie in front of the brand new television, transfixed by *Coronation Street*. I told her that she reminded me of Ena Sharples. You held your breath, waiting for the outburst, but she just cackled loudly, showing her four remaining teeth. When you'd gone she would play with those teeth to make me laugh. She'd poke at them and they'd swivel and bend as they clung tenaciously to the last remaining shreds of their roots. Aunt Lizzie singing 'All I Want For Christmas Is My Two Front Teeth'.

Perhaps it seems strange to you now, but I loved Aunt Lizzie. And I missed her, when she died. I was just fine with Aunt Lizzie, but at night I still cried for you. Tucked up in bed with the old red eiderdown tight around my chest and the ancient black brick for a hot-water bottle – scalding from the oven and wrapped in an old knitted rag. Gritting my teeth against the hot threat of tears. I wouldn't cry in front of anyone – not even then. 'I want my mummy,' I'd say, straight and rigid in the bed. 'I want my mummy.' 'Well, you can't have your frigging *mummy*. She's out at work earning money to take care of you. So you'll just have to make do with me.'

My mummy. Those were the days when I revelled in your stories. We would curl up on the sofa on Sunday afternoons and you would sing me songs from the musicals that you loved so much. *My little girl, pink and white as peaches and cream is she...* But that was before it all really began. Before you started to disintegrate in front of my eyes. Oh, I can feel for that uncertain little girl that you were. I can feel for you because I've been there too. No, you were never Aunt Lizzie. But I know what it's like to walk around on tip-toe. To watch and be wary, and never to understand what it is you've done wrong.

'Hi, Mum.'

Her shoulders are set; she doesn't answer. My heart sinks in my chest. What have I done now? She looks up at me and her mouth is mean and twisted.

'Where've you been?' *Her voice is still a little slurred: number two on the scale. On the way back up again. Sober soon. Hold on to that, Cat: sober soon.*

'Just out playing on the beach with Janice and Sally.'

'You've been gone long enough.'

'Not really, just a couple of hours.' *Just a couple of short hours. Such a short escape: such fun. For a while.* 'You were asleep when I went out.' *You weren't asleep, you were unconscious. But I don't say that.*

'Snuck out behind my back, did you? Didn't think about me while you were gone. Did you?'

I can feel it waking up inside me: the monster that hides away in my stomach. The monster that I inherited from my father. The monster that I mustn't let out. Not ever. Didn't think about you? The monster wants to say. How could I not think about you? All I ever do is think about you. Whether you're drunk or whether you're sober. Whether you're happy or whether you're sad. You don't exactly give me a choice, do you?

But of course I don't say that, either. 'Is there something you need?'

'Need? Yes, there's something I need. There's something I bloody need. I need someone who cares about me. Someone who gives a damn. Not like you. Not like you and your bloody bastard of a father.'

I find the notebook later, when I'm tidying up the magazines under her bed. My husband and my lovers and my daughter have destroyed me, *it says.*

I'm ten years old.

❦ ❦ ❦

'I hear you excelled yourself again at the HR meeting last Wednesday.'

Jack. Hair askew, eyebrows aloft and a grin twitching up the corners of his mouth. I'm so delighted to have him back, I could hug him. But that's definitely not allowed – someone would see and haul me up for contravening the company's sexual harassment policy. That's corporate life for you: filled with pitfalls for the unwary. I smile and wrap my arms around my waist.

'And a very happy Monday morning to you, too. Yeah, I got a little bit carried away again, I'm afraid. Tom read me the riot act afterwards.'

He slips into the office and perches on a chair in front of my desk, face serious for once. 'Cat. You know, if you want to keep your job you gotta play their game just a little.'

'Well, that depends on the game, doesn't it? Okay, so last time maybe I overreacted to all that bullshit about the mission statement.' I swing around to face him, leaning forward across the desk. The morning sun slips through a slat in the blinds and jabs me in the eye. I withdraw again, shaking my head at the question on his face as he gestures towards the window. 'But this was different, Jack. There are harmless games and not-so-harmless games. And what Bob and Tom are doing isn't harmless. All this business about the University of Arizona results makes my blood run cold. It seems to me like they're building up to a serious case of burying unwanted data.'

'Ah, now there I agree with you. That's different: a matter of principle and ethics. And that's an area I won't bend on.'

'You're right not to bend on it; what he's suggesting is inappropriate. But if you'd been there...' I sigh. 'And Tom has Bob completely on board. You really need to watch out for Bob, you know.'

'I'm not worried about Bob.'

'You should be, Jack. He's knifing you behind your back at every possible opportunity.'

He shrugs. 'Corporate games, Cat – that's all they are. It happens. You shouldn't get so worked up about it.'

'I can't help but get worked up about it. It's not right. Am I the only person in the whole damn company who thinks it's not right?'

'Okay – it's not right. But it's the way it is. You don't have to join in with it.'

'But even if I don't join in with it, I can't just ignore it. There's this – almost visceral reaction that I have against it. When people behave like that it makes me physically sick.' The sleek black two-line telephone purrs softly in the background; I glance at the caller ID. 'Tom,' I say, shaking my head to indicate that I'm not going to answer it. 'Sometimes I think he has ears everywhere.'

Jack frowns and looks at me carefully, scrutinising me like one of his laboratory rats. 'Cat, honey, you know – I'm worried about you lately.'

Oh, not another one. Not Jack as well. I laugh, a little shakily. 'There's nothing to worry about. I'm just losing the ability to tolerate these things and I can't seem to help it.

Why do we do it, Jack? Why do we work for these god-awful companies? Why do we tolerate this culture of control, all this mistrust, this suspicion?'

'You asking me? Why do I do it? Because when it comes right down to it, I like my work. I believe in my work. I want to create drugs that cure people. All the other crap is peripheral.'

'Perhaps that's the difference. I can't see it as peripheral. It's part of the deal. And I don't like it.'

'If you want to earn a living…'

'There are other ways to earn a living. Look at you, for example. You could've stayed in academic life. Had more freedom. Done your research there. You still could.'

He sits back in the chair and crosses one foot over his knee. He fiddles with his shoelace. 'It's not so different, really. Whoever pays for the research at some level pulls the strings. You're never in control. And there's the age-old issue of money – universities pay like shit. Then there are tenure problems: you have so little security. When we got married and started a family and took on a mortgage I needed a regular, steady income. And now, when we're used to the salary, it'd be hard to go back.' He looks up and grins. 'Though some days, I have to admit, it's crossed my mind.' He stands and stretches, green corduroy shirt pulled tight against slackening stomach muscles, and exhales loudly as he lowers his arms. He half-turns to leave, and then looks back again. 'Don't do anything rash now, will you, Cat? Let yourself cool down for a while. Settle back down.'

Settle back down to what? I want to ask him as I watch him walk through the door with a wave and a grin. Settle back down to panic attacks? Just carry on every morning with those phantom hands clamped around my throat as I sit in the parking lot and look up at the building, dreading the moment when I have to leave the safety of the car and walk inside? Settle back down to the sinking feeling of dread as I go to bed every Sunday night? Settle back down to all that?

But of course I don't ask him any such thing.

I badly needed to get away from the office, even though it's only mid-afternoon. And now I need to shake off the office persona, get out of these clothes and into jeans and a sweat shirt. The kitchen is empty; there's no sign of Adam though his car's in the garage. I hesitate for a moment; I can't imagine why he's home during the day. It's so unlike him. I am halfway up the stairs before I see that the door to my study is ajar. I stop. The sound of wood sliding against wood: the sound of a drawer opening. And the rustle of paper. What…?

I push the door open; stand in the doorway. 'Adam, what are you doing?'

He jumps; whips his head around to face me. Stares at me, open-mouthed. I look from his guilty face to the open drawer of my desk and the notebook in his hands. 'What the hell do you think you're doing?'

He flushes. 'I…' Shakes his head. Places the notebook – it's blank, but he probably knows that by now – back in the drawer.

'How dare you.' My voice is shaking, my whole body is trembling and a white-hot rage is burning in my stomach.

'Ah, Jesus. I'm sorry, Cat. It's just that – you've been so strange, recently. So distant…' His voice trails away as he sees the expression on my face. If it's as murderous as I imagine it to be, I can't say that I blame him. He turns away, rests his elbows on the desk. Places his head in his hands. 'I'm sorry.'

'What is it you were you looking for, exactly?' My voice is cold, precise.

'I don't know. Whatever it is that you're hiding from me. Evidence that you were having an affair, maybe. With Jack. Or someone.'

'You don't need to go rifling through my things, Adam. I haven't been hiding anything from you. I've been telling you what I've been feeling all along. You just haven't been listening.'

He stands, makes a move towards me. 'Cat, I –'

'Don't touch me.' I take a step back. The sense of violation is profound.

'I'm sorry. It's only because I love you. You don't understand. You're all that I have.'

All that I have. Chains creep around my neck and tighten. I turn on my heels and run back down the stairs.

When she wakes up she wants to talk. She asks me things, pulling, tugging, digging. How I am feeling. What I am feeling. Whether I love her. Say it, Cat. Say it. Say I love you.
I don't know how to answer. So much is bottled up inside me that I don't know how to let it out. I'd be frightened to, even if I knew how; I've seen what happens when you let it out.

And besides, I don't trust her. I know what she will do with anything I give her. She will use it to hold me to ransom. She will use it to belittle, to mock. Poor little Cat, *she'll say. Such a fearful child. Such small feelings, such a small life. You'll never know tragedy, will you, little Cat? You'll never really live. You'll always play it safe.*

Finding my diary one Saturday afternoon; reading it, laughing at it. 'Listen to this, Cat! You're so funny. "Tonight Janice and I went to the youth club. Brian and Paul were there and asked us to play table tennis. Brian had on his dark brown cord jacket and looked really gorgeous. He kept looking across the table at me and smiling. When we finished playing he asked if I'd be back next week. Said maybe we could have another game. I was so excited I could hardly keep still, all the way home on the bus. Kept thinking about the look in his eyes when he smiled at me. God, he's SO gorgeous! I do love him, I think."' *Laughs, closes the diary and throws it back down on my bed.* 'Honestly, Cat. You think that's love? You don't know what love is. You'll never have a grand passion like me. You don't know how.' *And all the rest of that weekend as she sinks*

208

more and more deeply into oblivion: 'How's your boyfriend, little Cat? Miss him, do you? Wish he was here, cuddling you?'

I shrink even further inside and squeeze myself up like a plasticine ball. I squeeze and I squeeze as she laughs and she laughs and I make it so small that by the time Monday morning comes around I'm not sure I'll ever be able to find it again.

Somehow, I don't know how, I find myself at Scottsdale airport. I park the car and I sit and I stare blankly out at the runway. Such a busy airport; it's a big centre for flight training. A small Cherokee lines itself up on runway 3 and hurls itself joyfully into the sky and loss invades me, swamps me, drowns me. More than anything else in the world right now, I want to be in that aircraft. Leaving the ground. Leaving it all behind, and in its place the sharp fear-tinged clarity that allows no thought to intrude that is not fully focused on survival.

The alternative to that clarity? This utter emptiness.

I have no idea why I feel so empty. As if I've sold out, somehow … let go of some part of myself that I can't even name, that I wasn't even aware existed. Bought into the insanity of it all, the absurdity. It's as if I've lost my way. Darkness everywhere: darkness, and such a sense of loss.

My hands are clutching damply at the leather steering wheel; I wipe them on my skirt. I don't even know who I'm supposed to be any more. I brush my teeth each morning and look into the mirror and I hardly recognise the shadowy creature that looks back at me. Always on the brink of disorientation, it's as if I'm watching myself from a distance staggering through some kind of half-life. Preoccupied, inaccessible. Eyes glazed over, smile fixed, laugh forced.

And always, the impossibility of making any of them understand.

Another small plane skips up into the sky; swings out north into the desert.

Jesse. Jesse would understand.

But that last flying lesson. The failure. How could I ever face him again?

Well, that's an easy one, Cat. The only way to face him is to get back into a plane and just get on with doing those stalls.

I shiver. The thought of falling. *Jump, Cat. Go on – just jump.*

I need her voice out of my head. I need her out of my head and the only place I can shut her out is up there. Up there, where there's no room for clutter. Where all that there is, is you and the plane and the sky and the lightness…

And Jesse.

Jesse, who taught a deaf girl to fly.

If a deaf girl can find the courage to learn to fly, then surely so can I.

Damn it, so can I.

❦ ❦ ❦

'You ready?'

Just one lean brown hand rests lightly on his yoke; he's waiting for me to reach out and take mine. His left arm is pressed against me in the cramped cockpit; I focus in on the warmth of it, try to tune into his strength, his solidity. But, scanning my body, I am aware of all the regular signs of tension. The tightening of my chest, the lump in my throat. The painful knot in my stomach.

I close my eyes for a moment and grit my teeth. I cannot go on like this. Something has to give. This is no way to live. Something has to change. It would be better to die than to go on like this. It would be better to just die.

I refuse to die. I have always refused to die.

I take a deep breath and I nod, reach out for the controls.

'Good. Now I'm going to talk you through it as we go.'

My feet are ready over the rudder pedals, tense. My arms are rigid as I clasp the control wheel. Concentration screams in my brain. Power out, wheel back. Don't stop now, Cat – don't give up. Let it happen. For once in your life, just let it happen. *Let go, Cat, let go.* I push her voice out of my head because I know what happens when you let go. But it doesn't have to happen that way, does it? and the nose shudders and still I pull back and the air hits the underbelly of the plane and burbles over the wings and it sounds different, too – a hollow sound, slower and deeper, like a music box winding down – and I think about falling – that strange sinking sensation when you're just dropping off to sleep – but the buffeting intensifies, stronger now and *there's a mystery there, in that moment before you fall – right on the edge of it, no meaning, no motion* the nose drops and the wing falls off to the right but I am ready for it – ready, and I drive the wheel forward foot crashes down on the left rudder pedal right hand jerks forward to push in the throttle...

...And the wings are level again.

Slowly, slowly, I pull the nose back up. Climb. Level off.

We're safe.

I laugh out loud in relief.

Jesse claps his hands on his thighs. 'Perfect. See – I told you it was easy. Hell, it can even be fun. I didn't have to do a thing. Now: again. All by yourself, this time.'

The second time is easier. The third is easier again. I don't think it's ever going to be fun, but I can do it. And I'm going to keep on doing it. Because he's not always going to be here by my side. Because he's right: this is the only way I can be sure to save myself from falling. Because at all costs, I mustn't let myself fall.

'Okay. Good work. Now, we're going to go back to the airport and do a few touch-and-goes. We'll have you landing this plane by yourself in no time at all.'

*

Back on the ground I am high on achievement. He laughs at the sparkle in my eyes and the spring in my step. 'It's really not so bad up there, now, is it?'

'Bad? Oh, no. It's not so bad at all. In fact, it's so *not bad* that I've hardly been able to think of anything else all week. I've missed it more than I can say.' I roll my eyes; smile wryly to cover my embarrassment. 'It's becoming more and more of an obsession. It gets under your skin like an itch that's so diffuse you wouldn't even know where to begin to scratch it. Do you know what I mean? Does that happen to everyone?'

'Always.' He leans up against the plane with his arms folded and a smile in his eyes that warms me all the way through. 'Though there are varying degrees of obsession, of course. One of the first signs that you have it really bad is when you feel as if you're responsible for every other aircraft that's up there. Every time you hear a small plane overhead, you stop. And you look up. And you watch over it, just to make sure it doesn't fall out of the sky. Right?'

I nod.

'You find yourself obsessed by airports. You want to hang around them. All the time.'

'Lately I've found myself driving to Scottsdale airport on the way home and parking for a while, just to watch the aircraft take off. I have a portable transceiver so I can tune in to air traffic control. Listen to the communications; imagine I'm up there with them.'

'Ah, we have a seriously bad case here. Next symptom: the days when you're not flying lack colour. It's as if your whole life is in suspension, just waiting for the next lesson to come around.'

I laugh, and shake my head. He's right and it's true; I'm only alive on those days when I fly. It isn't just the adrenaline rush: there's so much more to it than that. Something that's hard to put into words, hard to explain to someone who's never done it.

Because flying is … well. Flying is an enchantment; it's a spell. In spite of the fear – or maybe because of it? – something draws you back into the sky just as the lure of a siren's song draws a sailor into deeper waters.

And I am beginning to want it more than I have ever wanted anything in my life.

'There's something about flying that obsesses everyone who chooses to do it – it's as simple as that.' Jesse pushes himself away from the plane and sets off slowly across the asphalt. I wipe away the sweat that's beginning to bead on my forehead. Lord, it's hot.

'What made you want to fly?' I'm lagging behind a little, wanting to prolong the conversation. Not wanting to break the spell; not wanting the success to end.

He stops; turns around to face me. 'When I was a kid, sometimes I would watch television late at night – in the good old days, before the service ran for twenty-four hours. I remember at the end of the programming, on whatever channel it was that we used to watch, they'd close down with a video clip of the Blue Angels. You know – the aerobatics team? And there'd be a voiceover reading the poem "High Flight" by John Gillespie Magee. Do you know it?' I shake my head. 'Beautiful poem. A bit sentimental, maybe, but there's nothing that describes the joy of flying like it. *Oh, I have slipped the surly bonds of earth, and danced the skies on laughter-silvered wings…* I'll bring a copy in for you next time you have a lesson.'

'I'd love that. Slipping the surly bonds of earth. What a wonderful way to put it.' And isn't that just what it's about? Casting off the guy ropes that hold you down. Letting yourself rise up; throwing away the ballast. Letting yourself grow lighter.

'Well, anyway: I always wanted to be that guy – the one who slipped those bonds. *Up up the long delirious burning blue…* ' His face changes and he looks away for a moment, shading his eyes against the glare of the sun. 'We couldn't afford flying lessons. But when I was at college I saved every penny I had from every evening and weekend and summer job I could find, and as soon as I could manage it I took myself along to the local airport and booked a lesson. Hooked up with a crusty old pilot called Sam Elliott. He gave lessons in his own plane – a Piper Cherokee that was just about as old and crusty as he was. We got along pretty well, Sam and me, and he took pity on me when he saw how much I meant it. He gave me a good few lessons on account – told me I could pay him back when I was earning a proper wage as a pilot.'

'And did you?'

'Of course. With interest.'

'Is he flying, still?'

He shoves his hands in his pockets and looks down at his sneakers. 'His plane went down five years ago over the Beartooth Mountains.'

Shit. 'I'm sorry. That must have been hard for you.'

'Yeah. But that's the way Sam would have wanted it. Turns out the week before he'd found out he had terminal cancer. He was only given six months to live. Something tells me that he decided to die the way he'd most loved to live – flying.' He shrugs; smiles faintly. 'He was that kind of guy. Lived by nobody's rules other than his own.'

'You admire that.'

'Sure.' He cocks an eyebrow as if it's obvious. As if he's surprised that I should find it necessary even to comment on it. 'I wouldn't know any other way to be.'

8

Laura

The village is so very silent in December; the tourists deserted long ago. Though at New Year the usual refugees from the south will come again, in search of a traditional Hogmanay. Laura emerges from the newsagent and raises a hand to shade her eyes against the low brilliance of the morning sun. It's bitterly cold even without a wind; at this time of year the sun doesn't rise till nine in the morning, and there barely seems to be time for the air to warm before it starts to set again at three-thirty.

Laura has finished her weekly shopping and loaded it into the car, and now she has bought a newspaper in a hollow effort to stimulate an interest in what's going on in the wider world. Her intentions are good, but the chances are that it will sit on the coffee table, unread. After a day or two, its perpetual glare of silent reproach will cause her to cover it up with a magazine. It will lie there, hidden under a pile of gradually accumulating weight, until weeks later – when its discovery will precipitate nothing more than its transfer into a pile of similarly pristine items that will some day serve as kindling for the fire. She has also bought a copy of the weekly newsletter that provides the surprisingly plentiful listings of local events. Visiting folk bands; presentations and slide-shows covering peculiarly arcane branches of geological and archaeological science; soup and sandwich lunches in the village hall in aid of various worthy causes. She likes to read the listings; likes to think that there's life going on around her, even if she doesn't want to join in with it.

The harbour looks so beautiful this morning with no-one around to disturb the peace. The fishermen are long gone and the Stornoway ferry left a little while ago. There's hardly a sound except for the ever-present seagulls that cry and screech as they swoop and circle, furiously scavenging for scraps. On impulse Laura locks the car again and walks down to the pier. The loch, balanced on the threshold of a change of tide, is perfectly still. The outline of the mountains – layer after layer of them receding into the eastern sky – is sharp and distinct. A fishy, oily smell wafts up from the clustered old fishing boats that sit in the water like a flock of exotic waterfowl, peeling paint curled around their bodies like feathers.

On a quiet day like this it would be so easy to believe that nothing essential had changed. And yet it has changed. In thirty-five years, what else should she expect? There are more houses, more buildings; the shop-fronts have all been modernised and a brand new supermarket has opened up at the back end of the village.

But the sensory impact of the harbour is just the same. Hardly a day went by that she didn't walk around the harbour, all those years ago. She would stop and gaze down at the boats, wondering about the stories behind each name. What sharp longing, what long-postponed fantasy prompted the *Dreamcatcher*? Who inspired the *Imelda May*? A Spanish lover, seeding memories of hot blue skies and warm calm seas along this cold stormy shore?

Time passed slowly then, just as it does now. So many long days to fill. Alec didn't want any wife of his working; it would be a slur on his manhood, he said. People would say that he couldn't provide. She should stay at home and look after the house and wait for the babies to come along. Aye, she'd be busy enough then. Laura thought it an old-fashioned perspective, but in so many ways living up here had been like slipping back in time ten years. So she busied herself about the house, keeping it spotless, racking her brain for new ways of combining meat or fish with potatoes and the occasional limp cabbage or shrivelled swede. She would sit in the window of the small terraced house on Shore Street and keep watch in the evenings as the fishermen came in. Waiting for a sight of Iain Mòr's bright blue boat that would deliver Alec safely back to her. Watching with longing and impatience, so badly wanting him to be home, so badly wanting to be in his arms again.

But that was before. Before everything changed.

The house is still there, of course, though since she came back she's avoided walking past it. She's avoided even looking at it, averting her eyes as she drives down the street. So it is a strange but irresistible impulse that leads her now to turn up Shore Street, old feet tracing young footsteps, winter tracing all the longings of spring. Her footsteps are firm at first but begin to slow as she approaches the house. Sudden catch in her throat; heart pounding and all the old fear surging in her stomach like the waking Kraken rising from the deep. Breathless, she halts in the middle of the pavement. Stop it. There's nothing here to fear. Not any more. She tries to laugh at herself, but the cold air catches in her throat and she chokes. An elderly man in a worn Harris tweed jacket and stalker's cap looks at her curiously as he approaches. Pull yourself together, she tells herself. It's only a house. If Cat were here, she'd say you're being melodramatic. Again. She manufactures a reassuring smile and a nod, and a cheerily murmured 'Good morning.'

'Aye, it is that,' he says. And passes by, leaving her alone with her memories.

The whitewashed façade of the house doesn't seem to have changed much, except for the colour of the woodwork. It used to be painted black; now it's a rich royal blue. The wooden sash windows and the old door that opens right onto the street are still there. It looks a little neglected: unloved. A sharp pain shoots through her chest and she closes her eyes. More than anything she wants to turn right around, to run back to the car. She laughs abruptly. Oh, yes – wouldn't that be in character? Typical Laura, averting her face from anything that smacks of discomfort. Pretending it doesn't exist.

But she ran away before, and where did it lead her?

Right back here. Right back where it all started.

She takes a deep breath and raises her head high. She doesn't know what she's afraid of; doesn't know what it is that she thinks she might see. It was thirty-five years ago that she left, and everything here has changed.

Alec is long gone.

She takes a resolute step forward and bends; she peers in through the window of what used to be the sitting-room. It never occurs to her that anyone might be inside: the house has such a sad and empty air. She shades her eyes and squints through the dusty glass into the dim room beyond. And exhales in relief – a short, laughing breath. It's completely different. Of course it is. The flower-garlanded wallpaper is gone, replaced by magnolia paint. Well-used modern furniture is backed up against the walls – a dark velour sofa and matching armchair; a cheap wood veneer coffee table and a low-slung corner unit that bears a bulky and elderly television set. Nothing lies around that indicates any sign of occupation. It's probably a holiday house; so many in the village are, now.

But the fireplace is still there. The fireplace is still the same, with its plain cream-painted surround and its black cast iron grate.

Sunday afternoons on the sofa, before desire drove them upstairs to huddle together in ice-cold sheets.

Long evenings waiting for the sound of the door handle turning, wondering what mood he'd be in after a night in the pub.

The door to the house next door opens and swiftly Laura turns away. She crosses the road. Sits on the sea wall for a moment, ice-cold hands in the pockets of her padded black jacket, and she shivers. Alec. She closes her eyes. Sometimes lately she's found herself wondering what she could have done differently. Trying to remember at what point it all began to go so badly wrong. Were there signs at the beginning that she missed? Could she ever have predicted it, when they first met?

Once upon a time, there was a girl who lived in a cottage by the sea. And how she loved the sea! She would swim in it at all times of the year, no matter how cold the water. Swim and feel the soft salt water swirl around her body, soothing and nourishing.

She was tall and slender; her curly brown hair shone and her black eyes glowed. She was courted by many local boys; they were familiar to her, and safe. But in her dreams she was romanced by tall, handsome strangers from far distant lands. She longed for someone who would take her away from this place, away from her wicked stepmother and from the family that had discarded her so long ago.

Saturday nights were dance nights at the Queen's Rink in town, and by the time she stepped down from the crowded bus at eight o'clock Laura was tense with excitement. Saturday nights were Laura's escape. Escape from Aunt Lizzie's constant nagging and negativity; escape from the mindless monotony of her job in the typing pool of a local marine engineering company.

On Saturday nights Laura could pretend she was someone completely different. On Saturday nights she wasn't trapped in this small dreary steel town. Possibility didn't seep away with each relentlessly ebbing tide and women didn't grow bitter and old before their time. On Saturday nights she was Cinderella, incandescent with hope in her glittering ball-gown and one night, she just knew it, a prince would pick her out of the crowd. One night, a man would come who would look at her and know her. Really know her; see deep into her heart and into all of her dreams and he would sweep her away from this colourless life, away from the wicked old witch by the sea, and make all of those dreams come true.

Oh, it might be that Laura had been reading too many fairy tales. But dreams of escape were all she'd had to cling to for so many years now. No-one that she knew had ever escaped from this town, but that was beside the point. Laura was different. Other girls might get married to the lad down the street and settle for a life filled with babies and drudgery, but Laura Brown was going to be different. Because Laura was a changeling; Laura wasn't like the rest. Laura was a fairy child, and magic was her birthright.

And so every Saturday night she dressed up in her finest outfit and carefully made up her face in front of the bathroom mirror. ('You've got more paint on your face than on the *Mauritania's* backside,' Aunt Lizzie would say as Laura emerged from the bathroom in a cloud of 'Evening in Paris'. Uncle Billy would tell Laura to take no notice: that she looked like a princess. 'Princess my arse,' Aunt Lizzie would snort.) Every Saturday night Laura stood in front of that bathroom mirror, eyes tight shut, and wished with all her heart for a miracle. And every Saturday night came home again filled with the belief that the next week would be different. There was no room for disappointment in Laura's ever-hopeful heart. Next week, everything would work out fine.

And while she was waiting for this miracle to occur, the dances were just plain fun. There was always a large crowd of people that she knew: girls from her old school and from technical college, girls from the typing pool at work and some of the lads from the drawing office. And plenty of others that she didn't know, because all kinds of people went to the dance – not just those who lived in the town. They came from miles around: lads from the mining villages up the coast – 'pit-yakkers', Aunt Lizzie called them – and soldiers from the army base at Catterick. That was the beauty of the weekly Queen's Rink dance: you never knew who you might meet.

As always, Josie and Nan were waiting for her outside the dancehall, enviously eyeing Laura's latest outfit. 'I love your dress,' Josie said, and sighed. The cotton lawn sleeveless dress was a delicate shade of dusky pink. The fitted bodice and wide belt showed off Laura's small neat breasts and tiny waist, and the flared ballerina-length skirt swirled around her calves when she moved. There were beige shoes with pointy toes and stiletto heels, and a beige leather handbag to match. Laura knew that her friends envied her clothes, and she knew that she was lucky. Because, even though Aunt Lizzie moaned and grumbled, Uncle Billy was determined that she should have the best of everything. They weren't at all well-off, though compared to most of the families around them they ate well and they dressed well. But then Uncle Billy had a steady job and worked hard, and he didn't spend his money on drinking and smoking like most of the other men.

The office crowd were clustered in their usual gathering place at the edge of the dance floor. Danny, who lived just down the road from Laura, offered them something to drink, and Laura said that she'd have an orange crush. She looked eagerly around the hall; the band up on the stage had just started to play 'Chances Are', and already the dance floor was beginning to fill up with couples. She loved the distinctive odours of the dancehall: the smell of the dust lifted by feet stamping on the wooden floor, mingled with cigarette smoke and floral air freshener. Globes faceted with dozens of tiny mirrors sparkled over the dance floor, glinting off the beads of sweat on the dancers' brows.

She danced first with Danny and then with Robert, laughing and swinging around the floor. The band was playing rock and roll now: 'All Shook Up' and 'Great Balls of Fire'. Her dark hair swung around her head and her brown eyes glittered. Laura loved to dance: she threw herself into it, loved the freedom of it, loved to lose herself in the rhythm and the music. All the lads loved to dance with her and she never turned them down.

Laura excused herself from the group and headed for the cloakroom. She had almost reached the door when a young man in a shiny black suit with an equally shiny red face lurched over to her and grabbed her roughly by the arm.

'Hey, lover, come and dance with me.'

She shook her arm free and backed off, smiling nervously. 'No thanks. I have to get back to my friends.'

'Aw, come on, pet. Just one dance.' He lunged at her, laughing; he pulled her towards him. She could smell the alcohol on his breath. He must have brought it in with him, because the Rink didn't sell alcohol. She struggled to pull away but he had tight hold of her arms and wouldn't let her go. She was trapped now, held tight against him and all she could see was the black of his suit and the bulk of him blocking out the light. The rancid smell of old sweat mingled with the grease from his hair. Bile burned in her throat.

'Let go of me.' Her voice was tight with panic.

'What's the matter? Too good for me, are you?' He thrust her away from him, fingers burning into her upper arms. She flinched. 'All tarted up in your best pink frock. Too good for a lad from down the mines?' The laughter had gone now, his face so red it was almost purple and spittle flecking his lips. Laura froze. She glanced from side to side out of the corner of her eyes, looking for a doorman, waiting for someone to help her. But no-one had noticed what was happening.

'She's with me.' The voice was soft but firm. A large long-fingered hand clamped down on the shoulder of Laura's assailant. He tried to shrug it off, but the hand just tightened its grip and the body behind it moved closer. 'I said, she's with me.' Louder this time. Louder, and decidedly Scottish.

'All right, you bastard.' The miner let go of Laura's arms, clenched his fists and swung around to face his challenger. He pulled back his right arm and Laura's hands flew to her mouth – and then he stopped. The man looming over him was well over six feet, but it wasn't just the sheer bulk of him that would make you hesitate, Laura thought, and it wasn't anything in particular about his face – a lightly tanned face with high, sharp cheekbones, square jaw and a strong, straight nose. It was something in his eyes. The miner lowered his arms and backed off. 'All right, all right. I only wanted to dance with the lass. No harm done.'

'Aye, well next time maybe you'll learn to take no for an answer.'

The miner mumbled an obscenity as he turned away and staggered towards the exit doors. Laura's rescuer shook his head grimly and watched him leave. Then he turned and his eyes met hers, and for a moment everything else around her lost its focus. He looked as if he was a few years older than Laura: early or mid-twenties, maybe. Blond hair waved softly on top of his head; he was wearing a light grey suit with an immaculate white shirt and a dark blue tie. Finally, slowly, she blinked.

'Thank you,' she said.

'You're welcome.' And all at once his face changed: laughter lines crinkled at the corner of his eyes. 'I don't suppose you'd like to dance with me instead? Just in case yon laddie comes back looking for trouble.' His voice was deep and soft. Scottish for sure, but different, somehow; there was a definite lilt to it.

Laura smiled. 'I'd love to.'

He nodded in the direction of the cloakroom. 'Then I'll just wait here till you come back, so.'

Blindly, heart racing, Laura launched herself through the door of the cloakroom and into the first empty cubicle that she saw. She hung her handbag on the hook at the back of the door and stuffed her fist into her mouth. Oh, my God. He was gorgeous. Absolutely gorgeous.

Carefully, she adjusted her clothes. She left the cubicle, washed her hands and went over to the mirror, eyes right ahead of her. That was always best, because some of the rougher local girls would be spoiling for a fight. If you caught their eyes, even if you didn't mean to, they would say 'Having a good look?' or 'Who do you think you are?' and so it was best just to keep your head down and try not to listen to the colourful language and the insults that they flung at each other up and down the length of the crowded room. Hastily, Laura combed her hair, touched up her dark pink lipstick and dabbed a bit of powder on her chin. She went back outside: he was still there. She hadn't dreamed him. He smiled; a broad, white smile.

They danced to 'How High the Moon' and then to 'That'll be the Day'. He danced as well as she did, moving her around the floor with effortless athleticism and a grace that was unusual for such a big man. And then the band began to play 'Dancing in the Dark', the song that they played every week to signal the start of the interval. Very gently, he pulled her into his arms. Breathless, she closed her eyes and allowed herself to melt against him. They didn't speak; not a single word. The song seemed to last forever; every one of her senses was on full alert. She would always remember that first time that he held her in his arms: the hard warmth of his body against hers, the prickle of his fine woollen suit against her bare arms. Hair that smelled of the salt winds and sea – he didn't smother it with Brylcream like most of the boys she knew.

Her heart fell as the music ended and the lights came up, but then he bent his head down towards her ear and asked her if she'd like a coffee. Mouth dry, all she could do was nod. She walked with him up the stairs to the coffee bar on the balcony and sat down at a small table in the corner while he waited at the counter to be served. She watched him, his back wide and straight as he stood, towering several inches above most of the other men in the queue. He didn't stoop, like so many tall men. He returned, carrying two cups of coffee, and sat opposite her. He smiled at her; she could feel herself blushing and looked down, wishing they would keep the lights low during the interval as well.

'My name's Alec. Alec Munro. I'm sorry; I should have introduced myself before.'

She risked a quick glance across at him. 'I'm Laura Brown.' The cat seemed to have got her tongue. Laura wasn't normally lost for words, but right now she couldn't think of a single thing to say. But she needn't have worried: he seemed to sense her discomfort and took over the conversation. She listened as he told her that he came from the Highlands, from all the way up the west coast, almost at the end of the world. He came from a fishing village, he said, and he was a fisherman himself. He'd come down south to work on the trawlers, to make a bit of money before he went back home again. Because he had a dream: a dream of owning his very own fishing boat with his very own crew that worked for him.

She asked him what it was like, the village where he'd been born. The lilting cadence of his voice was hypnotic as he told her how the still glassy waters of the sea-loch reflected the northern lights in midwinter. She could see it in her mind as he spoke: bone-white driftwood on the beach, smooth pebbles in pastel shades of pink, lilac and grey, and shiny red and brown seaweed. Crabs and the big juicy langoustines, just waiting to swim into your nets. Herons and oystercatchers on the lochside; seals and porpoises that played in the sea around the Summer Isles. It sounded like something out of a fairy tale, and Laura's eyes glowed and glistened with dreams as he wove his long, slow web of words around her. He told her that he preferred the west coast to the east. 'It's wetter, right enough,' he said, 'and it's wilder. Storms, mists, winds. And the light is always changing. But on a fine sunny day the beauty of it would break your heart. Aye, the scenery is a whole lot grander out west. More mountains. Misty glens. Mysterious lochs.' And Laura could picture him, striding across mountaintops like a giant of old. Standing on the deck of a tall ship, sails billowing in the squally wind. And Laura by his side, laughing in the face of the coming storm.

Her own life seemed so boring in comparison. Hesitantly, she told him that she was eighteen years old, that she worked as a typist, though she really wanted to be a librarian because she loved books, and that she lived at home with her Aunt Lizzie and Uncle Billy. She told him that her mother had died two years ago, that she had three sisters, and that no, she didn't see them or her father very often. There didn't seem to be much more to tell, but that was just fine because all she wanted to do was listen to him. She wanted the night to go on and on, because this was how it was supposed to be; this was how she had always imagined it would come. This was love at first sight. This was how it happened in all the best stories, and already she was certain that Alec Munro was the man she'd been waiting for.

The lights dimmed and once again the band members took the stage. Laura followed him downstairs and onto the dance floor, oblivious to the stares of Josie and Nan and the whisperings of her group of friends. The rest of the evening passed in a whirl and then, all too soon, the band was playing the last dance, 'For All We Know'. The lights went back up but she lingered with him for a while longer – she couldn't bear the thought of being parted from him. She ignored Josie and Nan, who were gesticulating frantically by the door in a vain attempt to remind her that the bus would be leaving soon. This could be the most important night of her life; she didn't want to worry about small things like buses. And so by the time he took her hand in his, holding it gently, thumb caressing her palm, and by the time they parted, with promises to meet there again the next Saturday, the last bus had gone.

Laura ought to have been frantic; Aunt Lizzie would have a blue fit when she didn't arrive home at the usual time. But she couldn't seem to bring herself to care. She'd walked home before now in an emergency, and she could easily do it again. And tonight there was a glow around her that nothing could penetrate. She was immune to all harm; she was in love. She pulled her light woollen coat tightly around her and set off briskly down the road, stiletto heels clacking noisily on the pavement.

'Hey – Laura! Wait up!' She turned, and saw Danny running up behind her. 'I'll walk home with you. I missed the bus myself. It must've left a bit earlier than usual.' Laura doubted it; she suspected that he'd waited behind on purpose, but she was glad of the company – it was a dark and long road home. Josie had said once that Danny had a crush on Laura, but she didn't take any notice of that; she'd known him ever since they were kids. He was just a friend. She allowed him to fall into step beside her, and as they walked she happily answered his questions about 'the tall blond guy' she'd been dancing with.

An hour later they arrived at the crossroads, passed the now-deserted bus shelter, and turned the corner into Laura's road. Immediately, she saw the dark bulk of Aunt Lizzie lying in wait for her on the front doorstep, backlit by the dim orange glow from the dusty old glass lampshade in the front passage. Laura groaned. As soon as she caught sight of Laura and Danny, Aunt Lizzie scuttled out down the front path and stood by the front gate, hands on her well-padded hips. The screeching began before they were even properly in earshot.

'What time do you call this? Just where do you think you've been till this time of night? And who's that you're with, you taking-on little bastard, you!'

Laura flushed and turned to Danny to apologise, but he just grinned. He knew Aunt Lizzie; every child along the road grew up knowing Aunt Lizzie. And avoiding her, whenever it was possible.

The tirade continued all the way down the street. 'I warned you what would happen if you were late home. You know where you'll end up, don't you?'

As they got closer and she saw who was walking with Laura, she switched her attack to Danny, jabbing a long bony finger at him. 'Danny Johnson! Is that you, you dirty little get? If you've got her into trouble, you'll know about it!'

Laura answered in her softest, most soothing voice. 'It's all right,

Aunt Lizzie. I just missed the bus, that's all. Danny was kind enough to wait behind and walk back with me.'

Danny tried to help. 'Yes, honestly, Mrs Stokes. We came straight home from the dance.'

'And what were you up to that you missed the bus, the pair of you? Straight home? You've been across the fields messing about – you can't tell me any different! You get in that house, you little midden, you. You won't have any home to go to, if you carry on like this. I've been at my wits' end, worrying. And you frig off home, Danny Johnson, before I black your eye for you.'

Danny raised his hands in defeat and turned away, shouting 'goodnight' to Laura as he left. In the house Laura put the kettle on and made a cup of tea, oblivious for once to Aunt Lizzie's mutterings. She murmured soothing apologies whenever there was a pause and whenever it seemed to be required, but it was going to take more than Aunt Lizzie to wipe the glow from her eyes tonight. Because tonight, Laura's dreams had come true. She'd found the man she loved, and he was all the things she ever imagined he might be, and more.

Damp at the corners of her eyes but it might just be the cold – the sudden blast of chill north wind that sweeps down from the hill beyond slips down the neck of her jacket and makes her shiver. Laura stands and turns back along the street to the car, but as she walks all she can see is his eyes and his smile. Her nose still remembers his fresh, salty sea-smell and she can still hear his soft lilting voice gentle in her ear. Oh, it all sounds very Mills & Boon now, she thinks. But at the time it was all so real. The most real thing that had ever happened to her. She remembers how she melted in his arms; she remembers how she loved him.

And, fool that she is, there's a stubborn little part of her that in spite of it all loves him still.

*

The weather is turning. The water is beginning to ripple and surge and the sky out to sea glowers and broods. But the sun still shines as it slowly edges south, oblivious to the rising threat from the west.

The main road out of the village is deserted. After half a dozen miles or so Laura turns off; she drives home slowly along the single-track road carved into the lower slopes of the hill that rises steeply from the lochside. She lives close to the end of it, four miles down a rural cul-de-sac that thirty-five years ago led only to a few isolated crofting communities. But in the years that have passed since then, a growing population of both locals and incomers has produced a scattering of newer houses above and below the road.

There's an interesting mix of people along the lochside – or so Meg tells her; Laura hasn't met many of them at all. Except for those that were kind enough to call when she first moved in, with their offerings of plants or maybe a cake or a bottle of wine. All of them invited her to visit in return, but she hasn't taken up their invitations. She's just not good at spontaneous visits, and so she stays at home. Meg is the only one she's comfortable with – the only one that she'll visit uninvited. And Meg's storytelling circle is the only other activity that she wants to deal with right now. Laura had only intended to go that one time, but somehow Meg persuaded her into it again. And it's true that she enjoyed it, that she felt herself finally beginning to relax in the easy company of the other women.

But she hasn't told a story of her own, yet. She's not quite ready for that.

She slows as she reaches the last small cluster of houses; she passes three driveways that lead to old dwellings right down near the lochside. A local primary school teacher, her carpenter husband and two small girls live in the first. In the second, a retired couple from Scunthorpe that Laura has never set eyes on. They don't go out much, Meg says. And at the end of the third drive, a couple of incomers from Edinburgh – Laura can't remember what they do. Above the road, just before you get to Meg's house, sits a neat bungalow newly built by a couple who recently moved out from the village. He's a fisherman; she works for a local heritage organisation. All ages, all shapes, all sizes down this road. All kinds of professions: a small handful of crofters, a doctor, an editor, a business consultant working from home, a couple of weekending lecturers from the University of Glasgow.

She peers down at Meg's house as she passes by; the back door is closed and an ashy coil of wood-smoke swirls out of the chimney. And then her own long drive, winding down through dark green layers of gorse and broom to the house below. A typical one-and-a-half-storey croft house: two rooms up and two down, with a toilet and utility room tacked on at the back of the ground floor and a small bathroom squeezed between the two bedrooms upstairs.

She opens the front door, shopping bags in hand; a burst of warm air from the central heating greets her.

That's all that greets her. No-one else here. No-one else to care whether she lives or dies.

She swallows down the loneliness. You chose this, she reminds herself. You chose to come here. This is what you wanted. You chose to be alone. You brought it on yourself.

Laura has never been alone. Not really; not for any significant length of time. And she doesn't know how to be alone, doesn't know what to do. Can't seem to make herself feel real. Alone, she is nobody. *What is there inside you, Laura, really?*

So: Laura. Standing in the living room of a house that still does not feel like home. It's oddly bare – but that may be because a dozen boxes lie unopened still in the spare bedroom. Boxes of books, photographs, china. The living room is arid – it's desert country. An old navy blue two-seater and a matching upright armchair cling to the outer edges of the room, facing the open fire. A small wooden desk in one corner and the TV by the door. An old oak sideboard with nothing on top of it but an empty crystal vase, and a square pine coffee table by the side of the sofa. She's never known how to build a cosy home; she doesn't know what to fill it with. Laura has nothing to give to her space; she simply occupies it. Space is filled by other people. Without them, she's nothing.

She passes through into the kitchen, switches on the kettle and unpacks her shopping. When it's done she settles down at the kitchen table with a fig roll and a cup of tea, and begins to write.

Aunt Lizzie, of course, hated Alec on sight. A month or so after they'd met, Laura invited him home for coffee after the dance. Uncle Billy was working nights, and so Alec sat in his place on the settee in the front room. Laura didn't dare sit next to him – not with Aunt Lizzie looking on – so she sat in the armchair at the other side of the fireplace. And Aunt Lizzie sat in her customary spot in the old wooden chair at the table, watching them with gimlet eyes. Alec tried to turn his charm on her, but she wasn't having any of it. She sat in silence, like the figure of Justice.

And she judged. And after he'd gone she turned to Laura, her voice unusually quiet. 'He's a baddun,' she said.

Laura laughed, disconcerted by her intensity. 'Of course he's not! What makes you say that?'

'I can see it in his eyes. You mark my words: no good'll come of it.'

Of course she thought Aunt Lizzie was trying to undermine her again. To take away from her the one shining thing in her life. Armoured in the invulnerable certainty of young love, for the first time in her life Laura lost her temper with Aunt Lizzie. 'You're just a vicious old woman. You don't want me to be happy. You just want to spoil things for me.'

'It's not me that'll do the spoiling here. He's no good, and you can't tell me any different. He'll hurt you, lass. You just see if he doesn't.'

Laura set her jaw and she closed her ears and she marched out of the room. Laura didn't care what Aunt Lizzie said. Astonishingly, wonderfully, she discovered that she could just tune her out. And just for a while, for a glorious while, for the first time in her life, she allowed herself to believe that everything that Aunt Lizzie had said to her over the years was untrue. She knew perfectly well that she couldn't be stupid, because she had managed to attract a man like Alec Munro. She must be worth something, because Alec Munro loved her. And it didn't matter whether her mam and dad had wanted her or not, because Alec Munro wanted her now. She was happy and joyful and completely impervious: she was young, and she was in love.

And Aunt Lizzie never again said a word against him.

Not until it was too late.

Too late.

Laura's eyes are burning; they don't seem to have the moisture in them that they used to have. She squeezes them tightly shut and opens them again to swiftly skim over the last few paragraphs. She puts the notebook down and shakes her head, looking out of the window at the mist that's beginning to form on the top of the hills. She knows what Cat will think, when she reads this. How could you be so naïve? she'll think. How could you be so trusting, and so very, very certain? And it's true; Laura didn't doubt him for a minute. Ah, but she was young then. And more than anything in the world she longed for someone to love her. There had been so little love until then. There'd been a hole the size of a crater in her heart and it had seemed that nothing could fill it. Not until Alec came along. So she'd poured out onto him all her young dreams, all her wild fantasies. All of her longings for love, for a warm human body next to hers.

So much pressure on him, when she looks back on it now. The pressure of all her need. How could anyone have lived up to what she expected of him? To the weight of all her adoration? He was just a fisherman, that's all. Just a fisherman, but she'd wanted a prince. A prince, to save her.

Foolish, foolish Laura. What was it, anyway, that she'd needed saving from? From the empty place inside where her sense of self should have been? And has she really grown any less foolish over the years?

The night before she was to be married, Laura couldn't sleep. She lay awake in the high wooden bed where she had spent almost every night of her life, and thought about the day that stretched ahead of her. It was a misty night, and foghorns blared out at sea. It wasn't till the early hours of the morning that she slipped finally into a restless half-sleep. And afterwards she would never be sure whether she'd been asleep or awake when she opened her eyes and looked down at the foot of her bed. Her mother hovered there, transparent hands resting on the dark wooden bedrail. Too sleepy to be afraid, Laura couldn't look away. Mam looked sad; she shook her head.

'What?' Laura whispered. 'What are you trying to tell me?' But Mam couldn't seem to speak; a solitary tear rolled down her cheek and once again she shook her head.

'Why did you let me go?' she wanted to ask her. 'Why did you let me go?' But Mam faded away and Laura was left alone.

The next morning she was woken by Aunt Lizzie's screech at the bottom of the stairs. 'Laura! Are you going to lie in that bed all day, or are you going to get up and get yourself married?'

She sat upright, sheets and blankets tangled around her feet and the thick red eiderdown crumpled on the floor. By the time she put on her dressing gown and went downstairs she was feeling sick.

Uncle Billy took one look at her pale face and sat down at the table opposite her.

'Laura, lass, are you sure about this?'

She nodded uncertainly.

He frowned; reached across the table to prise apart and take hold of one of the hands that were clenched there. 'You don't have to marry him, my lass. If you're not sure.'

'Don't tell her that, you daft old bugger,' Aunt Lizzie snorted. 'She's just nervous. Everyone's nervous on their wedding day. Of course she has to marry him. It's all arranged.'

'Well then, it can be unarranged if she's not sure.' He looked into Laura's eyes and she looked back at him, back into the kindly blue eyes that had been her lodestar for all these years. How could she do this? How could she leave him behind? 'Are you sure, pet?'

Laura closed her eyes, and took a deep breath. She was aware of how little she knew Alec. Of how far away from home she would be when she went away with him to Scotland. But more than that: something deep in the pit of her stomach felt uneasy; she just couldn't put her finger on what it was. She loved Alec with all her heart, and she didn't doubt that he loved her, but in so many ways he was a stranger to her. She couldn't pretend to understand him: the long silences, the sudden, mercurial changes of mood. But then she thought about how she felt in his arms. Of the feeling deep in the pit of her stomach when he kissed her. Of the longing that wouldn't go away, and the months of waiting to be able to love him properly – which she would be able to do now, as his wife. Starting tonight. She shivered; smiled. She raised her head, and she nodded. 'Yes,' she said. 'Yes, I'm sure.'

She rubs her eyes again, vigorously. No need to worry about wrinkles forming now: they're already there. It's far too late for vanity.

She rests her head in her hands, tries to ease herself slowly out of the memories. The fact was that the wedding night had hardly lived up to either of their expectations. They'd spent it at a hotel in town, so they could leave early in the morning to get the first of the trains that would take them up to Scotland. No sooner had they left the wedding reception, Laura's stomach clenching at the look of promise in Alec's eyes, than her period started. Even then, she had had the periods from hell. She remembers vividly how it was: copious and agonising, one in every three would have her bedridden for two or three days at a time. This wasn't to be one of her worst times, but it was bad enough to blight not only her wedding night, but the three-day honeymoon that they took in Edinburgh on their way up to the Highlands. An inauspicious start, she thinks now; the omens were poor from the beginning.

Elbows on the table and palms propping up her chin, she stares out of the window, re-orienting herself to the present. She chooses to write here at the kitchen table, warmed by the Rayburn, rather than risk the wasteland of the sitting room. She likes to sit at the window; to keep an eye on the weather as she writes. It all changes so rapidly here: it's like watching a video. And she doesn't want to miss a scene. Now, for example, on this midwinter afternoon, the light is fading fast. The wind is beginning to pick up, and night is beginning its daily relentless march down the glen and out along the loch. It's coming up to solstice, the shortest day. She sits and watches the room grow dim as light slowly ebbs away from the world.

It's going to be a dank evening, and chill, but it will take more than that to put Laura off her nightly walk down to the lochside.

The seal is there again tonight, sleek dark head rising above the water, blue-black eyes gleaming with reflections from the glassy surface of the loch. Haunting eyes. Haunted. In the past few weeks Laura has often found her there, in the early light of morning or the dying light of late afternoon. Watching there, waiting. Something in her calls out to Laura, a strange kinship. Almost if she's trying to tell her something. Almost as if she knows her.

She looks so comfortable there in the water – so very much in her element. How it is that you develop that sense of belonging? Perhaps it's just that she's old now: old and accustomed, at home in her skin. Though it seems growing older carries no guarantee that you'll grow more at ease – Laura is a perfect illustration of that. Perhaps it's just that she's lacking in cares. She is, after all, a creature of instinct: she eats, and she mates, and she swims. How much sorrow can there be, in the life of a seal?

Beautiful creature, beautiful eyes. There are fairy tales about seals, she remembers. Stories about women – half-seal, half-human. Everyday stories of love and of loss.

It was long ago, and a beautiful night. The full moon reflected in calm, glassy water – you could almost believe it had fallen to earth, floating there, finally now in your grasp. The sand twinkled silver like a galaxy of dusty stars, and the midnight air was warm and still. How could you not want to taste its treasures?

So they swam in to shore, the selkie sisters; they heaved their clumsy bodies out of the sea and onto the sand. They lifted their heads, and with one last call to the sky, they began the strange process of shedding their skins. A shiver of danger, a sharp stabbing pain – then the rapturous, shuddering waves. The anguish and joy as each was transformed, as each of them now became human. Long black hair and midnight eyes; their bodies tall, sleek and pale as white pearls in the moonlight.

It was her first time, for she was young then. How to describe it, that sudden reconstruction of the world all around you, the abrupt transformation of your senses? Cool shiver of night air on warm hairless flesh, heart pounding loudly to a strange new beat. But above all, the wonder of arms and of legs; the breathtaking miracle of fingers and toes. She was utterly intoxicated, lost in the dance. She whirled, and she laughed, and she sang.

Ah, but it's an old, old story. He was hiding and watching from behind the rocks, his eyes wide with wonder to behold them there, a watery mirage on moon-burned sands. And how terribly human, that longing to possess the exotic and the new.

They didn't see him: they were all too entranced by this curious new world. They didn't see him inch up behind them as they sank down breathless on the beach, running long-fingered hands through each other's hair as they sang their strange new songs. They didn't see him edge up to the rock where he had seen her place her skin. They didn't see him steal it away. They didn't see as the dark began to fade and the first pink shreds of dawn crept into the sky – as they sighed and remembered the watery places. Innocent, they smiled; it was time to go home.

Her sisters took their skins and in a swift shimmer, a strange trick of the light, became seal-folk again. But there was no trace now of her skin. She waved her sisters on, back into the sea, and frantically searched the beach – every rock, every hollow – but it wasn't there. The sky was growing paler now, and she knew that they had no choice but to leave her, for transformation is only possible at night, and with the power bestowed by the fullness of the moon. Their keening rang in her ears as they swam away slowly, looking behind them all the while.

Distraught, she turned back to the beach – and there he stood on the sand, quite still. He was handsome enough for a human, and exotic to her with his white-blonde hair and his coal-black eyes. He was holding her skin in his arms. She ran swiftly towards him, to thank him and take it back. If she could only have it now there'd be just enough time, for the sun had not yet crept above the horizon and the night retained some of its spell. But he held it away from her; she stopped in her tracks.

'Don't go,' he said gently, and his soft, deep voice caused a strange, wild fluttering in her chest. 'I wish you would stay. Stay here with me. Live with me – marry me, if you will.'

She mocked him at first; she laughed at his boldness. 'I can't do that – I'm a creature of the sea. Tell me, why would I give up the sea, and my sisters, to stay here with you?'

'Because I have your skin.' And shock rippled through her as she looked in his eyes, and saw he'd no thought now of giving it back. 'Stay with me,' he whispered. 'I'll love you, I'll cherish you, provide for you. I've a cosy warm cottage just there on the brae. You'll always be able to look out to sea.'

'Seeing it isn't enough,' she cried, panicky now as the sky grew lighter and the cries of her sisters grew fainter, then ceased. 'I can't survive here on land.'

But his ears were closed, consumed as he was by the fierceness of his need. 'Listen,' he said. 'I'll make you a deal. Stay with me a while – just for seven years. And at the end of that time, if you still want to leave me, then I promise I'll give you your skin.'

And for sure it is true that she had little choice, for the sun had appeared now, a blood-red fireball on the eastern horizon. But if she is honest with herself, there was more to it than that. Because something inside her cried out for release – responded to the longing and the hunger in his eyes. So she reached for the hand he held out to her, fell into the arms that trembled for her, and her strange human body voiced new strains of song. She turned her back on all that was familiar to her, yielded to her senses and the lure of the new. And, young as she was, she trusted that he'd love her, and keep his promise.

9

Cat

'Okay, Cat. I'm getting out now. Time to solo.'

Solo? I don't move; I don't say a word. I just stare blankly out of the windscreen, replaying the words over in my head. Solo? It never entered my mind. Not even when he cut the lesson short after half a dozen stalls and three seamless touch-and-goes and asked me to head back to the terminal.

It should have entered my mind. After thirty hours of flying time, the moment was bound to come soon. Most of the kids solo around fifteen hours – I'm already way behind. The truth is that I've been trying not to think about it. In the early days the thought of flying solo loomed ahead of me like a monster, a three-headed guardian at the threshold of paradise who'd laugh in my face and forbid me to pass. More recently I've quite simply blocked it out, my only focus on getting through the lesson just ahead of me and trying to get the plane down on the ground in one piece.

So many lessons; so many struggles. Lying in bed at night, dreaming about the shape of the runway at different altitudes. Hour after hour of touch-and-goes; practising landings, over and over again. Days when I've thought I would never get the hang of it; days when I've wanted to weep with frustration. A perfect set-up and the airplane within fifty feet of the runway – and then I'd blank out. 'Flare,' he'd bark, as it looked as if I'd forget to pull up on the yoke altogether and just crash head-long into the asphalt. 'How about you fly it down to the runway rather than driving it, next time?' Or I'd pull up too soon and float down the runway for a while before the airspeed bled away and we'd drop down with a bang as the usually sanguine Jesse flinched in the seat beside me.

Jesse. Never giving up on me, never letting me give up on myself. 'Come on, Cat – you can do this. You've done worse, remember?' Through landings and stalls and simulated engine failures … so many hurdles to overcome.

And now, the biggest hurdle of all.

Solo.

I turn and watch helplessly as Jesse unbuckles his seat belt and harness. 'Three touch-and-goes and then that's it – come right back in. Stay in the traffic pattern; next time we'll see about you going further afield.'

I don't seem to be able to make my mouth work but he's opening the door now and all I can do is gape at him. He ignores me completely; gives me no chance to demur. As he slips out of the plane he turns around and smiles that small, quirky smile, winks slowly and without another word closes the door behind him and leaves me there alone.

Alone. I've never been alone in a plane before. The silence is oppressive, more than a little spooky. The usually cramped space stretches out to infinity. He's gone, and this morning there's only me for the sky.

Stop it. I clamp a shutter down on my thoughts. I know perfectly well that if I let myself think I'll be out of this seat and running after him across the asphalt and before I know it I'll be failing again.

I close my eyes and take a deep breath and the familiar odours of the cockpit comfort me: flying has a unique perfume all of its own. I regulate my breathing into a slow, stable pattern. Loosen my muscles, let go of the tension. A familiar routine by now, and one that seems to be working. It's been a while since I experienced that desperate gasping for breath, the phantom fingers clutching at my throat.

Don't think about it, Cat. Just do it.

I switch into automatic mode. Quickly and efficiently I run through the checklist, lean out of the door and yell, 'Clear prop!' One swift turn of the key and the anticipation of that moment – *will it catch? Will it start?* – before the engine bursts into life and the propeller begins to spin. I listen to ATIS; I press the red button to ask ground control for clearance to head on back to the runway. To my astonishment, my voice emerges clear and steady. I'm glad of that: I know he'll be listening to the radio inside. He'll be listening and he'll be watching. The thought gives me comfort; it almost makes me smile.

The late February sky is cool, light and crystal clear: perfect flying weather. And it's early enough in the morning that the airport is still pretty quiet. The radio is eerily silent as I taxi out to the runway. Not thinking; listening, concentrating. Focusing. Perfectly calm as I approach the runway. How can I be so calm? Not thinking, just doing. Because this is what you do when you fly a plane. Simple. Routine. I've done it before. I can do it this time. Nothing is different except the empty space to my right, massive with meaning. But I'm not thinking; I can shut that out.

Calmly I complete the run-up checklist; calmly I pull up to the line at the entry to the runway; calmly I talk to the tower. 'Two November Romeo, ready on Four Left.' I pause, and add, as I've heard others add before me, 'First solo.' My voice cracks slightly but still I'm not thinking. Deep breath, shoulders down. Engine purring softly, a smooth solid sound; hazy blur of the propeller through the windscreen. Control wheel smooth and warm in my hands and the shiny metal of rudder pedals hard under my feet.

'Two November Romeo, position and hold.'

'Position and hold, Two November Romeo.' Slowly, smoothly I move to take up my position at the beginning of the runway. I am calm, calm, calm. It's a source of wonder to me, how very calm I seem to be. The long strip of asphalt stretching away there into the distance, coming to a point, stretching out into infinity. I do not use the time to think: I simply wait. I've done this before; I can do it now. I am calm, and my mind is so very, very clear.

A large black crow steps onto the runway and looks at me. Challenging? There, in the middle of the runway, stands my fear. But for the first time in my life I do not run away from it: I stand and I stare that fear directly in the face. I meet it head-on, and I find it a poor, pitiful creature that feeds off carrion and lurks in dark places; that, like a shadow, puffs itself up when its wings unfold, seeming larger than it really is.

The bird turns away; flaps its wings and squawks in disgust or dismay and launches itself into the sky. So many things on the edge of my consciousness, ready to fall into place. But I don't have time for them now; I don't have time to think. I'm too busy doing the one thing that I always knew I could never do. I'm surrendering; I'm preparing to fly.

'Two November Romeo, cleared for takeoff.' Just as they've said so many times before. 'And good luck.'

I smile slightly as I push in the throttle and hurtle down the runway. It is a moment of perfect purity. I am calm, I am clear, I am doing what I have been trained to do. The little plane wants so badly to fly; freed from the burden of one more body she leaps from the ground, thrusting herself through the sparkling clarity of the air, rising effortlessly, purring her pleasure. Airborne. I clear the field and bank to the left, ascending all the while. The sky has never been so blue; the distant desert has never been so clean and so starkly beautiful. Time doesn't just slow down: time simply is not. Suspended here between heaven and earth, I could have been here for seconds or minutes or hours or maybe even for the whole of my life. Part of the plane, part of the sky, I am flying. This time, for sure I am flying.

I seem to be calm but I think there is terror, lodged there somewhere at the back of my mind. Elation still grapples with fear when I fly. But you become the terror and the terror becomes you and there's no other option than to travel on through it; the only way back is to die. You point your aircraft into the cold blue fire of that fear and it burns you, it changes you. And it is the residue of this strange alchemy that impels me onwards, soaring and wheeling, fearful and transported, learning to fly.

I'm on the downwind leg now; it's time to come down. And the only person who's going to get me back on the ground is me. But that's fine: I'm part of this plane. I know precisely how much power she needs, the exact angle of her nose. Mind still but alert, perfectly focused on the task of flying. I am more aware than I have ever been in my life. I am so – clear, so bright, so *vivid* that I fear I will catch light, burst into flame. I turn to base with the runway stretching out to my left and I know that I need flaps now and I pull out the power and then I'm turning onto final approach – gently now, gently … float all the way down and then – just there – pull the nose back – pull it back – flare.

The landing is a little bumpy but I'm down and I'm safe but there's no time to think because I'm pushing the throttle in one more time and I'm off again and with every takeoff I leave a piece of my burden behind.

I have been asleep for forty years. This is what I need: this fear, this risk, this wind rocking my wings. This is what I have been missing. This is what it means to be alive – up here, on the edge of death.

I cut the mixture and turn off the ignition. A strange lightness begins to rise up from my stomach and I do not know what it is, I do not know what it will become when finally it bursts out of me.

I step out of the plane and close the door softly behind me. I rest my head for a moment against the side of the plane and whisper my thanks. I turn; Jesse is walking towards me across the asphalt. His smile is wide, luminous, proud. The lightness springs up now, all the way up from my stomach, passing through my chest and into my throat and then out of my mouth as I open it to laugh. I turn my face up to the sky and then one more time, I fly: light as a bird, I fly into his open arms.

He gathers me up in them, into those arms that have so capably launched me into the skies and cradled me there in the air. I inhale the warm green smell of him and my heart is too full, too big for my body and it presses against my lungs so that I cannot breathe. He swings me around and I close my eyes and I let out an almighty whoop and I am all joy, all of it rising from somewhere I never knew existed inside of me and it's so free in there, so very, very light. My whole body tingles with it, blood rushing to every vessel in my skin and I want to dance, to spin.

He lowers me gently to the ground; I open my eyes again. He grins down at me as if this is a perfectly normal reaction. And perhaps it is. To anyone else, perhaps it is.

'You did a fantastic job up there. And who'd have believed it? That this is the same woman who had to be helped out of the plane four months ago?'

I shake my head, so light and so empty that I feel I could float. I cannot believe I've done this. I can't believe it. And if I don't stop smiling my face will split in two.

He watches every wave of emotion that passes over my face. 'Feels pretty good, doesn't it?'

'Good' doesn't even begin to describe it. I've just conquered the whole damn universe. I'm Superwoman. But I'm not sure that I'm capable of intelligible speech. All I can do is grin like an idiot and shake my head.

And in the midst of my joy, a fleeting pang of sadness at the thought that nothing will ever be this good again.

He puts a warm, strong hand on my shoulder. 'Come on. You look like you could do with a cup of coffee.'

I take a deep breath; my lungs, light and open, fill with air. I could weep for the relief of it, for the loss of the now-habitual band of pressure around my chest. 'Okay. But I'd better run to the restroom first.'

I creep up on my reflection in the mirror. I do not recognise the Cat that I see there. Large dark eyes glitter feverishly as if in the aftermath of tears. My cheeks are pink and my usually pale lips are swollen and flushed. Strands of subtly-layered blonde hair that have escaped from the black velvet hairband curl in damp feathery tendrils around my neck. I am awestruck: I look like a wild creature. I remove the band and pull a hairbrush through the tangled hair, splash my face with cool water and pat it dry with a paper towel.

I glance back at the mirror.

I do not know what I am becoming; I do not know what I am shapeshifting into.

Jesse is in the training room with two steaming mugs of coffee before him on the table.

'Real china? Must be a special occasion.'

'Real coffee too; I made it fresh – and strong.' He grins. 'May not match up to European standards, but it ought to be better than the usual trash.'

'As long as it's wet and warm. I don't think I'm capable of finding fault with anything right now.' I throw myself into the chair opposite him and let out a loud breath: I'm still smiling. 'This is amazing. I wonder how long it'll last?'

'Everyone gets a real high from their first solo. But for you, it's an especially big achievement.'

I peer up at him over the rim of my mug. 'Did you think I'd ever get this far?'

He studies me, as always, with lips tilted slightly at one corner of his mouth. 'Truthfully?'

'Truthfully.'

'Yes.'

I blink. 'You did?'

'Sure I did. I wouldn't have agreed to teach you otherwise. I don't believe in setting people up for failure.'

'But after that first lesson? Surely you didn't ... what on earth made you think I could ever get over all that terror? It all seems pretty excessive, looking back on it now.'

'The fact that you got out of that plane shaking like a leaf and the first words that came out of your mouth were "When can I have another lesson."' He shrugs. 'I've rarely seen that much courage.'

'Courage?' I laugh, disconcerted. 'I'm not in the least bit courageous. You saw how afraid I was. How afraid I've always been. Ever since.'

'Right. And who do you think the most courageous people are, Cat? The ones who manage to overcome their fears to do whatever it is that they need to do? Or, even better, the ones who choose to do it when they don't need to, precisely *because* of their fear?'

I flush; I feel like a fraud. 'I don't want you to get the wrong idea. That's the first time I've ever done anything like that in my life. Normally I'd just turn away. Run.'

He smiles faintly, pale blue eyes gleaming as the sun catches them. 'That's exactly what I mean.'

And all at once as I look into his eyes I'm confronted with a new version of myself. A Cat who is strong, not weak. A Cat who is courageous, not afraid. A Cat who, like everyone else, has fears – but a Cat who is strong enough to overcome the worst fear of all. I am transformed in his eyes and I want badly to weep – my emotions are running wild. But I'm not sure what to do with this new image of myself. I clear my throat, look away. A silence.

'Well. Thanks.' I look down into my coffee mug again; push

it all away. Too big; too big. It's all too confusing; too many things have changed. 'So. What's next?'

'We've still got a long way to go, but now I sign you off for unsupervised solo flight. Until we've done some cross-country work you'll be restricted to staying within fifteen miles of the airport. Stay around the practice area. Don't go out if the winds are high, or if there's a crosswind. Practise stalls.' He raises an eyebrow as I grimace. 'Practise stalls,' he repeats, more firmly now. I resist the urge to giggle like a naughty teenager. 'And while you're doing that, we keep on with the lessons. Right now we need to concentrate on navigation and pilotage skills, and in three, maybe four weeks we'll be doing our first cross-country.'

'I'm looking forward to that. Where will we go?'

'We'll make the first one a fairly short trip. Probably down to Ryan, near Tucson. It's a fairly obstacle-free flight path.' He stretches; yawns. 'You also need to think about sitting your written exam. How are you doing on the study for that?'

'Not too bad; I've covered most of the ground. Maybe after a couple of cross-countries I'll feel more confident about all the navigation theory.'

'Good. Next lesson on Saturday morning as usual?'

'Saturday sounds good. Then if I can book the plane maybe I'll try a solo on Sunday.'

'Got you hooked, huh?' He laughs. 'I think I have a couple of other lessons on Sunday so if you can catch me in between I should be around in case you have any questions or problems. Keep it short at first.'

'Okay.'

He smiles again, a slow, warm smile that wraps itself around me, light as a goose-down duvet. 'Ready to go out and conquer the world now?'

'It has no chance.' I can feel the wing-stubs pushing through the sweat-shirt at my back.

*

I am still light-headed and grinning after lunch as I walk up to Tom's office for my annual appraisal. We really should have done it before the end of the year, but somehow it kept being postponed. Tom registers my unusually cheerful demeanour with a sardonic lift of his eyebrow but, beyond that, doesn't comment.

Everything starts off evenly, as we work through the key results areas and specific task objectives that I set myself at the beginning of last year. The department is doing well: we won the one case that went to trial against us, we've met our other targets, and I've even managed to cut the product liability budget and make some financial savings that weren't anticipated. I've achieved every objective, met every deadline. The lawyers and administrative staff that report to me are all doing good jobs; the one performance issue that arose was addressed and resolved to everyone's satisfaction. On paper, at least, I'm a star. And as always, Tom is appropriately complimentary.

It all begins to fall apart when we turn to the obligatory discussion about personal development and career planning. I've been head of litigation for two years now, and in theory my next move up the corporate ladder would be into Tom's board-level job as Senior Vice President for Law. That's always been the plan; in the succession documents I'm listed as his replacement. Not that he's planning to go anywhere in a hurry: Tom is just fifty-five years old and so wedded to his work that he's unlikely to leave until they wheel him out. And I'm in no rush to move on and upwards; I've never been that kind of driven, fiercely competitive type. But it's still something of a blow when he informs me coldly that he is beginning to wonder whether I am, after all, an appropriate candidate for the board. He suggests that my attitude over the past three or four months has left something to be desired. 'In fact,' he concludes with a steely stare, 'I'm just not at all convinced of your commitment to our management values.'

I raise an eyebrow. 'Well, that all depends on the values. If I agree with them and find them meaningful, I'll accept them and I'll do my best to act upon them.'

'Nice words, Cat, but right now I can't think of any recent initiatives that you've wholeheartedly supported. Your attitude to the mission statement was nothing short of contemptuous.' I open my mouth to disagree, but he cuts me off. 'And take the downsizing exercise. You're obviously not on board with it. In fact, you reacted to certain proposed reductions in staffing and budget in a way that's inappropriately emotional.'

Inappropriately emotional? I can't help but laugh out loud. This is the first time in my life I've ever been accused of being overly emotional. He's not amused by my laughter; his mouth tightens in a way that I know all too well. I sigh and try to take the conversation seriously. I'm still on way too much of a high to be seriously irritated; in fact, I feel oddly detached from the whole process.

'I expressed the view that certain cuts – such as those planned for R&D – might be ill-considered. I don't consider that to be an emotional reaction; I consider it to be a perfectly appropriate reaction from the person in this company who's responsible for litigation and who, like you, knows perfectly well that our commitment to research is our strongest defence. Besides, I still don't know the detail of the reductions that are actually being proposed. It's been – what, two, three months now since we first started to discuss them? – and since then it's all been handled at board level. I quite understand that cuts may be needed to keep the business healthy and profitable; what I'm concerned about is what we cut.'

'The downsizing strategy will be announced on Friday.'

This is unusual; my eyebrows fly up my forehead. 'Without further discussion with department heads?'

For a moment Tom looks uncomfortable – an event so rare that I'm immediately suspicious. 'There are some tricky issues to deal with here; we had to keep our discussions confidential. We're taking the opportunity to completely restructure a couple of areas.'

'Such as?'

'Such as R&D.'

I don't like the sound of this. I'm assuming that Jack doesn't know what's going on with the downsizing, any more than any of the other department heads. He would almost certainly have told me about it if he knew. And I'm shocked at the idea that a reorganisation package for R&D might have been drawn up without his input. 'For example?'

Tom sets his jaw and meets my eyes without flinching. 'For example, we're letting Jack go. He'll be replaced by Bob Finkelman.'

My mouth drops open; I can't believe what I'm hearing. 'You're letting Jack go? You mean – you're firing him?'

Tom raises a steely grey eyebrow. 'I wouldn't put it like that. The board has identified opportunities for restructuring across the whole organisation that will bring it into closer alignment with our business objectives. That restructuring includes R&D. We're not entirely sure that Jack's values match those of the company.'

'Ah, bullshit. You mean he won't agree to suppress data.'

Tom sits back in his chair and looks at me coldly. 'What exactly are you saying, Catriona?'

I lean forward; my voice is just as calm and just as cold as his. 'I'm saying that over the last few months you've come dangerously close to suggesting that we ignore negative data on one of our products. I'm saying that Jack knows this to be true so you're firing him because he won't play along with you. I'm saying it's completely inappropriate, Tom.'

He flushes, another rare occurrence. If I weren't so furious I'd be fascinated at the sight of the slipping mask. 'I'm going to give you a chance to rethink that comment.'

'Or what? You'll fire me too?' He shakes his head and opens his mouth to speak, but I interrupt him. 'Aren't you taking a bit of a risk? Jack could easily make trouble for the company if this got out.'

He smiles faintly. 'Jack wouldn't do a thing like that.'

'Which is exactly why you ought to be keeping him on, rather than firing him.'

'He'll get a generous severance package. Besides, there's no evidence at all that what you're suggesting is true.' He's regained his equilibrium; he leans forward again, elbows on his desk. 'The decision's been made, Cat. It's not open for debate.'

Anger rages inside me now, fierce and hot. The band of pressure around my chest returns for the first time in an age and that just makes me more furious still. Why am I letting all this nonsense get to me? Today of all days? What do I think I'm doing?

What am I doing?

'Does Jack know?'

'We told him this morning. He'll be gone by the end of the week.'

And, suddenly, I know exactly what I am doing. I'm doing what I should have done a long time ago. I'm doing the only thing that I can do. 'Then I'll be gone too. Unless there's also a proposed restructuring of the law department that will make my resignation superfluous. Unless, for example, you're planning to fire me too.'

Tom sits back in his chair again and sighs loudly. The conversation has moved completely out of his control; he's not used to that. He rubs his forehead with his hand. I am drinking in every second of his discomfiture. 'Come on, Cat. I don't want to lose you. That certainly wasn't part of the plan. I know you and Jack are close, but don't you think you're overreacting?'

'No. I'm simply not prepared to work for a company that acts like this. This isn't just about Jack: it's about the principle.

You fire a good, loyal senior employee because he won't go along with something he feels is ethically questionable, and you replace him with a mealy-mouthed yes-man who doesn't have a fraction of Jack's intellect or ability.'

Tom flushes again. 'It's true that Bob isn't quite as … charismatic, shall we say … as Jack. But he's a good and senior worker, and his values are closer to what the company expects of its employees.'

I shake my head. 'There's obviously no point in discussing this further. Like Jack, I won't espouse values that go against my personal morality, whether the company "expects" it or not. So I'll save you the problem of firing me too, either now or at some point in the near future. I resign. You'll have it in writing by the end of the afternoon.'

'Cat, this is ridiculous. I'd like you to take some time to think about this. Take a few days off. How long is it since you had a vacation?'

'I will not tolerate being called ridiculous. I don't need a few days off to think about it. I'll clear up my desk and then I'll be gone by the end of the week too. I strongly suggest that, under the circumstances, you contest neither my right to leave within that timeframe nor my right to all contractual benefits upon leaving.' I am aware that I hold all the cards. I have met or exceeded all my job objectives and I am a lawyer who is leaving because she has concerns – with or without evidence – about the company's ethical standards. It would do no-one at Sanderson any good to stand in my way or to make my life difficult. 'I strongly suggest that we get this done as quickly and as amicably as possible. If you leave me a voicemail telling me who'll be taking over from me I'll do my best to make sure they're up to speed with what's going on. I will not, however, under any circumstances be briefing Bob Finkelman.' I stand and walk out of his office.

The sight of his open mouth as I turn to close the door

behind me makes me smile. I wonder if anyone has ever walked out on Tom before.

Jack's office door is closed; I knock, and then softly I open it. He's sitting behind his desk, chair turned to the side and facing the window. He turns his head as I enter.

'Jack.'

The crooked grin is a little more crooked than usual. 'So you heard.'

'I heard.' I close the door again, and lower myself into the distinctly uncorporate battered old leather armchair in front of his desk. 'I can't believe it. Not even of Tom.'

He shrugs. 'You warned me, I guess. Should've been expecting it.'

I shake my head. 'I didn't imagine anything like this. I'm so sorry.'

He rests his head against the back of his chair. 'Well, the termination package is a good one; I've been with Sanderson for fifteen years. We won't starve. And there are other jobs out there, I guess. Maybe not in Phoenix, but then maybe it would be better to move away, after this. I don't know. I'll have to think about it. Right now, I'm still pretty stunned. It seems so strange to think of leaving this building, this office – all the people I've worked with over the years – not seeing them again.' He smiles faintly. 'I'll miss you.'

'I've just handed in my notice.'

He jerks himself upright. 'No, Cat. Not because of this.'

I shake my head. 'No. This was the final straw, but it wasn't because of this. It was for so many reasons. It was because I can't work for a company that can spend so much time talking about glossy but ultimately meaningless corporate responsibility initiatives, and yet quash data that doesn't fit in with its plans for one of its products.'

He shrugs. 'It's not such a big deal really, Cat. You know

that, deep down. If there's a flaw with SP 32534 it'll come out in other research, whether it's internal or external research. It'll certainly come out in the clinical trials – it'll be glaringly obvious, if subjects are still experiencing sedation as well as anxiety relief. It's not as if they're covering up something life-threatening. It's certainly not worth you resigning over.'

'I know. But that's not the point, is it? The point is that they'd even try to cover something up. Whether it's serious or not.' I sigh. 'I just can't believe in this company or in its management any more. And I have no idea what I'm doing in corporate law anyway – I have no real interest in the business world and never really have. Though once upon a time maybe I thought a pharmaceutical company was on the side of the angels – trying to cure all the ills of the world.' I laugh. 'It seemed a worthy enough cause. Naïve. How many employees of this company – especially at senior management or board level – do you really think give a damn about helping people? It's a nice-to-have, but it's not their reason for being here.' He's looking at me blankly; sometimes I forget that Jack doesn't share all of my feelings about corporate life. I shake my head. 'Never mind, Jack.'

He shrugs. 'Well, I can't say I'm really surprised. You haven't seemed happy for quite some time now.'

'Do you want to know what really brought it to a head? What really made me do it?'

He looks surprised. 'Sure.'

'I did my first solo today.' In spite of all that's just happened I can't keep the silly grin off my face.

And in spite of all that's just happened, he can't help but grin in return. 'And you feel like you could just go on out there and conquer the whole wide world.'

'Oh, no. The universe, at the very least.' Turning away from him, I stare out of the window at the slowly setting afternoon sun and the deepening blue of the sky. 'I sat in that plane at the beginning of the runway waiting for clearance to take off, and it was as if someone had turned on a light switch in my head. Just for a moment, I saw everything so clearly; the world made so much sense. *I* made so much sense. I suspect I'm going to be spending a great deal of time from now on trying to remember just what it was that seemed so blindingly obvious.'

'And you weren't afraid?'

'No. Isn't that the craziest thing you've ever heard? After all the worry and all the build-up and all the certainty that I'd never be able to do it? No, I wasn't afraid. I was perfectly calm. I've never been so gloriously calm in my life. I've been trained to fly, I was there to fly, and so I flew.'

He smiles, a little sadly. 'I never doubted you for a moment.'

A lump comes to my throat. 'No. I know you didn't.'

For a moment, all that has gone unsaid between us for so long now hovers on the verge of being spoken. Ah, but that wouldn't do, now, would it? I tear my eyes away from his; I break the spell.

'Have you told Melissa?'

He nods. 'She's furious about the whole thing, but she's a tough cookie. She'll do whatever needs to be done. If we need to move, she'll move. You know Melissa. She's at her best in a family crisis.'

I smile faintly. 'I know.'

'And you?'

'What about me?'

'What are you going to do?'

'I don't know.' The reality of my situation begins to creep in on me and for a moment I wish that, like Jack, I had a family for moral support. Somehow I can't see Adam being impressed by what I've done. 'I've plenty of savings; there hasn't been much to spend my salary and bonuses on over the years, and in any case, Adam earns more than I do. I'm not going to starve, either. I'm going to take some time off, really think about what

255

I want to do with the rest of my life. Indulge in a proper midlife crisis. Really go for it.' I laugh.

'And Adam?'

Slowly, I shake my head. 'I don't know, Jack. But you know what it's like. Once you prise open one crack in your life to see what's down there, a whole bunch of others seem to widen in response. Right now, though, I'm going to go home, bask in the glory of my solo flight and my battle against the forces of evil, and just see what comes.'

'No plan?'

'For once in my life, no. I'm not going to have it all planned out. For once, I'm just going to take each day as it comes. In fact, I'm going to actively embrace chaos.' A heady sense of freedom hovers at the threshold of my mind. I should be scared witless by what I've just done; instead I'm on the verge of elation.

'I'm really going to miss you.'

I look away, smile. 'I'm going to miss you too. But I'm not leaving the country.'

'No?'

'No. I like it here. And nowhere else really feels like home, so I might as well hang around for a while.' I stand. 'I'd better go and break the news to Janie. But you keep in touch, won't you? Though no doubt we'll run into you both at the country club.' He nods, smiling faintly. I turn to the door.

His voice, when it comes, is soft. 'Cat?'

My eyes are guarded as I turn back to him. Don't say it, Jack. Please don't say it. But he doesn't say it; he just shakes his head and swallows. 'You go fly.'

'You did what?' Adam is seriously unimpressed. He stands before me, immaculate in his dark grey suit and the white shirt that is still crisp even after a long day at the office. His eyes hold an expression of utter incredulity.

'I resigned.'

'You resigned?'

I nod.

'Why the hell did you resign? Jesus, Cat.' He pulls a chair out from underneath the kitchen table and sits down, looking at me as if I'm from another planet.

I take the seat opposite him and calmly I explain about Jack, and about SP 32534.

I have barely finished before he is leaning back, arms folded firmly across his stomach and shaking his head. 'Cat. I know you and Jack have worked closely together for a long time now. I know you don't like the fact that they let him go. But it was something the entire board must have agreed on. There are always going to be times when you don't like a decision that the company's taken. You can't go around resigning whenever that happens.'

'I don't consider myself to have a habit of "going around and resigning". I've worked for Sanderson Pharmaceuticals for twelve years, here and in the UK. Nor have I ever thought of resigning when the board made a decision I didn't like in the past. But this is different. This is a matter of principle – and a question of corporate ethics. Doesn't that interest you at all?'

'Of course it interests me – I just don't see what all the fuss is about in this case. It's not as if they're hiding data that's going to mislead or cause harm to a consumer. I certainly wouldn't advise it to any of my clients, and doubtless it'd look bad in a lawsuit if it got out, but I wouldn't have thought it was something to resign over. Jesus, Cat. When you throw a hissy fit you sure don't do it by halves.'

I want to take hold of him by the throat and rip him apart. I try to keep my voice calm, try to stay reasonable. 'This wasn't a hissy fit, Adam. This was something important that's been building up for a long time.'

'You're telling me. You've been acting oddly for months. Ever since you started taking those goddamned flying lessons.'

Oh, for heaven's sake. I pass a cool hand over my eyes. It's been a long day, and it's starting to catch up with me now.

'Ever since I started taking flying lessons? Well, let's talk about flying lessons. Do you know what I did today? I took my first solo flight. Yes, me. All alone in a plane. Do you have any idea what that meant to me?' He looks at me with complete incomprehension. 'I thought not. Do you even *care* what it meant to me?'

'Well, of course I'm interested in what you do; I just can't see why you want to fly.'

'You can't see why I want to fly; you can't see why I want to leave Sanderson. Adam – is there anything about me right now that you can see? Anything that matters, at all?'

He slumps, grey, exhausted, and for a moment I feel a pang of the old guilt. I bite down on it; those days are gone. They have to be. 'Cat. Honey. I admit that I don't understand you a whole lot of the time. I don't know why you think the way you do; I have no idea what goes on in your head. Maybe it's a cultural thing; maybe it's a sex difference. I don't know. But what I do know is that I love you.'

As if that makes it okay. As if that excuses everything. As if it's all that's needed to bind us together and chain us to this bizarre stone wall of mutual incomprehension. 'I know you do. But that's not enough, Adam. It just isn't enough.'

He gets up from the table and moves behind me; he bends down and puts his arms around my shoulders. He wants me to stand, to move into his arms, but I can't. All I can feel is the weight of him, the weight of his need and of all his false expectations.

I remain, flat and rigid, in my chair.

Dinner is a tense, largely silent affair. When Adam tries to bring up the subject of what I'm going to do next, I cut him off. I don't want to talk about it any more right now, I say. I want to sleep on it.

After the dishes are neatly stacked in the dishwasher and it is switched on, I leave Adam glued to *Ally McBeal* and retreat to my study. Tonight there is no comfort to be found in this room; I don't know what to do here. I pace for a while; I can't settle. I don't have the focus to pick up a book, and even the solace of listening to music seems like too much hard work. My eyes fall on my desk and on the small stack of mail that I threw there when I got home. Peeking out from beneath the usual pile of junk is a large brown envelope bearing the familiar bright blue of an air-mail sticker. Inside, a short letter of the 'Hi darling, hope you're doing well' variety; attached to it, another piece of story.

The perfect distraction: I settle down in the armchair to read.

At the bottom of the page at the end of the extract you have scrawled a brief note.

> *Cat,*
>
> *I'm sending you all this because I wanted you to know how very much I loved your father. And not just when we first met. Whatever happened, and whatever came later, I want you to know that you were the product of a lot of love. I realise that your memories of him aren't all good – but in so many other ways he was a fine man. He was the love of my life, and for all that happened afterwards, I will never regret that feeling. I wouldn't have missed it for the world. You take a risk whenever you fall in love. (I should know; I've done it often enough!) But the risk is almost*

always worth it, for the possible reward. In this
case it was more than worth it, because you were
the reward.

When you think about him, remember that.
Lots of love,
M.

But I don't want to think about my father now. Later, perhaps. Later I'll have to think about him, when we get to that point in the story. But not now. Because all I can think about now is the stake that's driving its way into my heart as I re-read your words about love and risk.

Because at least you had a 'love of your life'. At least you took that risk.

Look at me. Who has been the love of my life?

Nate? All those years ago, back in college?

Ah, no. Not really. Nate was no more than just a youthful dream.

Adam?

Poor Adam. Did I ever tell you how he and I first met? Probably not; I've shared so little of my life with you these past years. And besides, it really wasn't very interesting at all. I'd been invited to a Christmas party by one of the senior partners at Regan Dinsdale; they represent us in Arizona litigation. Adam wasn't one of those who worked on our cases; his major clients were companies in the chemical sector. But Drew, Ginny's husband, had done some work for us in the past and Adam is Drew's best friend. So, Drew introduced me to Adam. I remember thinking that he looked so distinguished in his 'black tie' gear. Tall, slim, kind brown eyes and short blond hair with a slight wave to it. He'd been divorced then for a couple of years, and at that point it had been a long time since I'd been in a serious relationship. Oh, I wasn't ever a nun. I dated – but I kept my distance. I was frightened, you see. Frightened of falling too hard. Frightened of getting hurt. Frightened that I'd let them in, that they'd see right into me. See all the dark places; see what I was hiding. The shame. The guilt. The difference.

But Adam was safe. He'd already done the marriage-and-kids thing; there seemed to be no pressure there. He knew about relationships; he seemed grown-up; he seemed to know what he was doing. Nice, smiled a lot, considerate. He made me feel looked-after, cared-for. Sex wasn't especially earth-shattering but it was okay. And, although I was always used to my own company, it was nice to have someone to go places with. It's tough being single in corporate America: there are so many functions where you really need an escort. So we fell into a steady dating habit. When he asked me to move in with him, it seemed like it wouldn't be too much of a hardship. I'd fit in, if I lived with someone. I'd belong. I wouldn't be different any more. And he spent a lot of time travelling; so did I. So surely I wouldn't ever feel hemmed-in?

And for a while, it worked out just fine. I felt safe; he loved me. I thought that I sort of loved him back, that it was an easy, safe kind of love. But it wasn't love at all, was it? Not really. It was affection, comfort, convenience. It wasn't long before he began to press in on me; that always happens when one of you cares more than the other. And, when it comes down to it, we have so very little in common. Adam doesn't worry about that; he's not especially analytical, either of himself or others. He's a simple, straightforward kind of guy and he doesn't really understand people who aren't. I perplex him.

The truth is, there's never been a love of my life. And whatever might have happened in your life, at least you've known that. You were prepared to risk it all for love – and for what you believed in. The stakes were high, and heaven knows you lost. Time and time again, you lost. But you sure as hell gave it your all.

And it strikes me as odd, that I've never really seen it as a strength before.

To my surprise I sleep like a baby; I wake later than usual in the morning and feel the lightness of the empty space beside me where Adam should be.

I wake knowing that I have to leave.

↞ ↞ ↞

I let myself back into the house in the middle of the afternoon. It's been the day from hell. Too many people, each of them demanding explanations for why I'm leaving – reasons that I can't possibly give. Janie weeping. A brief visit from Tom during which he told me that Byron, my deputy, would be taking over from me. He put an envelope down on my desk and explained that the company would be happy to treat my departure as part of the cost-cutting exercise and that I could expect a termination package of one month's salary for each of the years I'd worked with Sanderson. He informed me that perhaps it would be best if I left today. I laughed. I understand their motives perfectly, but they needn't have bothered. I don't need to be bought off; I'm not the whistle-blower type.

And so: Catriona. Cat. Whoever she is; whoever they are. Standing here in this cold, beige kitchen, cutting through each of the ropes that tie her to the ground with a sharp, white-hot knife. One by one, slicing through them. Hurling them all away.

I walk over to the air-conditioning control panel and turn the thermostat up to seventy-two.

I'm sitting at the kitchen table when I hear the sound of his key turning in the lock. Fear clutches at my stomach: fear of the scene that's to come. The gravity of what I'm about to do hits me full-on in the solar plexus, depriving me of breath. How can

I do this to him? He loves me so. How can I possibly leave him, when he needs me to stay?

But I have to do it. I have to do it for my own good. I can't be responsible for his happiness. I can't be responsible for his life.

I am sleeping when I hear her bedroom door open across the landing. In an instant I am fully awake. I sit up, listening, tense. I hear the first heavy footstep on the stairs. Then another. And another. I sigh quietly; it's okay. I lie back down again, wanting to just tumble back into the warm oblivion of sleep – and then it comes. The unmistakable sick dull thuds that a body makes when it rolls down the stairs. I rush over to my bedroom door and wrench it open, heart pounding and the rough salty taste of tears in my throat. She's lying at the bottom of the stairs in a huddle. Slowly, hand over mouth, I creep down to her and stand over her, shaking. I hardly dare look.

Have I let her die? I shouldn't have just lain there: I should have jumped up as soon as I heard her door open.

If she died it would be my fault. I should have tried to persuade her to sleep downstairs on the sofa like she normally does when she's drinking.

What would I do if she died? She's all I have in the world. You and me against the world, little Cat. Just you and me.

Please, don't let her be dead.

She isn't dead. But she's breathing heavily and her arm is caught under her at a strange angle. 'Mum,' I shout at her. 'Mum!' There's no response at all, not even a groan. I place a shaking hand on her forehead. Cold, clammy. I smooth back a matted lock of hair from her face.

I don't know what to do, and there's no-one else I can ask. Once, a few months ago, I called next door for help, thinking that she was dead when she was just unconscious. She made my life hell for weeks. Nobody must ever know. It would be better to die than have anyone know. But I don't want her to die. And this time she's fallen down the stairs: I can't take the chance. I pick up the telephone in the hall and call 999.

The ambulance is here in minutes, the ambulance men gentle and efficient as they move across to her. One of them asks me what happened; he has rough greying hair and kind brown eyes. 'She fell down the stairs,' I tell him. My voice is calm; I am perfectly composed. I know that surprises him; it always surprises people.

One of the men examining my mother turns to us. 'Has she been drinking?' He can smell it on her, of course. The whisky.

I look away then, away from the disgust or pity in his face, and I meet the kind brown eyes of the man next to me. He reaches out and puts a warm hand on mine. I pull away; I don't like to be touched. 'It's all right, pet. You can tell us. Does your mam take a drink?'

Something's gnawing away at my stomach and there's no room inside my chest for air. I can't tell him. I can't. You mustn't ever tell. But she's lying there and she's so pale and if I don't tell and something happens to her it will be my fault. I'm supposed to be the one who looks after her; the one who takes care of everything when she's not well. If she dies, it will be my fault. I look back at the kind man, and I nod.

'Do you know how much she's had to drink?'

I shake my head. Acknowledging it is bad enough; speaking it out loud is unthinkable.

'How long has she been drinking for?'

'Since Friday night.' My voice is a whisper. It's Saturday night now.

He reaches out again, puts a firm hand on my shoulder and this time the simple comfort of it brings the unthinkable: tears well up in my eyes. 'It's okay, pet. We'll look after your mam. Looks like she had a lucky escape this time. But we're going to take her to the hospital just to make sure there's nothing broken.'

I nod, fighting back the weeping. 'I'll come with her.'

'Better not,' he says. 'It'd be better if you stayed at home. Is there anyone else here?' I can see that he's choosing his words carefully.

I shake my head.

'A friend or a neighbour you can stay with?'

I look at him and assess the situation. I'm good at that: weighing up the consequences, the pros and the cons, the risks and the balances. 'I'll come to the hospital. I have to. I'm all that she has. I have to find out when she'll be home. See if she needs anything. Then by the time I get home, next door will be up and I'll go and stay with them. Or with my auntie. Auntie May. She lives over in Owton Manor.'

'How old are you, love?'

I look into his honest brown eyes and I grit my teeth and I lie. I've learned how to do that, too. 'Twelve,' I tell him. 'I'm twelve.' I'm not really twelve, I'm just ten. But I'm tall for my age and twelve sounds so much more grown-up.

He sighs, and then nods. 'All right, then.'

At the hospital a lot of people ask me questions. They ask me questions about my mother, and about how much she drinks. I tell them this has never happened before. I tell them I don't know. I tell them I've never been left by myself to cope. I tell them we have lots of friends and family and people that I can call on for help if I need it. I smile brightly and I lie and I lie and I lie.

A lady drives me home and goes to talk to Mrs Brown next door. When the lady has gone Mrs Brown knocks on the back door. I am making myself tea and some toast for my breakfast. She tells me that the hospital says I should go and stay with them until my mother comes home. I look her calmly in the

eye and tell her that there's no need for that, thank you. I can
manage.

I can look after myself.

And when my mother comes home, I can look after her too.

The door opens and the acrid odour of gasoline wafts in from the garage. I sneak a quick assessing glance at Adam's face; catch him doing the same to me. I want to weep at the futility of it.

'Hey,' he says. 'How's it going?'

'Fine.' I hesitate.

Get it over with, Cat.

'Adam, we have to talk.'

Swiftly, he puts down his briefcase and walks over to the table. 'I know, sweetheart.' He squats down beside me and takes one of the hands that are so tightly clenched in my lap.

I pull it away. 'No, Adam. I mean *really* talk. I –'

'I know,' he interrupts me. 'I know. I've been doing a lot of thinking. Last night, and all day at the office.' He stands up, runs a hand through hair that is significantly less neat than usual. 'I'm sorry, Cat. I've been acting like a prize fool. For a long time, now. You were right, last night. What you said. About me listening to you. Or rather, not listening. Not *really* listening.' He's pacing up and down now; I've never seen Adam quite so agitated. But I don't want to hear this; it's too late. Can't he see that it's too late? I try to interrupt but he brushes me off with a wave of his hand. 'No, Cat. Let me finish. Please.' And what can I do? He's hell-bent on seeing it through. I shake my head slightly, but let him continue. 'I just wanted to say that I'm sorry. That I want us to start again.'

Start again? I want to ask him. After five years? Start again with what?

'Pretend none of these past few months ever happened. I know I haven't been very sympathetic about your anxiety attacks, and all. Haven't taken much of an interest in your new hobby.'

My new *hobby*? Can he possibly mean flying?

'But I want you to know that all of that's going to change now.'

'Adam –' I try again.

'No, Cat. Really. I know it's hard to believe, but I think I've finally seen the light. Everything's just been so hectic at work and I haven't been taking any time for myself, or for us. And I can change that. I'm going to make sure that in future – unless there's a trial running of course – I'm going to take every weekend off. Just like I used to, when we first met. Maybe we can start going on up to Apache Lake again. Hell, it's not like I really need to be in the office on Saturdays. Not like I need the money. I'll just cut down a bit on the case-load. And won't play as much golf. Then you and I, we can get out of a town a little more, just like you used to love –'

'Adam. Please stop it.' My voice is hard now; I just can't stand it any more. All these sad little plans; plans that are never going to come to fruition. Surprised by my tone, he's quiet. 'I'm sorry,' I say. 'I'm sorry. But it's too late.'

'Cat.' He strides back over to me and I brace myself, try not to flinch away. He rests his hand, air-conditioned cool from the car, on top of my head. I close my eyes; shrink a little. 'It's not too late. I've said that I'm sorry. I know you're going through a rough time right now with leaving your job and all, but we can still work this out. You'll find another job. Hell, there are plenty of law firms in this town who would just snap you up. Not to mention other companies. You could walk right into another job tomorrow.'

And that's just the point, of course. He'll never understand why it is that I don't want to. It isn't his fault; it's just the way he is. 'Adam...'

And when it comes right down to it, I don't know what to

say. Don't know what words to use. Adam, I'm leaving you? Way too melodramatic. Adam, I'm sorry, but things just aren't working out? All I'll get is another tirade about how he's going to make it all okay. Adam, I just don't love you any more? In fact, I don't really think I ever did?

But I don't need to find any words at all. For all his difficulties in figuring me out, he isn't a stupid man. Once he looks – really looks – he reads it quite plainly on my face. 'You don't want to be with me any more.' He sits down heavily in the chair opposite me; his face turns grey.

'Yes. I mean, no. I mean – I think we should split up, yes. Stop living together.' Jesus Christ, I'm babbling. Get a grip, Cat. I take a deep, shuddering breath. 'You know – it's true, isn't it? What I said last night. That we really don't understand each other, you and I. We don't have the same interests or the same values. It's getting more apparent with time, not less. And that's not going to change.'

'But I love you.' His face is boyish, perplexed. Flushed.

A pause. 'I'm sorry.'

'You don't love me.'

I'm silent. What can I possibly say? One more lie? There have been too many lies in my life. No more lies, Cat. No more lies.

And then, unthinkably, Adam is crying. Loud, guttural sobs; a sound that I've never heard from him before, or from any man. 'Adam, please don't.' But I can't move to comfort him. I can't, because as soon as he touches me it'll make it worse and he'll cling on to me and

her face is red with weeping. She's weeping and weeping and she can't seem to stop, and I don't know how to make her stop. She's weeping as if she's bearing all of the agonies of the world, and I don't know how to help her. And all the while, she's looking at me as if it's my fault. Because it's supposed to be my job to make it all right. But I don't know how to make it better. She reaches for me, all that need in her eyes and I can't possibly – I can't possibly be what she needs me to be. I don't even know what it is that she needs me to be. It's as if there's this big hole inside her and I can't fill it up, I can't – there'll be nothing left for me

and I sit, helpless; stare outside but all I can see is our reflections in the plate glass doors that lead through to the back yard. A strange tableau; a strange piece of theatre. And what part am I playing tonight? I watch it as if from a great distance and I wait for him to finish. Finally, he stands abruptly, walks over to the counter and blows his nose loudly on two large sheets of snow-white kitchen paper. He bends over the sink, leans the weight of his upper body on his hands. Lowers his head; takes a deep, jagged breath. 'Well. I guess that's it, then.'

'I'm sorry.' Again. Futile words, stupid words. But I don't know what else to say.

'Sorry?' He laughs, abruptly. Bitterly – and it doesn't sound at all like the Adam that I know. 'No, Cat. I don't think you're sorry. Look at yourself. I don't think you feel anything at all.'

I flinch. *You have no emotions at all, little Cat. Have you? Just like your father. Don't give a damn about anybody but yourself.*

No, no, no. Not again. I will not take this from anyone, ever again. 'That's enough,' I whisper.

'It's not enough. It's something I should have said a long time ago. You've never really loved me at all, have you?' *You don't love me, Cat. Do you? Say it, then, if you love me. Say you love me, Cat.* And there they are again: ice-cold hands, reaching, clutching at my throat. I shiver; my eyes flick over to the control panel on the wall. Has he turned the thermostat down again? 'It's the same when we make love. You lie there in bed like some kind of … automaton, just waiting for me to finish. I don't think I've ever heard you cry out with pleasure –

269

not once.' And my breathing is more and more rapid now and the bands are tightening around my chest. I gasp for breath but my lungs are closing up and I can't seem to fill them and I gulp down some more air and – 'You sit there so calmly and you tear my life to pieces and sometimes I wonder whether you have any emotions at all –' *Don't you feel anything at all, little Cat? Just like your father. What did I do to deserve either of you?* and the band is tightening and I'm suffocating and…

'Stop it!' I yell and I leap up out of my chair and the words echo around the cold, empty room and Adam's mouth falls open and he gapes at me. 'Who the hell do you think you are, to judge me? What do you know about me? What did you ever think to find out about me that might give you the right to say those things?'

He recovers himself quickly. 'What did you ever tell me, Cat?'

'You never asked!' I whirl around, stomp over to the garden doors and, shuddering, rest my hands against the glass as if against the walls of a prison.

'I asked, Cat. I asked all the time. You just brushed it off.'

My hands fall to my sides and I rest my forehead on the cold, smooth glass.

He's right. I brushed it off. Just as I always do. Mustn't tell, mustn't let anyone in. Mustn't ever let them know the shame.

I slip back into the chair, head in my hands.

'Cat.' He hesitates; I hear him creep closer to me. 'Cat. Let's start again. Please. You can tell me. Whatever it is you haven't ever told me. I want to know. I want to understand. And in return, I promise I'll listen. We can work this out, Cat.'

Wearily, I shake my head. 'No, Adam. We can't. I'm sorry. I'm really sorry. You're quite right. So much I haven't shared with you. But you need to believe me, and to understand when I tell you that it really is too late. I'm sorry, Adam. I really am. But I'm going to have to leave.'

Silence. Then the soft whoosh of the dishwasher as it takes in more water; the harsh hiss of Adam's breathing next to me.

Silence. And then: 'Cat – don't go.'

'I have to go. I have to.'

'No, you don't. You're not thinking; you're just reacting.'

'Don't you tell me what I'm doing. I know what I'm doing. I'm leaving.'

'Don't leave me, Cat. Not like this. So sudden.'

'There's no point in dragging it out. That would be worse for both of us. I won't change my mind.'

'Cat, please –'

'Leave me alone, Adam – no, don't touch me.'

'Cat –'

Tears in the night, and a last desperate clinging.

He stands at the counter and sips at his coffee before leaving for work. Dressed in a dark grey suit, white shirt and sober blue tie, he looks very remote – a stranger. I sit in a huddle at the kitchen table, eyes hollowed out from lack of sleep. We avoid looking at each other's faces and calmly agree I should leave my things there until I find somewhere else to live. We congratulate each other that there are no messy financial or legal details to be sorted out. He asks me to keep in touch with him sometimes, if I feel that I can. And to let him know that I'm okay. Then he places his coffee mug carefully inside the dishwasher, picks up his car keys from the bowl by the back door, and he leaves for work. Walks out of the door without looking back, and for that much, at least, I am grateful.

When he is gone I lower my head onto the table and I close my eyes. I urgently need a plan, but I'm so tired. So very tired, as if the chronic lack of nourishment in my life for all of these years has finally caught up with me and taken its toll. I'm so tired and I don't know who I am any more; I don't know who

I'm supposed to be. All I know is that I want a place where I *can* be. Myself. Whoever that might happen to be, today. Or any day.

10

Laura

O n this dark winter afternoon, the flickering glow of the
fire is the major source of light in Meg's living room.
Laura wraps her aching fingers around a mug of hot tea and
stares into the flames. A sudden crack, and the fire spits a small
fragment of coal onto the solid slate hearth. It reminds her of
childhood fires: the Rice Krispie snap, crackle and pop of sea-
coal. She'd forgotten all about sea-coal; no-one seems to use it
any more. When she was a girl it was there on the beach for
the taking: small grains of coal from veins that ran close to the
surface, washed up by the sea. Sometimes the local men would
go down with their bags and bring it home for the fire, but
Aunt Lizzie bought hers from the sea-coal man, who came in
his horse-drawn cart and delivered it in rough hessian sacks.
They'd wrap it in tight cones of newspaper so that it wouldn't
just fall straight through the grate before it got set alight.

'Aye, there's something hypnotic about a good fire.' Meg's
voice is sleepy, but amused.

Reluctantly, Laura tears her eyes away from the flames. 'I
was watching scenes from my life passing by.'

'Good memories or bad?'

She shrugs. 'Neutral, I'd say.' But there are good memories
from those days, too. She just hasn't chosen to recall them.

'Talking of memories: you haven't mentioned your writing
for a good while now.'

Laura grimaces. 'That's because I haven't done any for a
while. Not since before Christmas.'

273

'Ah.' Meg shifts slightly in the old tapestry wing chair, and Mab mews, disgruntled, on her lap. 'A difficult part, is it?'

Laura nods, staring blindly back into the fire. Too difficult by far.

'Ach, well. The memories are there. If they need to come out, they'll come out whether you want it or not.'

'There's no question about that.' Laura sighs. 'That's why I got started on all this in the first place.' Memories: crowding, pushing, shoving. Demanding to be set free.

'I remember. Samhain, wasn't it? The first day of the old winter. And here we are now, well into spring.'

'Spring? You've got to be joking. The weather forecast this morning threatened snow.'

'In the old calendar, the second day of February was the first day of spring. Imbolc, they used to call it.'

Laura smiles faintly. 'And I suppose you've another story for me about that.'

'Aye, well, if you're wanting a story, I suppose I could oblige.' The fire glints in Meg's eyes like a Bonfire Night sparkler as she smiles across at Laura. 'Though it's not really a story. More a myth. An old belief. If you remember, at Samhain it's the Cailleach – the old hag of winter – that begins to assert her sovereignty over the land. All through the winter she rules, when the days are dark and the nights are cold and the mountain tops covered with snow. But at Imbolc she begins to fade, and Brighid the Spring Maiden returns. The legend says that she restores the lifeless land, brings back the green plants and the miracle of birth.'

'It certainly doesn't feel like spring out there.' Out of the front window she can see the wind whipping through the rowans around Meg's house. An icy wind that cuts right through you and lodges itself in your very bones.

'Some years the Cailleach fights off her rival and keeps her grip on us for a wee while longer. Many's the year we used to get the snows well into March and April. I mind when they came once in June. Lambing snows, they called them when I was a wee girl. But no matter what the weather is doing: the point is that this is a time of renewal. Whether we see it or not. The welcoming back of the Spring Maiden; the welcoming back of the light. See how the days are gradually growing longer, now? Slowly the light begins to emerge again. And life regenerates. A new cycle begins.'

But the place I've yet to go is still dark, Laura thinks. Dark as the coal-hole that Aunt Lizzie would lock me in when I was wicked. I was such a wicked child.

The truth is, Laura doesn't want to write about her marriage. Doesn't want to face it. Wants to turn away from it, just as she's always done.

'You never married, Meg?' She knows, of course, that Meg was never married, but she wants to hear her talk. There's a magic, sometimes, in Meg's words. Magic, and a strange sort of healing.

'No. Though I might have thought of it, once.'

Surprised, Laura raises an eyebrow. 'Who was he?'

Meg is silent for a while, and Laura wonders if she's overstepped the mark. She watches as Meg's hand moves absently over Mab's black fur. Mab purrs loudly. Sometimes Laura longs for a pet of her own. Something to stroke, something to love. Something to love her in return.

It always comes back to that.

'His name was Patrick. Patrick O'Connell, and he never answered to Pat, or to Paddy. His name was Patrick, and that was that.' Meg smiles, a soft smile whose edges are laced with sadness. 'Ach, but he was a handsome man. Black curly hair and bright blue eyes the colour of a Kerry sky.' She nods slowly. 'Aye, and that was where he came from originally. Though he was a travelling man, so he wouldn't ever own to coming from any one place unless you pressed him hard.'

'He was a gypsy?'

'Not a Romany, no. A traveller. The Summer People, we used to call them here. That was when they came. He was a musician. And also a storyteller, as I was myself.'

'And how did you meet him?'

'At a folk festival down in Glasgow. I'd been asked to perform, and so had he. He'd his two brothers along with him; one played the fiddle and the other the tin whistle, and Patrick played the bodhran and sang. In between the songs he told stories.'

'And was it love at first sight?' Laura's eyes sparkle mischief across the room and Meg laughs.

'Aye, that it was. One look into those baby-blue eyes and I was lost. And it was the same for him, too. Or so he said.' She shakes her head, smiling still. 'Ah, but I was a bonny lass in those days, you know. You might not think it to look at me now, but I was bonny in my day. Hair red as the fire, I had. But anyway – the folk festival. I told a tale about a selkie, and he told one about a mermaid. It made us smile, that we'd chosen such similar stories. Though it's not so surprising when you think on it – the old tales are similar in Scotland and in Ireland. We borrow their myths and they borrow ours, and who knows any more where the one begins and the other ends.' She sighs, and rests her head against the back of the chair. 'And that was how it was with Patrick and me.'

Laura remembers that feeling. Lying there close, limbs entangled and breath mingled. Wondering for a moment whose leg is this, whose arm, and deciding in the end that it doesn't really matter.

She never had that feeling again. Not after Alec. 'So you saw each other again after the festival?'

'Aye. From time to time. All through that spring and summer, I'd see him at festivals here and there. Then one September morning he came knocking on my door. He'd camped down by the shore at Clachan.'

'Surprise visit?'

'Aye, indeed. He stayed for two months. The longest he'd ever stayed anywhere.'

'What happened?'

She closes her eyes and is silent for a while. Then softly she says, 'He left, as a traveller will.'

'Did you never think of going with him?'

Meg's eyes open and flash and for a moment Laura sees a younger Meg, wind whipping around her hair and fire in her eyes and heart. 'Aye, I thought about it. I thought about it day and night. I thought about it for years. I think about it still.'

'Why didn't you?'

Meg waves a hand. 'Ach, too many reasons. I don't know any more whether they were good ones or bad. He asked me to go with him, but I wouldn't. We argued about it. My mother was the main reason. I'd three brothers originally, you see. Aly, the eldest, was lost in the war. The other two, thankfully, were too young for the fighting. Ruaridh became a fisherman; he was lost at sea three years after the war ended. Duncan stayed and minded the sheep and looked after the croft. My mother had always loved him best, and grew to rely on him with the others gone. But Duncan was a strange boy. Quiet. After Ruaridh died, he took to drink. Nothing we could do would stop him from drinking. And then one day, just before Patrick came, Duncan shot himself upstairs in the bedroom just above our heads.' Laura flinches; Meg sighs and carries on. 'My mother was the one who found him, and she was never right, after that. I was all she had left. How could I leave her too? So I stayed at home. I stayed, and I didn't go to the festivals any more. Not until she died.'

'When did she die?'

'Two years later.'

'Did you never see Patrick again?'

'No. By the time I was back on the festival circuit, no-one had seen him for a year or more. Eventually I asked after him at a campsite – some folk I'd seen him keep company with. They told me he'd married a girl two years previously. Sara. They'd settled.'

'Settled?'

'Aye. They were living on a small farm back in Kerry.'

Laura is silent for a long moment. Watching the sadness on Meg's face. Unusual, to see Meg anything other than peaceful; anything other than content. But she's eighty years old, Laura thinks. Of course she's known sadness. 'And you never met anyone else after that?'

'I hadn't the heart for it. He stayed in my mind. Nobody else could get around him.'

Just as Alec stayed in Laura's. Though she never gave up trying; she was always so very ready to launch herself full-tilt into the arms of the next Big Mistake, whenever he might happen along. She looks up; Meg is watching her closely.

'Marriage,' Meg says. 'A difficult business indeed. Sometimes I wonder whether it isn't better the way old Janet Mackenzie did it. Old Janet, whose house you live in now.'

'And how did she do it?'

'Old Janet lived on that croft all alone with just a cow and six sheep for company. Fine woman, she was. Fit and healthy. But she just never found a man to suit. She must have been in her forties when she took it into her head that she would like to be married. She put it about locally that she was looking, but there was no suitable bachelor to be found. So she took out an advertisement in the *Stornoway Gazette*. Aye, indeed – she advertised for a husband. Well, one day a wee mannie comes knocking at her door. From Lewis he was; he'd seen her advertisement and he'd come across on a fishing boat to the

278

mainland. He'd hitched a ride with a lorry to the end of the road, then he walked the five miles along the lochside. Knocked on her door and asked to be considered for the position. Well, she looked him up and down and invited him inside, and after an hour and a couple of drams it was all decided. She gave her cow to one neighbour and her sheep to another; she signed over her croft to Sandy next door and away she went with him, off to the islands.'

Laura laughs. 'Maybe that's the way to do it. A simple business arrangement, expectations clear on both sides. And did it last?'

Meg nods and clicks her tongue at Mab, who is snoring quietly now. 'It lasted right up until the mannie died. Not so very long ago. So is it your own marriage you're writing about now, then?'

A pause. 'I've written some of it. How I met him. Before the start of the – of the problems between us.'

Meg eyes her shrewdly. 'He was hot-headed, was Alec.'

Laura flushes; turns her head away.

Meg nods. 'Aye, I thought as much. Pity. He was a fine boy when he was younger.'

'He was?' And still it's there, that hunger to believe that there was good in Alec. To believe that she had been right to love him. In some small way, at least.

'I mind one time old Ishbel Mackenzie was laid up with the shingles. She lived next door to the Munros, and Alec used to play with her dog when he was small. Silly wee creature, it was – a Yorkshire terrier or some such thing. He used to take it for walks. Ishbel was a distant cousin of mine, though she'd no family in the village to look after her. Alec's mother was already run off her feet looking after the family and had a job cleaning as well. Well, Alec started going in to Ishbel before school. He'd get up half an hour earlier in the morning and go and light the fire and make her tea and a pan of porridge. Then when he came home from school he'd run straight in to see whether she needed anything, and he'd carry a meal over for her after they'd eaten. Did it every day till she recovered. No-one ever asked him, he just took it upon himself to do it. Can't have been more than ten at the time. And after that he looked out for Ishbel till the day she died. Every day, fetching in a bucket of coal. Checking did she need anything from the shops. Had she enough milk for her morning tea.'

And Laura can see how it might be true. Alec, always the man to rely on when his friends needed help. Taking Jock McKenzie's shifts as well as his own when Jock's wife miscarried and he needed to stay home. Driving all the way to Inverness when Laura was pregnant with Catriona because she had a craving for cucumber and there was none to be found in the village. 'That was Alec. He could be so kind, so caring one minute, and the next – well.' Still, so hard to go there. Still, so many words that she can't say.

'Are you in touch with him still, at all? Through Catriona, maybe?'

Laura shakes her head. 'No. No, and she doesn't keep in touch with him much now, either. They'll maybe exchange a brief note at Christmas. Some years he remembers her birthday, but most years he forgets. She always remembers his. But I took her away when she was a child, so she never had a chance to see much of him. He came down to Hartlepool once or twice, but it never really worked out. She made contact a couple of times when she was a teenager, but he didn't bother much. And then he moved away down to Edinburgh, married again. To someone with four children, Cat tells me. Ironic, really, since he never could be bothered with his own. And I wouldn't have come back here if Alec had still been here. Or his family.'

'Aye, they're all gone now. His mother and father dead these long years. And Robert in Canada, I hear.'

'Really?' Laura smiles. 'I liked Robert, but I never could get him to talk much to me. He always seemed so shy.'

'He had a hard time of it as a child. So did Alec, but not as much as Robert, I think.'

'Really? Alec didn't talk much about his childhood.'

'His Aunt Isobel lives in the village still. Do you remember her?'

'A little. But we didn't see much of her when we lived here.'

'Aye, well. It was Alec's father that was her brother, and they didn't get on. She knows all about Alec's family. How it all was. You should go and see her.'

Laura shakes her head. 'I don't know, Meg. I'm trying to put all that behind me.' Not that I'm succeeding, she thinks, staring back out of the window at a seagull struggling furiously against the wind.

'All part of moving on, lassie. You can't put the past behind you till you've stood up to it and faced it down.'

And Meg is right, of course, Laura thinks as she makes her way slowly back down the lane to her house. She normally walks through the gate and across the field – a much faster route, but it's far too slippery in all this rain and she doesn't have her wellies on. As always, Meg's right. She has to move on. But how do you find the courage to move on? To move on, one more time, when you've already done it so many times before? Picked yourself up, brushed yourself down and started all over again. How many times can you keep on doing it? And what happens if the time comes when all you really want to do is just lie down and die?

Back at home, the kitchen is still warm from the Rayburn. She sits at the old table by the window, and switches on her laptop.

The days passed quickly at first, for everything was vivid and new as the selkie girl played at being human and explored all the wonders of this strange new world. The ripe brown smell of the soil; the fresh green scent of trees. She pressed her ear to the earth and she learned the thrusting, exultant songs of growing things. Her days and her nights were filled with passion; it seemed he could never get enough of her.

It wasn't long before she grew to love him in return.

Laura was awestruck by the train journey up to Inverness. She had hardly ever been out of Hartlepool before, except to go on a day trip down to Scarborough or Whitby; she had certainly never seen anything like the scenery they were passing through now. The train wound its way through one misty water-ridden valley after another, and on either side of them dark mountains loomed and brooded. Alec stared silently out of the window and she was struck by how he resembled this land. She loved him, but in so many ways he was hidden from her.

At the railway station in Inverness they were met by Alec's younger brother, Robert. Alec had told her that Robert worked as a stalker, and had the use of a dilapidated old Land Rover that went with the job. He had the look of Alec, but smaller somehow, quieter. Less sure of himself. He nodded shyly at Laura but spoke only to Alec, who sat next to him in the front seat. Laura was quite happy with this arrangement, entranced as she was by the scenery and the vast emptiness of the landscape they were travelling through. They passed only a couple of tiny villages on the sixty-mile journey through lush green fields and then through tree-covered mountains and high, bleak moors. Eventually, as they descended down through more woodland and the road began to run along the shores of a huge sea-loch to their left, Alec pointed ahead of them, out of the front window.

'There it is, Laura. There's Ullapool, now.'

And Laura would never forget that first sight of Ullapool: the sun shining down on the row of white shiny houses on a finger of land that pointed out into the loch just before it opened out into the sea.

Not long after they entered the village, Robert pulled the car up outside one of the small white houses on the road that faced the harbour. Alec got out of the car and stood beside him on the narrow pavement; Laura was left to fumble by herself for the door handle and wrench the door open. Alec turned to her as if he had momentarily forgotten she was there.

'Here we are, Laura. This is our new home.'

And Laura stared at the peeling black paint on the door and wanted to weep. Home. A home of her own. A place that was hers. All of it, hers and Alec's. No Aunt Lizzie. A place where she could be quiet. A place where she could be safe.

Robert shuffled his feet nervously and kept his eyes down as he talked. He had a slight stutter. 'There's not much inside, now, Alec. We did the best we could: there's a few wee bits of furniture and a bed and all –' he blushed furiously as he said this '– and Ma left over some sheets and a few dishes, but there's plenty of stuff you're going to be needing still.'

Alec put his arm around Laura and pulled her to his side, smiling down at her with eyes full of promise. 'If we've a bed then that's all we'll need for now.' Robert blushed again and looked down at his feet; Laura looked up at Alec with stars in her eyes and thanked God that her period seemed finally to be coming to an end. Now it can begin, she thought. Now, finally, we can begin. This is where my real life begins. This is where it begins to be good.

Because here was a place where she could be safe. Have children of her own, create a family. A family where there would be no betrayals; a family where always there would be love. Laura would be the perfect mother. Laura would never abandon her child.

Ah, this is hard, hard. She places her head in her hands.

So: Laura and Alec. Happy at first, and everything seemed to be

283

perfect. She stayed at home and painted and scrubbed and polished the house, working as hard as she could to make it her own. When he wasn't at sea they would lie in their bed, skin damp and flushed from lovemaking – he would sigh, then, and tell her his plans for the future. One day, he said – and not far off, because he was saving hard – he would have his own fishing boat and Iain Mòr would never again order him around. One day. Such tales he could spin, and a smile from those soft dark eyes was all that it took to believe in him completely.

She badly wants a cup of tea, but she's afraid to stop now. Afraid in case she never again has the courage to sit back down and write what's still to come.

But the selkie girl was too young to know that a mystery possessed is a mystery no more: he grew tired of her. She waited at home as he went out more often to sea; she sat on a rock on the shore and she sang, and she caused the fish to come swiftly to his nets. Her husband grew rich. He bought more fishing boats and hired more crew and turned all of his energies to the gathering of wealth.

She grew lonely, and she began to pine then for the sea. For it called to her: the soft, breaking voice of the waves sang her name. She remembered how it was in the watery depths, and she wept then for all that was lost. For the soft swell of seaweed in the shallows; for the cool salty sea-spray in your nostrils and the deep, crystal stillness of the seabed. For the joy of the chase as you pursued glowing fish, scales shining like jewels in water that is spotlit by sunshine. For the soft, cool touch of a male seal, his body just as sleek and as lustrous as yours as you slide over each other and around each other, the seaweed caressing your body as you slip and you roll and you tumble together through cool, surging waves. For hot mornings lying on the rocks, the sun warm on your belly as you lie with your head thrown back and your flippers dangling into cool blue water.

She languished; she wilted. And slowly, slowly, the bloom began to fade from her cheeks and her hair began to lose its lustre.

The first time it happened a storm had blown up out at sea. Alec and his crew returned with no catch, nets tangled and torn on the rocks around the Summer Isles where the boat had been blown and battered.

He walked through the door, clothes and hair stiff with salt, and his face just as dark as the sky. Laura was so relieved to see him – she'd feared he was lost – that she threw herself at him, half-crying, half-laughing.

'Alec! Oh, thank God! I didn't see the boat come in, I didn't see you, I – '

He scowled and he pushed her away, hard – too hard, so she stumbled to the floor – and her arm caught the corner of the table as she fell. Pain shot through her, sick and sharp. Dazed, she couldn't seem to understand what had happened to her; how it was that she had fallen. He frowned down at her with eyes like flint. 'Clumsy, you are,' he said, and blindly kicked out as she lay at his feet. She cried out as his boot made contact with her shin. 'What's the matter with you, that you're so clumsy all the time?' He kicked her again, in the stomach. 'Clumsy and stupid,' he said. 'Stupid, just like your Aunt Lizzie says.' And then he turned and strode back out of the front door, slamming it behind him. A thunderclap that foreshadowed the end of her dreams.

He came back late, with the smell of the wind and of rain in his hair. Laura lay rigid and shuttered on their cold, empty bed. Once again she had become nothing: she had lost herself. But gently, so gently he sat down beside her and, murmuring apologies, took her in his arms.

Oh, how sweet their lovemaking that night. How tender he was, and how loving. How thoroughly he kissed away all the hurt.

And how easy it was, lying warm in his arms, to believe him when he promised he would never do it again.

Laura stands; she wanders from room to room. She feels strangely panicky – that old hollow feeling deep in the pit of her stomach. After a while, she finds herself in front of the old oak desk in the corner of the living room. On the wall behind it is a shelf unit. She starts at the top and works her way methodically across the shelves, counting her possessions like sheep. A *Concise Oxford English Dictionary*, a copy of *Fowler's Modern English Usage*, *Roget's Thesaurus*, a *Chamber's Dictionary of Quotations* and the *New Oxford Book of English Verse*. And on the next shelf down: a small vase that Cat brought her once from a school day-trip to Whitby.

Cat. Remember the good that came out of it all. Focus on the good. Focus on Cat. A photograph in a simple wooden frame: Cat at eight. A school photograph, glasses dark against the pallor of her face. And another one next to it: Cat at her graduation. Laura doesn't know who took this photograph; she hadn't been there. Ah, push it away again, don't think about that now. A recent photograph of Cat and Adam, dressed up to the nines for some black-tie event. Cat, with her father's face, clearer and clearer the older she gets.

No. Not Alec. Remember Cat now. Remember the good. A photograph of Laura holding Cat in her arms at the christening. She was how old then? Six months? All wrapped up in the white lace shawl that Laura herself had worn as a baby, and her mother before her.

Remember this, Laura. Remember what made it all worthwhile.

And then, something wonderful happened to the selkie wife: she

286

had a child. And the child filled the emptiness that was growing inside her. She looked down at her daughter's face and she saw herself reflected in the dark blue-black eyes that were so like her own. 'Sister,' she breathed. 'Sister and daughter.' Mara, she called her, after the sea, and it didn't matter now that he stayed away. All that she was, now, she focused on Mara: her daughter, her saviour, her only friend.

By the time the seven years passed that she had promised to her husband, Mara was only three years old. She was just a baby; she still needed a mother. How could she ask him now for her skin? How could she return to the sea and leave her here, alone and motherless?

So she stayed. She stayed for the child, not for him.

It happened again, of course – more than one time. No matter how Laura tried, she was always at fault. Something she did would displease him; in some small way she would fail him. He began to drink heavily and more and more often. Several times a week he would go with his crew straight from their boat to the pub. And Laura grew nervous and pale, for she never knew what to expect when he came home. He would find fault, and he'd beat her – but then he'd make it up to her and oh, how gentle and oh, the pleasure and oh, how she loved him.

She thought that it would all be different when they had a child. A strong, tall son with Alec's blond hair and dark brown eyes: how could he fail to treasure her then? But three times she became pregnant, and three times she miscarried. And with each of her failures his frustration grew. She had managed to carry the third child for six months, but then Alec came home drunk from the pub one night and he kicked her three times in the stomach.

Another child lost; another dream bleeding away.

Then, finally, came the miracle. She conceived another child, and this one was tenacious – ah, this one wasn't going to let go. Three times she almost lost it, but each time the child held on, and

Laura felt the warm steady strength of its heartbeat deep in her womb. And this time Alec left her alone – ashamed, perhaps, by what had happened before.

She was born in early November, with her father's dark eyes and with pale blonde hair. Catriona, they called her.

Cat.

11
Cat

It's as if you're underwater. Way, way down in a dark, still pool. Everything is muffled, muted. Sensory input is dim and faded, as if it's travelled a great distance. You can see the light, there above you, but it hurts your eyes – and anyway, you're too heavy to swim up to it. You try to identify the source of this weight: a tombstone in the place where your heart used to be. A heavy iron chain garlands your throat and your chest; a tight band of steel crowns your head. Your stomach is hollow and raw. And the weeds grow tangled around your feet, holding you down. But the darkness is comforting, somehow. It's almost a necessity, this dim lonely place from which you cannot yet choose to emerge. So you don't try. Not yet. Oh, you know that you can't stay here forever; there's a part of you that knows that you'll have to break free. You can't not come out: it isn't an option. You just don't know when, yet. Or how.

Those are the bad days. The days when I don't want to get out of bed. Those are the days when I close the shutters on the burning blue skies and the merciless sun and the blinding hurting brilliance of the desert.

Then there are the good days: the days when I fly. This morning I awaken with a start in the dim glow of dawn, and ready myself for the slow sinking back down – until I remember that today is one of those days. Relief lends me the energy I need to propel myself upright, and away from the queen-sized bed that seems too large for me now. I open the curtains; the moon is fading into a sea of blue half-light and a deep orange glow is beginning to kindle at the back of the mountains out east. The desert is silent still, but expectancy hangs in the crisp morning air. Its beauty and purity pull at me, but something inside recoils from it. I don't want to go out there: it frightens me. So I stand bare-footed by the open window and listen as, one by one, the morning sounds begin. An early cardinal whistles as it flits from mesquite to cottonwood and back again; a gecko clicks in the undergrowth outside the window. I stand and watch as the sun pushes higher and other desert creatures creep from their night-time hiding places to join in the twittering, rustling chorus.

A pot of coffee and a jug of hot milk on the coffee table, facing the glazed doors that look out over the desert. Sitting on the sofa, squeezing the last dregs of sunrise from the lightening sky.

New morning rituals that I'm beginning to create in this house that is slowly becoming home to me. A cloak of routine to cover the chaos that threatens beneath. To restore some kind of order. Because this house has seen the bad days as well as the good. And it has seen the in-between days: the days when I lie on my sofa, with its soft sandy cover and the bright Anasazi pillows that contrast so well with the terracotta walls – no more creams and beiges for me – and I read or I listen to music. All the old music – the music that I used to listen to way back in college: Leonard Cohen and Jackson Browne and Joni Mitchell. When I tire of the music I lose myself in poetry: Margaret Atwood, Kathleen Raine. I run my hands over much-thumbed old paperbacks by Camus, but I'm not sure whether I'm ready to go there yet. I wallow in words. I don't know what I'm hoping to find, among all those words. Not answers – I'm not naïve enough to expect answers.

A residue, perhaps, of what I might have been.

Because after all these years of frantic striving I have stopped doing: I am trying simply to become. Learning to be, all over again. I have silenced all the voices that would tell me what to do. That tell me to be like them. To live like them, and to think like them. Or better still, not to think at all.

But all that remains now is silence, a vacuum. I have no voice yet to replace them.

At night I dream strange, dark dreams. I walk the misty paths of a cold, grey, liminal land. I walk between worlds, neither dead nor alive. In shade-ridden forests, through skeletal trees that bear no fruit. Through tunnels and tombs, where jewel-eyed serpents hiss and spit in dusty corners.

Is this how she felt, I wonder – my mother? Is this how she felt when she left my father, when she ran from her home and her love? Oh, I quite understand that the details are different. I have no daughter – don't have to be responsible for anyone but myself. I have the money to do as I will, and Adam was hardly the love of my life. But now, for the first time, I find myself wondering: is this how it was for my mother too?

But I am not my mother. I have no need of alcohol for solace. I have no need for oblivion. Flying is the only drug that I need, speeding light as quicksilver through my veins.

I don't really understand why I feel like this. After all, no-one did this to me; I have chosen to be here. I chose to leave Adam and to tear myself away from my old, safe life. I chose to move here, right out in the desert, dry grit underfoot and the dusty taste of sand in my mouth. I chose to flee from city lights that drowned out the stars, from soulless and sterile suburban streets. Away from Phoenix, where they do all they can to curb the reality of the desert. Oh, they want it close enough – framed, picturesque – like something they can hang on their walls and admire. But not so close that it threatens their comfort. So they pour their concrete over the sand, they plant their palm trees and perfect green lawns. They escape to their swimming pools, or manicured golf courses – man-made oases, insulated, shielded from the uncomfortable reality of the dry, harsh land.

Here, there is no such protection. The Superstition

Wilderness is rugged terrain. The Superstition Mountains do not bother with foothills: born of eruptions of fire and light, their jagged peaks thrust upwards from the flat desert floor and tower to a height of six thousand feet. These are no soft, green mountains with towering pines to give shelter and shade. Pitiless, this desert provides no such respite. Out there, there is nowhere to hide. The sun shines down on you fiercely, illuminating all your hollowed-out emptiness, casting far too much light on your daily fumblings for adequacy.

I've marooned myself in a place with few frills, a terrain that is stripped right down to the bones. But I dare not confront that landscape yet. I stay inside. Inside and safe, in my silent, dark cave.

It didn't take long to find the house; I knew exactly where I wanted to be. I'd always loved the Superstitions, with their legends of mystery and hidden gold. Adam and I used to go there for weekends – we'd head out north on the Apache Trail and drive all the way to Apache Lake. He kept an eighteen-foot bow rider moored there; sold it about a year ago. He could never seem to find the time any more to take a full weekend away from work.

On the morning after I told Adam that I was leaving him, I headed out to a local firm of movers and took away some packing cartons. It took only a few hours to box up what I owned. I did it quickly and efficiently, trying not to look at what I was packing, trying not to pore over the residues of our life together. But then most of what I was packing was just clothes and the contents of my study – old boxes of photographs, and books and music that were very much my own. There was so little, really, that we'd shared. The furniture, like the house, belonged mostly to Adam, and there was nothing there that I wanted. Six boxes filled with my old china and glasses still sat, unopened, in the closet. So all that I had to take with me now were a couple of old pine dining chairs, a large cherry-wood sea-captain's trunk and a chunky coffee table made from reclaimed oak. A lamp created from an old copper fire extinguisher, a few small folk-art paintings of desert scenes, and some pieces of bright Mexican pottery that I'd managed to secrete around the house in a vain attempt to make it seem more like home.

I left the packed cartons there in my study; I'd make arrangements to collect them later. And before he came back home that evening, I was gone. Out on the road with a heady sense of freedom, and some basic necessities loaded in the trunk. As I drove away from Scottsdale through the Friday afternoon traffic, I felt no regret at all. Just an odd sense of lightness, the much-longed-for feeling of a burden being lifted off my back. I turned on the radio, and for the first time in so very many years there was no-one looking over my shoulder. Nobody judging me, present or not. I switched from Adam's favourite public radio to a local country music station, grinning all the while like a naughty child. I didn't have to care that he thought country music uncool. I didn't have to care that he thought it was for hicks. I sang along with all the songs, whether I knew them or not. I tapped my left foot and slapped my thigh and on the outskirts of Mesa, as if in acknowledgement, they played Trisha Yearwood's 'Hello, I'm Gone'. I threw my head back, and I laughed. Just after evening fell I was comfortably installed in the Cactus Tree Motel outside Apache Junction; I slept for eleven hours straight.

The next morning I cruised through the strip malls in town, looking for a realtor's office, in search of someplace to rent. All I knew was that I wanted a house I could make my own – even for just a few short months. Till I figured out what the hell I was going to do now. And at the second office that I found I looked in the window and there it was: a small Santa Fe-style house, nestling at the base of the mountains.

I found the realtor at her desk, a large woman with a wide smile and a sleepy black dog at the side of her chair.

'Hey, there. I'm Marylou Peebles.' She pulled herself up from the desk, came around and took my hand in a firm grip. All the while, looking at me in that way realtors have, flicking up and down and away again, assessing. Well, she wouldn't be able to tell much from a pair of beige chinos and a black tee-shirt. I don't do designer handbags and the trainers on my feet were chosen for comfort, not to impress. 'How can I help you today?'

'Hi. I was wondering about the house that's for rent – the one in the window. In Gold Canyon?'

'Oh, yes. The Alvarez house. Well now – let me just pull up the listing and print out the details for you.' She bustled back around her desk and sat down, tapping away at her computer. 'It only became available a couple of days ago and hasn't been advertised properly yet, so you're just about the first to inquire.' She passed me the sheet of details, warm from the printer and smelling of ink. As I quickly looked it over she confirmed that the house was available on a minimum six-month let. It was unfurnished, and apart from the owner's house next door it was perfectly secluded. A mile down a dirt road, right on the edge of Gold Canyon. With uninterrupted views of the mountains, and surrounded by undeveloped desert.

'It sounds ideal. I'm looking for somewhere quiet.'

Another assessing glance at my left hand: no ring. 'It's just for yourself?'

'Yes.' I threw her a forbidding glance from under my eyebrows; my life story wasn't part of the deal.

'Well, I reckon that's the best way. I read the other day that women living by themselves are healthier and live longer than women who are married. So that probably means you're smarter than I am.' Her sudden burst of laughter startled me, and the chair creaked loudly as she settled back into it. The dog raised his head briefly from the floor to see if he'd missed anything, then glanced up at me with profound disinterest before sighing loudly and settling back down to sleep. 'It's not a huge house,' she continued. 'It's real well-appointed, but it's cosy. You wouldn't rattle around in it, anyway, all by yourself. You want to go have a look?'

'Sure. If you have the time.'

'No problem. A colleague is due to arrive any minute, so I won't be leaving the place unattended for long.'

She locked up the office; we got into her car – the dog, yawning, climbed into the back seat and took up sleeping right where he left off – and headed out of town. We pulled off Interstate 60 into Gold Canyon, turning out to the east as we came near the end of King's Ranch Road. After a few more twists and turns we drove down a dirt track and a mile or so later came to a dead end. Ahead of us, two identical small houses were set well apart from each other, each surrounded by a neat yard filled with cacti and native shrubs. And beyond the houses, only desert. A primitive place, still, where tall saguaros stand sentinel against the ravages of time and erosion.

'That's where the owner lives,' Marylou said, pointing to the house on our right. 'Maria Mercedes Alvarez. She's an artist – sells locally and in Phoenix, I believe. Folk art, mostly. Paintings, and some statues. She also does some kind of herbalism or something – I'm not real sure. Some kind of therapy, anyway. Real nice lady – you'll like her. Specified a single person – preferably a woman. Maybe a couple. No children, no dogs.' She looked around ruefully at the enormous black Labrador, stretched out and snoring on the back seat. 'Not that a fella like Sam here would be any trouble. But she likes peace and quiet. For her work, and all.'

We stepped out of the car to an apparent silence, but gradually the daytime sounds of the desert began to filter into my consciousness. Birds flitted from tree to tree; insects buzzed and rattled on the ground, and lizards scuttled through the undergrowth. Bees and butterflies swooped around the early yellow blossoms of a paloverde in the yard. 'Sure is quiet out here,' Marylou commented, leading the way down the gravelled drive to the thick wooden front door. 'Too many bugs and critters and not enough people. I prefer to be a little closer to town, myself. But this is what you're looking for, right?'

We stepped into a good-sized entrance hall with several honey-coloured wooden doors leading off it. She opened the door to the left of the hall, and we walked into an open-plan kitchen, dining and living area. Oak boards covered the floor, and the rough-plastered walls glowed in a rich shade of terracotta. The kitchen units were painted deep forest green, with worktops of maple and rich brown granite. Large windows with slatted wooden shutters lit up the kitchen space, and a pair of glazed doors in the living area looked out onto a clear view of the mountains and desert. There was a small adobe fireplace in one corner, complete with a basket filled with logs. Two doors on the other side of the hall led to two compact bedrooms with built-in closets. One, painted a pale pinkish shade of terracotta, looked out to the desert at the back of the house; the other, a rich sage green, looked out to the front yard. There was a small bathroom at the back, its walls painted a vivid lapis lazuli blue – a perfect contrast to the white suite and terracotta-tiled floor.

A week later I moved in.

That first week, before I moved, was easy: there were so many things to keep me busy. Furniture to buy, and rugs. Pots and pans and crockery and bedlinen. I wore myself out shopping during the day and fell into a deep dreamless sleep at night. It wasn't till the day after I moved in that the problems really began.

'Hello?'

'Hi. It's me. Cat.'

'Cat?' She sounded surprised; it's not often that I call her, and certainly never during the week when normally I'd be at work. 'Hello, darling. How are you?'

'I'm fine.' Another pause as I desperately began to wish I'd rehearsed something. I didn't know what to say.

'Great. I was just thinking about you, actually. I was talking to one of my neighbours. Not Meg; Ishbel. She lives along the road a way, and she goes to Meg's storytelling circle. I don't think I've mentioned her before, have I? Anyway – she came to have a cup of tea, isn't that nice? – people are so nice here, when you get to know them. I'd forgotten that. How welcoming they can be, here in the Highlands. It's not at all the image people have of Scotland, you know. Anyway – I was telling her that you were learning to fly, and she said, "Oh," she said, "my grandson is in the air force," and –'

'Mother.'

'– I said, "Well, isn't that funny? It must be the in thing to do these days," and she laughed, though he'd be much younger than you, of course, because she must be around my age or maybe more, and he's her grandson. Anyway. She said that he'd learned –'

'Mother!'

Silence. 'What's the matter?'

'I just called to let you know something. I needed to tell you something.'

'You did? Oh. Well. I'm sorry. I never thought... Go on, then.'

And if I'd been honest about it, I'd have realised exactly why it was that she 'never thought'. Because when was the last time that I rang specifically to give her news? Probably when I told her I was leaving for America, ten years ago. Hi, Mother, how are you? And oh, by the way, I'm leaving the country. Probably for good. But of course, I wasn't being honest about it, and already the irritation was beginning to build.

I closed my eyes; jumped in. 'I've left Adam.'

Another pause. And then, 'You've what?'

'I've left Adam. Moved out. I'm living somewhere else now. It wasn't working.' There was a deep, deep silence on the other end of the line, so I exhaled and pressed on. 'And I quit my job, as well.'

'You did *what?* You left Adam *and* you left your job?' I could picture her struggling, just as I was struggling, trying to find the right words to say. But she's never been all that good at restraining herself. If she wants to say it, she'll say it. Don't think about the consequences – just say it. That's my mother. 'What on earth for? Whatever are you going to do now? For God's sake, Cat – what is going on?'

'I hate my job. I've hated it for a long time. I need to find something else to do with my life. Even if it's still being a lawyer. But something more ... I don't know ... meaningful. When I first qualified I wanted to specialise in human rights. Maybe I'll try to do that again, I don't know. Or maybe I'll do something entirely different. Maybe I'll become a flying instructor.' I have no idea why I said that; it was the furthest thing from my mind. It was just something to say, something to throw out there. But of course, it was precisely the thing that she jumped on.

'A flying instructor? Now I know you're mad. You haven't even passed your test yet. You don't even know whether you're going to pass your test. It's far too dangerous. And you're a lawyer, for heaven's sake. All those qualifications. You can't just throw them away.'

'I can if I want to.' I might just as well have stamped my foot. 'I can, if I hate it.'

'And what are you going to live on? Have you thought of that?'

Had I thought of that? Oh no, not me. Me, think of that? It's not as if I'd been taking responsibility for worrying about what I – what we – were going to live on since I was seven years old. Not at all. It wasn't me who stole money from your purse and hid it so there'd be something left to pay the coalman and buy the groceries after you'd spent what you had on whisky. Not me.

For the first time in days a stray spasm clutched at my throat and suddenly it seemed that I didn't have the strength for this. For the first time that I could remember, I didn't feel strong enough to deal with this. I felt something begin to crack inside me; I wanted to throw the telephone to the ground and curl up in a tight little ball and wail. I struggled to keep my voice firm and steady. 'I have money. I haven't even paid rent for five years. I have savings. I'm not proposing to never work again. I'm just taking a break.'

'And what about poor Adam?'

'Interesting, that you should assume it's "poor Adam" rather than "poor Cat".'

'Oh, come on, Cat. I know you. You're always –'

'No.' To my utter horror I found myself almost shouting. 'You don't know me. You never really did.' You were too wrapped up in yourself, I wanted to yell. Far too engrossed in your own problems. Did you ever even wonder what I was feeling? Did you ever even wonder how it all affected me?

All of it building again and I didn't know whether it would ever go and I was so very, very tired of it weighing me down. I took a deep, shuddering breath and closed my eyes tight shut against the deafening silence in the background.

'Listen,' I managed after a moment. 'It doesn't matter. That's just how it is. Unlikely as it might seem, I do know what I'm doing.' Did I? 'I haven't done too badly with my life so far, have I? I was just calling to let you know what's happened. I'll send you my new contact details soon. Okay?'

'Okay.' She hesitated. 'Cat. I'm sorry. I never seem to handle these things well, do I? I overreact. It's just that…' She trailed off; sighed. 'I worry about you. All the way over there. When I can't see you. I can't look at you. I don't know if you're really all right. And I know perfectly well that you wouldn't tell me if you weren't.'

Something lost and desolate in her voice pulled at me and made me want to weep. I know that voice, too. I know that voice all too well. 'I'm all right. It's taking some getting used to, but I'm all right. I know it all seems very sudden, but it really wasn't. It's been building for a while. It's something I had to do. Listen – I need to go now. I'll be in touch, okay?'

I came away from the telephone call wrung out and exhausted. It had ended in anger, as it so often does. And then the anger turned to despair and guilt set in and the long, slow slide began.

Three long weeks have passed since I moved here. Three weeks in which I have emerged from this cocoon only to sneak down to Basha's for soup and cereal and fruit and milk in an effort to force something light into a stomach that recoils from the very idea of food. And to fly. Apart from those times, I have gone to ground. I have spoken to no-one and seen no-one. I've sat and stared into shady corners; I've ridden out the storms that sweep right into me, with their black-and-blue skies and the twisters that tear up and rip your insides and leave you quite empty and eerily still. I have let it all happen; I have let myself be. I haven't fought it at all. But there's a hole inside me now – a big empty space that my old life used to occupy.

I don't know, yet, what will fill it.

I take a long, hot shower, throw down a bowl of Fruit & Fiber, and drive to the airport through the rush-hour traffic. Today will be my first cross-country. We planned it two days ago, plotting our course on the sectional chart. A simple flight down to Tucson: easy to plan, and just as easy to fly – or so Jesse tells me. There are no major obstacles to skirt around, just a straight

300

course: seventy-five nautical miles south-south-east on a true bearing of one-five-four degrees. An ideal first cross-country. And I'm excited: this is the first time we've flown so far away from Chandler. It feels as if I'm being let out of a cage. At last, instead of just flying around in circles, we're embarking on a journey.

Jesse looks at me carefully when I arrive – just as he always does these days. But he asks no questions, no matter how deep the shadows under my eyes. I have told him, of course, about my changed circumstances, though it was surprisingly difficult to find the words on that first Saturday after I left Adam. I waited till we were out by the plane, doing our pre-flight. We were taking up a different aircraft that day: Five Seven Four Yankee Mike. It was another glorious early spring morning – still and cool and perfectly clear.

'Jesse,' I began – and then I stopped. What should I tell him? Did he really need to know? Well, yes, of course he needed to know. What if anything should happen to me? – Well, yes. He needed to know.

He turned to look at me, faraway eyes soft in anticipation of the flight to come. 'Mmm?'

I glanced away again, suddenly nervous. 'I just thought you ought to know. I've – given up my job. Left home, too. Moved out.'

'Ah.' A flicker of light in his eyes. There for a moment and just as quickly gone.

'It's just that – well. If I seem a little strange sometimes. You know.'

He nodded; his eyes didn't leave my face.

'But it means I can be a bit more flexible when I fly. So I thought I'd try two lessons a week and maybe one solo. Or the other way around, when I need more solo time. If that's okay with you.'

He nodded again.

'I don't want to push it too hard. But I figure if I can concentrate on this for a while – just concentrate on this – then I'll buy myself time to figure out what to do.'

'Makes sense.'

'It does?' I blinked. I had been fighting off a stream of voice messages on my cellphone from concerned people who thought I had clearly gone crazy. And yet there he was, looking right at me as if what I'd just done was perfectly normal.

Almost as if he'd been expecting it.

'Sure it does. You need breathing space.' He shrugged. 'There's nothing like flying to give you breathing space.'

It was my turn now to just nod.

'So where did you move to?'

'I found a house yesterday, in Gold Canyon. I wanted to get away from the city. Away from Scottsdale.'

'You never seemed like a Scottsdale kind of person to me.'

'I didn't?' Tears hovered not too far below the surface. Ridiculously, it seemed as if that was the nicest thing anyone had said to me in a long, long time.

He just smiled – same old enigmatic lop-sided smile. 'Gold Canyon's a good place. I live out near Apache Junction.'

'You do?' In all the time we'd been flying together, it had never occurred to me to ask where he lived. It's not that he's not approachable. It's just that – well, this is a professional relationship. Apart from the few times it's trickled out in the context of talking about flying, we don't really do personal.

'I was raised in the mountains; I still find it hard to do without them. I live close to the base of Superstition Mountain. Just off Mountain View Road.' He paused, and as always, his eyes drifted inexorably back up to the sky. 'Well, shall we get going?'

And that was all there was to it. Yet I had the sense that if I'd wanted to say more, he'd have listened. Jesse always listens. Listens more than he talks. And watches.

Just as he's watching me now.

'Pretty morning for it.' I smile.

He nods slowly, as if I've answered his unspoken question.

'Sure is. Got your charts?'

'Yup. Charts, timer, plotter, calculator...' I pat my bright blue Sporty's flight bag, slung over my shoulder.

'Filed your flight plan?'

'All done – telephoned it in just before I left. Weather report looks just fine.'

'Then let's go fly.'

There's a wind from the east that's pushing us off course; I learn how to correct for it by crabbing the airplane so that the nose is pointing into the wind. On the way out I concentrate fiercely on the route that we've plotted on the sectional chart, grappling with the effort that it takes to stay on a specific course rather than just heading out in some vague general direction. I learn to look for landmarks and relate them to the markings on the chart. And there aren't very many of them out here: a couple of lone peaks, a handful of airports: Casa Grande, Coolidge, Eloy, Pinal. But we can see Interstate 10 down to our right with its steady stream of traffic and the endless stretches of strip malls that have sprung up so rapidly between Tucson and Phoenix. As we approach Picacho Peak our course crosses over I-10, and then it's a straight line on down to Ryan.

One of the many good things about the emptiness of the desert is that it's almost always easy to spot the airports: there isn't a whole lot that competes for your attention. Which is just as well, because my attention is completely taken up in dealing with a new air traffic control routine, as well as Jesse's insistence that we cross-check our navigation using the non-directional beacon on the field. I split my awareness between what I can see outside of the aircraft and the needle on the ADF dial that I'm using to track the radial into the airport – trying to compensate for the mild cross-wind coming from the south-east. I'm nervous at first, trying to judge what's happening at this unfamiliar place. It takes me a while to recognise the runway configuration, to work out which runway I'm aiming for as I follow the tower's instructions and finally manage to enter the traffic pattern for six left without too many problems. Jesse is mostly silent, leaving me to it as much as he can, answering briefly when I ask him a question. It's disconcerting, landing on a runway that you don't know: all of the usual visual cues are changed. So it isn't the smoothest landing I've ever done – out of the corner of my eye I see Jesse wince as the main gear slam down onto the asphalt – but at least it's a safe one.

There's no reason to hang around once we're down: neither of us needs a comfort stop and we have enough fuel to get us home, so we simply make our way back to the runway and line up behind three other aircraft for takeoff. Once we're established on the course back home, mission half-accomplished, I begin to relax.

From time to time on the way home, I sneak a peek at Jesse. He is, so very clearly, literally in his element when he's flying. He gets that faraway glaze in his eyes, a translucent reflection of space and peaceful emptiness, blemished only by an occasional flare of joy – the pure, almost transcendental joy that he derives from dancing through the skies on these ever-changing currents of air.

'Well, that wasn't so bad, was it?'

I turn to him and smile. 'Not at all bad. In fact, it was fun.'

'You did good. Another achievement to cross off your list. You're building them up right now.'

And it does seem that way. We've covered pretty much all the manoeuvres that we need to cover, though I'm still going to need plenty of practice to get them up to standard. I still hate stalls, but at least I can do them now. We've practised short-field and soft-field takeoffs and landings, and faked emergency descents. I'm not doing too badly at turns around a point and my S-turns are looking quite good too. We're just getting into navigation, but by the time we've completed all of the dual and solo cross-countries that are required before you can qualify to take your test, I should be quite comfortable with all of that. What I really need now is more time in the air – and especially, more solo time. To build my confidence, as well as hone my technique. I'm happy to practise all of those manoeuvres with Jesse beside me, but I still get a little nervous when I'm by myself.

'And I see you're looking down a little more these days.'

'Got to. Can't see where you're going if you don't look down.'

He laughs, a low, soft sound in my ears through the headset. I shiver. 'Like what you see?'

'It's pretty flat, but it has a charm all of its own.'

Ah, but it's more than just charm. There is a stark beauty – such a sense of simplicity – in flying over the desert. It's not just the sharp clarity of the sky: the landscape itself is austere. You look down below, see the geometric forms of the land and the rocks, and the vast arid emptiness cuts through the clutter of your tiny, everyday thoughts. This is what flying means to me, now that I'm over the worst of the fear. And if I think – as so often I do – about what I've accomplished these past five months, it's as if every takeoff has been part of a lesson in learning to let go. Learning to let go of all the old fears, learning to let go of all the old patterns. Because there is no room for them in the sky. Flying demands a perfect, pure concentration. If you slip, you fall. If you panic, you die. And so you focus with all your strength and with all your will and with all your heart. You keep yourself in the sky by the sheer power of your belief that you can, and in the purity of this focus you begin to lose sight of all that might previously have held you back. You let the old life slowly begin to melt away. And the process of transformation that ensues is redolent of an old, old alchemy. It begins with a perfect dissolution of the self: molecules of Catriona spinning out across the desert sky. But now that I have begun to be dissolved, how shall I reassemble myself? What form shall I take when I return to earth, as all flying mortals must?

Now at the end of my lessons I take a different direction home. I drive away from Phoenix: away from the city, away from my former life; I turn east on highway 60 rather than west. There is a whole world's worth of difference.

When I pull up into my driveway, Maria Mercedes is in her yard. I slip out of the car, intending as usual to wave and to smile and just walk right on by. There's no good reason to avoid her, other than the fact that I avoid everyone right now. I've only spoken to her once. On the day that I moved in she paid a brief visit and brought me the gift of a loaf of bread – soft and white, and scented with rosemary and garlic and sage. She shook my hand and we exchanged names; that was about all I was ready for back then. She invited me to come and have coffee with her one day, and said that I should ask if there was anything I needed. She was friendly but not pushy; I was grateful for that. I've seen her from time to time; she waves and says hello, but she doesn't intrude. I slip by her like a shadow. She's quiet over there, though some days she has visitors; people of all ages arrive one by one, stay for an hour or two and then just as quietly leave. Maybe they're something to do with her therapy business – the one that the realtor alluded to.

I steal a longer glance at her now, and for the first time notice that there's something that looks like a shrine right in the corner of her yard by the house. She's over there next to it, kneeling down on the paving slabs, rearranging objects in a cave-like niche built into the stucco-coated wall. It's too far away for me to make out individual items, but the outline of a tall statue right at the back catches my eye. Curious, I hesitate for a moment on the drive; she turns and sees me watching her. A wide smile splits her face.

'Hey there,' she calls. 'How you doing? You settling in?'

I nod, walk over to the low ranch-style fence that divides the two houses. 'I think I'm getting there.'

She smiles as my eyes drift back to the shrine. 'You're wondering about my *gruta*?'

'The statue,' I say, embarrassed to be caught staring. 'I was just curious about the statue.'

'*La Virgen*. The Virgin of Guadalupe.' Of course; I should have known. 'Do you know the story?'

'Not really.'

Slowly, she lifts herself off the ground and brushes the pervasive desert dust from her black flowing skirt. 'You want a glass of iced tea? Come on over, have a look.'

The late spring air is cool in the breeze, but as I step out from the shade of the house the sun nuzzles my shoulders, warm and soothing. I close my eyes for a moment; take a long, slow breath, inhaling the sun and the warm clean smell of the desert. Tentatively, I push open the gate between the two houses and walk into Maria Mercedes' garden. It's surprisingly beautiful. There are the usual native shrubs: prickly pear cactus, agave and jojoba, and a couple of paloverde trees now in full bloom. The ocotillos – like a group of giant spiders turned on their back – are just beginning to blossom: red buds like painted toenails at the tips of long spindly legs that wave in the breeze. But in this garden there is more: there are raised beds filled with dark soil and grit and edged with terracotta tile. In those beds there are herbs: rosemary and rue, sweet bay and sage, and many other plants that I don't recognise. Terracotta pots of mint and lavender huddle in small groups, and a grapevine feels its way along a trellis at the side of the porch. Twittering birds and insects scatter as I brush by the blossoming shrubs.

By the time I reach the house Maria Mercedes is bustling out with a pitcher of iced tea and two glasses which she sets on an old wooden table on the porch. She gestures in the direction of a white-painted wicker chair and I sit down, gratefully accepting a glass from her. 'Cheers.'

She grins, sits down at the other side of the table. '*Salud.*'

The tea is cool, fresh and fragrant with lemon and a sprig of mint. She watches me with unashamed interest as I drink. I return her gaze. She's around my own age, I'd guess: forty, maybe forty-five. Short and slightly on the plump side, dressed in a poppy-red tee-shirt; glossy black hair threaded lightly with grey flows long and loose down her back. She looks at home in this place in a way that I, with my blonde hair and too-pale skin, do not.

I break away and stare into my glass, mindlessly clinking the ice cubes together. It's been a long time since I made polite conversation.

Maria Mercedes steps into the gap. 'So. Tell me something about yourself.'

I shrug; I hate open-ended questions like this. 'I'm a lawyer,' I begin – then it suddenly seems sad that my instant reaction is to define myself by profession – confine myself by profession – and the hesitant words slink away.

But how else should I define myself? Who else can I say that I am?

'You're not working now?'

'No. I left my job.' And it's odd. Because under normal circumstances I hate to talk about myself: that age-old habit of concealment. *Mustn't tell anyone, Cat. Just tell them Mummy's sick. Mustn't ever tell; mustn't give yourself away.* But when I look at Maria Mercedes there is something in her that prompts me to continue. Something about her ... slices into you. Sees. She has the same quality that Jesse has – that same intense concentration, that ability to put all of her focus into listening.

But she's not really like Jesse; she doesn't have the same characteristic of – oh, I don't know – stillness, maybe. She is lively, bird-like, her head tilting from side to side, eyes gleaming and intense. I take a deep breath. 'And I left my partner.' I smile wryly. 'I suppose I had a kind of midlife crisis.'

She shakes her head vigorously. 'No, no. I hate that term. Makes it sound so trivial, when these changes are so natural and important a part of life.'

'They are?' Most people see them as a sign of weakness. Or something laughable. I've heard them at work – heard them laugh at the business executives who buy their first Harley at fifty years old. Bambis, they call them: Born-Again Middle-aged Bikers. Searching blindly for their lost youth. *Oh,* they say, *it's his midlife madness. I suppose it could be worse. Better than an affair with another woman.* A midlife crisis is a joke, they say: it's just an excuse for behaving badly. *She'll come around,* they say. *It's just a phase. Just give her time.*

'Sure they are. It's just that most people resist them. Don't take them seriously. Do something trivial to cover up the cracks. And then end up breaking down – or sick, or in hospital.'

Or diagnosed with panic attacks.

And then it occurs to me: tough as it's been, in the three weeks I've been here, the symptoms of panic have mostly died away.

'Change can be good. You've heard of the Navajo goddess Changing Woman?' she asks, and I nod. 'Well, think about it: she's a celebration of change. She's celebrated as a baby, and then a child. She's celebrated as a teenage girl experiencing her first menstruation. She's celebrated as a mother who gives birth to the first humans, who grows older and dies, and finally is reborn. At each stage of the life cycle, she is celebrated. Because everything changes. Change is natural. We have to grow.'

'Well,' I say lightly, 'I'm not sure in my case that it has

anything to do with growth. I seem to be living in a vacuum right now.'

'Ah, but that's how it works. The caterpillar goes into the chrysalis. Forms a hard shell, retreats from the world. It's dark in there, and nothing seems to be happening, but all the while the changes take place. And then one day ... the butterfly.' She smiles, eyes alight with amusement. 'Give it time. These changes don't take effect overnight.'

I flex my toes and look away. Away from the penetrative light in her eyes. I turn my empty glass around in my hands and then place it down on the table. I clear my throat. And then, smiling so as not to offend, I say, 'You've a wonderful collection of herbs. Do you grow them just for pleasure, or do you use them?'

She accepts the change of subject with grace and a slight inclination of the head. 'Both. I use them in my work.' She points above our heads to the roof of the porch; a dozen or so bundles of cut herbs are hanging from the cross-beams to dry.

'What work is that?'

'I am a *curandera*.'

I don't know much Spanish; I shake my head. 'I'm sorry. I don't really know what that is.'

'In my tradition, it is a healer.'

'Ah.' I pause. I've surrounded myself with lawyers and scientists and other rational folk for most of my adult life; the concept of traditional healing isn't one that I'm exactly comfortable with. But she seems sane enough; I decide to give her the benefit of the doubt. 'What kind of healing?'

'*Curanderas* can specialise in different kinds of healing. There are *hierberas*, who work with plants – kind of like herbalists, I suppose. Then there are s*abadoras*, who give massage; *parteras*, who are midwives; *consejeras*, who are counsellors; *espiritualistas*, or mediums, and *hueseros*, a kind of chiropractor. I practise mostly as a counsellor and herbalist.'

'And what kind of problems do you treat?'

'I treat *susto*: soul loss.'

Soul loss?

She grins. 'Sounds dramatic, huh? But that's what we call the sense of being off-balance. The sense of something missing. In our tradition we believe that illness occurs when you don't live in harmony with all aspects of yourself, and with nature. That is what I treat. I try to help my clients to restore balance in their lives.'

I smile wryly. 'Sounds like I could do with some treatment myself.'

She laughs, a chortling infectious laugh that I can't help joining in. 'Well, you know where to find me.'

'And you're an artist, too?'

'A folk artist. One day you should come over and see my studio. But today you've come to see the *gruta*. Come on.'

She puts down her glass; she leads the way around the porch and into the far corner of the yard. She steps to one side, and I see that 'grotto' is a good word for it. It is a small cave-like structure hollowed out of the stucco-plastered wall that is painted the same sandy terracotta as the house. Small pebbles and seashells decorate the outer edges, and the inside is painted a vibrant turquoise. The floor of the opening is covered with a cloth of what looks like homespun wool, bearing beautiful and intricate floral embroidery work.

But I have eyes only for the statue: a woman clothed in a deep turquoise cloak painted with gold stars. There is a half-moon beneath her feet and she wears a dark band around her waist; she looks to be pregnant. She is carved out of wood; her features are plain but surprisingly delicate. Surrounding her are three brightly coloured glasses filled with candles, a small iron pot of incense and a bundle of dried herbs tied with a red ribbon.

Maria Mercedes kneels down to one side, and I follow suit

so that I can see inside properly: the floor of the niche is only a couple of feet from the ground. 'Here she is,' she says. 'This is Our Lady of Guadalupe.'

'She's beautiful. So delicately carved.'

'Thank you.'

'Did you make her?'

She nods and smiles faintly. 'Usually I make statues or images that are simpler in their lines – typical folk art. She seemed to need more attention.' She sighs. 'She took a long time to carve. Making her was a kind of – a meditation, I suppose. At a time when I very much needed to focus on what she meant to me.'

'She's the same as the Virgin Mary? More or less?'

'Not exactly. The legend is told that she appeared to a Mexican Indian called Juan Diego, on Tepeyac hill in Mexico City. She appeared to him as a *mestizo* woman – one of his own people. This was interesting because Tepeyac hill is the location of an old shrine to Tonantzin, the ancient Aztec mother goddess. But Tonantzin's shrine had been demolished by Cortez, and the native people of Mexico were forbidden to make pilgrimages there. Anyway: the Lady made several appearances to Juan Diego, and eventually she asked him to have a church built on the site and dedicated to her.' She reaches out a hand and brushes away a stray petal of paloverde blossom, caught in the sharp ridges of the shells around the shrine. 'Well, he went to the local bishop and asked, but of course the bishop wouldn't do a thing without proof. So the Lady provided the proof: she told Juan Diego to go to a place nearby where he would find roses growing, even though it was winter. She told him to put the roses into his cloak, and to take them to the bishop. When Juan Diego opened his cloak and released the roses in front of the bishop, the Virgin's image was imprinted on the cloak. You can see it still today, in the basilica on Tepeyac hill. The image was just like the statue you see here: a woman standing upon a

half-moon. And the half-moon was the symbol of Tonantzin.'
She looks back at me and smiles. 'So she is something more
than the Virgin Mary. She is a merging of the new world in the
form of Mary, and the old in the form of the goddess Tonantzin.
She belongs to the church, and yet she is a symbol of Mexican
identity and culture – a *mestizo* woman. So she became a
symbol of freedom during the revolution, and to this day she
represents a symbol of empowerment for *chicanas*.'

There's something about the statue that draws me, in a
way that religious statues never usually do. I don't know why.
The half-moon, perhaps. The stars on the cloak. Our Lady of
the Sky; all she needs is a pair of wings. 'And what does she
represent to you?'

Maria Mercedes smiles. 'She is the mother of the world.
That is what she said to Juan Diego: "Am I not here, who is
your mother?" To me, she represents the divine feminine: the
life-giver. The great mother goddess who can heal the wounds
of the past.'

An unthinking small shake of my head: a reflex. Maria
Mercedes catches it, and nods.

'Ah. To you, that's not such a positive image, motherhood?
But you see, that is the point. Especially in countries like
Mexico where life can be hard. Everybody wants to be the
perfect mother. Everyone wants to have the perfect mother.
But who can be perfect? Who can be perfect, when the world
is hard and you struggle so, just to survive? That's what I think
of when I look at her. I see every mother who ever looked at
her child and knew that however much she tried, she would
never be enough. I see all of the suffering mothers in the
world. More than that: I see all those who love and yet feel
insufficient. I think she understands.' She turns to me and
smiles, and something in her eyes is both understanding and sad.

There is another story in the bundle of mail that I collected

313

on my way back into the house after I said goodbye to Maria Mercedes. There hasn't been one for such a long time. I thought you'd given it up. I *expected* that you'd given it up; after all, giving up is what you do best, isn't it? Looking for oblivion rather than facing up to all that was wrong with your life. Rather than doing something about it.

Oh, it's all very well for Maria Mercedes to talk about everyone wanting the perfect mother. Excuses, it seems to me. All excuses. I never wanted perfect, but just a *mother* would have been nice, sometimes.

And yet … I had a mother, in those early years. I do remember, you know. You and I, walking along the shore, my hand clutched tightly in yours. 'Look,' you'd say, pointing out into the distance. 'Your daddy's out there. All the way out to sea. Catching fish so that you can have some for your tea. And so that he can sell them to other people, to look after us. Look – all the way out there, he is. Can you imagine, little Cat? Isn't he brave? Aren't you proud?'

And in spite of it all, I was proud. Proud of you both. Proud of my pretty mummy with her dark curly hair and dark, flashing eyes. Proud of my tall, handsome daddy, who would pick me up and swing me round and round in his arms and take me down to the harbour sometimes, down to his boat with its strong briny smell of old fish and the other men laughing down at me and calling me Pussy-Cat. Proud of my daddy, God damn him to hell.

I was so like him, wasn't I? Still am, I guess, though I haven't seen a photograph of him for years now. Not of him; certainly not of his new family. But when I look back at those old photographs now, I can see how it was that whenever you looked at me you saw his face. I reminded you of him. Constantly. Did I only remind you of the bad times? Because there were good times, too. Good times together. You and Daddy climbing the Ullapool hill, and me on his shoulders, towering above the whole world. The two of you laughing, giggling like children in the bedroom next to mine. Pulling me onto your bed and tickling me as I peeked through the open door, wanting to join in. Did you see that too, when you looked at me? Or did you only ever see what he did to you?

Yes, I was so like him. And you never let me forget it, did you? *Just like your father. You're just like him, as hard as nails. Don't you dare shout at me; who do you think you are, your father? Don't you dare lose your temper with me. Don't you dare get angry in my house.*

No, anger was never an option. And so all these years, it's been hiding inside of me – eating me away. The big bad monster, waiting to gobble me up.

But it's not anger that I need now. There's been too much anger. What I need now is to let it all slide away. I need to let it go.

12

Laura

Laura sighs loudly at the kitchen table, and reaches for the lukewarm mug of tea by the side of her laptop. She can't get started today. Everything's so quiet here in wintertime. Silence surrounds her, penetrates her, sets up an aching in her heart and most days she just doesn't know what to do with herself.

For a moment, the silence is broken by a slow, mechanical rumble along the road behind the house. Sandy's tractor, Laura imagines. Sandy Jock. So called because there are two other Sandy Mackenzies in the family, and so each of them is differentiated by the addition of another name to their own. Sandy Jock, by the addition of his father's Christian name. Sandy Stalker, because that's his job. And Sandy Broch because he was born in the house just below the broch along the road. Laura is still bemused by the fact that two of the three Sandys married women called Ishbel, and so their wives too became Ishbel Stalker and Ishbel Jock.

Few people along this road seem to be known by the name they were given at birth. Kenny Macrae along the road is called Digger, for reasons that she's never been able to fathom and that even Meg can't explain. Old Willy Munro is known as 'the Finnock', and Laura managed one day to extract the story from Meg. All to do with some apocryphal tale that he'd spun to his friends when he was a teenager, about wrestling with a giant fish in the sea-pool down at Clachan.

So many stories in this place. Stories new and old hover in the air and seep into lives as the rain on the wind seeps through clothes and into skin. 'The old stories tell truths about our lives,' Meg says. 'Stories that are forged from the landscape, as we also are forged.' This is a place where stories come as easily as breathing.

Unless you are writing the story that Laura is writing.

Mara grew up strong and healthy. She was a beautiful child, and her father was completely besotted with her. He would look down into those big dark blue eyes so like his selkie wife's, and for a little while, would remember how much he had loved her. Remember how she'd looked on the beach that night, beautiful pale skin shining in the moonlight. Life became easier then in the little cottage by the sea, and the selkie woman began to bloom again. But time passed, and he fell once again into his old ways. Times were hard at sea; the fish seemed to avoid his nets, and the responsibility of providing for a family ate away at him. His anger and frustration grew.

And eventually it became the case that, when he came home at night, the child would change. She would become silent, and stay close to her mother.

The front door slammed behind Alec as he came home from work, and Laura flinched. Cat looked up at her mother, a flash of apprehension in her eyes. Laura sent her a smile that was intended to be reassuring, but she knew that fear had been added to the pain reflected on her face. Another cramp took hold of her and she clutched at her stomach, head down to her knees, and groaned. The waves began to recede just as Alec walked into the sitting room. She pulled herself upright into a sitting position on the sofa and tried to smile.

'Hello, darling.'

He loomed in the doorway, dark-faced and sullen. 'What's all this, then?'

Still breathing heavily, waiting for the next wave of agony to come along, she opened her mouth to explain. He didn't give her time.

'What are you doing lying around at this time of the day in your dressing gown? Only a slut would be still in her dressing gown at this time of day.'

'I'm not still in my dressing gown. I only just changed into it a couple of hours ago. I haven't been well, I –'

'You're always fecking unwell. For Christ's sake, Laura, can't you pull yourself together? I've been out working all day in the wind and the rain, and you haven't even got my tea started.'

He waited for an answer but Laura couldn't speak: the clawing cramp in her pelvis had begun again and the force of it literally took her breath away.

'Are you listening to me? Sitting there like a tragedy queen, all pale and pathetic. Like the useless slut that you are.'

Laura felt tears begin as the sweat broke out again on her brow. She was too weak to move; she'd been enduring the cramps for over two hours now and they'd just plain worn her out. Cold sweats, hot sweats. She'd thought of going up to bed but lying down only seemed to make things worse and besides, she hadn't wanted to leave Cat alone.

'Alec –' She cried out as another wave hit her and she clutched herself and bent double.

'Mummy –' Cat began, and started over to Laura, but Alec turned on her.

'You go up to your room.'

Cat shook her head and stood her ground, but Laura could see the fear in her eyes. Dear God, she thought. Dear God.

'Get up to your room, or I'll tan your hide!' He stalked over to Cat and took her roughly by the arm. She didn't cry out but Laura could see that he was hurting her. She tried to get up off the sofa to go to her but she couldn't – her legs were too weak. The cold sweat was coming again and the cramp and all she could do was shiver and moan. Alec shoved Cat out of the room and Laura came over so dizzy that she almost fainted. She watched his feet coming towards her, almost in slow motion. Still in his black outdoor boots, white with salt and smeared with fish scales.

'Well?' His voice was low now. 'What have you got to say for yourself?'

'I'm sorry, Alec. I can't help it. My period –'

'You and your fecking periods! I'm tired of them! That's all I hear from you. How ill you are. How much pain you're in. What use are you, with a womb that can't even carry children to term and gets you into this state every fucking month? A pathetic excuse for a woman, that's what you are.'

Laura looked up just far enough to see his fists clenched by the side of his legs. They clenched and he flexed them and they clenched again. Please God, no, she whispered as the first blow caught her on the side of her head. 'A pathetic slut.' The second blow spun her head around and she saw Cat, a flash of purple dress, cowering behind the open door with her hands over her mouth. She tried to push herself upright, to go to her, but the pain took her again and she fell to her side on the sofa and then Alec's boot left the floor and caught her in the pelvis just as the wave took hold of her and she heard herself scream, and that was the last thing she remembered until she came to and Alec was gone, and Cat was standing over her and crying. 'Mummy, Mummy. Please don't die, Mummy.'

Laura is shaking. Carefully, she moves the mouse and presses 'save'.

She takes a deep, shuddering breath and looks out at the day that now has turned as grey as she feels. So many monotonous grey days. Is this all that is left to her now – grey? Grey for age. Grey for the thinning hair that is left behind in clumps on her pillow each morning. Grey for the slow loss of passion and increasing inability to feel – except for past emotions. Oh, she can feel *them*, all right.

Grey, all grey.

She stands stiffly and walks over to the kettle. She supposes that she needs to eat lunch, but she can't imagine what she might want. Too hard a decision; all too hard.

She opens the door of the fridge, looks inside for inspiration. Half a packet of ham; might as well have that. A ham sandwich: how very original.

How very grey.

It's frightening, all this grey. Day after grey day to be filled. To be lived, quiet, watching the loch, watching the rain lashing the fields. Alone. With nothing to aim for, nothing even to live for. What's my goal now? she thinks. Death? A long, slow descent into death, blaming everyone else for whatever pain I've experienced in my life? Blaming Aunt Lizzie, blaming Alec, blaming Cat? And all the while, looking for others to fill me emotionally because there's nothing inside me to feed on? There's no source of nourishment inside of me. It's empty. And anyway – isn't it too late now, to fill myself up? It's late, and there's so little time.

But then she thinks of Meg: nearly eighty years old and still going strong. Laura could live that long. She doesn't think it's likely: she's subjected her body to way too much abuse over the years. But it's certainly possible. She could suffer through another ten, twenty years of this suspended animation. Each winter day dawning duller and greyer, and only the sullen loch for a background. A house filled with shadows, and echoes of ghosts in the lamplight.

And what is it, exactly, that she's doing now, writing this story from hell? What does she hope to achieve? – flicking through the filing cabinets in her mind and finding only nightmares. Sorting through all the memories. All these grim, grim memories.

Sorting: the task given to the heroine in all the best fairy tales. Sorting. Maybe that's the task of old age. Maybe that's what she's doing here. And as in all the best fairy tales, she has no choice but to carry on doing it. The consequences of failure are too great.

A princess sits alone in a cold, empty tower-room and listens to the storm howling outside. The princess is old now; she's been a prisoner here for many, many years. She doesn't know who it is that's kept her prisoner; it's just that she's always known that if she goes to the door and tries to open it, it will remain closed.

Nothing has changed here for many, many years. Until last night. Last night, she had a visitor. A little old woman appeared in the corner of her room – a really old woman, much older than herself. She looked the princess up and down, and shook her head. 'What are you still doing here?' she asked. 'What are you doing here, after all these years?'

Tears would have sprung to the princess's eyes if it hadn't been for the fact that they'd all dried up years ago. 'I don't know how to get out,' she whispered. 'I don't know what to do.' She passed a gnarled, shaking hand over her face. 'At first, you see, I waited for someone to rescue me. There was a prince, years ago. I could see him from the window, if I stood on my little stool and stretched up high and peeped over the ledge. Every morning, he'd ride up and down on his snow-white horse in front of the tower. I tried to call down to him for help, but although he looked up from time to time, I'm not sure that he ever really saw me.' The princess lowers her aching bones onto the three-legged wooden stool by the empty fireplace. There's been no fire in that grate for as long as she can remember. 'There were others, too, as the years went by. Princes and bishops, and even a little girl who used to come and play in the garden from time to time. I waited and I waited, but no-one ever came. No-one ever tried to rescue me. So eventually, I gave up hope. What else could I do?'

The old woman shook her head. 'That's not how the story

is supposed to go,' she said. 'Haven't you figured that out by now? Haven't you understood it yet? No-one else is going to rescue you. You have to rescue yourself.'

'But I don't know how,' whispered the princess. 'And besides, I'm too old now, and tired.'

And the old woman laughed. She opened her mouth and she laughed: a high, thin cackle at first that grew and filled out and eventually transformed itself into a rich, throaty chuckle. And the more she laughed, the younger she became. Younger and younger, the years dropped away until finally she stood before the princess in a pure white gown with garlands of ivy dripping from her golden hair. 'Here's how you escape,' she said. 'Here's how you find your way out. See that cupboard over there?' And she pointed to a shady corner of the tower room, a corner that the princess hadn't ever really noticed before. The room was empty, after all; whyever would she want to explore? But, peering into that corner now, she saw for the first time that there was a door. 'Inside that cupboard,' the golden-haired woman continued, 'you'll find a pile of grain. In fact, it's filled to the brim with grain. Good grain and bad grain, old grain and new. Your job is to sort the grain. Pick out the pieces of spoiled grain: the grain that's mouldy and is of no further use. Pick it out, and burn it on the fire. Then you'll be free.'

'But there is no fire,' said the princess.

'Oh, for heaven's sake,' the golden-haired woman said. 'Can't you figure out anything for yourself? You'll just have to find a way, that's all.'

'But that's going to take me forever,' said the princess. 'And it's late as it is.'

'You don't have forever. You have till tomorrow morning.'

'Tomorrow morning? But that's impossible!'

'Is it?' asked the golden-haired woman. 'Is it really?' And with a final wink at the princess she spun on her heels and vanished in a puff of smoke.

It wasn't long after that Laura left. She had watched anxiety replace laughter in Cat's eyes; she had heard a doctor tell her that Cat's eye problem – the one that meant that she now had to wear glasses – was due to anxiety. He had looked at Laura with his lips tightly pursed together. 'And what is it that the little one has to be anxious about, Mrs Munro?'

She didn't plan it; she knew that if she did, she would lose her nerve. She simply woke up early one morning as she heard the door close behind Alec, and she knew that today was the day that she would go. It was a winter morning, and the house was icy. But this morning she didn't light the fire; she just put the kettle on the stove for tea. She washed and dressed herself quickly. She pulled a suitcase out of the wardrobe and she packed as quickly as she could. She packed only what was essential to her, and what was essential to Cat: clothes, and a small handful of toys that went into a large bag. She hesitated before taking the box of slides and photographs; she might not want them, but perhaps Cat would. It was quickly done – there was so little of her in this house. So little that she wanted to take; so little that she wanted to remember.

Shivering, she sat at the table and wrote a note to Alec. She told him that she was leaving him for Cat's sake, as well as her own. She told him that she was going back home, and that if he attempted to follow her or make any kind of contact with her other than by letter, she would call the police. She told him that she would be consulting a solicitor about a divorce, and that the solicitor would be in contact with him. She suggested that he find a solicitor of his own. She signed her name. Laura.

Then she put her head in her hands and she wept.

A car crunches its way down the gravel drive and pulls up outside. The postman. Hoping for something in the mail that'll divert her, she makes her way to the front door and is waiting there before he can haul his heavy bulk out of the red postal van, puffing and muttering to himself as always. He's holding a small bundle of what looks mostly like junk mail, neatly held together with a red elastic band.

'Fine day it turned out to be.'

'Yes, it is, isn't it? Lovely.' She holds out her hand but, oblivious, he turns to face the rich blue waters of the loch, using the letters as a shield to protect his eyes from the surprising glare of the unexpected late afternoon sun.

'Aye, hardly a cloud in the sky now, so there isn't.' He turns, lowers his hand and examines her appraisingly, taking in the old bobbled cotton sweater and the faded black jogging pants. Her hair hasn't been washed for days and her face is devoid of makeup. His eyes come to rest at her feet and remain there, transfixed by the yellowing, bunion-ridden toe that protrudes through a hole in her red quilted slippers. Embarrassment surges through her; she's letting herself go. There was a time, not so very long ago, when she would have rushed to put lipstick on and comb her hair just to answer the door to the postman. When she wouldn't have dreamed of venturing out beyond the front door without using the best part of a can of hairspray. But these days it seems such an effort just to get herself dressed in the mornings. She really can't summon up the energy to care just what it is, precisely, that she's dressing herself in.

He tears his attention away from her feet and back to her face. 'Settling in then, are you?'

'I am.'

'Don't see you out and about much. On the roads, or in the village.'

'I don't have much need to go out, except for groceries.'

Her defensiveness irritates her, but this is one of the downsides of living in a small place with a tiny population. Anonymity is impossible. Not at all like London. And she so used to love it, the dark reckless anonymity of life in the city. There are so many ways to lose yourself in a city, where the judgements of others are as transient as their friendship. In the city everyone is a stranger, and you're just as faceless as everyone else. You can be anyone you want to be precisely because you're no-one. But in the country, everyone knows who you are. Word travels fast. You're 'that woman who moved into Janet's old croft. All by herself, hiding away down there by the lochside.' Yes, she knows what they say about her. She knows what they're thinking. They think it's odd; they wonder what she's hiding from.

'You don't get lonely, then?'

'No.'

It's a lie, of course, and he seems to know it: he raises an eyebrow and smiles.

'Aye, well, I was just saying to Kenny Joe up the road. She must get lonely sometimes, all by herself and all. Lonely life for a woman all by herself in an old place like that, I said to him.'

In spite of herself Laura's lips twitch in amusement. Kenny Joe is one of the few eligible bachelors in the area. More eligible than most, for sure: a favourite phrase of Aunt Lizzie's pops unbidden into her mind: *I wouldn't have them if their backsides were decked with diamonds.* But every blade of grass stands to attention on Kenny Joe's emerald green lawn; no smear would dare mar the shining windows of his small croft house. He cuts a surprisingly dapper figure, strolling up and down the lane in his grey Harris tweed jacket and flat cap, his elderly border collie ambling along contentedly by his side. Laura pushes the sudden flicker of interest – the sudden familiar flare of hope that springs up in her heart – to one side. She's done with all that, now. Finished with it. Isn't she?

'You shouldn't worry about me. I prefer being by myself.'

He sighs and scratches his head; shifts from foot to foot. Even Willy knows when he's making no headway at all. It's a fine line to walk, though: she doesn't want to offend him. You can't afford to fall out with people in a small place like this and besides, there's no harm in him. Just the natural curiosity of all those who are born and who stay in remote places.

Willy belches loudly, winces and rubs his stomach. 'Aye, well then. I'd best be getting on. Got a letter for Meg today. Fine woman, Meggie. Fine woman.' He risks a hopeful glance over at Laura to see whether Meg is a subject that she might be more prepared to discuss, but it must be clear from the set of her mouth that she's not. He produces a last mournful sigh and hands over her letters. 'Best be off. No time to stand around talking. There's sacks of post to be doled out today, so there is.'

As he lowers himself back into the van and pulls away up the drive, she shuts the door behind him and sifts through the pile of mail. Stops, heart leaping with pleasure, as she sees the postcard. It shows a copper-coloured mountain protruding from the desert floor.

> *Hi,*
>
> *Here's a postcard of Superstition Mountain. This is where I live – right at the bottom of it. I'm doing fine, really: taking some time out and keeping myself busy flying. Hope the winter there hasn't been too dreary. Here I sometimes get reverse seasonal affective disorder: too much blue sky!*
>
> *love,*
> *Cat*

Love? It's a long time since Cat wrote that on a postcard. Or on anything at all. A long, long time.

Laura turns and walks through to the kitchen. It's warm in here: warm from the ever-constant Rayburn, and the afternoon sun that pierces through the morning's gloom and sweeps away the shadows from the corners of the room.

*

When she turned up on Aunt Lizzie's doorstep the next afternoon she was grey-faced and exhausted. Cat was silent beside her; she had been silent for the whole trip. Not once had she asked Laura where they were going; it was almost as if she knew. She had put her hand in her mother's; she had watched her carefully, and she had rested her hand on her mother's knee, almost as if to comfort her. Almost as if to tell her that she understood, and that she was doing the right thing. Fanciful, perhaps, but then Cat so often seemed older than her years.

The front door was shut against the fierce and icy east wind. She knocked, but she didn't go in. All at once, she felt like a stranger here. She could hear the shuffling and the muttering as Aunt Lizzie made her way to the door. She hadn't seen her for four years. She hadn't been home once in that time, though she'd written and she'd sent photographs of Cat. But she had nowhere else to go, and it was only the thought of Uncle Billy that had kept her going.

Aunt Lizzie opened the door, scowling. When she looked at Laura's face there was surprise at first: for a moment she looked old, and vulnerable. But it didn't last long, and Laura felt the same old sense of defeat descend on her head as the surprise in Aunt Lizzie's eyes turned to triumph.

'Left him then, have you?'

She nodded. She hadn't the energy to fight her.

'I told you no good would come of it. Leaving your home and your family and going off all the way up there. I told you no good would come of it. You mark my words, I said. You'll come running home, I said. And I was right.'

Wearily, Laura nodded.

'You'd best come in then. The bairn looks tired.' She turned abruptly and went into the house. Laura heaved the suitcase and her bags into the passage, took Cat by the hand, and followed her into the front room. There was a fire burning in the grate, and the smell of fatty busters baking in the oven. Aunt Lizzie took up position in front of the fire with her hands folded over her stomach.

'Well now,' she said, looking down at Cat. 'I'm your Aunt Lizzie. You don't know me, because your daft mother there ran off to Scotland with that no-good get who calls himself your father, and she hasn't bothered to come back here since to see the folk who raised her.'

Cat stood tall and straight by Laura's side and lifted her face to Aunt Lizzie's. 'Don't you call my mummy daft. My mummy isn't daft.' She put a hand out to Aunt Lizzie. 'My name is Catriona, but you can call me Cat if you like.'

Aunt Lizzie, for once, was speechless. She reached down and took Cat's hand; Cat shook it firmly and then let it go. Laura felt a lightness bubble up inside of her. Cat would be all right, she thought. Cat had the measure of her.

Cat was strong.

13
Cat

The night air is warm when we leave the plane, but nevertheless I shiver and fold my arms around my waist as Jesse secures her, tying the knots with nimble, practised fingers. I really didn't want to come back down; I would happily have stayed up there for hours on this first night-time flight. Blinded by the beauty of the stars in the indigo desert sky. So many of them, as if some great sky spirit had reached out her arm and sifted a cupful of flour in a neat arc across the roof of the world. And the moon so large and its features so distinct that I imagined we could have reached it if we'd had only a little more fuel.

'Starry-eyed?'

I tear my eyes away from the sky; he's standing there watching me, just a few feet away. Although my eyes are still dark-adapted and the moonlight is bright, I can't see his face. But I can hear the smile in his voice.

'That was incredible. Just beautiful. I can't believe it was so beautiful.'

We took off into the north-east about an hour and a half ago with the swiftly setting sun behind us. We climbed up through the clear evening air, the land below suffused with light, gradually fading into a soft golden dream. And Superstition Mountain thrusting upward from the flat desert floor ahead of us, its colours rapidly shifting in the ever-changing light. Instead of turning south to the practice area as we normally do, Jesse decided we had time for a spot of sightseeing. So we continued on course, heading for the mountain, watching it change from copper to red to magenta as the sun sank ever lower in the sky.

We flew west of the mountain, circling up round the back of it. By the time we passed Weaver's Needle – the old volcano that's supposed to be close to the legendary Lost Dutchman's gold mine – the mountain had turned deep purple, its jagged ridge stark against the sky. Jesse lifted a hand from his lap and pointed up there. 'Do you know the story about how the ridges on top of Superstition Mountain came to be?'

I shook my head. 'Go ahead.' I'd heard a couple of different versions before, but I wanted to listen to him tell it. I love to listen to Jesse, and he doesn't talk nearly enough – at least, not while we're flying. I love to hear the sound of his voice stealing through the headphones, right there in my ear. As close as he can be; almost as if he's inside my head. Calming me; lightening.

'See all the spikes up there on top, lined up along the ridge? They look kinda like people in this light, don't you think?' I murmur my agreement, concentrating on keeping us steady against the up-draughts and thermals that are bumping us around and rocking our wings from side to side. Jesse seems completely unconcerned, looking up at the mountain, comfortable just to let me fly. 'Well, the Native people thought so, too. They had a legend about a medicine man turned bad – Earth Doctor, they called him – who hated the People and tried to destroy them. He caused a great flood that drowned the earth. Most of the People perished, except for White Feather, who fled to the top of Superstition Mountain with a band of followers. He tried everything in his power – every piece of magic that he knew to prevent the flood rising further – but nothing worked. So he told the remaining People that he had only one piece of magic left to save them. And then he took a stone from his pocket. He stole a bolt of lightning from the sky and hurled it at the stone, and with a loud clap of thunder it broke into pieces. And the spirits of the People entered into the fragments of rock: each one of them transformed into a stone pillar. And that way, they survived the flood. So they're the figures you can see along the ridge of Superstition Mountain today. It's said that they stand there as sentinels, protecting the sacred ground of Thunder God.'

And you could feel the mystery that surrounds these mountains in the fading light; it hovered there, almost palpable. You could see why so many stories and legends have sprung up in this vast wilderness: ghost stories, stories of little people who appear and disappear, guarding the secrets of the mountain. As the sun went down we circled back south. Night fell fast, and the sky turned a deep rich midnight blue splattered with points of light. We did some night-time navigation around the valley, made a couple of landings and takeoffs, and then all too soon it was time to come back down.

It was thoroughly magical. I look at him now, and sigh. 'When do we get to do it again?'

'Well, we probably need to go up one more time, maybe twice, and then we have a night-time cross-country to complete as part of the training requirements. We'll probably just head down south to Marana for that one. Maybe in a week or two. We'll see how the schedule works out.'

'Okay.' I reach down and pick up my flight bag, ready to head inside and hand over the paperwork and keys.

'You hungry?'

The question takes me by surprise. It must be at least eight o'clock, but I haven't really thought about food. 'Yes, I guess so.'

'Want to grab a bite to eat? There's a Mexican place I know just down the road in Mesa. Stays open a little later than most. It's on the way home.'

It takes a moment for the invitation to sink in; it's so unlike him. At the end of each lesson it's as if he flips a switch: polite, but he keeps his distance. Retreats. I don't know much more about him than when we started; all I know is that when I fly with him I feel safe. And that all the words that come to mind when I think of him aren't the kind of words you normally use when you're trying to describe someone. Words like 'distance' and 'wide open spaces'. Words like 'easy', words like 'light'.

'Sure,' I say, as hope mingles with terror and clutches at my stomach. I shiver again. Stop it, Cat. He's just being friendly.

'Want to just follow behind me, in your car? Should be pretty quiet on the roads – I don't think there's much risk of you losing me.'

'Okay.'

The restaurant is small and cosy, and only three of the dozen or so tables are occupied. The décor is vividly Mexican: bright blues and yellows and greens. The mingled aromas of spice and chilli and sizzling meat make me realise just how hungry I am. The waitress, a young girl with a long black ponytail wearing a starched white apron and a huge smile, seats us at a quiet table in a corner. She hands us our menus and we order a couple of beers. Jesse tells me that he can recommend pretty much everything they do, and by the time she returns with our beers we've decided on chicken fajitas and side-orders of green salad.

I've managed to accomplish the whole process without meeting his eyes for more than just a second or two at any given time.

Once she's left I find that I don't really know what to say. I sip at my Corona, buying time. It seems so strange to be with him in this kind of situation. And so odd to be facing him; I'm used to sitting side by side. Not just in the plane – even when we do ground training we seem to end up alongside each other, poring over diagrams and charts.

'Congratulations on passing your written test, by the way. You must have studied hard – ninety-six percent is a pretty stunning score.'

332

'Thanks.' My cheeks are warm, and I hope to God that I'm not blushing. 'I enjoyed all the work. I've always liked to study.'

'And always had high marks?'

I shrug. 'Studying was the thing I was good at, as a child.'

'Were there so few others, then?' His elbow is on the table, his chin resting in the palm of his hand and his eyes are warm, teasing. Oh, shit. I'm definitely blushing. I feel like a shy teenager out on a first date. Except that this isn't a date. Just a friendly meal at the end of a lesson. It's past dinner time; neither of us has eaten dinner; so we might as well eat dinner together. It's nothing more than that. And he's my flying instructor. There are probably a whole string of regulations against any kind of relationship developing between student and instructor. And if there aren't, there probably ought to be.

I can't imagine why I'm even thinking like this.

I conjure up what I hope is a wry smile. 'There weren't a whole lot.'

'You were an only child?'

I nod.

'So, tell me about where you grew up.' He's watching me intently, but I can't – oh, shit. Why can't I just meet his eyes? Why do I always have to back away? Why can't I just … let things happen?

'You've never been to Britain?' I ask.

'Nope.'

I lean forward, folding my arms on the table, and look down. 'Well, like you, I was born in the mountains. In a fishing village on the coast – the west coast of Scotland is pretty mountainous. One major difference between there and Montana: it rains all the time.'

He laughs, a warm ripple of sound that shimmers in the air between us. 'That's what I've heard. But my grandfather used to talk about snow, too.'

333

'The one who grew up in Aviemore? Well, there'd have been plenty of snow there, for sure: that's skiing country. It's actually warmer out west, by the coast. Some Gulf Stream influence. North Atlantic Drift, or something.' I risk a glance up at him. His eyes are the same colour as his faded denim shirt, and they're still firmly fixed on my face. I look away again, try to find my way back into the story. 'My father was a fisherman. But – well, my mother left him when I was four and they were divorced. We went back to the place where my mother grew up, in the north-east of England.'

'And what was that like?'

'Completely different. Very industrial: coal mines, steel works, sugar factories, chicken processing factories… It was also by the sea, but not quite so picturesque – except for the beach and the dunes, which were beautiful. There was a busy docks area, and much larger fishing boats: drifters, and trawlers. We lived there till I was eighteen. Then I went off to university in Bath – that's in the south-west of England – and my mother moved to London.'

'Is she still there?'

I sit back in my chair, look down at my hands. 'No. She moved back up to Scotland a year or so ago.'

There's a pause. 'You don't get on.'

I roll my eyes and attempt a laugh. 'Is it so obvious?'

'I have an ear for mother problems.'

'You had some of your own?'

He smiles faintly. 'Yeah.'

I open my mouth, hesitate. I badly want to know, but it doesn't seem right to ask. It would feel like prying. But then he sits back in his chair and lays his hands flat on the table as if he's come to a decision.

'My maternal grandfather was Crow Indian – I think I told you that. He married my grandmother – she was Anglo, a schoolteacher – and they lived on the reservation. My mother was their only child. Those were tough times on the reservation – hell, they're still tough today – but my grandfather was proud of his heritage, and didn't want to move away. When she was in her teens my mother fell in with a bad crowd at school, and got into drugs.'

Drugs.

Half-fearful, half-hopeful, I look into his eyes. 'What kind of drugs?'

'Alcohol, marijuana, amphetamines – whatever was going. And there was plenty going then on the rez, just as there is now.' He reaches out, takes a long gulp of his beer; I watch the muscles in his throat contract as he swallows. 'She was given counselling, managed to stop, and went to college. She wanted to be a teacher, too, like her mother. She met my father there – again, an Anglo – and after they married they both got jobs teaching in Billings. She had a love-hate thing going with the reservation – didn't want to live there, but didn't want to be too far away, either. When she was carrying me they moved away from Billings, down to Red Lodge. After Ellie Mae was born Mom began to take drugs again.' He runs a hand through his hair; it flops right back down over his forehead, partially obscuring his right eye. I fight an urge to reach over and brush it aside. 'I don't know why. But I remember that those were crazy times. Sometimes she'd stay at home and everything would be normal for a while; then sometimes she'd run off, back to the rez. I don't know where she stayed when she was there – with the same old crowd that she used to run with, I guess. This went on for five years, maybe. Then when I was ten and Ellie Mae was seven, she left us for good. Moved back to the rez. Made drugs her life, instead of us.'

I reach out, fiddle with the clear plastic pepper mill at the side of the table. This isn't at all what I expected to hear. Not from Jesse. He always seems so ... together. With that kind of background, how do you get to be so serene? And there isn't a hint of bitterness in his voice. How do you get to be so accepting?

'And your father?'

He shrugs. 'Dad did all that he could for her while she was with us, but it was never enough. Whatever treatment programme she was offered, she wouldn't stay with it. So he just carried on without her. Looked after us, protected us as much as he could. His sister, Aunt Edith, lived close by and she would help out from time to time. Especially with Ellie Mae.' He smiles softly, just as he always does when he talks about his sister. 'And now Ellie Mae does her best to look after Dad. When he lets her.'

I put the pepper mill down and start on the salt cellar. 'He never remarried?'

'No.' There's a hint of wistfulness in his voice. 'My mother was beautiful. Crazy, but kind of hard to forget.'

Yes, I want to say to him. Yes. It's the crazy ones that are always the hardest to forget. Because for all that there's a part of you that hates it – hates all the wildness, maybe even fears it – there's another part that watches with envy and longing. That thinks: how do you get to be so free?

'Did you see her again, after she went back to the reservation for good?'

'Every now and again she would come by. Usually when she was high. Sometimes with a car-load of friends who were out to cause trouble. It didn't do any of us any good – especially not Ellie Mae. My mother couldn't manage the sign language when she was doped up, and Ellie was too young. She couldn't get a grip on what was happening.'

All of this new information is racing through my brain, fighting to be assimilated; a crowd of half-formed questions mills around in my mind. 'How did you feel about her, back then? When all that was going on?'

336

'My mother?' He hesitates. 'I loved her, of course. She was my mom. She was beautiful and she was fun – and there were so many good memories from when I was a little kid. The problems didn't really start till I was five or so. But all mixed up with that there were times when I was real mad at her as well. Times when I'd get up in the middle of the night to go to the bathroom or to get a drink of water, and see my Dad sitting out on the porch. Just rocking there, with his eyes wide open, staring out into space. Times when I'd listen to Ellie Mae cry herself to sleep at night. How do you explain all of that, to a little girl?'

I don't know, I want to whisper. I don't know. I watch, entranced, as one long finger runs up and down his glass of beer, creating shallow gorges and dripping rivulets in the condensation that clings to its sides. I sneak a glance up at him, trying to smile. 'So you went into psychology.'

He laughs. 'Yeah. Absolutely right. Thinking that I could learn how to save my mother.'

'And, of course, it didn't work.'

He shakes his head ruefully as the waitress brings our food – just a momentary distraction. 'Not exactly, no. But I worked on the drug and alcohol programme while I was studying for my degree. And fell in love with Sarah – a recovering heroin addict. We lived together for a couple of years, but I guess I couldn't save her, either. She relapsed, took an overdose and died. I finished my degree, pulled out of psychology and took up flying instead.'

Jesus. I have no idea what to say. I watch as he calmly reaches for a tortilla and places a line of grilled chicken and roasted vegetables down the middle. A dollop of guacamole, one of salsa and one of sour cream. Then neatly rolls it up. I swallow, and begin to do the same. 'Do you see your mother at all now?'

'She died five years ago.'

I close my eyes. 'I'm sorry.' And he smiles, such a slow, sweet smile. How can he be so calm? 'Aren't you still mad at her?'

He looks at me in genuine surprise. 'Still? What for? What would be the point? Sure I was mad, as a child. Madder'n hell. But there's been plenty enough time to think it through, over the years. My mother was a drug addict before I came along. She didn't become one to hurt me. The damage was already done long before I was born. How could I still be mad at her?'

I stare at him blankly, a fork loaded with lettuce stalled halfway to my mouth. 'But ... she left you.'

'Yes. But she loved me, too. She loved all of us – I was never in any doubt about that.'

And he's right, of course – on some level I know that he's right. Because it occurs to me for the first time that I was never in any doubt that my mother loved me too.

'So. That's my story. Want to tell me yours?'

I put my fork down again. I close my eyes and before I can think about it and change my mind, I jump. 'My mother was an alcoholic.'

Forty years old, and finally I've said it. Suddenly I'm cold; my teeth are on the verge of chattering.

'Ah.' I daren't look at his face, but the gentleness in his voice brushes over me like a caress. 'So we have something in common.'

I clench my jaw and pick up my fork again to steady myself. My hand is trembling; I grip the fork more tightly. Oh, God. Can he tell how difficult this is for me? Am I making a complete idiot of myself here? I've come this far; there's absolutely no point in turning back now. I take a deep breath. 'I guess. The difference, for me, was that there wasn't anyone else. Just the two of us. I didn't see my father for years after we moved away – which was just as well, maybe. He wasn't a great father. Or husband. Which is why my mother ran away from him in the first place.'

'He was violent.'

'Yes.'

Dear God. I can't believe I'm telling him all this.

'To you?'

'No. To my mother. Though perhaps he would have been, if we'd stayed. There were moments when – when it seemed that it might have happened.'

'So she took you back home, and there were just the two of you. Didn't she have any family there?'

Slowly, carefully, I chew and I swallow the mouthful of lettuce. Steady, Cat. It's okay. This is okay. Listen to him; think about what he's just told you. He's not judging you. It happened to him, too. It's okay. 'My mother was never close to her family. It's complicated, but … when we first moved back we lived with my Great-Aunt Lizzie till my mother got a steady job and made enough money to put down a deposit so we could rent a small house. Then we lived together, just the two of us.'

'And that was when she started to drink?'

I nod. Sneak a glance back at him. He's watching me, watching, but there's nothing in his eyes except understanding and the slightest trace of a smile. He's not judging. He's not blaming. He's just listening. It's okay. No-one's waiting in the shadows to lock me away now that my guilty little secret is out in the open…

… So I tell him. I tell him what she told me, in her story. I tell him what I remember. And I continue, slowly, to eat, needing something to do with my hands and my eyes. Something to anchor me. But in between mouthfuls of food I pour it all out. And he listens. He listens and he watches and he nods and whenever I pause he asks a question and his questions sweep through the clutter in my brain like a spring breeze tumbling into a room that's been closed all winter long. Sweeping it clean.

Then our plates are empty and there seems to be no more to tell.

I put down my knife and fork. 'I'm sorry. I didn't mean to go on about it. Believe it or not, I've never told anyone before.'

'Never?'

I shake my head, bite the inside of my lip. I don't cry in public. *Don't ever let them see you cry, little Cat. Don't ever let them know they've got to you.*

I hold my breath as he reaches across the table, passes the back of his index finger gently down my cheek. Its coolness sears my flushed skin; goose-pimples shiver out across my body. He withdraws it again, leaving behind a sudden sharp stab of yearning that takes my breath away.

'And was it so bad? Talking about it now?'

'No.' My voice is a whisper. I clear my throat. 'No, it wasn't so bad.' And it wasn't. Because he understands; because it has happened to him. Because, you see – you assume that you're the only one. That everyone else is normal. That you're the only one who isn't. That you're the only one who's ashamed, and hides.

I open my mouth, struggle to explain. 'When there's just the two of you – you end up colluding, somehow. That old habit of secrecy is a hard one to break. You always have this feeling that you're hiding some strange guilty, shameful secret. Concealment becomes second nature to you; self-disclosure is … completely inconceivable.'

He smiles, mischief glittering in the depths of his eyes. 'And I thought it was just because you were British.'

I laugh, freeing some of the tightness that's lodged in my chest. 'That famous British reserve? Oh, there's some of that too. It normally takes us a while before we spill.'

'Well. I'm glad to know you better.'

I meet his eyes; he's not smiling any more. A sudden wave of vertigo takes me by surprise. I look away from the edge of this new precipice. 'Perhaps I'd better be getting home. It must be late.'

'Just after ten. No coffee?'

I shake my head.

'Not even tea?'

'I ordered tea once before in a Mexican restaurant. Tea with milk, I said – not lemon. They brought me a cup of hot milk with a tea-bag floating in it.' He laughs, waving to the waitress for the check. 'Now I only drink tea in the security of my own home.'

He shakes his head when I reach for my purse. 'My invitation – my treat. Next time, maybe we'll talk about splitting it.'

And in spite of myself, the idea that there might be a next time leaves a warm fluttering feeling in the centre of my chest.

I lie in bed, basking in the moonlight that surges through the window and bathes my restless body, freed from the stifling constraints of the comforter. Sleep has deserted me. I might just as well get up again, make a cup of tea, but there's something magical about this dusky blue half-light that spills into the room from the silent desert sky. Jesse's words spin around in my head, all mixed up with my own; again and again, I replay them. I can't believe that after all these years I've broken that old taboo. And the earth didn't open up and swallow me. Far from it: the cool caress of the moon on my skin feels like approbation. And for the first time in what seems like months a slow, tingling heat begins to build between my legs. I roll over onto my stomach, fists clenching the pillow. When eventually I drift off a pair of pale blue eyes travels along with me, floating closer and closer, expanding out to fill the whole sky. I point my plane into the blue and the air inside is cool and light.

𝄢 𝄢 𝄢

It came at last today: the part of your story I've been dreading. It was a bad time, wasn't it? Such a long time since I've thought about it. Really thought about it. Creeping around on tip-toes. Always on edge, always looking at you, standing over you. Afraid to leave you alone with him. I remember the sense of helplessness, of guilt, of wondering if it was my fault.

And, mixed up in it all, I remember my fear.

My mummy and daddy and I are standing at the bus-stop waiting for the bus to come. Mummy has to go to Inverness, which is a big city miles and miles away across the mountains. Mummy and Daddy are arguing again. I'm frightened, frightened with that cold hurting feeling that starts in my feet and runs all around my body and settles like an ice-cube in my stomach. Frightened because I know what comes next when Mummy and Daddy shout at each other. But surely he won't hit her in the street, because if he does the policeman will come and lock him up. Because even though the policeman is my daddy's cousin they don't like each other very much. Daddy says Petey's so far up his own arse it's a wonder he can see the light of day. Mummy tells him not to talk like that in front of the bairn, but Daddy just laughs.

For a minute I let myself think about how it will be if Daddy is locked up. We won't have to be frightened any more, and Mummy will be safe. But then I remember that he's my daddy and I love him and I don't want him to go away. I love him because sometimes he makes me laugh and sometimes he takes me down to the harbour and shows me off to all the men who work with him on his boat. I love him because he's my daddy. I'm the spitting image of him, my nana says, and I don't want him to go away even though a lot of the time he scares me. The thought of him going away and being locked up and not seeing him any more makes me cry and when I start crying it makes Daddy even angrier. I don't usually cry – don't let them see you cry, little Cat, my mummy says when the other children laugh at my glasses – but today I can't seem to help it – it just bursts out of me and there's nothing I can do. He shouts at me to shut up and Mummy tells him to leave me alone and he says that he's going to do more than shout at me when he gets me home. And I know what that means and so does my mummy, because she looks at him with that same look in her eyes that she gets when he hits her. But then the bus comes and she has to get on it but I don't want her to leave me and I'm crying even harder and she looks at him and says 'Don't, Alec,' but still she gets on the bus and it pulls away and she leaves me with him.

She leaves me.

Daddy turns away and walks quickly down the road and I run after him, because I have to, don't I? There's nowhere else for me to go. My nana lives down the next street but if I go there he'll only come and get me. I'm frightened because I've seen my daddy angry before and I know he'll hurt me if he hits me like he hits Mummy. And then we're back home and he's opening the door and the fear bursts out of me and I can't help it – I run. I run through the door and on up the stairs and up to my bedroom and I can hear him following me – 'Come back here, you wee bastard,' he says – and I'm crying as I run – 'No, Daddy, no' – and I shut the door behind me but he's pushing it open and I'm trying to push it back but I'm only a little girl and he pushes harder and I fall over. He comes in and stands over me; I look up at him with all the fear that I'm feeling right there in my eyes for him to see.

But then something funny happens. He stands there and looks down at me and he sees my face and the tears on my cheeks and his face crumples. He stumbles right past me and over to the bed and he sits on the edge of it and puts his head in his hands. And then my daddy starts to cry. A sharp pain stabs into my stomach and for a second or two I feel sick. And then I get up and I move over to him quietly and I sit next to him on the bed. I put my hand on his knee. 'Don't cry, Daddy,' I tell him. 'Don't cry.'

343

14

Laura

'Dreich old day,' the postie says. 'You wrap up warm and stay inside, lassie. The road looks all set to flood down by the crossroads, so I wouldn't be venturing out today if I were you. Aye, the weather's turned again, all right. Thought we'd had it too good for too long. Rain, rain and more rain, that's what we're used to here. I mind old Davey Johnson and his wife Maggie – used to live in Jamie Blair's house. They moved away three years ago now. Why're ye leaving, so? I asked him. Well, says he, we moved here two years ago. The sun shone for a week and then it started to rain. It rained all day and it rained all night and the next day it rained again. It rained for eighteen months. So I'm going to take up residence somewhere less biblical, he says. And off they went to Tenerife.'

Some days the rain just falls. Some days it dives against the window and stings it swiftly before flying away again in the wind. Other days it slips down softly, hardly touching the window at all, hanging out across the loch like a pearly voile curtain. Some days it hurls itself against anything that stands in its way and spreads itself in vast slick films across the fields like a blanket of doom.

Sorrow rises up in Laura – rises up and gnaws at the pit of her stomach and stabs like a white-hot knife into her heart but she welcomes the pain: welcomes it as a sign that she is still alive.

That she is more than just grey.

Laura had finally saved up enough money to rent a tiny terraced house and furnish it. She was training to be a librarian now, and although the work was hard, she enjoyed it. She ought to have been relieved to leave Aunt Lizzie's house for a second time; ought to have been happy to have a place that was hers and Cat's alone. But she wasn't. On the day that they'd moved in, when Uncle Billy had gone and left Laura and Cat in their new home, she'd looked around the living room with its small settee and armchair and the small drop-leaf table and two rickety wooden chairs and she'd felt only emptiness.

This wasn't how it was supposed to be.

The house was near the seafront, just a fifteen minute walk away from Aunt Lizzie's. It was handy really, because Cat's school was right opposite Aunt Lizzie's and she could go straight there after school until Laura arrived home from work to fetch her. It was strange how that relationship worked, Laura thought. Aunt Lizzie seemed to love Cat in a way that she'd never loved Laura. Uncle Billy, of course, was besotted with her, but oddly, Cat was wary of him. She seemed to be wary of everyone, especially men; that was just Cat. She played alone most of the time, though there were plenty of other children her age around the groves where Aunt Lizzie lived. But then Cat wasn't a physical child, either; she seemed to live entirely inside her own head. And that was one place where you never knew what was going on.

'Mummy?' Laura turned, saw Cat standing forlornly in the doorway.

'Yes, pet?'

'What shall we do now?'

'Come and sit down here with me, Kitty-Cat, and I'll tell you a story.' Laura switched on the small two-bar electric fire and sat down on the settee; Cat sat close beside her but still kept her distance. She didn't like Laura to cuddle her. She was such a self-contained child. You approached her only on her terms. Laura was in awe of her sometimes; she couldn't imagine how she had managed to give birth to someone like Cat. She was in awe of her, but she loved her with a fierceness that never ceased to surprise. From the moment Cat was born Laura had known that giving birth to her was the best thing she had ever done, that she would ever do. The one act that would give her life meaning. That would make it complete. And yet Cat was a constant reminder of Alec. The image of him: the absolute image. But Cat was the best of him. The part that Laura had loved.

'Which story will it be?' Laura wondered out loud, and Cat looked up at her, big brown eyes wide under the thick dark-rimmed glasses. Laura reached out and tucked Cat's long blonde hair behind her ear. 'I know. Once upon a time, there was a little princess with pale blonde hair who lived in a small palace by the sea…'

Cat had loved Laura's stories then; it seemed that she could never get enough of them. She liked fairy stories best of all; Laura was surprised to find how easy it was to remember them, and later, when she'd exhausted her supply, to make up new ones. Yes – those were, for sure, the best times for Cat and Laura.

Restless, Laura is wandering again. A ghost, haunting her own house. It's almost as if she's trying to imprint herself on it: at last, to make it her own. Finally, she finds her way to the small spare bedroom under the eaves that has no hope of occupation. It is filled with boxes that remain unopened, and as she eyes them wearily Laura wonders whether this is the problem. All of her past is locked up here, in these boxes. The past that she's tried so hard to ignore but that will not, finally, be denied.

A battered old box on top of the pile closest to the door. A box that still displays a Hartlepool address; this is an object that has seen some years. The thick Sellotape is yellowed and crumbling: it needs little encouragement to peel away from the lid. She hesitates before opening it; no longer knows what ills it might contain, what plagues she might unleash on her world. Slowly peers inside: a decaying elastic band around a bundle of cards and letters from Cat. Tries to remove the elastic band, which breaks in her hand. Old, she thinks. Everything now so old. At the top of the pile, one of the first birthday cards that Cat ever made by herself. How old would she have been then? Probably not so old; she was a precocious child. 'To my lovely Mummy, from Kitty-Cat.' The writing is crooked and poorly formed, but carefully coloured in red and blue crayons. On the cover are the usual childish triangular figures, one small with yellow hair and the other tall with black curls. They are standing in front of a house, and in the background is the sea.

Laura puts the pile of cards to one side and picks up the bundle that lies beside it. Cat's school reports. Opens one out of curiosity. Cat, aged eight. 'Cat continues to work hard and succeeds well in all subjects. However, her teachers have noticed a change in her over the past year; previously an animated, sociable child, she seems to have become silent and withdrawn.'

Laura thrusts the reports back into the box and slams down the lid; sinks to the floor and leans her head back against the wall.

The selkie woman stayed with her daughter in the little cottage by the sea, but as she slowly grew older, once again she began to dwindle. Her skin grew sallow and dry and cracked; her eyes grew dull and her hair grew brittle. The loss of her skin ate away at her until she no longer knew who she was. Grasping at the life that was fading away, she begged her husband to give back her skin. But he'd reverted back to his old ways: had grown harder and cold, lived only for status and wealth. And she was a part of the life that he'd built, his possession, a symbol of success. His strange, beautiful selkie wife. How could she have imagined that he would ever let her go?

Then, one day, a storm blew up at sea and the fisherman and his boat were lost. Freed from her husband's growing tyranny, at first the selkie woman rejoiced. Finally she would be free; finally she would be able to return home! All she had to do was find her skin.

But it wasn't there. She searched the house high and low; she searched in the attic and she searched in the cellar. But there was no sign of her skin; no sign that it had ever been there. Despairing, she sank once more into sickness and gloom.

Laura sat in the empty living room. It was almost midnight, but she knew that if she went to bed she wouldn't sleep. She hadn't slept properly for months. She wandered through the days like a wraith, her eyes full of shadows and her face sallow. She was lonely, and she missed Alec more than she ever would have thought possible. Sometimes she thought it would be worth it – worth all the pain, just to feel his strong arms around her again. But then she thought of Cat, and the fear in her eyes and the turn in her eye, and she shut those thoughts away.

On the table before her was a bottle of sherry and a small glass. She didn't normally drink, but she'd bought the sherry tonight on the way home from work. It had been Joanie's idea – Joanie, one of the women she worked with down at the bingo hall two nights at week, to earn extra money. Joanie had been talking about how her sister was suffering from insomnia.

'So I said to her, "Ee, our Maggie," I said to her, "I used to suffer from that meself, you know." "Did you?" she asked me. "So what did you do, like?" "Well," I said to her, "I took myself down to the offie and I bought a bottle of sherry." "Ee, our Joanie, you never did," she said. "I did," I said. "I went down and I bought myself a bottle of sherry, and every night before I went to bed I poured myself a little glass of it, and before you know it I was out for the count," I said. Well, she did the same thing, and she hasn't had a problem since.' Joanie had looked at Laura, at the blue circles under her eyes. 'You want to try that yourself, Laura. Looks to me like you could do with a bit of sleep as well.'

So Laura had gone to the offie on the way home, and she had bought a bottle of sherry. She'd been embarrassed when she paid for it: embarrassed in case the woman at the counter thought that she might be drinking alone. So she'd told her, as she fumbled in her purse for the correct change, that she was having a few friends round for drinks. The woman had pursed her lips. 'Oh, aye?' she'd said. 'Nowt to do with me what you want it for.' Laura had blushed and left in a hurry. She didn't think she'd do it again; she wasn't even sure it would work, but she was desperate enough to try anything right now.

She poured a finger's width of the golden brown liquid into the glass and sipped at it. She'd had an occasional glass of sherry before, mostly at Hogmanay up in Scotland, but she'd never really liked alcohol much. Neither Uncle Billy nor Aunt Lizzie had ever touched alcohol when Laura was growing up, though nowadays Aunt Lizzie swore by a bottle of Mackeson's before she went to bed every night. 'Thickens the blood,' she'd said to Laura. 'Nowt like a bottle of stout for putting hairs on your chest.' And she'd made a funny face at Cat and Cat had giggled. But this tasted nice; it was sweet, and it burned a little as it slipped down her throat. She sipped again and again, until the glass was empty. Her stomach felt warm and she closed her eyes; she could feel her muscles begin to relax. She smiled, and went to bed.

She woke up the next morning after the best night's sleep that she'd had for ages. Silently, she sent up a prayer of thanks for Joanie and her good advice.

Laura opened her eyes: her head hurt. For a moment she didn't know where she was. She blinked and tried to focus: she was in the living room. In the armchair. She seemed to be in her dressing gown. She wrinkled her nose as she moved: she smelled terrible.

349

Cat was sitting on the sofa with her feet curled up, reading a book.

'Cat,' she croaked.

Cat's eyes flew from her book. 'Are you better now, Mummy?'

'Sorry, little Cat. Mummy was sick.' She heaved herself into a sitting position. Her head swam. 'Why aren't you at school? What day is it?'

'Sunday. It's three o'clock.'

Sunday? So what had happened to Saturday? She remembered Friday night. She remembered that she'd had her usual glass of sherry, but it hadn't worked. So she'd had another one. She looked down at the bottle by her side. Empty. Surely she hadn't drunk the whole bottle? But she must have, it's the only thing that can explain why she'd slept all that time. 'Have you been all right? Did you have something to eat?'

'I was fine. I was a bit scared at first but you told me you would be all right and just to leave you alone.' Cat's eyes were huge brown saucers. 'I made myself some beans on toast and ate some cereal and things, so don't worry.'

'I told you that? When did I tell you that?'

'Yesterday morning. I got up and you were sleeping there, on the chair. I shook you and you woke up and you told me you just needed to sleep and so I left you alone.'

'Did I wake up again?'

'You got up and went to the bathroom a couple of times but you were all dizzy, you said. I think you were sick, as well. I asked whether I should go and get Aunt Lizzie if you were sick but you shouted at me and told me to leave you alone. You said you'd be fine. I didn't know what to do, but I thought if you didn't wake up by tea-time I'd go anyway and I'd ask Aunt Lizzie what to do.'

'No, little Cat. You mustn't ever do that. You leave Aunt Lizzie out of it, do you hear? There's no need to tell. No need to tell anyone. All right?'

350

And Cat nodded, her pale little face serious and filled with the weight of this new responsibility.

Cat was seven years old. Seven years old and Laura had left her to fend for herself for a full day and a half. And had shouted at her for trying to help. Whatever had she been thinking of?

Laura promised herself that she would never do it again.

She couldn't help it, really she couldn't. And besides, she didn't see why she should stop: it was the only comfort she had. The only escape she had. The only escape from the weight of her isolation and sorrow, from his laughing eyes and long-fingered hands that haunted her nights and now haunted her days too. This was all she had to take the edge off the memories, to gain some relief. Now that the divorce was final.

She took another gulp of the amber liquid and screwed up her face. She hated the taste of whisky, but it had been a long time since the sherry was enough. She needed too much of it now, and a bottle of whisky could last a whole weekend whereas the sherry would only last a day.

She hid it from Cat as best she could. She poured the whisky into a teapot and drank it down from a mug. Cat was only a child; she didn't understand what was happening. Laura told her that she was sick sometimes, but that there was nothing to worry about – it would wear off. Other mothers were sick, after all; her friend Janice's mother had migraines that would keep her in bed all day, sometimes two. She told her that it was best just to leave her alone when she was sick. She wasn't to tell Aunt Lizzie or anyone else. If anyone should come asking for her, she was just to tell them that her mummy was sick and had gone to bed. She wasn't to tell.

And it wasn't as if she did it every weekend. Just sometimes. Just sometimes, when the memories got too much to bear. Cat knew how to look after herself. It's not as if she starved, or anything: there was always food in the house. Cat was self-reliant. Cat was just fine.

*

Laura hadn't had a drink for a whole month. She looked in the mirror and carefully applied her lipstick. She smiled at her reflection. She was a little thinner these days, and her eyes had a hollowed-out look to them, but she was still pretty enough. Pretty enough for Alan to ask her out. She'd met him in the library: he'd come in once a week and take out a couple of westerns, and he'd whisper to her and ask her questions about herself. And now he'd asked her to go dancing with him. To the Queen's Rink.

She'd rather not go to the Queen's Rink ever again, but she didn't want to tell him that.

'Will you be all right, darling?'

Cat looked up briefly from the pages of her book. 'Yes, Mummy.'

'Don't go to bed late now, will you?'

'No, Mummy.'

'I won't be back late. I'll be home by midnight. Or else I might turn into a pumpkin, mightn't I?'

Cat smiled. 'You look like a princess going to a ball.'

Laura twirled, showing off her stiff flared skirt. 'Well, I am going to a ball. With a handsome prince.' She bent down and kissed the top of Cat's head. 'You'll like Alan. You'll get to meet him soon, I promise.'

She left the house with hope in her heart. It would be nice not to be alone any more. She hated to be alone.

The whisky was bitter but Laura drank it down. She didn't understand what had happened. He'd seemed so charming. He'd been so well-dressed, and so well-spoken, and he'd come from the best side of town. Not like Laura. But even though Laura came from a council estate, she had had a good education. Uncle Billy had seen to that.

She hadn't expected him to behave like that. She knew she shouldn't have done it. Nice women didn't sleep with men and then expect to be respected. But he'd seemed so attentive and he'd wanted her so badly and she'd so badly wanted someone to just hold her.

She hadn't thought that would be the end of it. She'd thought that if she went to bed with him he would love her even more. She'd thought they might even get married after a while. After all, they'd both been free. She'd thought he might be the one who would take care of her. Her and Cat.

Cat was up in her room. Laura took another giant gulp. Cat hadn't liked Alan very much, and Laura had been angry with her. 'You might at least have talked to him!' she'd yelled.

'I did talk to him.'

'No, you didn't. Not properly, anyway. You just answered his questions with as few words as you could muster. You were rude.'

'I wasn't rude. But I didn't like him. I didn't like the way he smiled at me. He didn't mean it.'

Well, it seemed that Cat had been right all along. Laura smiled thinly and took another gulp. Ah – there. She could feel it now. The lightness in her head, the soft relaxation of her muscles. Yes – that was better. She finished the glass, poured another. Slipped slowly into sweet oblivion.

Oblivion. Laura remembers oblivion. She and oblivion are old friends – a friendship that will be renewed soon enough now. When it's time for her to die.

She shudders. It's not that Laura fears death; she just fears dying. The slow, inexorable descent into the unknown. She fears that she will have to do it alone. Alone, and maybe in pain. She worries that she may die and her daughter will not have loved her. Or that she will die and that Cat will remember how much she loved her. And regret.

Laura knows all about regret, too. She is filled with regret. Regret for all of the things that she might have done and now will not. For the loss of possibility. Regret for all of the lovers that she never knew, and the ones that she might have chosen more wisely. She regrets the loss of passion, because now that it is gone there are only ashes. She has lost that vivid inner flame that always burned inside her no matter what. That kept her going, hoping, even in the worst of times. She has always loved fire, always loved the heat, always loved storms. But what is she now? Just a burned-out cinder? The dusty remains of a stroke of lightning?

It was cold on the seafront. The wind crept under her headscarf and brushed icy fingers over her scalp. 'Cold,' she thought. 'This is a cold, grey town. This isn't a town where you have much of a chance at happiness.' She'd been happy, once, but that had been somewhere else.

It began to rain. Laura ran across the road to the small parade of shops and peered through the steamed-up windows of the brightly lit café. Several tables were occupied; people were talking and laughing. She hesitated on the threshold, but then lifted her head and stepped forward into the fug of warm greasy air and fresh cigarette smoke. Nausea clutched at her stomach. But after all, she thought, you had to take your chances. And then – well, who knew what might happen?

She removed the headscarf and shook out her hair.

Her tea arrived; she picked it up with hands that trembled. She took a sip and wrinkled her nose, but it was still too early in the day for a proper drink. She reached into her handbag for her pack of Players Number 6 Plains, but couldn't find her lighter. She sat back and closed her eyes in defeat.

The man at the table next to her leaned over.

'Need a light?'

'What's the point?' Laura thought, as tears began to form in the corner of her eyes. And for a moment futility overwhelmed her. She glanced down at the long-fingered hand that hovered in the air above the table, holding out a shiny gold Colibri lighter like an offering. She looked up at him, and he smiled.

The old reckless feeling took possession of her. She'd been right. If only you tried, anything might happen.

The next one was called Johnnie. He was much better than the others. Johnnie was a welder at the steelworks. He was a quiet man, a strong man. Laura longed for a strong man. She was tired of being strong for herself and for Cat. At least, that was how she saw it. She longed for someone to share the load – not just the financial load, but everything. Someone to take away the heavy, exhausting need to make all the decisions by herself.

She'd met Johnnie at the bingo hall; he used to come in sometimes for a pint. Then she'd noticed that he was there every evening that she was working; he'd sit at the bar and he'd smile at her, but wouldn't say much. Sometimes he would come in with a couple of friends; they called him 'Guinness', because that was what he drank. He was a simple man, but he seemed kind. Kind would be nice, she thought to herself. She could do with a bit of kindness.

Johnnie belonged to a working men's club, and that's where they were going tonight. There was going to be a woman on who sang like Shirley Bassey, Johnnie said – and Laura loved Shirley Bassey. 'A House Is Not a Home' was one of her favourite songs. Cat hated her – thought she was morbid. Melodramatic. Well, maybe she was. But she sang songs that Laura identified with: songs of loneliness, songs of betrayal. Songs of yearning.

She looked in the mirror; she looked tired. She tried to smile, but it was hard. It was hard to keep hoping. But that was what Laura did best: she hoped. Time after time, she hoped.

Cat didn't look up from her book as Laura came into the room.

'Cat. I'm going out now.'

'Bye, then.'

'Will you be all right?'

'Of course I'll be all right. I always am, aren't I?'

Yes, Cat was always all right. Cat was fine. Cat was ten years old.

Laura came round; her head was clearer, now. Far too clear: it was wearing off. She reached for the bottle, but to her horror it was empty. She couldn't go round to the offie herself: she was still too drunk. She'd never make it there and back. But she needed to be drunker still. Drunk enough to forget what she found out about Johnnie. Drunk enough to blot out the knowledge that he'd served time for grievous bodily harm. Not once, but three times.

Where was Cat? Cat would go to the offie for her. The woman who owned it knew her because she sold tobacco and sometimes Laura would send Cat down for her cigarettes. Players Number Six Plain, that's what she smoked. Not many of them – maybe half a dozen a day. It had been Ernie who got Laura onto smoking. He'd been the one before Johnnie. No – the one before that. The one with the Colibri lighter. Robert. Mustn't think about Johnnie.

'Cat!' she shouted.

'What?' Cat was upstairs in her bedroom. Probably reading; Cat always had her nose stuck in a book. She didn't ever go out much, didn't seem to have a lot of friends. But when Laura asked her, she always said she was fine.

'Come down here a minute.'

Laura heard the feet clumping heavily down the stairs. Cat came in and stood in front of her. 'What?' She looked sullen. She was still tall for her age. Pretty, too, with her high cheekbones and straight nose, just like her father's. Her long blonde hair was tied up in a ponytail. Laura grimaced. Cat reminded her of Alec. Too much for comfort, sometimes. God, she needed a drink.

'I want you to go to the offie for me.'

'You've got cigarettes. There's another packet in the kitchen. I got them for you yesterday, but I don't suppose you remember.'

Anger flared up in Laura. 'Don't you talk to me like that! You get down to the offie this minute and you get me a bottle of Bell's.'

Surprised, Cat blinked. 'I'm too young to buy alcohol.'

'You're too young to buy cigarettes, but Mrs Evans knows they're for me, so she lets you have them. She'll do the same with the whisky. Take my purse – it's in my handbag in the kitchen.'

'No. I don't want to go.' Cat's face was flushed; she looked as if she might cry, but she wouldn't do that. Cat never cried. 'It's embarrassing.' For a moment Laura hesitated, but then the hunger grasped at her, gnawed at her.

'Embarrassing? Don't be so stupid. I don't care whether you want to go or not. You do as I tell you, or you can get out of this house and go and live with your Aunt Lizzie. See how you like that.'

Laura regretted the words as soon as she'd said them, but she didn't seem to have control over her tongue when she'd been drinking. She saw the colour flare up again in Cat's pale cheeks and the hurt in her eyes as she turned and strode out of the room. She wanted to call her back and apologise, but she wanted a drink more. And Cat knew she didn't mean it: Cat understood. Cat was her baby.

The looking back is hard – so hard. Laura can hardly bear it. This is what she's hidden from herself all these years; this is what she's refused to see. What was she thinking of? Was she really so naïve? Never seeming to learn from her mistakes. Time after time; one unsuitable man after the other. Always searching for the one who would make it all better. For the one who would make all the hurt go away. For the one who would look after her.

And so began the long slide into chaos and decay, oblivious to anyone's needs but her own. Laura hardly saw what was happening to Cat, so intensely was she focused on her own pain and loss. But she can see it now, and she wishes she could make it go away. She can see how Cat looked at her as the years passed by: first the hurt, then the anger and contempt. And now,

357

looking back, so much becomes clear that she didn't see then: she remembers Cat's withdrawal, and her solitude and shame.

But on Laura had gone, dancing in those red shoes. Following wherever they took her. Dancing on, dancing away. Powerless to change.

↞ ↞ ↞

Laura should maybe have telephoned beforehand, but for some odd reason she didn't have the courage. The little house is well-kept; the front garden neat and tidy. She doesn't remember it. She doesn't remember ever visiting her before, at all.

Laura takes a deep breath and rings the doorbell. A few moments pass, and there is no reply. Relief settles over her: she's out. But just as she's turning away she hears a fumbling at the door catch. She turns back, and the door opens. A tightly permed white head peers out at her.

'Yes?' The voice is high-pitched and frail.

'Mrs Mackenzie?'

'Aye, that's me.'

'I'm Laura. Laura Munro. You won't remember me. I was married to Alec. A long time ago.'

'Laura. Well, now! I heard you'd moved here, of course. And of course I remember you. I came to your wedding along with Alec's father and my sister. Come away in.'

The door opens wide to reveal a tiny old lady neatly dressed in a grey tweed skirt and black lambswool sweater. She beckons Laura into the tiny hall, and leads the way into a small sitting room; the air inside the house smells of air freshener and detergents. 'And none of that Mrs Mackenzie nonsense. Call me Isobel. Will you have a cup of tea?'

'Yes, please.'

'Sit you down, then. I'll be back in a moment.'

Oddly nervous, Laura looks around the room as Isobel

358

clatters in the kitchen. A small room; tidy and spotlessly clean. A coal fire burning in the grate. There are photographs on the mantelpiece: Isobel and a man who Laura imagines was her husband. She doesn't remember that there was a husband, but Meg said that Isobel was a widow now. No children. Beside it another photograph, and faces that she recognises more clearly: Alec's mother and father. An old sepia-tinted studio shot of Alec and Robert as children; she's seen that one before. And, finally, a photograph of a man around Laura's age. A tall man and stoutly built, with thick sandy hair laced with grey. With a woman. With four girls who look to be around the same age as Catriona. And with four small children. And two babies.

'Aye, that's Alec.' Isobel's voice from behind startles Laura. Alec? She turns; Isobel is placing a tray of tea things on the table in front of the sofa. 'Taken last Christmas. With all the children and grandchildren.' She sees the expression on Laura's face. 'Or should I say, stepchildren.'

Of course it's Alec: she should have known. She picks up the photograph, looks closely. Older for sure, but still very much himself. It shouldn't have been such a very great surprise, this photograph: she'd known that he'd married again. Cat had told her. Said there were stepchildren and so naturally there would be grandchildren too. But it shocks her still, to think of Alec with a family and children.

'Sit you down now, lassie. How do you take your tea?'

'Milk, please. No sugar.' Reluctantly, Laura places the photograph back on the mantelpiece. She perches on the edge of the sofa and takes the delicate china saucer and a cup filled to the brim with weak, milky tea. And they chat for a while, about inconsequential things. How Laura is enjoying life back in Ullapool; what she is doing with herself these days. And, inevitably, about Cat.

'So, Catriona,' says Isobel. 'How is she?'

'Good. She's a lawyer. Working in America right now.' Laura

pulls a photograph out of her handbag: a two- or three-year-old photograph of Cat out in the desert in denim shorts and a black tee-shirt, face solemn as always.

'She's the image of her father.'

'She is.'

'Are they in contact still, at all?'

'Not much. Alec never really bothered to keep in touch. She tried to write to him a few times when she was a teenager, but he hardly ever replied.' Laura looks away, stares into the glowing coals of the fire. 'Maybe it was my fault for moving her away, but I didn't think I had much choice at the time.'

Isobel nods. 'He had a temper on him, did Alec. Can't say I blame you for getting out of it, lassie.'

Laura swallows; looks down into her empty cup. Did they all know, then? she wonders. Did they all know, and do nothing?

Isobel tilts her head at Laura as though anticipating her question. 'Oh, I don't know what went on, if that's what you're asking. And Alec never spoke about it. Never spoke about you again. I just made my own assumptions. Based on his background, and all.'

'His background?'

Isobel nods, slowly. 'Is that why you've come, then?'

Laura blushes. Is she so obvious? 'Meg Macleod suggested that I come to see you. She's my neighbour.'

'Ah, Meg. We don't see enough of her, now, in the village. Well, then. If Meg sent you, she must think there was something that you needed to know.'

Laura waits, silent. She's not sure that she wants to know anything at all, but here she is, after all.

Isobel sits back in her chair and sighs. 'It's a sorry tale. When Murdo, Alec's father, came back from the war in '45, his younger brother Iain came to live with them. He wasn't right in the head, you know? Shell-shocked during the war, they said. I think it was more than shell-shock myself, but what do I know.

Alec's mother, Margaret, did her best to care for him, but he had some funny moods. She wasn't really comfortable with him there, but she couldn't say as much to Murdo. Murdo would beat her, you see. Go down the pub, come home, and beat her. Iain would stand by and watch, so she said, urging him on.' She closes her eyes briefly. 'I wanted her to leave him, but she wouldn't do that. You didn't do that, in those days. Well, of course it all continued after the boys were born. Alec was the oldest, and protective of Robert. He argued with his father, tried to protect his mother. But then Murdo would take a stick to him. Or his belt. Beat him senseless. But Alec always made sure that Murdo beat him, and not Robert.' She pauses, seeing the expression on Laura's face. 'Did you not know all this, then?'

Laura shakes her head, bewildered. 'Alec said his dad had a bit of a temper. He wouldn't ever talk about his childhood.'

'Well, of course, the beatings were bad enough. But then Iain began to abuse Robert.'

'Abuse him?'

Isobel flushes. 'Aye. You know.'

Abuse him? Robert – shy gentle Robert – abused?

'He was ten years old when it started. Maggie didn't find out till months later, when Alec finally told her. She threw Iain out of the house and told Murdo she'd kill Iain if he ever set foot here again. Murdo must've believed her, for Iain went away to the mental hospital in Inverness. We never saw him again. But of course, the damage was done. To both of them – to Alec, as well as Robert. Alec hated his father; he began to go around with an unruly gang. Always getting into trouble. A wild thing. He hated his father, all right, but the pity of it was that he was the image of him. Whenever you looked in his eyes you saw Murdo. So I always wondered if he'd turn out the same way. Because some of them do, don't they? It runs through the generations, so they say.'

'What happened to Robert? Where is he now?'

Isobel shakes her head sadly. 'Ach, he never married, didn't Robert. I think it broke something in him. He was a lovely boy. Lovely man. He worked in the bank here for years then went off to Canada. Died of AIDS six months ago.'

Robert. Abused. And Alec, watching it all.

So much violence, so much abuse. Thoughts and images are swimming around in her mind but she can't let them in: doesn't want to deal with them now, not here. She takes a final gulp of lukewarm tea. 'Do you ever see Alec now?'

Isobel shakes her head. 'Not since his parents died. His father went first, then Maggie. She died just before Robert. Alec hasn't been back since. He writes to me every year at Christmas, but it's as though he wants to forget the place now. Too many bad memories, perhaps. He's started afresh.'

And how very fine for him that he can, Laura thinks. She glances over at the photograph again. Anger rises up in her, fights with sympathy. He could take on someone else's children, but not his own. And his new wife – did he ever beat her, she wonders? No, probably not. Probably she doesn't even know.

Laura feels strange as she drives home. Head buzzing with memories, making connections, seeing pictures. It's just as Meg says, she thinks as she makes the now-familiar turn along the lochside road. Everyone has their story. Aunt Lizzie, Alec – even Meg has a sad tale to tell. The idea wouldn't be a surprise to anyone else, maybe, but then Laura has never been good at seeing the world through the eyes of other people. Not until now.

Back at the croft, she enters with a sigh of relief and makes her way to the kitchen. Tea: more tea, that's what she needs. Well, actually, she'd like a drink. And for the first time in a long, long while the old longing comes over her. But fortunately she hasn't a thing in the house. And she wouldn't do it anyway. Would she?

No. She wouldn't do that.

There's only one thing to do; only one way to deal with it.

She reaches again for her notepad.

15

Cat

'Phoenix Approach, this is Cessna Four Tango Two November Romeo, two miles east of Chandler. Student pilot.' I release the red 'talk' button on the control wheel and immediately another pilot leaps into the gap.

This is madness. A cacophony of voices, crackling through the airwaves without pause as aircraft after aircraft reports its position and waits for instructions from the smooth-voiced air traffic controller. The difference between those aircraft and me? I'm a rookie all alone in a two-seater, single-engine trainer just trying to cross through Phoenix air space to get to Wickenburg. They are deep-voiced airline pilots flying 767s and MD-11s and all manner of serious planes, who would quite like to land at Phoenix Sky Harbour International Airport.

And I'm about to get in their way.

My heart rains frantic blows against the bars of my ribcage as half a dozen new transmissions follow mine and the controller answers each of them, one by one. Has he even noticed me?

'Cessna Two November Romeo, go ahead.'

A sudden jolt of electricity courses through my arms and down to my fingertips; I jerk my thumb down on the red button again and start to gabble. 'Er – Phoenix Approach, Cessna Two November Romeo en route north-west to Wickenburg.' And then the inevitable happens: my brain races ahead of itself and drives straight into a white-out. I open my mouth again; I falter.

Shit. What am I supposed to say now? Something's missing. Isn't it?

The early morning sun strikes the scratches on the Perspex windscreen and refracts into a thousand slivers of blinding light. East, I think. Tell him you're flying east right now. 'Flying heading zero-niner-zero,' I add, with more than a hint of desperation in my voice.

There's a small pause, and then: 'Cessna Two November Romeo, if you're planning on making it to Wickenburg before you run out of fuel, you might wanna think about turning back around and heading *west* sometime soon.'

I flush. *Smart-ass*, I think. Smart-ass. I can't turn around, or I'll fly right into your airspace. Phoenix Class B airspace – the airspace, heavily restricted, that surrounds all the busiest airports – and if I do that without permission you'll throw the book at me. I bite my tongue, imagining all the serious guys in their oh-so-serious cockpits sniggering at his little joke.

'Climb and maintain two thousand five hundred,' he continues blandly. 'Fly heading two seven zero. Remain clear of Class Bravo.'

I repeat back the instruction – dripping as much acid into my voice as I dare – and bank in a sharp circle to the right, squawking the new transponder code that follows.

A direct heading from Chandler to Wickenburg would take me right over the top of Sky Harbour Airport, but he's clearly decided that would be a bad idea. And thinking about all those testosterone-laden heavies out there, I'm one hundred percent with him. This new routing takes me well to the south; a quick glance at the Phoenix Terminal Area Chart on my lap indicates that flying on this heading and at this altitude will keep me outside of the Class B boundary altogether.

Concentrating fiercely, looking out for other traffic, I cross over Interstate 10 just north of Firebird Lake. In theory, getting through Phoenix airspace should be the most difficult part of the trip. Not that it's an easy trip: far from it. Today is my third and final mandatory solo cross-country flight, and the longest.

I'm required to fly a kind of triangle, with two destination points instead of the usual one. So we've chosen to start with Wickenburg, and then I'll be heading up north to Prescott.

South Mountain passes just below my right wing; I'm focusing so hard on keeping my bearings that I almost miss the next transmission. 'Cessna Two November Romeo, climb and maintain three thousand five hundred. Fly heading two eight zero.' I confirm and then follow the instructions, bank gently to the right, and the controller calmly advises me there's a Boeing 767 descending into Sky Harbour right there ahead of me at two o' clock.

Oh, great. I hunch forward and peer out of the windscreen, desperately scanning the sky to my right, fearing that I'm about to become the loser in this time-limited game of 'spot the airplane'. I can picture the controller waiting for my confirmation, drumming his fingers impatiently, muttering about incompetent female foreigners cluttering up his airspace and taking up valuable radio time. Concentrate, Cat. A 767 ought to be hard to miss.

A bored voice intrudes into my increasingly frantic search. 'Cessna Two November Romeo, traffic now at twelve o'clock.' And then finally I spot it, cutting right across my flight path a few miles ahead.

'Traffic in sight,' I inform him and laugh nervously, hoping for all I'm worth that whoever this man is who's running the show, he had a good night's sleep. Because wherever I look there are aircraft. Aircraft ascending and aircraft descending, swarming in circles round the skies like a scattered flock of birds. I focus on breathing evenly and remind myself that all this isn't completely new to me; I flew through Class B last week on my cross-country north to Sedona. It seemed straightforward enough at the time, but Jesse was with me then – and just the simple fact of his presence saturates the air with calm.

Except for this morning. This morning he didn't seem quite so serene. He walked out to the plane with me; he seemed oddly reluctant to let me go.

'Call me on my cellphone as soon as you get to Wickenburg, you hear? You'll need to stop and tie the plane down anyway to find someone on the ground to endorse your logbook. Head for the FBO – chances are you'll run into other pilots there, and if anyone's come from the north you can get a real-life update on conditions around Prescott. I have a couple of students today but you should be in Wickenburg before I have to go up.' He looked down at me with a faint frown on his face. 'It can be real bumpy around all those hills and mountains up north when the ground warms up, so expect that and just stay calm. If you don't like what's happening, turn around and come on home.'

'All right.' I grinned up at him with as much confidence as I could muster. Perfectly content to wallow in the warmth of his concern, I didn't remind him that we'd gone through all this before. He stopped just short of Two November Romeo, sighed and thrust his hands into the pockets of his shorts. Mouth suddenly dry, I looked away. Over the past couple of weeks I'd been trying not to be too aware of the fact that the flight school dress code for instructors – such as it is – had changed from long pants to shorts now that the full onslaught of summer heat was beginning. I'd been failing.

'You sure you're okay?' he asked.

'I'm fine.' And strange, now, that I should be the one reassuring him. 'It's an adventure, right? This is what flying is for. I've had enough of scooting around in circles. I want to go places.'

He nodded again, slowly, and finally rustled up a smile. 'Okay. You just take care.' He reached out and tucked back behind my ear a stray strand of hair that had escaped from my ponytail. And there it was again: that sudden vertiginous tilt as the world slid away beneath my feet. Rapidly, he withdrew

367

his hand and slipped it back into his pocket. He looked away, taking a sudden interest in the condition of the paintwork on the small Cessna's nose.

Something has changed since that dinner, a couple of weeks ago. Something has been set in motion and I daren't even begin to think where it might be leading us.

The empty Gila River bed is coming up ahead of me now. With the racetrack to the north and the Sierra Estrellas to the south, the final transmission cuts into my concentrated effort to stick as close to my heading and altitude as I can – I don't want to give this guy ammunition for any more jokes at my expense. 'Cessna Two November Romeo, radar service terminated. Contact Luke Approach on 120.5 for traffic advisories; squawk one-two-zero-zero.'

And that, thankfully, is that: I'm on my own again. It's the thought of the communications with ATC that's been making me nervous about this trip; I've been fearful of getting mixed up. I've been afraid that I'd miss an instruction or clearance, find myself in the wrong place at the wrong time and cause a mass pile-up in the sky. Airplanes tumbling like fallen angels, bringing their fiery residues of chaos to orderly city streets. So many possible ways to fall from grace.

My only problem now is that ATC's routing through Phoenix didn't match the flight plan that Jesse and I had so carefully mapped out. I push in the throttle and climb to five thousand feet to give myself a little more altitude. I unfold the terminal area chart and decide to stay clear of the Luke Air Force Base alert area coming up just to the north of me – somehow I don't fancy joining in with their military jet training routines. A quick calculation with the plotter gives me a rough heading that will take me out west towards the Buckeye VORTAC, where I plan to turn north to Wickenburg. It's not exactly the straightest route, but it's probably the safest.

On course again, with a plan, I can begin to relax.

Wickenburg is a small town, and the airport is easy to spot against the hills and ridges that sweep away to the south and west. The Unicom is silent; there's nobody flying out there right now. I enter the traffic pattern for runway two-three, announcing my intentions over the radio. Slipping down the invisible slope to the runway, I land right on the numbers. Jesse says that's the difference between a good pilot and a bad: the ability to believe in what can't be seen. It's not an ability that I ever thought I would have. Not me: not the logical, rational Cat who turned up her nose at stories of fairies and magic. Cat the lawyer, Cat the fearful. Cat the earthbound.

Ah, but there's so much in my life right now that I never would have believed possible.

On the ground I tie down the aircraft outside the FBO and punch his number into my cellphone. He answers shortly after the first ring.

'Hey.' He sounds relieved. 'So ATC didn't chew you up and spit you out in little pieces?'

'No, but I think he might have quite liked to. He routed me south, so I stayed out of Class B altogether. The flight plan went by the wayside, but I got here via the Buckeye VORTAC. I'll tell you exactly what I did when I get back.'

'And Wickenburg's okay?'

'Yup. No traffic at all right now. I'm just heading into the FBO to get my logbook signed and then I'll be off again.'

'Way to go. Call me when you get to Prescott, you hear? I have a lesson in thirty minutes, so if I'm out flying and don't pick up, leave me a message. And if you're in any doubt about anything, stay there and wait for me to call you back. Oh – and once you're in Prescott, go into the flight service station and update your weather briefing.'

'Yes, Mom.'

He laughs. 'And you take care, you hear?'

'Will do. See you later.'

I stick the phone back in my flight bag and head into the FBO with a ludicrously soppy smile on my face.

From Wickenburg I turn north-east and follow the heading we planned, which runs alongside Route 89 through the mountains. An altitude of eight thousand feet should keep me well above the highest terrain. It's so different from flying over the flat desert around Phoenix; here the earth curves and bubbles and flows, gently raising itself up to the sky as it spreads out to the north.

The other day Maria Mercedes told me that to the Native people, the earth is the body of the Great Mother. 'Look at it,' she said. 'Look at it one day, when you're up there. You'll see. You'll see her shape, see her form. You'll see for yourself the curves and the contours, the wrinkles and the ridges. They say that Mother Earth lies on her back and opens herself to the embrace of Father Sky. She endures everything: extremes of heat and cold and aridity. And out of that endurance she produces life. Life springs from her body even in the most unexpected places. She bends; she adapts.'

And looking down now, it is easy to see what she means. A small circular breast rises from the desert floor crowned with a swollen nipple. Ridges criss-cross the land, protruding like thick veins from suntanned flesh. Everything is laid out; nothing is hidden. And just for a moment, a new version of the world seems possible. A version of the world in which the earth is my friend and not my enemy. A version of the world in which the earth and the sky aren't at odds with each other: they're a part of the same story. *The Great Mystery*, Jesse called it, on one of those first flights so many months ago. The threshold; the place where the earth meets the sky.

*

The aircraft starts to shudder and dip. Instinctively, I clutch at the wheel. Relax, I tell myself. Relax. It's just your average light turbulence – I may not like it, but I'm used to it by now. Especially on hot desert afternoons. I release my stranglehold on the control wheel and try to concentrate on the changing scenery below. Such a small palette of colours: just a single shade of green splattered across the scorched brown sand. Below me on 89 there isn't much traffic; the road stretches through the mountains like a shiny grey serpent, its coils rising and falling with the swell of the land.

A gust of wind hits the plane from the right, slithers under her belly and nudges up her nose – ah, but that's too high, the airspeed is beginning to fall and if I'm not careful we'll stall – and I press the wheel forward again, lower the nose. Sweat breaks out on my brow and I wipe it away with a trembling hand. Another sudden jolt; the turbulence is increasing in intensity now. I exhale loudly as the city of Prescott comes into view. I badly want to be on the ground. The palms of my hands are moist and my breathing is shallow and rapid. The ATIS broadcast tells me that the winds are at fifteen miles an hour from the south. They feel a whole lot stronger than that but that's probably just because they're gusty – though of course it's entirely possible that the wind speed and direction are different on the ground.

At six miles out I call the tower and receive instructions to join right traffic for runway two-one left. The turbulence seems to ease a little as I slowly descend to pattern altitude, but just as I enter the downwind leg for the runway the wind whips up unexpectedly, gusting around us, pushing and shoving us from side to side. The windsock by the side of the runway is rising and falling like a punch-bag as the gusts hit it and just as suddenly ebb away. Hanging onto the control wheel for dear life, I try to keep us steady. The wind is coming from behind me now, and slightly to the right, and I crab the airplane into it to avoid being blown away from the airport. But then it fades away completely and suddenly I'm veering off course. I'm much closer in to the runway than I should be. I bank left, but I'm not sure whether I have enough room to execute a proper base leg. Long pointed fingernails claw at the lining of my stomach and a pulse drums away at the base of my throat. *Calm, Cat, calm,* I tell myself – but there's no time to worry about being calm; this isn't working out well at all.

I extend my downwind leg, pulling out the power a little, lifting the nose to slow the plane right down, descending in as steep a slope as I dare. A little more power; a sharp right turn to base, descending steeply all the while. I'm so close to the runway now that almost immediately I have to turn again for final approach. I pull the power all the way out for landing but a sudden sharp gust swirls underneath the plane, giving us unexpected lift, and for a moment I fear that I'm going to overshoot the runway, land long. Another gust, under the nose again this time, and the nose is lifting and the airspeed is already too slow and if I'm not careful we're going to stall and we're way, way too close to the ground to recover. I slam the control wheel down, think about pushing the power back in, going around, trying again, but it's a long runway and I should be okay and in any case I really, really don't want to go through this again, but then as rapidly as it came the wind dies down again – dies down completely and the plane suddenly sinks, sinks far too rapidly and now it looks as if I'm going to land short. That would be a seriously bad idea but I seem to be out of options. Heart pounding, I slam in the power and just make it, landing right at the very edge of the asphalt with a jolt.

By the time I taxi off the runway I'm shaking.

———

Please pick up, please pick up. But his cellphone diverts to voicemail. I wrap my arms around my waist and squeeze hard; I don't know what to do. I hang up without leaving a message.

I pace up and down the length of the plane. An occasional gust of wind rocks her from side to side, but she's safely tied to the asphalt. I talk to myself incessantly as I pace. I tell myself that this wind isn't anything I haven't already experienced; I tell myself that the Flight Service Station briefer wouldn't have advised that conditions were safe if they weren't. Tall, thin, in his mid-twenties, with thick black-rimmed spectacles and the kind of supercilious air commonly encountered at New York City hotel reception desks, he was surprised to hear that I'd experienced wind shear. 'Well, ma'am, all I can tell you is that you're the first report of it that we've had today. I'll make a note of it, of course, but as you can see by just looking at the runway, people are taking off and landing out there without any apparent problems at all.' He looked me up and down as if doubting my ability to even know what wind shear was, taking in the tangled sweaty ponytail, denim shorts, black tee-shirt and slightly scruffy tennis shoes with an air of genteel bemusement. I was tempted to ask what else he expected to see in the way of attire on a hot May day in the middle of the desert south-west. Top hat and tails, perhaps?

But I really don't doubt that his advice was correct. I've no doubt at all that most pilots can handle that level of turbulence accompanied by gusty winds and – maybe – the occasional spot of wind shear.

I'm just not one of those pilots.

Rivulets of sweat are coursing down by back, but my hands are as cold as ice.

What am I doing, thinking I can fly?

Scaredy-Cat! Why don't you just jump?

Everything looks pretty calm out on the runway. A Cessna 172 has just landed; some kind of Cherokee has just taken off. I look doubtfully at Two November Romeo; she's smaller than either of them. And so very delicate, with the thin wiry struts that brace her wings against her body, her spindly white legs

373

and whiskery antennae. I tug at the propeller blades, making sure they're firmly attached. For a moment a different voice slips into my head, thin and distant like the voice of a fading ghost. *Propeller blades don't just drop off, Cat.*

Jack. The thought of him makes me smile.

'Do you miss it?' Jesse asked me last week on our dual cross-country to Sedona. 'Do you miss it at all, your old life?' And I really did try to think about it, I really did try to remember but it all seemed so far away. I looked away from him; closed my eyes. I tried to focus; I tried to hone in on Adam's face and the smell of his skin and the sort-of-hazel shade of his eyes but all I could see on the movie screen of my mind was a pool of clear blue water with sunlight rippling on its surface like a scattering of fairy gold.

I wrap my hands around the spinner; I bow my head and close my eyes as if I'm seeking a blessing.

And maybe I am. Because if I'm going to fly in the desert I need to be able to deal with turbulence.

But it scares me. It always scared me, and *I'm sitting down and I can't stop the terror as the storm rages around us and the wind buffets the body of the aircraft and we stumble and rock and fall through the turbulence, and I haven't a thought for the man or his child or for Tiffany or for anything else at all except for the overwhelming need to just hold on.*

Is this where I am? Right back where I started?

Jack looks at my hands, clasped tight on the arms of my seat, white knuckled. My jaw aches from tension. 'You know,' he says, 'I've got just the answer for that.'

Right back where I started.

And there's nothing to stop me from just staying here – just holding on – just a little while longer – but the longer I stay the less likely it is that I'll ever be able to muster the courage to strap myself back in this plane.

Or I can go. Close my eyes and turn back around and just

take off again. Take off, fly on – right into the face of it all. Close my ears to all of those voices screaming inside, telling me that I should just get the hell out of here and run for my life.

But that would take a courage that I don't think I have.

Jesse would know what to do. If Jesse was here, I'd feel safe.

I pick up the phone again; still he doesn't answer. And as it rings I see him standing there with a slightly worried frown on his face, just as he did this morning. And for a moment, it occurs to me to wonder why. Doesn't he think I'm up to this? In spite of all his fine words, does he still wonder whether I've got what it takes?

Ah, but he's right to wonder, isn't he? And he'd be wondering precisely that, if he could see me now. I know just how his eyes would look: kind and understanding and a little bit sad. Just as they looked at the end of the lesson on that day I refused to do stalls. But that's not what I want to see in his eyes. What I want to see is what I saw in them the next time that I went back to the airport. The day that I climbed right back into the plane. The day that I finally practised those stalls.

His voice cuts in. 'Hi – this is Jesse. Sorry I can't take your call right now. Please leave a message and I'll get right back to you.'

I take a deep breath, and I leave a message.

Okay, Cat – hold on. The guy in the Cherokee ahead of you there did just fine. You saw him sway a little as he rose off the runway; you saw the wings dip to the left – you're going to have to expect that – but you saw him depart safely out of the traffic pattern. You heard the tower tell you quite calmly that you were cleared for takeoff. All in a day's work. Just another day in paradise. Jesus, girl, you're rambling. It's okay. Throttle in, feel her pull to the left. A little more right rudder – keep to the centre line now – more right rudder, you're going to veer off the runway. Fifty knots so rotate now – pull the nose up;

it's okay. A little dip to the right this time – no need for those sudden jerky movements, the plane will right itself. And for heaven's sake, loosen your death-grip on the wheel. Keep on the right rudder, keep to the runway heading – and oh, dear God, another small sink but nothing to be worried about, you're high enough now. Another sharp gust, but bank left – *bank left*, for God's sake: the wings aren't going to fall off and you're not going to tip over. Turn more sharply, don't be such a wimp. Over the highway; don't look down if you don't like it. Just look ahead. Look ahead and above you, look at the clear bright blue of the sky and tell yourself that it's all okay.

It's worse than it was coming in; I'm skittering around from side to side as if someone has me dangling on a string, just blowing around in the wind. I continue to climb, hoping that it'll be clearer higher up. It isn't. Route 69 joins I-17 and I adjust my route slightly to join and follow it. It's comforting to see the cars below: company in my terror.

I may fool myself that I'm immune to the earth up here, but that's just another illusion. I'm no more immune to the earth than I am to the sky. Because even the clear blue sky can turn on you, with raging gusts that batter and shake you and threaten to dislodge you from your precarious perch four thousand feet above the ground. Another sharp jolt from below, then we're falling; my breath catches in my throat and my head bumps against the ceiling of the plane. My stomach is deep into its usual agitated dance and my body is drenched in sweat. I was never one for roller-coaster rides as a child; I don't know whether I can take another hour or more of this. And it's so strong now, that part of me that wants so badly to turn back around and land, but I ignore its shrill insistent voice in my mind.

This is a place where I could so easily die. And yet, as I concentrate on just keeping the plane in the air with a fierceness that I've never known before, it comes to me that I've never felt so alive.

Above me, a large bird tumbles, searching for a thermal. A buzzard, or an eagle – I can't tell. But, buzzard or eagle, she's still up there. She's struggling, but she's still up there.

And then I remember.

Eagle Woman.

It had been such a spectacular flight to Sedona last weekend, like flying through a strange petrified forest of red rock. Red stone spires – cathedrals, they call them – and exhilarating distant skylines filled with buttes and mesas and god-sized table-tops. Jesse suggested we ride into town and have lunch before heading back. We wandered around for a while, peering into the shop windows. There was nothing of real interest to see, just the usual tourist tat. Until, through the window of an art shop, I spotted a print. Against a golden background of rock and sky, a woman knelt on the edge of a cliff. She held a drinking vessel before her, as if in the form of an offering. Or maybe even supplication. Superimposed over the figure of the woman was another figure – one with the same shape and attitude, but with the wings and the head of an eagle.

It was a painting of transformation. Woman transforming herself into eagle.

I went into the shop and looked more closely; the title of the print was 'Eagle Woman'.

The woman behind the counter told us she'd always admired it. 'Looks like a Native American angel, don't she? Looks like she's just thinking about maybe jumping off that cliff and testing out those wings for the very first time.' She smiled at me: a smile of feminine conspiracy from across the counter. 'Guess we all know how she feels, hey, hon?' Her face softened and her eyes became sad for a moment as she took the print from my hands and reached under the counter for a tube to put it into. 'Trouble is, most of us just turn right around and walk on back down that mountain. We're all too scared to fly. After all, who's going to catch us if we fall?'

I looked over at Jesse, and the smile of complicity in his eyes turned my heart over. And I wanted to say to her – *No*. Don't you see? That's not how it's supposed to be. *Listen*, I wanted to say to her: listen. We learn to save ourselves. We learn to fly under our own steam, and we make our own safety nets. We card and we spin and we wind – and we weave. From our hopes and our dreams we weave ourselves back into life. From our hopes and our dreams and the fragile gossamer threads of our courage.

I close my eyes and gather those threads round me now. I steady my breathing and relax my grip on the control wheel. I wipe the dripping sweat from my brow and follow the dancing steps of the plane. Where she leads, I follow. Eagle eyes; eyes that see to the front and the side at the same time. Eyes that see the past and beyond it into the future. Sharp and clear, unfolding before me in perfect Technicolor. I stretch out my arms, and I fly.

I fly, and I save the only life that I can save.

❦ ❦ ❦

When finally I get home, exhausted but flushed with success and the pleasure of Jesse's approval, the familiar brown envelope lies waiting in my mailbox. And I think, for a moment, about setting it aside for another day. Even, perhaps, about throwing it away. Because I don't want to know about all that now: I just don't care. It all seems so very long ago.

But I can feel its presence as I wolf down my hastily heated pizza; it watches me from the countertop as I prowl around the kitchen looking for something sweet to fill the sudden deep hunger inside me – I feel as though I haven't eaten properly in weeks. It lurks darkly in the corner and it pulls at me and eventually, of course, I give in. I take it, along with my ice-cold Coors Light, and I sit on the sofa in front of another glowing desert sunset and the memories invade me again.

And it is in this way that, finally, I learn what made you begin. I always did wonder. But it was hardly something we could have a jolly little chat about, was it? Your drinking was something that we never got to talk about: it simply didn't exist. And all these years, it's lain there between us. A silent party to every conversation. So much unspoken; so many stories untold.

It makes me think about a story I heard once, somewhere along the way. A story about a story bag. Once upon a time, there was a young boy who refused to share his stories with anyone else. He hoarded them all in a bag that he carried on his back; he kept them all to himself. And the more he hoarded them, the larger the bag grew until there was no space inside it any more. And the stories got twisted, and when eventually they burst their way out of the bag they were so broken that they went on a rampage through the town where he lived, and they killed every child that they found.

How big is my story bag now, do you think? I've carried it around for so many years. Heavier and heavier it's grown, weighing me down. And the stories inside it just as twisted and filled with anger. Yes, I was angry that you drank, goddamn it. Didn't it ever occur to you? *I just can't understand it, Cat. Why you're always so angry at me.* But how could it never occur to you? Oh, I knew that you didn't drink out of spite; I knew that you drank because you were unhappy. But there were only the two of us in the world – *you and me against the world, little Cat* – and you shut me out. You blotted me out in whisky, as if I didn't exist.

You left me.

And for so very long, I couldn't forgive you that. I don't

think you ever really knew what it was like, for me. Perhaps now you can see. Perhaps now. Just as I can finally see how it was for you. Perhaps now, both of us can begin to understand. Perhaps now, I can maybe even begin to leave it behind. Because I let one of those stories out, didn't I? I let it out and told it to Jesse. And now the other stories know that there is a way out: there is the possibility of escape.

And because there are other good things that I have learned. I can reach out; I can overcome fear. I can become Eagle Woman.

So you see, Mother: all is not lost. Nothing is ever all lost.

16

Laura

It was when Mara found her mother one day in a heap on the floor, at the foot of the stairs where she had fallen, that finally the selkie woman had to explain. She told the child her story: the tale of the loss of her skin. She explained that she'd stayed all those years only because she loved her; she'd stayed because Mara needed a mother.

Mara's eyes seemed so old to her mother then: old beyond her years. 'What good is a mother who's fading away? And how can you truly be a mother to me, when you're dying a little more every day?' Sadly, she shook the small dark head that was so like the selkie's own. 'No – you must go back to the sea. We have to find your skin.'

With each day that went by, the selkie woman withered still more. Mara looked after her; each morning she bathed her parched flaky body with water that she fetched from the sea. And whenever she could, she hunted for her mother's skin. 'I'll find it for you, Mother,' she whispered each day. 'I promise I'll find your skin.'

The burden of responsibility weighed heavy on her young shoulders, but there was nothing that the selkie could do to halt the sickness that was draining away her life.

His name was Roddy. Laura didn't know whether this was the real thing or not, and this time she didn't really care: she just wanted the company. Just wanted to have some fun. And Roddy was fun. He was an insurance salesman, and he always dressed nicely: pinstripe suits and nice pastel-coloured shirts. He liked to go dancing, and Laura still loved to dance. Roddy was the perfect partner: he could dance to anything, whether it was ballroom or disco.

Tonight they'd been to a disco; they'd danced and danced until eleven o'clock, and then they'd gone back to Roddy's flat for a drink. And she'd been to bed with him. Laura had some standards, after all: she didn't take her boyfriends home to sleep with her. Cat wouldn't like that.

She felt a bit giddy. She'd had way too much to drink, and Roddy was in the same state. Roddy liked a drink. Tonight he'd walked her home. She should have taken a taxi really, but he only lived fifteen minutes down the road. Except that it had taken them much longer than that because neither of them seemed capable of walking in a straight line and they kept stopping and clutching on to each other and giggling.

When they got back to Laura's house, he asked if he could come in for a nightcap before he walked back home again. Laura didn't see why not; it was after midnight now, and Cat would be in bed. She wouldn't mind.

She fumbled in her handbag for her keys, but she couldn't seem to find the keyhole. She was laughing hysterically when she pushed the door really hard because it was always sticking at the bottom, and it gave way and Roddy almost fell on top of her.

'Sssshhh,' she told him, putting a finger over her lips. 'You'll wake Cat.'

'So?' Roddy said. 'I like Cat. She won't mind.' He moved to the bottom of the stairs. 'Oh Ca-at!' he called.

Laura pulled at his arm to move him away and into the living room, and reluctantly he followed her. But she couldn't seem to find the light switch; she knocked over a small table with a crash. This set Roddy off giggling again.

Laura turned around to the wall to have another try, and saw Cat standing in the doorway. She had a thin cotton robe over her nightdress; her long blonde hair was tousled. She looked furious. 'What's going on here?' she asked. 'What are you doing?'

Laura felt like a naughty schoolgirl, which made her giggle again, because she was supposed to be the mother, and Cat the schoolgirl. Though she wouldn't be a schoolgirl for long, now: Cat was sixteen.

Roddy walked towards her with his arms open. 'Cat, darling,' he said. 'I was hoping to see you. Come to your Uncle Roddy.'

Cat took a step backwards. 'You leave me alone. I just came to see if Mum was all right.'

'Course she's all right. I'm looking after her. I just came in for a nightcap.'

'You look like you've had quite enough. Both of you.'

'Ah, come on now, Cat – don't be a bore. Give your Uncle Roddy a kiss.'

Cat pushed him away as he made to put his arms around her and he staggered back into the room. 'I said, leave me alone.'

Laura said, 'Leave her alone, Roddy. She doesn't like to be mauled.'

But Roddy looked angry now. 'I was only trying to be friendly. What's the matter with you, you uptight little bitch?'

Something penetrated the alcohol-induced haze, and Laura began to understand that the situation was getting out of hand. She shook her head, trying to clear it. 'Roddy – that's enough.'

But it was too late – he was walking over to Cat again and he was taking her by the shoulders. She struggled but he pulled her against him and tried to kiss her. He was much stronger than she was. Laura could see the horror on Cat's face and her own heart started to beat rapidly and her stomach turned over in a sudden burst of fear.

She staggered over to Roddy and tried to pull him off Cat, but he lashed out behind him and Laura fell to the floor. Her head fell back against the corner of the old wooden bureau and the last thing she remembered was Cat screaming 'Mummy!'

Laura is breathing heavily now. She rests her elbows on the kitchen table, and lowers her head into her hands. They're trembling.

She'd forgotten about Roddy. She's forgotten about that whole incident. Dear God, how could she have forgotten that? What else has she so efficiently forgotten, over the years? What had happened after she'd blacked out? Did she ever know? Did she ever even think to ask?

All she remembers now is that she'd come round at some point during the night and there'd been no sign of Cat and no sign of Roddy. Her head had hurt like hell. She struggles now to remember, to focus. She'd gone upstairs – yes, that's right; she'd gone upstairs and peeked through the open door of Cat's bedroom. There had been no trace of her. Then she'd noticed the light under the bathroom door. 'Cat?' she'd called out. 'What are you doing?' And Cat had just replied – hadn't she? – as Cat always did – as Cat always does – 'I'm fine, Mother. Just go to bed, will you, and leave me alone.'

And Laura had done just that. The next morning she'd woken with an even more blinding headache and a vague recollection that Roddy had misbehaved, that he'd somehow tried to hurt Cat. But her mind had skitted away from the memory; she didn't want to think about the detail of it. But she was left with a vague sense of shame and a feeling that somehow she might have put her daughter in danger. She promised herself that she'd never drink again.

But Cat had been all right, hadn't she? Cat had been no different. Except that she wouldn't talk to Laura. Whenever she looked at her, her eyes were full of betrayal and contempt. Laura couldn't stand it. Everyone she had ever loved had turned against her and what had she ever done to deserve it? So she'd gone into the living room and opened the cupboard and took out the bottle of Bell's. A new bottle, shiny and golden and full of the promise of oblivion.

That was the last thing that she'd remembered for a week.

And that was the end of it, for Cat and Laura. The next two years, while Cat was in the sixth form, were a nightmare. Laura did, after all, give up men. But she compensated by drinking even more. To this day, she has no idea what her daughter did during those two years. Laura barely held her job down; she took a lot of sick time and she drank herself into a stupor every weekend, without fail. Cat would talk to her only when she had to; most of the time she would spend in her room. Ashamed, Laura let her.

It all came to a head on the day that Cat was leaving to go to university.

Laura woke up. She was sprawled horizontally across her bed; she had no idea what day it was. All she knew was that she needed another drink, but the bottle was nowhere to be seen. She must have left it downstairs. She pulled on her grubby dressing gown, wrinkled her nose at the stale smell of sweat and whisky that emanated from it, and staggered to the stairs. She was halfway down when she noticed Cat standing in the hall. She was dressed as if she was going out – wearing jeans and a black jacket. Squinting, Laura focused on the bags piled on the floor by the front door. She shook her head, trying vainly to clear it.

'What day is it?'

'Do you know how often I've answered that question?'

Laura was irritable. 'Don't talk back to me, young lady; just tell me what day it is. What's going on?'

'Why start worrying now about what's going on? It hasn't concerned you much for the last two years.'

Laura sighed; she was too tired for this. Too sick. All she wanted was a drink, for God's sake. 'What are you doing with all those bags?'

'I'm leaving home, remember? Today's the day I'm going to university.'

Laura's hand flew to her mouth. 'Oh, my God. I'd forgotten.' She saw Cat's mouth turn up into a sneer, and flushed. 'Well, you might have reminded me.'

'Oh? And when would I have done that, exactly? Last night, when you were so paralytic that you puked all over the bathroom floor for two hours on end? Or Thursday night, when I came home and found you lying stark naked in the front room with the curtains open and all the lights blazing?'

Laura felt dizzy; she grabbed onto the handrail and sat down on the stairs. She didn't know what to say. Normally they didn't talk about her drinking – they just ignored it. They treated it as if it wasn't there. This was breaking all the rules.

'Anyway. I'm going now. Goodbye.'

'Wait – how are you going to manage? I was going to come with you. At least let me get dressed and I'll help you to the station with the bags.'

'Come to the station? Like that? Stinking of alcohol, big black bags under your eyes, a cute little stagger in your step? Oh, I don't think so, Mother. Do you?'

Tears sprang to Laura's eyes. She couldn't think straight; why couldn't Cat just be quiet for a while, and let her think?

'Oh, that's right. Cry, why don't you? That's what you always do. Cry, and tell yourself that everybody hates you. That it's all their fault. And then go on into the front room and have another drink. Because that's all you're good for.'

Laura saw that Cat was shaking.

'Cat. I don't understand. Why are you always so angry with me?'

'Why? Just look at yourself, Mother.' Cat took hold of her mother's arm, and with a strength that surprised Laura, she pulled her to her feet and shoved her in front of the full-length mirror in the hall. 'Take a look at yourself. What do you see? Do you see a mother? Because I don't. I don't see anything remotely resembling a mother.' Laura shut her eyes against the uncharacteristic fury on Cat's face. 'Do you know what I see? I see a drunk. And I've had enough of it. For – what, now – ten years? – I've looked after you. I've cleaned up after you. I've lied for you; I've kept your secret. Mopped up your vomit. Listened to your weeping. Listened to you blaming my father, Aunt Lizzie, me – everyone in the world but yourself – for what's wrong with you. You're not the mother: you're the child. I've been the mother. And I've had enough of it now. I'm leaving.'

'Cat –' And Laura had simply looked at her, helpless; somehow she couldn't seem to find the words. She was confused. Shaken. What was going on? How had this happened?

'And I won't be back. Do you understand that? I'm never coming back to this house. I've had enough of it. I've had enough of you.' She turned away, picked up a bag and slung it over her shoulder. 'The address of the halls of residence is in the kitchen by the kettle.'

After the door had closed behind her, Laura sank to her knees in front of the mirror. And saw herself fully, for the first time in years.

Laura inserts a page break into her manuscript, and begins to type again.

Ah, Cat. You must have been saving it up for years. All those words. All those words that imprinted themselves like a brand in my head and wouldn't go away. My first instinct, of course, was to have a drink. But that's exactly what you expected me to do.

When I'd been sober for three months I sent you a letter. I told you that I'd stopped drinking, that I'd had help. You wrote back to me – you always did. Polite little notes reporting on your progress. 'That's nice,' you said. But still you wouldn't come home. You didn't trust me, I think.

The months after I stopped drinking were tough. I can't tell you how tough. Not that I expect your sympathy; not that I deserve it. I had support, of course: I'd gone to an alcohol and drugs centre, and there were meetings and counselling sessions and all the help that I needed to pull myself through. It wasn't so bad during the week while I was working, but the weekends were agony. I walked the streets and hurled myself along the beach and gritted my teeth and tore at my hair, but I didn't ever take another drink. Not one. And I never have since.

I was thirty-nine years old: almost the same age that you are now. Can you imagine that? I felt as if I'd lost ten years of my life. More than that, I'd lost everything I'd ever loved. You. Your father. Even Uncle Billy, whose death I'd experienced in an alcoholic haze five years before. I was completely alone. But I didn't give in, Cat: I didn't let it drag me down again. I had the memory of your eyes and your words to keep me going.

But at thirty-nine years old it seemed as if my life was over. I had no friends and I hardly ever saw my family. My three sisters still lived in town, but they'd never been any more than strangers to me. Aunt Lizzie was still Aunt Lizzie; I visited her every week but it was a chore. All of my memories in that house that you and I lived in were bad. Except for the memories of you – but even they hurt. Because there were good times in that house too, Cat – don't you remember? I do. I remember you sitting on the settee next to me as I sang your favourite song. 'Paddy McGinty's Goat'. Val Doonican – do you remember how you loved him? You knew every word, off by heart. So many things I remember, but I won't bore you with them now.

Desperate, I took an evening class. I can't remember what it was called; they call it creative writing now, but it was all about writing children's stories. You know me – I always loved stories. (And so did you, once. Do you remember?) And I found that I could write them as well as tell them. So I bought myself an electric typewriter and every weekend I sat down and I wrote. I created imaginary worlds, just as I had done as a child. I lost myself in them. I finished a book and I sent it off to a publisher, and to my astonishment it was published.

I didn't ever make enough money to live on, of course: I still needed to work. But it gave me some of my confidence back.

And so I decided to leave – to leave completely. I decided to move to London. Crazy really – such an expensive city. But my publishers were there, and my illustrator. And nobody knew me there – I had no ties. I could reinvent myself. Reinvent myself for real; I'd only ever done it in my head before.

All those years I spent in London. In that cosy little flat in Battersea. You never saw it, of course, though we met up from time to time. Whenever you happened to be in town. Which wasn't often. Oh, I'm not blaming you – not at all. Because you were right to leave, Cat. You were right to say the things you said. The chances are that you saved my life. Because what would I have been if you hadn't said those words? Dead, maybe, or drunk in a gutter somewhere. Where would I be, if I hadn't had the image of your face that day driving me on?

But I never told you that you were right. I never said that I was sorry.

Would it help at all, if I told you I'm sorry now?

She hesitates, and then adds a final line.

And that incident with Roddy. He didn't – well, he didn't hurt you, did he, Cat?

Ah, it's so hard to relive these things. She's not sure that even the brisk breeze by the lochside can blow these cobwebs away. But she pulls on her jacket anyway and slips on her wellies over a pair of old green hunting socks; she heads on down to the field to the old rusty gate that opens onto another world.

It's a chilly breeze, a chilly evening, but she doesn't care. There's a sense of relief at being here. The simplicity of the place. The wind-blown patterns on the surface of the water; the careless bursts of air that lift the young branches of the trees and rustle their fledgling leaves. It's empty; it's elemental, and it's precisely what she needs. To sink down – to lose herself completely in the vivid reality of the moment.

Spring is in full swing now, and soon it'll be summer. The oystercatchers have been back for a good while, and Laura watches as a mating pair chases each other round in the sky. Swooping and diving and calling to each other with voices that resonate with joy. She smiles; ever-fanciful, she thinks. That much will never change. And she thinks of Cat, swooping and diving in her tiny little plane, six thousand miles away. Flying on through the pure burning blue of those vivid desert skies: Laura can barely imagine it. Is Cat flying now, she wonders? And she closes her eyes and she can almost hear the drone of the engine. Cat. Her Cat, a pilot. Smiles again; hugs herself with the pleasure of it. And thinks back to this last winter, when she had slipped so far down into darkness that it had seemed that there would be no more springs. Her Demeter winter, spent in mourning for Persephone. Spent in mourning for herself.

But she has to face it: she's no Demeter. When did she even register the grim and lonely Underworld that Cat must have been living in, all those years? When did she ever rescue Cat? No, she's no Demeter. And the image of Roddy flashes into her mind again. Dear God, she thinks. Dear God. Please let him not have hurt her. It's strange, Laura thinks: if it came right down to it you wouldn't hesitate. If someone asked you to, you'd give your life for your children without a second thought. And yet, on a daily basis you torture them in ways that you're hardly even aware of.

No, the truth of it is that Cat had rescued her. Laura had said as much to Meg the other night, over the inevitable cup of tea. 'Cat used to be my rock,' she told her.

And Meg had just nodded, watching Laura for a while in silence. And then she asked: 'And who was Cat's rock?'

And Laura had wanted to laugh. Had wanted to say, 'Oh, but Cat never needed a rock. Cat was her own rock. Cat never needed anybody.' But something in Meg's eyes had stopped her.

Who was your rock, Cat? she wonders now. And where did you find the strength to endure? Where did you find the strength that I lacked?

A sudden small splash, a whirlpool in the water – and there she is again. The seal. 'Hello, sweetheart,' Laura whispers. 'Have you come to sit with me for a while?' The seal simply watches her with huge dark eyes, head bobbing like a ball on the surface of the water, and perfectly still. 'Tell me about it,' Laura says. 'Tell me about your skin. Tell me how you found your skin again.'

The seal silently slips her head below the water and is gone.

17

Cat

The body lotion is blissfully cool against my skin as I rub it carefully around my breasts. My skin is getting drier these days; no doubt a combination of advancing age and too many years spent in the desert south-west. Sometimes it feels as if it's peeling away; as if I'm shedding the last vestiges of youth.

It's taken me all this time to cool down, and the lukewarm shower is a wonderful respite from the searing heat in the cockpit during today's solo flight. Most of which I spent desperately wishing that I'd chosen to fly in a smarter kind of plane: one fitted with air-conditioning. A Piper Archer, maybe, like the one that Jesse showed me around last week. Though that was hardly a beginner's plane; it had autopilot and a GPS and all kinds of other really fine navigation and communications equipment that would make someone like me feel so much more confident up there. Which, of course, is totally wrong according to Jesse; the idea of relying on equipment and instruments rather than on your own skill and judgement is absolute anathema. I'm with him, but I still feel that I need all the help I can get.

So hot, in that tiny Cessna. I booked the aircraft for the earliest slot available, knowing how unbearable the heat would become as noon approached, but Two November Romeo hadn't been available till eleven-thirty. And wherever possible I choose to fly only that plane – she's become kind of like a lucky mascot to me. I only stayed up there for an hour, practising turns and landings. I was supposed to be practising stalls too, but I still daren't do that alone. I'm still fearful that I'll mess it up – that

I won't recover properly and that I'll spin. And if Jesse isn't in the plane beside me, I won't know how I'd recover from a spin. Even though he's told me how you do it, I know that I'd panic, that I'd freeze – that I'd fall. Just the thought of it is enough to bring back all of those symptoms of panic again – and that hasn't happened for such a long while now. So I don't practise stalls unless Jesse is with me.

And at the end of every solo flight I come back down again, look right into his eyes, and I lie.

The crunch and hiss of tyres on the gravelly sand driveway announces the arrival of the mailman. I slip quickly down the drive to the mailbox, not wanting the still-rising heat to mess up my thermostat again. A credit card bill from Bank of America, a direct mail brochure from Walgreen's, and another big brown envelope with a blue air-mail sticker, postmarked *Ullapool*.

Inside again, I settle down on the sofa and slowly open the envelope. I hesitate before I pull out the short manuscript inside. I'm not sure that I want to read this. The hard parts are coming up now – the parts that have haunted me for so long. The parts that I don't want to think about any more; the parts that I want to forget. The parts that I need to let go.

Roddy. Oh, dear God, Roddy. The weight of his body pressing down on me and the sudden sharp pain and all the while crying out her name, crying out for her but she never came.

She never came.

Blackness, and there's only the night.

I awaken at dawn with the comforter tangled in a sweaty heap around my legs and my mother's words resounding inside my head. *You're never going to forgive me for it, are you, Cat? You're never going to let it go. You're just going to keep on punishing me, as long as we both live. Can't you see that you're punishing yourself too?* So many years ago now, that last ice-cold row. The last big disagreement that we ever had – the last time that we ever really spoke about anything other than the trivia of our daily lives. Just before my graduation. When I told her that I didn't want her to come to the ceremony.

Yes, I was punishing you.

My head is heavy from broken sleep; pressure throbs and burns behind my eyes. I make a pot of coffee but it tastes like mud. My mouth is as dry as the desert floor and my stomach is churning and raw. Something has shaken loose inside me, but it's on the run and moving too fast and I can't grasp hold of it to put it back. Agitated, I stalk from room to room. I can't get her face out of my head and I can't get his face out of my head and even the shower won't wash them away. I need to get out of here – the walls are closing in on me. The first blinding rays of early morning sun penetrate the front windows and stab into my eyes, and this final perceived violation tears me out of the room and propels me through the front door.

Halfway down the drive I stop, folding my arms around my stomach, gasping for breath.

This is crazy. What am I doing? What am I running away from? And where on earth do I think I'm running to?

I look behind me, back towards Maria Mercedes' garden. There's no sign of activity yet from inside the house. The sun has slunk into the *gruta*, lighting up the statue within. I creep through the gate. The warm scent of early morning lavender drifts up to meet me and I stop, inhale, and break off a small sprig from one of the many pots clustered around the edges of the path. Treading as silently as I can on the crunchy gravel, I make my way to the shrine. The Virgin's face is warm in the golden light, and the sun glints gently off the stars on her cloak. I sink to my knees, lay the lavender as if as an offering at her feet. A small smile hovers on her lips but her eyes are large and brown and sad.

Without warning, hot tears collect in the corners of my eyes and erupt like burning lava down my face. I can't see. My throat closes and I gasp for breath. Someone or something is taking my stomach in its hands and kneading and wringing and the sharp, raw pain of it doubles me up. I want to wail; I want to howl. I want to weep as I have never wept before in my life – every cell, every atom a fully charged participant in the fierce electrical storm that racks my body. I don't even know what I'm weeping for. I don't know what I'm weeping for but whatever it is, every shuddering sob is shaking it free, pulling it out of the cold marble vault in which it has lain entombed for all these years and every moment of pain that I have turned away from, every shiver of hurt that I have refused to feel has been stored in there somewhere all this time and oh, dear God, what will I do now that it's loose? How can I possibly pick up these pieces? How will I ever recover from this?

'Cat.'

Startled, I turn my head; Maria Mercedes looms behind me, blurred and flickering oddly in the stealthily advancing sunlight. I duck away again, ashamed, brush the tears from my cheeks. *I don't cry in public*, I try to remind myself, but that Cat doesn't seem to be listening. That Cat is long gone.

Maria Mercedes kneels down beside me and places her arms gently around my shoulders, pulling me to her. I don't even have the strength to resist; I allow my head to sink sideways onto her shoulder. She smells of herbs and of lavender shampoo. She murmurs in Spanish, words that I don't recognise, words that I don't understand. Words that sound like the words you would use to comfort a hurt child. Strokes the back of my head and I remember that, from so long ago. *It's okay, darling. Mummy's here. Mummy'll kiss it better.* Back in the days when I would still let her touch me. Before I turned into that cold, shrivelled creature, trapped behind the forcefield of her own hurt and anger.

Another wave of sorrow crashes over me, another surge of loss.

And then soon, as rapidly as it arrived, the storm passes. A final, lingering shudder or two. Then I'm quiet again.

I stay where I am, assailed by a sudden exhaustion.

Gently, she eases away. 'You want to come inside and have a cup of coffee?'

I shake my head. 'No. Thanks. Not right now. Maybe later.' She nods, and I fish for an old, crumpled Kleenex in the pocket of my shirt. I blow my nose furiously. 'I'm sorry. For someone who has hardly ever cried in her life I seem to be doing it – or on the verge of doing it – rather a lot recently.'

She tucks a soggy strand of hair behind my ear and smiles. 'It's a good thing. Bottling up your emotions leads to imbalance.'

I laugh, and a slight edge of hysteria catches in my throat. If that's true, then I must have been the most imbalanced person in the world.

'Go home now,' she says; 'rest. But why don't you come and see me this afternoon? I'll do a *límpia* for you.'

'What's a *límpia*?'

'It's a kind of ritual cleansing. Something from our *curandera* tradition.' She sees the expression on my face and laughs. 'Don't worry – there's nothing too weird about it. I promise. It's very relaxing. It won't take long. Maybe an hour.'

I shrug. 'Okay.'

And really, why not? It seems likely, after all, that I have nothing more to lose.

I'm floating. Floating on a bed of soft, cool cloud where fragrant fingers of air stroke my body with all the gentleness of a lover's caress. I'm sailing aloft in a cool blue sky, and it's so strange that I can't hear the sound of the engine, but it doesn't seem to worry me at all because someone is with me, and the gentle golden sweep of her wings is holding me there...

I'm not floating, of course: I'm lying on a massage couch draped with crisp white linen in Maria Mercedes' treatment room, which is painted in a shade that just has to be called 'Heavenly Blue'. She's sweeping smoke over my body with a small hand-broom made of grasses. Smoke from an abalone shell that contains smouldering sage and rosemary. Smudging, she calls it. 'To remove the sadness and negative energy,' she told me before she began. Before she told me to close my eyes and lulled me into this strange trancelike state with her drums and her rattles and the heady scent of copal incense mingled with the smell of smouldering herbs. She chants softly as she sweeps. Prayers for vision, she said: for strength and for wholeness. Prayers that invoke dreams for guidance.

'Who are you praying to, though?' I asked her, but she only smiled.

'Does it matter?'

On an altar in the corner that faces east – the place of beginnings, Maria Mercedes said – another beautiful carved statue stands, surrounded by burning votives. This one, she told me, is Tonantzin: the patron goddess of *curanderas*. Perhaps it's to Tonantzin that she prays – to the goddess of healing, the pagan alter ego of Our Lady of Guadalupe.

And I? I wanted to ask her. To whom should I pray?

I don't pray.

But if I were to pray – and such poor prayers they would be, spoken in a voice cracked and rusted with disuse – I would pray (if I could; if I dared, if I hoped) to the figure who has flown with me through this cool, giddy dream. I would pray to this woman with golden eagle wings, her chalice of faith gently cupped in her hands. I do not know what I would say, in these prayers. But somehow, I think she would understand.

I open my eyes; slowly adjust. The wooden slatted shutters are two-thirds closed against the glare of the afternoon sun; the partial shade and the light blue-grey walls lend an air of soft twilight to the room. I feel strangely light-headed, as if I've awoken from a long, deep sleep.

'Welcome back.' Maria Mercedes touches me gently on the shoulder and then walks over to the altar. She blows out the votive candles that she told me represent the element of fire. 'Candles for fire,' she said, 'rock for the earth. A bowl of water, and an eagle feather for air.'

An eagle feather. I smile. Slowly, I raise myself up on my elbows.

'Take your time,' Maria Mercedes calls to me. 'You'll probably feel a bit woozy for a while.'

Being in this room is like being in another world. The treatment couch on which I lie takes pride of place in the centre of the room; two small armchairs face each other in one corner, next to a small table with a lamp. In another corner is the altar, draped with a piece of ivory lace. Apart from that, the room is bare. The overwhelming sensation here is one of cool, quiet, blue light.

No wonder I had flying dreams.

'When you can, come on into the kitchen. We'll have a glass of iced tea. Or coffee. Maybe you'd prefer coffee?'

I nod slowly, licking my lips and waiting for my mouth to wake up. 'Coffee sounds wonderful.'

In contrast to the treatment room, Maria Mercedes' kitchen is a riot of colour. Warm colour-washed ochre walls, and bright Mexican tiles above the counters. Still a little groggy, I lower myself into a chair at the old pine table. Maria Mercedes flicks a switch on the coffee-maker, and with a cacophony of hisses and spits and gurgles the wonderful aroma of freshly brewed coffee permeates the room.

'So. How do you feel?'

'Light-headed. Light-bodied. Wonderful, actually.'

She grins. 'Don't sound so surprised.'

'I didn't mean that. It's just that I've never done anything like it before.'

'Nothing? Never even had a massage?'

'Not even that.'

'You should. It's good for you.' She returns to the table with a couple of bright blue mugs, a jug of cream and a couple of colourful Mexican pottery plates. 'I think you need to pamper yourself more.'

Pamper myself? 'I suppose I've always had this vision of desperately boring hours spent in a day spa with people picking at your fingernails and pulling at your hair and bundling you up in Saran-wrap in a last-ditch effort to preserve your youth. That's just not my scene. And besides – I've never really had the time to pamper myself. Always been too busy. And there was always someone else who needed my time more.' I smile ruefully. 'Until recently. Until I went completely crazy and turned my whole life upside down.'

Maria Mercedes stretches, walks across to the carved wooden bread bin by the window, and extracts from it a package of cinnamon rolls. She puts a couple on a plate and pops them in the microwave for a few seconds. The aroma of warm sugar and cinnamon that seeps through the air is mouth-watering. I watch as she sets the plate down on the table between us. She moves away again, returning this time with the coffee pot, and fills our mugs.

'Perhaps it was just time,' she says, settling into a chair opposite me. 'There are times in our lives when we go through these changes. And when all of those things that are holding us back begin to show their face.' She reaches for the sugar and puts a couple of lumps into her coffee. 'And those things keep at us until we sit up and take notice. Until we face them. Move on. Change.' She pushes the plate at me. 'Eat. Whether you feel like it or not.'

But sugar seems to be just what I need right now. I pick up a roll and bite into it, the soft, sticky sweetness filling my mouth and making my stomach rumble.

Maria Mercedes nods her approval. 'It's like I said to you before: change needs to happen. If you let it happen, if you don't fight it, you build up the strength to break out of that dark place – out of that chrysalis. You can become that butterfly.'

I lick the sugar from the corners of my mouth. 'I still don't feel like a butterfly.'

'No? But you're learning to fly. And you almost have your wings. Don't you?' And the thought of my checkride at the end of next week pops briefly into my mind – but I push it away again: I'm far too chilled out to worry about that now. For a minute or two there's a peaceful silence as we finish eating, interrupted only by the cheery *purdy-purdy* of a cardinal outside the window. Childlike, I lick the sugar from my fingers and reach for my coffee.

'That's part of the process, too,' she continues, brushing away the sugar from her mouth. 'Learning new ways of sustaining ourselves. Like you and your flying. Breathing new life into our bones.' She smiles. 'Bones. Did you know that Native people believed that the life force resided in the bones?'

'No.'

'Have you never heard the story of *La Huesera*, the Bone Woman?'

I shake my head and it spins for a moment. It feels so light that it could blow away, just take off across the desert floor, dancing like tumbleweed.

'She's known by other names: *La Loba*, the wolf-woman; *La Trapera*, the ragged woman. Anyway: the legends tell of an old woman who wanders through the desert alone, dressed in rags, looking for the bones of dead animals. Wolves especially, she likes. She gathers up all that she finds, and when she has all of the bones that she needs to make a complete skeleton, she lays them on the desert floor. And she begins to sing. She sings over the bones, and as she sings they begin to grow flesh and fur. She sings life back into the bones, and the animal begins to breathe again. It becomes strong and it leaps up and runs away into the desert. And, so the stories go, *La Huesera* laughs. They say it's her laughter you can hear in the distance on a calm desert night. As she breathes her life back into another set of dead bones.'

'All these stories that you tell – about women. Women who have power. Women who change things.'

'Think about it,' she says. 'Women give birth to new things. They're ... agents of transformation. When you grow a child in your body, for example, you are an agent of transformation. You transform a couple of struggling cells into a living breathing creature. It's a miracle. So yes, those are the stories I like.'

I don't know why it occurs to me to ask. Her constant reference to mothers, maybe. Something in the way she spoke about motherhood by the shrine that day. Making me wonder. 'Are you a mother, Maria Mercedes?'

'Yes.' She looks down at her hands for a moment, frowns, and then stands; she walks over to the fireplace in the corner of the room and takes a photograph from the mantel. She brings it over to the table and holds it out to me. 'This is my daughter.'

The photograph shows a young woman in her early twenties. Slender and smiling, with jet-black hair and dark brown eyes, she's a younger version of Maria Mercedes.

'She's beautiful. Where is she now?'

'In Los Angeles, where she was raised.' She sits down again, heavily. 'I gave her up for adoption, you see.' She raises her head, looks directly into my eyes. Unflinching, I hold her gaze. 'I grew up in El Paso, in the *barrios*. I was young when I became pregnant. I had been raped; her father was a member of a local gang. I knew him. And I knew what would happen if I told. In those days you didn't tell. Probably you still don't.'

Raped. I ignore the sudden sharp pain in my stomach; I

swallow it down with another mouthful of coffee. That's gone now: all over. All over, all gone. 'How did you come to see her again?'

'She came to look for me.'

'And was she angry? That you'd given her up?'

Maria Mercedes' eyes fill with tears; she blinks them away. 'No. When I told her what had happened – and I felt that I owed her the truth, not just a pretty story – she told me that she understood completely. She'd had a happy life with a family who loved her, she said. Probably a better life than she'd have had in the *barrios*. And then she held me while I wept. How back-to-front is that? She didn't seem to blame me at all.'

'But you blamed yourself?'

She shrugs, a quintessentially Latin gesture. 'Of course. You do, when you give up a child. You feel inadequate. You feel like a criminal. It never leaves you. Never.'

It comes back to me, then: the conversation about the statue, that day in the garden. How she told me that she carved it at a time when she needed to focus on what the Lady of Guadalupe meant to her. 'And that's why you carved the statue.'

'Yes. While I was trying to come to terms with seeing her again. With my own regrets, that I'd given her up. Most mothers are not perfect, Cat. I was not perfect. No doubt your mother was not perfect. We try – but we are human too; and so, often, we fail. I carved the Lady because she is a mother. Because it seems to me that she understands.'

❦ ❦ ❦

The sun set hours ago, and the desert air is pleasantly cool. The moon is waxing, almost full now, and there's just enough light to see by. The quality of silence in the desert is tangible; night wraps itself around me like a soft fleecy blanket made of midnight blue. I crane back my head and look at the stars. I let myself sink into it – that strange, giddy feeling that they're sucking me up. An owl hoots from somewhere in the bushes close by. A lone coyote howls and a chorus of voices replies from the hills. Out on the southern horizon three shooting stars hurl themselves at the ground in a beautiful, graceful arc, but burn out long before they get there. I feel light and clear and for the first time now I acknowledge my connection to this place. This magic of the desert: elemental. Stripping you down to the very essentials. Stripping you bare. All the way down to the bones.

I sit down in the sand, close my eyes and softly begin to sing.

Tonight I sleep, and I dream. I am walking beside a railway track that runs through empty desert. Away in the distance, I see a station: a simple wooden hut by the side of the tracks, with no platform at all. A train is standing there. I start to run towards it – I know that I have to catch it – but I am carrying in my arms a heavy stone that weighs me down. I can't seem to make any progress – it's as if I'm running through molasses – and before I can reach the train, it starts to pull away. I run and I run and eventually I catch up with it. Through an open door the conductor watches me. The train is moving slowly, and I am trotting alongside it. I try to grasp hold of the door, to pull myself up, but I can't seem to do it and the conductor just stands there, refusing to help. Behind him, I see the shadowy figure of my mother moving back and out of sight. The train speeds up; I try to run alongside but it's pulling away from me.

'I have to get on this train,' I shout at him.

'You can't,' he says. 'It's already left. We're late. Should've been long gone.'

'You don't understand,' I say. 'I'm carrying the foundation stone of my mother's house.'

As I speak those words the train stops, and with some difficulty I climb on board. Except that it's not my mother, standing there behind him. Because she's wearing a deep blue cloak encrusted with stars – but it changes into a golden cloak as I walk towards her, and I see the gold-feathered wings that sprout from her shoulders. She takes from me the heavy stone that I am carrying and I am light now, I am light and free and feathers sprout from my shoulders too. I float out of the carriage door and up and up, with my arms spread wide and my face turned up to the burning blue sky.

The next day dawns into a stunning magenta-streaked sky. I take my cup of coffee into the garden and breathe in the crisp clarity of the desert air. A quick glance across to Maria-Mercedes' *gruta* shows the Virgin still wreathed in shadow.

I sit on the wooden slatted chair on the porch and close my eyes.

All those years. Blaming you, hating you. Judging you for always blaming your failures on other people. Ignoring the fact that when the time came, you came through. You stopped drinking. Focusing on your failures – and failing to see the strength. The sheer refusal to go gently, to give up, to sink under. And through all those years, through all your own pain, you tried to teach me that I could be anything that I wanted to be. Pushed me, encouraged me. *You can fly, if you want to, little Cat. You can do whatever you want. Because you're strong. You're stronger than you know. You're tough and you're smart, just like your mummy.*

Well, now I can fly, Mother. Now I can really fly.

And it may be, after all, that this is a gift I can share with you.

The postcard is a reproduction of a painting by Georgia O'Keefe: the sunbleached skull of a cow lying on the burning desert sand. *No,* I write: *no. Roddy didn't hurt me. It was all just fine.*

'Cat, this is Buddy Simpson.'

The red-faced man at Jesse's side puts his hands on his hips and looks me up and down with what can only be described as a smirk. 'Well, hello, little lady.'

Little lady? Oh, dear God. The guy only comes up to my shoulder, but what he's lacking in size I rather suspect he's going to make up for in character. Out of all the flight examiners in the Phoenix area, I landed the one that everybody dreads. I landed the ex-US Marine.

I daren't even look at Jesse; I don't know whether to run away screaming or to burst into hysterical laughter. In the end I settle for a noncommittal 'Hello.'

'Cat? That what you call yourself?'

'That's right.'

'British, are ya?'

'Yup.' My heart is pounding in my chest and my stomach has been churning for a solid twenty-four hours. I have a serious case of the pre-checkride jitters, and something tells me it might be safest right now to keep my answers short.

He grunts. 'Sky's full of foreigners these days. Don't know how the controllers make out the accents sometimes. Still. Yours is pretty enough.'

I smile politely but I'd really like to just curl up on the floor and weep. It's going to be a long, long day.

'Well, let's just go on upstairs and find out what you know, shall we?'

'Sure.'

He turns on his heel and stalks across the reception like a man with a mission. I cast Jesse a look of utter panic mingled with desperation before I turn to follow him. He shakes his head and mimes, 'It's okay. Chill.'

*

Upstairs, Buddy tells me to sit down at a desk. He doesn't say a word, just looks at me as he reaches over and takes my log book out of my hands. For the next five minutes he pores over it and over my medical and pilot certificates, ticking off all the requirements for the checkride.

'Hmm. See your last solo cross-country was up to Prescott.'

'Wickenburg and Prescott, that's right.'

He raises an eyebrow as if to suggest that a simple 'yes' or 'no' will do. Rule number one, Cat: don't talk back to the examiner. 'How'd you find it?'

'It was a tough flight.'

'Why's that?'

'I hit a little wind shear on landing at Prescott. The winds were gusty and the turbulence was even worse than normal.'

'Got to get used to a little turbulence if you fly over the desert. The desert ain't no lady, you ever heard that saying? If you want to fly over the desert you got to be tough. You think you're tough enough, Catree-Ona?' He pronounces it incorrectly, with the emphasis on the 'o.'

My head flies up. 'I wouldn't be here if I didn't.' *You son-of-a-bitch*, I add silently.

He hears it. He was clearly expecting nothing more than a 'yes, sir'; he raises a bushy grey eyebrow in surprise. 'Well, now. Good. That's real good. We'll see about that now, when we go up and fly.'

Oh, shit. Have I just issued some kind of challenge? In Marine language, was that the equivalent of swords in the park at dawn?

After a few more routine questions he closes the book and shrugs. 'Well, all that seems to be just fine. You got the results of your written test?' I pass him the slip of paper. 'Ninety-six percent? My, but you're a smart one.'

I resist the increasing temptation to slap him and concentrate on trying to feel amused instead. 'Thank you.'

'What do you do for a living, Ms Catree-Ona?'

'I'm a lawyer.'

He grimaces. 'What do you call twenty lawyers at the bottom of the sea?'

I close my eyes briefly. I can't believe that he really expects I haven't heard that joke at least a thousand times before. 'A good start.'

He laughs out loud and slaps a hand against his thigh and I begin to wonder what time his day pass out of the local funny farm expires.

He pushes the documents back across to me. 'Okay. You know what comes next, right? I'm going to give you thirty minutes to prepare a flight plan and a weight and balance computation for the flight. I'll go downstairs and have a cup of coffee with young Jesse while you're doing that. Then I'll come back and I'll ask you some questions. Depending on how well you answer them, that'll take maybe an hour. Then we'll go fly.'

'Okay.' My voice comes out as a croak and Buddy smirks again. Rule number two, Cat: never let the enemy smell your fear.

'Let's make the flight plan a trip to Winslow.'

I'm standing on a corner in Winslow, Arizona... I've definitely been listening to too much Jackson Browne. Get a grip, Cat. This is serious. But I have to say that I expected worse than Winslow. It would be a tough flight if we had to do it for real, right across the mountains, but to the best of my recollection there aren't too many obstacles in the way of a straight heading. Maybe Jesse's right, and his bark really is worse than his bite.

An hour and thirty minutes later I feel as if I've been mauled by a rabid dog. Federal aviation regulations, airspace, sectionals, aircraft electrical systems – we've covered it all.

Buddy sits back and frowns. 'Well, I suppose that's all okay.

You certainly seem to know your theory. Not much more'n I'd expect from a lawyer. Now, theory's all very well – but what I care about is how you fly. So. Let's go fly.'

Abruptly, he bounces out of the chair and stomps down the stairs and I follow like a prisoner being led to the gallows.

In reception Jesse is bustling around looking uncharacteristically nervous. He lifts an enquiring eyebrow at me as Buddy heads off to the restroom.

I shrug. 'I think it went okay. But I'm not sure he's happy about it. I can't decide whether he's disappointed or not that he can't fail me here and now.'

'I told you – he looks a lot worse than he is. Honest.'

'Don't try to tell me that under that rough and tough exterior there beats a heart of gold. I'm just not going to buy it. The guy's a first-class asshole.' I sigh. 'I'm really not sure that I'm going to survive this checkride. Still, I suppose it's all good experience, even if I fail.'

'You going to let that put you off?' He raises his chin and pierces right to the heart of me with the cold blue ice of his eyes. 'You just going to roll over and give up?'

I smile, a little wanly. 'No. I guess not.'

Christina on reception passes me the ignition keys and aircraft documentation. 'I'm afraid Two November Romeo's out of commission. Avionics problem – the talk button on the passenger side seems to have failed.'

'Oh, no.' This seems like the final straw.

'You're in Five Yankee Mike.' I groan. It's a plane I've flown in before, but I don't know it so well. And I've come to think of Two November Romeo as my good luck charm.

Jesse puts a warm hand on my shoulder. 'You'll do fine. Just keep your cool. Oh – and try not to sock the guy. It's not considered good practice.'

Buddy returns and stands with his hands on his hips. 'Well, Jesse, your pretty little student here certainly knows her theory.'

I cannot for the life of me understand how he can refer to a forty-year-old who's a good six inches taller than he is as a 'pretty little student'. But that's our Buddy for you.

'She does.'

'But this is where the real test comes, hey, boy?' He looks at his watch: it's eleven a.m. 'And it's going to be kind of hot out there. A little turbulent. You reckon she can handle it?'

Jesse isn't going to be drawn. 'She can handle it.'

'Well, now, we'll see.'

He taps his foot impatiently as I slowly run through the pre-flight. 'Thorough, aren't you?'

'That's how I was taught. I figure you'd rather be safe.' I turn around with the sweetest smile I can muster on my face. 'Especially since it's likely to be kind of hot out there. And a little *turbulent*.'

Out of the corner of my eye I catch a small quirk at the corner of his mouth, but he just grunts and gets in the plane.

We take off to the north-west, as if we were planning to fly our flight plan to Winslow for real. It's turbulent, all right. I figure by this stage that I have absolutely nothing to lose. If I fail, it'll have been a good experience, and with a bit of luck I won't get this goon again next time. So I sit perfectly calmly, following his instructions slowly and carefully. After a few minutes en route he turns me around and we abandon the mock flight plan and head south into the desert to practise the manoeuvres. One by one he barks them out. Emergency landing, power-on stalls. Steep turns, S-turns. I calmly respond to whatever he asks me to do; I'm on automatic pilot. Eagle Woman, I repeat to myself like a mantra. Eagle Woman. I belong in these skies. I belong in these skies and no son-of-a-bitch ex-Marine is going to stand in my way.

An hour and a half later we're making our way back to

Chandler. In my head I can tick off every manoeuvre that he's asked me to perform, and he hasn't missed a single one on the list. He hasn't yelled at me or wrestled the controls from me; in fact he's sitting there looking pretty relaxed. But I don't know whether I've passed or not. Mostly the manoeuvres seemed to go well. There was one that I had to repeat: the inevitable turn around a point. Strong winds and turbulence blew me off course and my path was more an ellipse than a circle. Second time around, though, it was a textbook example. But if he was looking for an excuse to fail me, maybe that would be enough.

'Five Yankee Mike, cleared to land.'

There's a slight crosswind; I crab the plane into it and land on the numbers.

It isn't till we're back at the flight school and the ignition has been switched off and the propeller is still that he turns to me.

'Well, little lady: looks like you're a pilot. That was a real classy ride.'

Clutching my pink slip tightly in my hand, I watch him walk across the asphalt and on into the building where Jesse will be waiting.

I can't believe that it's real. This pink piece of paper – this temporary licence – is a badge of honour. A sign that says: look at me. I am a person of courage. I can fly.

I turn to Five Yankee Mike and I bow my head for a moment and drop a light kiss on her shiny hot nose. And then I hear his footsteps behind me.

'Hey.'

I turn to face him with a huge grin on my face.

'Congratulations,' Jesse says.

I meet his eyes. Blue, blue eyes teeming with warmth and I think to myself – he isn't my instructor any more. And a sudden sharp loss pierces my chest and takes my breath away.

And the sudden sadness that overtakes me isn't what I expected at all.

Something is over. Something is coming to an end.

'Post-checkride blues already?'

Does he really know me that well? I shrug, and try to maintain the smile. 'How crazy is that?'

'It isn't crazy at all. It's actually quite common. Though most people wait for a few hours before they succumb.'

'Well, that's me. Always one step ahead of the crowd.'

'It doesn't end here, you know.' He looks at me, eyes intense. Uncomfortable, I glance away. He sees too much, I think. He knows me too well. 'There's so much more you can do. Instrument training, for one. You might not need it too often out here in the desert, but anywhere else in the country it's a necessity.'

I nod my head without conviction. 'Yeah. I guess so.' I'm so mad at myself. This should be the happiest day of my life, and now look at me.

'Right now, though, I'm not your instructor any more.'

'No.'

'So.' He looks away, shuffles his feet on the asphalt.

Panic sweeps over me. 'Listen –'

He reaches out, puts his hands on my shoulders. His fingers burn into my skin through the thin cotton of my tee-shirt. 'Cat.' I turn my face up to him and as I meet his eyes again something happens and I'm moving towards him and then it's just his face, blocking out the sky.

His lips meet mine and I'm drowning.

Drowning ...

... or falling.

I pull myself out of his arms and I run for my life.

I drive away from the airport with tears in my eyes and those same old fingers clutching at my throat. What am I doing?

What in God's name am I doing, running away from Jesse? Isn't this what I've been wanting, if I'm honest with myself? Isn't this what I wanted almost right from the start? Because it's not just the flying, with Jesse – not just the hours spent side by side, crammed together in that tiny little cockpit. It's not just that he's been beside me, teaching me and encouraging me as I've plumbed the depths of my courage to get myself out of the hole I've been so blindly digging all these years. No: it's more than that. It's the lightness that seems to surround him – the sense of space, the lack of pressure ... oh, I don't know. He's just so easy to be with.

And, let's face it – he's gorgeous. Far too gorgeous for me. I can still feel the warmth of his mouth as it brushed against mine for that briefest of moments – the shiver that ran through me as he placed his hands on my shoulders. What on earth would a guy like that want with me?

Way above me, out over the desert, a plane is practising aerobatics. My stomach lurches as I watch it, spinning and falling through the sky. Another plane joins it, keeping pace with it. Whirls and swirls of white smoke spinning out from them, spinning and spinning and falling and falling until it seems they'll never stop ... and then, in perfect synchronisation, they pull themselves out of the spin and they point their noses into the air and upwards they soar, back up into the sky where they belong.

Once, many years ago, I watched a television documentary about bald eagles. The footage of the eagles mating is something that I've never forgotten. They began their elaborate courtship with a series of aerobatic rituals. They circled each other, gently. They cart-wheeled around each other, then they soared up into the sky, locked talons with each other, and began a death-defying spiral down to earth. Down and down they spun, falling like stones, tangled together as if they were taking part in some crazy mutual suicide pact. Moments before striking the ground they disengaged from each other ... and up they soared. And then did it all again. If their timing wasn't perfect, there'd be nothing but death that awaited them there.

What do eagles feel, as they fall? Fear? Exhilaration? Is that what they need, to give them the courage to mate? Because eagles mate for life, and how much of a risk is that? You need to be very sure, to take a risk like that.

Maybe it's their way of making sure.

The patched-up cracks in the road shine like silver snakes as I slowly make my way home. The truth is the same as it's always been: I'm afraid. Afraid of my own feelings. Afraid that if I trust him, he'll hurt me. Afraid that if I take a deep breath and close my eyes and join with him in that tumbling fall ... he'll let go.

As soon as I get home, I pick up the phone and I dial his cellphone.

'Jesse?'

His voice is cool. 'Cat.'

'I want to learn to spin.'

'You what?'

I take a deep breath. 'I need to learn to fall.'

There's a pause and then slowly, deeply, he begins to laugh. 'You sure know how to spring a surprise on a guy.'

'Will you teach me?'

Another pause. 'Yeah. Okay, Cat. I'll teach you to fall.'

18

Laura

The waiting has been desperate. She just hasn't been able to settle at all. An odd feeling in her stomach – sort of fizzy. Tension in her shoulders, and a deep throbbing ache behind her eyes. Laura can't sleep for thinking about it: Roddy's face grinning drunkenly in her dreams; Cat's terrified eyes and the high-pitched scream of her 'Mummy!' echoing into the night.

When Willy arrives with the post each day she rushes to the door and half-snatches it from him, heart pounding. Torn between the desperate need to know and the equally desperate need not to know. After all, that's the way she's always dealt with difficult things in the past. If you don't want to know, then just push it away. Hide it, lock it up. Easy-peasy. Smile brightly and pretend it never happened – and then, magically, you'll wake up the next morning and find that it never did happen, after all. It's gone. All gone.

But that strategy isn't working now. She's opened too many doors into her past. Layer upon layer of doors, each of them reflecting the others back at her like some nightmarish fairground hall of mirrors. She can't seem to find a way to close them again. And so: this purgatory. And the only sources of solace, her morning and evening visits to the lochside. Her strange communion with the solitary seal – her mother confessor; her soulmate.

Laura is back late from a weekly shopping trip to the village extended by another brief visit to Aunt Isobel. For distraction, and the consolation of a cup of her weak milky tea and a slightly soft, damp shortbread finger. As she crawls slowly down the pothole-ridden drive she sees that the postie has already been and gone: the white corner of an envelope peeks out through the lid of the shiny black mailbox by the side of the front door. She fumbles with the rusty old key that she leaves in the box – for who's going to raid a mailbox around here? – and utters a staccato and uncharacteristic 'Shit!' as the mail falls out and flutters to the floor. And then she sees it: a postcard. Recognisably Cat: one of those arid, barren desert scenes again. Some kind of animal skull, for heaven's sake. Exasperation toys with fear as she fumbles for the card with fingers that grow stiffer with each day that goes by. She holds it for a moment in her hands. Closes her eyes; prays.

Turns it over.

Reads.

Sinks down onto the doorstep with her head in her hands and weeps.

᠁ ᠁ ᠁

Laura clears her throat and scans the faces around her. The days are still long this deep into summer, and the evening light in the village hall is tinged with the soft blue glow. In previous years the storytelling circle has taken a break during the height of the tourist season, but this year, Meg says, no-one wanted to stop. 'And ach, after all,' she said to Laura, 'it's only once a month. Their bed and breakfasts aren't going to go bankrupt for the sake of one Saturday night out of every month.'

Tonight it's Laura's turn to tell a story. She's managed to avoid it so far, though she hasn't missed a single meeting since that day back in November when she so reluctantly accompanied Meg for the first time. She's nervous. She's accustomed to telling stories to children, but not to adults. And it's a long, long time since she told stories at all, even to children. She looks at Meg for courage: Meg winks and grins. Laura takes a deep breath and, without preamble, begins.

'It was long ago, and a beautiful night. The full moon reflected in calm, glassy water – you could almost believe it had fallen to earth, floating there, finally now in your grasp. The sand twinkled silver like a galaxy of dusty stars, and the midnight air was warm and still. How could you not want to taste its treasures? So they swam in to shore, the selkie sisters…'

It's a long story, as Laura tells it – indeed, as she began to write it, the first afternoon that she saw the seal. Longer than the average story that's told here, anyhow. But there isn't a murmur in the room as her voice, faltering at first, slowly grows stronger and clear. Not a single flicker or fidget. All eyes are on her; each face is entranced. It's an old, old story that she's telling, but with a twist in the story that is uniquely Laura's. She has no concept of time; she's aware only of the gentle dancing glimmer of the single candle on the low wooden table in the centre of the circle.

'… And so, with each day that went by, the selkie woman withered still more. Mara looked after her; each morning she bathed her parched flaky body with water that she fetched from the sea. And whenever she could, she hunted for her mother's skin. "I'll find it for you, Mother," she whispered each day: "I promise I'll find your skin."

'The burden of responsibility weighed heavy on her young shoulders, but there was nothing that the selkie could do to halt the sickness that was draining away her life.'

Laura pauses for breath and closes her eyes. Cat's face, wary and withdrawn, flickers back and forth in her mind like the guttering flame of the candle, and the sharp suddenness of pain in her chest makes her wince. She blinks; recovers herself. 'But after a while it seemed that Mara had given up. Powerless to intervene, she grew silent and withdrawn as she watched her mother slowly fade away. And at night, when the selkie had

416

finally fallen into a fitful, restless sleep, Mara turned increasingly to the solace of the sea. She would wander for hours on the beach; a slight, solitary figure, coming and going with the tides.

'One night it began to rain heavily as she made her way back to the house at midnight, and she took shelter for a moment in the old stone boathouse on the shore. No-one had been inside since her father had died. She slipped through the rotting wooden door and sat down on the upturned wreck of an old boat with her head in her hands, until a gentle glow around her feet – from a beam of light shining into the shed from the newly uncovered full moon – told her that the sudden rainstorm had passed. As she stood to leave, her shadow shifted, and the moonbeam fell now on something dark and shiny that protruded from under one corner of the boat ... and that was how, finally, Mara came upon her mother's skin.

'She ran home swiftly through the rain; she came to the selkie with tears in her eyes and her voice low and breaking with anticipated loss.

'"Mother," she whispered, bending over her bed, "I've found it. I've found your skin."

'The selkie's heart leapt to hear it, but by then she was so weak that she could barely move. Getting down to that beach was the hardest thing she'd ever done. Her skin cracked and broke in the chilly night air, and pain lanced through her body with each step that she took. But her daughter supported her: all the way to the shore Mara held her up, murmuring words of encouragement and love. Who now was the mother? Who now the child?

'The selkie sagged down on the sand while Mara ran to the boathouse and came back, holding the skin in her arms: the soft warm skin that smelled of her mother and the sea. Still sleek, still glossy after all those years. Weakly, the selkie held it to her face and inhaled the old familiar seal-smell, and for the first time in years found the energy to weep. Salt tears rolled warmly down her arid cheeks and lent her strength. She took hold of Mara's hands; they were cold now, and trembling. "Listen," she said: "listen to me, Mara. This isn't the end. When the moon is full and the night is still, slip down to the beach and I will come to you. That way, you'll always know you can see me again. You'll always know that I'm with you."

'"No – it's too risky. What if someone else finds you there? What if someone else steals your skin?"

'"This time, I'll protect my skin. This time, I know its value."

'And Mara stepped back then, as her mother clutched the old seal-skin tight to her breast. The selkie closed her eyes and lifted her face to the sky. A sliver of moon shone down on her through a crack in the rain clouds and she opened her mouth and the song spilled out and she felt it again – the pain and the rapture – and she turned back into a seal. She hauled herself heavily into the cool sea-water, and wept – wept large salty seal-tears to feel once again the gentle caress of the waves. She turned on her back and she kicked with her flippers and she swam out to sea, away to the sisters who waited for her there, just beyond the limits of the bay.

'She swam away, and she left Mara behind.'

Laura pauses again; swallows.

'Mara mourned long and hard. Each night she would go down to the shore, hoping to catch a glimpse of her mother. And one month later, on the night of the fullest moon, her patience was rewarded: a seal sat on the largest rock on the beach. As it saw Mara approaching, it slipped off its skin and instantly was transformed into her mother. Her mother and yet somehow not her mother: a mother with eyes and hair and skin that shone; a mother at peace and seemingly at home with herself.

'And so it continued to pass: that each month the selkie woman would come to the beach and talk with her daughter and tell her stories. She taught her to sing the song that she had

418

sung that first night, when Mara gave her back her skin: the song that would call to her selkie family. The song that would sing her soul back home.'

Laura falls silent. There is absolute silence in the room. She looks up; meets Meg's eyes.

Meg nods. Just nods.

ϟ ϟ ϟ

The morning air is still and warm down by the lochside. Sheep bleat softly in the fields and Laura's ears ring with birdsong. She is sitting in her usual spot under the bent rowan tree, with a pen in her hand and a pad of paper resting on her knee. Her handwriting isn't what it used to be, but it's still just about legible. And for this letter she doesn't want the impersonality of a word-processed typescript. She wants this letter to be more … real, somehow. More *Laura*. Not the fake, cheery Laura who populated letters in the past: the true Laura.

The Laura who has found her skin.

> *Dear Cat,*
>
> *Well, I've finished my story now. It's not that there isn't more that could be told: there's plenty more. But it's not necessary now. I've come to terms with my story; made my peace with the past. It's a funny thing, Cat, the past: it's like a skin. You might try to shrug it off, to shed it, but in shedding it you lose it and you lose part of yourself in the process. And if I've learned anything through telling my story it's that it is possible to find your skin again. Maybe even a cleaned-up, better skin: a skin that you can look at with fresh, new eyes.*
>
> *Often, when I sit here by the lochside, a seal*

419

comes and swims there beside me. Stares out at me, across the water. Do you remember the old stories about selkies? There's one that's often told about a selkie woman whose skin was stolen by her husband. Exiled from the sea, she sickened and pined. And everything seemed lost as she foundered under the weight of being what she wasn't meant to be. But she found her skin again, so the old story says. And I take comfort from that, Cat. Because perhaps it may be – it may well be, if you watch and you wait, with hope in your heart – all that you once thought lost will return to you.

A Devonware jug sits on my mantelpiece now, nestled warm above the wood-burning stove. I keep it filled with flowers. On its side are inscribed the following words:

'No dream is ever lost
we once have seen
We always may be
what we might have been.'

I feel as if I have found my skin, Cat: and in finding that skin I can let go of the past. Not hiding from it, as I used to do: but just not needing it any more. Letting it go. As if all those doors in my mind that were keeping it under lock and key gave way under the pressure and let the past slip out. And at first it swirled around me like a mist – like something sinister out of that movie, The Fog – a world filled with ghosts and a lingering sense of doom. But somehow, I wrote it all away. And now I sit here, by the lochside, and

I look out over the water and the sea blends into the sky and the sky blends into the sea and the endless blue of it goes on forever. It's as if all the edges have dissolved: there's nothing to contain me or hold me back.

Perhaps I've grown wiser with the passing of this year, as well as older. I'm easier now, Cat: quieter. I am growing old; maybe I am developing a crone's wisdom. I sit here on this rock under this tree and I find peace in the solace of growing things, of wild things. The seal, the otter, the herons, the oystercatchers… I'm at peace here, Cat. And my stories are beginning to return to me. Ah, Cat: this is a place where stories come as easy as breathing. Stories new and old hover in the air and seep into our lives as the rain on the wind seeps through our clothes and into our skin. Listen: across the loch is a line of hills. Cast in relief against the skyline, their contours reveal the shape of a breast and the profiled face of a woman. When the sun shines golden on the grass and the bracken she's Brighid, the spring-maiden, reborn every year at the beginning of February. When the first snows clothe her in white she's the Cailleach – the old hag with blue skin and boar tusks who brings winter to the land; who strides across the mountains, whipping up the winter storms and causing it to snow.

The old stories tell truths about our lives. Stories that are forged from the landscape, as we also are forged.

And meanwhile, there is the soft taste of salt mist on your tongue in the morning; the raindrops that hang like chandelier crystals from the trees after rain, the distant sound of fog-horns in the harbour and the ponderous flight of a heron as it lifts itself up from the harsh, rocky ground beneath.

I wish you luck, Cat, with your flying. And I wish you love.

Always make room in your life for love, little Cat: it's the one thing I've never regretted.

All my love to you,
Mother

19

Cat

Has the sky ever been so blue? I can't imagine it: not in the entire sweep of human history could it ever have been so blue. A deep polarised blue that bears no trace of the usual Valley smog. The distant mountain ranges stand stark against the southern skyline and, to the east, the spirits on top of Superstition Mountain are lined up in a row along its rim to greet the sun. Maybe this afternoon the thunderclouds will gather and a temporary softening will pass over the land as the summer rain brings its blessings to the desert. But right now all is sharply defined, crisp, and precise.

I zoom in closer now; zoom in to the dusty tarmac at my feet and beyond, to the solitary airplane that lies ahead of me. It looks just like Two November Romeo, but it isn't. It's different in one crucial respect: it's a Cessna Aerobat. Built to take the strain of aerial exercises. Built to dive, to loop, to roll.

Built to spin.

Both of us are silent as we strap ourselves in; both of us know what is at stake. Jesse, as ever, is calm and matter-of-fact: he's in instructor mode again. All cool professionalism and polite reserve, as if nothing ever happened between us. Nothing that really mattered, anyway. But I daren't meet his eyes – hardly dare look at him at all, for fear that I'll lose the steely determination that I'm holding so tight and with such a fierce grip. I shrug; try to loosen the knotted tension in my shoulders. My stomach rumbles loudly, breaks into the uneasy silence. I haven't eaten or drunk anything since last night: I'm determined I'm not going to throw up or in any other way disgrace myself.

'You ready to go?'

Grimly, I nod.

'Off you go, then. You'll find she's no different to fly from a standard 152.'

Eyes fixed on the control panel, I breathe slow and deep and find my focus there. Instruments: all present and correct. Seat belts and harness: fastened. Doors closed. Radio and electrical equipment off. Mixture full rich; carb heat off. Prime, and open the throttle a little way. Beacon on, open door and yell 'Clear prop!' Hold brakes, master switch on ... and turn the ignition. A tiny surprised splutter, then she roars into life.

I'm focused on one thing alone, and that is the present moment. I'm focused entirely on what I'm doing right now. Focused on my breathing; on the throaty growl of the engine and the crackle of the radio in my ear as I turn the dial and tune into ground control. I take a deep breath. 'Chandler Ground, Cessna Eight Three Seven Two Five at Falcon Wings...'

Airborne. Not a bump, not a breeze, not a smear in the sky. Perfectly still. And perfectly focused – just on the pleasure of this moment of flight. Not looking ahead, not thinking about what is to come.

Until, quietly, Jesse breaks the silence. 'Go out over the Gila River reservation, away from the practice area. Go up good and high.'

I nod as serenely as I can, ignoring the sudden lurch of my empty stomach.

'You always want to be recovered from the spin by three thousand feet above ground level,' he continues, without inflection. 'For a single turn, assume you'll lose a thousand feet of altitude. For two turns, fifteen hundred feet. For three turns, eighteen hundred feet. You see how the turns get tighter and faster? You don't want to be doing more than three turns. Not at this stage of your aerobatic career. So, let's level off at six thousand feet.'

I clutch at the specific instruction that he's given me, and climb to six thousand feet.

'Good,' Jesse says. 'Now do your clearing turns.' I wheel to the left and then to the right, looking out for other aircraft in all directions and especially down below us. But the skies are clear. Nothing to stop us; nothing to hold us back.

'Tell me the conditions that are necessary for a spin.'

'The wings have to be stalled,' I say, 'and there has to be yaw – the nose has to be pointing left or right, not centred up.'

He nods. 'Good. What'll happen now is very simple. I'm going to talk you through the process. Then I'm going to take us into a spin. All the while you're going to keep your hands and feet on the controls with me so you can feel what I'm doing as I do it. Once we've recovered from this spin and we're back at our target altitude, you're going to do it by yourself. Just like when we were learning stalls.'

Ah, no. Why did he have to remind me of that? That awful day; that awful failure. Stalls were bad enough, but now we're going to spin. We're going to spin and while we're spinning we'll be falling and –

And I have no choice. I have to do this.

The pit of my stomach is all angry rawness as I try to focus on the explanation that he's giving me now, so matter-of-fact and confident, but my brain knows what is coming and wants more than anything in the world to simply shut down. And before I can even begin to pull myself back together, to take any of it in, he's ready to go.

'Okay. First off, I'm going to stall the plane. Put your hands on the control with me, Cat. Concentrate, now.'

I nod, vaguely. I don't want to concentrate now. I just want to close it out. I want it to be over.

'Cat!' he barks. I jump and without thinking I wheel my head around to face him. His eyes are blue. In the entire sweep of human history, I can't imagine that there have ever been eyes so blue. The bluest of blues and here we are again: just me, and Jesse, and the sky. 'Concentrate,' he says, gently now, and one hand lifts away from the control wheel and softly brushes my cheek. I close my eyes for a moment, and inhale the warm spicy smell of him. 'You're going to be fine. You know that, don't you? You've always been fine, deep down. It's not going to be any different now.'

I open my eyes, see the certainty in his, and I hold on to that – hold on to the blue and the clarity and the quiet strength and I know that if I can only hold on to it I won't fall, no matter how much they try to shake me out, no matter how the wind batters me and the sun burns me and the desert wind strips me bare. They can peel me and flay me and lay me out to dry but I'll always have that to hold on to: the quiet core of strength that's visible in his eyes and that simply reflects my own. Yes: my own strength, deep in the heart of me, no matter how I clothe it with uncertainty and fear. Hold on to that, Cat, when you fear that you're going to fall: the quiet core of strength, the pure crystal clarity of this moment and the improbable miracle of flight.

My mouth turns up in a pale approximation of his quirky, lopsided grin. 'Well, get on with it, then,' I say. 'We haven't got all day.'

Our airspeed falls rapidly and he pulls the control wheel all the way up against our stomachs. The nose rises; the usual shudder signals the beginning of a stall. He steps on the left rudder pedal – hard, too hard, and completely contrary to the usual rules. The nose yaws left, the plane pitches down and the desert begins to revolve in front of my eyes. For long silent moments that hang out in space I just can't take it in: it's total disorientation and the thought-stopping shock of seeing the ground where normally it isn't. Then slowly, slowly it all begins to come back into focus and I'm perfectly still and the earth is spinning below me and I can't find the button to make it stop...

Jesse's voice in my ear cuts through the confusion, a handle for my flailing mind to grasp hold of. 'If you released the controls now we would straighten out. But we're not going to do that. Not yet.' And a moment later he adds, 'That's one turn.'

One turn? Only one? A few seconds of time and a thousand feet of altitude but I feel as if I've been turning for ever.

Turning? Me, turning?

And then, finally, I understand. It isn't the world that's turning, it's me. I'm spinning and I'm falling and round and around we go and I'm falling and falling and –

'Two turns,' he says. 'Now we're going to recover.'

– and dimly I register the fact that he's let go of the control wheel – and that I should probably let go too. But I don't want to let go. If I let go I'll keep on falling and I want to grip it even more tightly still but he says sharply, 'Hands off the yoke, Cat!' and against all the odds my hands sink to my lap and he pushes the yoke forward and shoves in the throttle and hits the right rudder pedal hard.

And as suddenly as it all began, the desert stops turning. We heave to the left and over to the right and I can't believe that this tiny plane can take the stress as the desert assumes ever more astonishing configurations below us.

I don't understand what's happening here: I'm lost. One minute we're still diving down and then the airspeed indicator is rocketing up and we're pulling back now and the sky is pressing down on my head, pressing and 'It's okay,' he says, 'we're pulling two, maybe two and a half Gs right now' and my stomach is heaving and my ears are roaring and my head is aching but I'm not going to give in I'm not and I clench my jaw and the sweat is pouring down my skin...

427

… and then slowly, slowly, we're getting back to normal and we're climbing again at a reasonable rate and I'm trying not to gasp for breath and I want to weep, to just weep at the sheer utter insanity of it.

'You okay?'

I nod. What else can I do? What else am I capable of? But before I can start to recover, before I can start to regain whatever fragile equilibrium I might have had as we began, he says, 'Good. Your turn.'

And I'm not going to argue with him this time; I'm not going to fail. If I mess it up then maybe we'll die, but if I die then, so help me, at least I won't die fearful. Think about this, Cat, when you fear that you're going to fall. Fear of death is a function of not-living. There's been enough not-living in your life.

So I bring the power to idle; I raise the nose until the wing is stalled – and then I close my eyes and step down on the left rudder and over we go.

The world crashes to a halt and all I can see is your face. *Dance, Cat! Dance! Just let it go! Loosen up a little, why can't you! Come on – just listen to the music! Can't you feel the rhythm of it? Throw your head back and dance!*

For God's sake, Cat, what is the matter with you? You're not at any risk of falling! But if you keep telling yourself you're going to fall, then you probably will. Stop being so self-defeating, will you? Close your eyes and let it go!

But it's another voice now that slips into my head. Jesse's voice, quiet but urgent.

'Cat! Goddamn it, Cat. I'm not going to do this for you. That's two turns, Cat, and we're into the third. Recover, Cat. Push that control wheel forward. Get us out of this. It's all down to you, Cat. You can live, or you can die. If you want to live, first thing you have to do is let go of pulling back on the control wheel. Let it go, Cat!'

I take a deep sobbing breath and, fighting against every instinct I possess, I push the control wheel forward.

Back on solid ground, I wait while he ties the aircraft down. I watch him, but he doesn't meet my eyes. I watch every move that he makes. The long lean legs in their faded denim jeans; the tendons and muscles in his arms as he threads the rope through the metal rings in the tarmac and knots it. I watch as the fierce afternoon sun lights up his hair like a shiny brass plate. I watch with shining eyes and when he's done and he straightens up I watch as he stands facing me, legs apart and hands on his hips. He watches me back. Watches and doesn't say a word; he just looks. And the laughter bubbles up in me and I throw back my head and laugh and he catches me by the waist and swings me around and I'm reminded of that day – so long ago, it seems now – that I completed my first solo. Except that this time I place my hands on either side of his head and as he lowers me back down to earth I cradle his face in my hands and I close my eyes and I kiss him.

I leave my car at the airport and we drive to Jesse's house in his old black pick-up truck. We are silent throughout the journey, and I find myself in a strange half-aroused half-dreaming state that's different from anything I've ever felt before in my life. I focus my gaze on the road ahead of me, for if I close my eyes the world spins wildly around me still.

He pulls up in the driveway of a long, low house, not too different from my own, painted in the palest shade of cream. Superstition Mountain towers over us, dominates the skyline at the back of the house. Then he opens the door and I follow behind him into the house and a hallway that smells of sagebrush.

He throws his car keys down onto a small wooden chest and he turns to me and somehow, wonderfully, astonishingly, I'm in his arms.

'I'm all sweaty,' I say.

He laughs. 'I don't give a shit.'

The bed is cool and I sink down into the soft white clouds of the down comforter and night falls and crashes and the stars spin through it and I fall along with them but he is there to catch me.

And through the open bedroom window I am certain I can hear the wild laughter of *La Huesera* in the desert beyond.

20

Laura

Now when she heads down to the lochside in the early morning, once the sun peeks over the hill across the water, it's as bright as if it were midday. There's so little night at this time of year, and Laura finds that she misses it. Which is a surprise to her: she loved the constant summer daylight, all those years ago when she first lived here. But now she feels slightly dislocated, as if she's lost track, somehow, of time. No – more than time: you lose track of the rhythms of the day, and of the seasons. You go to bed in the daylight and you wake up in the daylight, and you never see the moon or the stars. Nothing to anchor you; nothing to orient you.

And her friend the seal seems to have disappeared along with the night. A creature of dusk and dawn she was, and Laura misses her too. But still she makes her way down to the shore on her twice-daily vigils. She's a part of the place now; a part of her resides under this old rowan tree and maybe always will. Just as she told Cat, she finds herself at peace here. In the sheer simplicity of its beauty and its seasons and in the relentless turning of the tide she finds peace.

Cat. Laura smiles. There was a note from Cat yesterday. A proper little letter, not just a postcard. 'I'm in love,' Cat said in the letter. 'No – really in love, this time. His name's Jesse, and he's a pilot. I think you'll like him.' A pilot? Her Cat, and a pilot? Of course Laura would like him. And even if she didn't like him she'd learn to like him, for Cat's sake. And maybe she'll even get the chance to do that – to see if she can like him –

because the piece of news that Cat saved till the end of the letter – the piece of news that makes her heart sing now – is that Cat is coming home. Coming home, and bringing her Jesse with her.

Cat is coming home. Cat, home. Cat, home. She tries out the two words, so strange in their combination; she pictures the jug that sits on her mantelpiece and she dreams of being a mother again. She dreams and she smiles and she whispers to the gentle rippling waves of the loch, over and over again, like a mantra: 'All that is lost may one day be found. All that is lost…'

Yes, her heart is singing … or is it breaking? A sharp pain – like all the other sharp pains, only sharper this time, and her eyes blur for a moment, her vision fades and she gasps and grits her teeth and looks out at the loch

and she's there again. There again, the seal, staring at her, big blue eyes filled with sorrow, and a strange keening coming from somewhere and the seal nods at her

nods three times and disappears below the waves and

Laura sighs and closes her eyes.

21
Cat

The telephone rings. Warm in my bed, I think of ignoring it – after all, isn't that what answering machines are for? – but decide to answer it anyway. It's probably just some salesman who'll keep on ringing and keep on bugging me if I don't get it over with and put him off. I roll out of Jesse's arms and grapple sleepily for the receiver.

'Hello?'

'Hello? Hello, is that Catriona?'

It's the accent that I register first. The accent and the distance and instantly I know that this is Meg and before she says another word I know what has happened. I know and before she is halfway through her sentence the receiver slides out of my hand and falls to the duvet and there's a sound now as well, a strange sound rising up from my stomach – the monster again, after so long? – and it growls and it roars and it roars in my ears and it howls and I'm gasping for breath again, gasping for breath and Jesse is up now, up and clutching my shoulders and in the distance, way over there in the distance, in the hot dry sand of the desert and blowing away, further and further away like a piece of tumbleweed in a squally burst of summer wind I hear him say 'Cat! What is it, Cat?' and then he picks up the receiver and way way out in the distance I hear him speaking and 'Yes, I see,' he is saying, 'I see.'

The past clings to you, like a skin. The trick is to learn how to shed it. How to just sit back and let it happen. Let the water rub your skin away; let the hot desert sun strip you back to the very bones. To the very essence of the story.

To the two of us, at last; alone in this tiny Cessna.

See the mountains stretching out there ahead of us, hard triangular edges protruding through the mist? See how they come into focus as we approach them – how they change from misty monochrome to full, glorious colour? They're so very different from the mountains around Phoenix. There are trees here, for one thing: geometric strips of forestry land stretching out across the landscape like great furry caterpillars. And there's water – lochans, scattered through the mountains like pieces of broken mirror, reflecting back the sky. Look down there now, as the earth slips away beneath us. Look at her; see how beautiful she is. See how she curves and bubbles and flows, raising herself up to the sky as she spreads on out to the west.

Yes, it's so very different from Phoenix. And it's Phoenix that is my home now, with its hard edges and hurting sunlight and everything crisp and clear. Home is no longer this green, milky, watery land. Phoenix and the desert and Jesse. That's my home, and that's where I'll stay. Right where I crash-landed, all those years ago, just one more stage in my perpetual flight from you. My exodus; my hejira. Do you see how far I ran that time? All the way to Arizona. Do you see, all those years, how I measured my progress in the distance I placed between us?

Ah, but all that I was, I chose to become in complete opposition to you. Because it's a strong, tight cord that binds us together. And some connections can't be broken, no matter how hard you try.

We're right in the heart of the mountains now, and looking down into ink-blot lochs so clear you can almost see the brown trout playing on the bottom. But look over there – a solitary rain cloud. It floats in the sunlight, just like a mirage. Shall we fly on towards it, shall we fly, you and I, as we've so often done in the past? *Cat,* you would say, your face drawn and suffering. *I don't understand why you're always so angry with me.* Yes, the sky ahead is changing now, as it so easily does on this western Highland shore. And sooner or later the blue will transform to the colour of ashes as storm clouds build up in the west.

A sudden sharp gust of wind and – what's happening now? No – no, it's okay. There's no need to jump: it's just a little turbulence as we pass through the mountains. Just a little shudder, just a small drop of the nose. It startled me, that's all. You needn't worry – I'm quite in control. I've always been in control, haven't I? One of us had to be. Just another gust of wind, that's all it is – slithering under her belly and nudging up her nose. No, that's not sweat on my brow – I'm past all that, now. I got my licence, remember? I learned how to fly. I learned how to fall. Nothing you can do now will change that – nothing you can say. *Scaredy-Cat! Why won't you jump?* Another sudden jolt; the turbulence increasing in intensity now. Do you want to be on the ground? It just isn't an option; there's nowhere out here we could land. Everything's fine now; I'm doing just fine. Nothing is going to paralyse me now – not even the memory of you dancing in your red shoes, red shoes carrying you away into the dark forest and never stopping, just dancing on and on and out of control…

… until, at the point where you finally took back control, you died.

You died.

I am eight years old and my mummy is dead. She's lying on the sofa so pale and still and I can't wake her up no matter how hard I try. Tears trickle down my face even though I'm a good girl and good girls don't cry. But I'm alone in the house with her, it's the middle of the night, and it's dark – so dark. I'm frightened; I'm not feeling well and my mummy smells funny and she won't wake up. I swallow hard; I can't cry. I have to be brave and take care of her. I take a deep breath and I swallow my tears and ignore the strange spasms in my throat. I sit down beside her and I keep watch till morning; I hold off our demons alone.

So many small deaths, over the years. I thought I had mourned the loss of you years ago. And now I don't know whether I'm crying for you or for myself; for the years that I suffered you or for a future that's empty of you. Because who will I measure myself against now? Because I have loved you as fiercely as I have raged at you.

Because no other love can compete.

Do you see the house now, over there on the brae? The whitewashed stone walls gleam white in the last golden rays before the rain clouds come to veil the face of the sun. It's time now – it's time. We're over the loch and I'm flying as low as I dare. I pull back the power and slow us right down, then reach out and open the window by my side. Air rushes into the cabin; I can't hear you any more over the whistle of the wind. I take the strong brown paper bag from the seat beside me – yes, I know: it's not quite as elegant as the urn, but the window will only open a crack. I open the bag and I shake out the contents.

The wind takes you; a pale brown stream of ashes drifts down and settles on the surface of the water like sea-foam. The bag remains for a moment, flutters wildly against the palm of my hand like the wings of a captive bird.

I let go.

Acknowledgements

Big thanks are due to Irene Barrall and Helen Conway for being such devoted and enthusiastic readers when this book was being conceived, way back in 2004. And my gratitude always to former fellow MA Creative Writing students at Manchester Metropolitan University, for constructive comments and support: Jenny Reeve, Jenny Westby, Neil Bunting, Siobhan Fennel, Sylvia Horner and Taneth Russell. Thanks to Nick Royle and Margaret Graham for encouragement, and Mandy Haggith for the final read-through before publication in 2008.

I'm grateful to Hannah Macdonald and Charlotte Cole at September Publishing for re-releasing this title, twenty years after I first began to write it, and to my agent, Jane Graham Maw, for everything.

It's always hard to know whether to thank or strangle my one-time colleague Linc Lewis for the entirely ridiculous suggestion, on a twin-prop plane somewhere in the north-east of America on a very stormy day in the spring of 1999, that I should learn to fly to overcome my fear of flying. And for helping to nurse me through the process and sharing the pleasure when, a year later, I finally got that pink slip.

Thanks to my husband, David Knowles, for climbing out of his fast jet for a while, sweeping me off into stormy skies in a tiny Cessna, and showing me how all that flying malarkey worked in Britain.

And most of all, thanks to my mother – for sharing some stories, educating me on life in the 1940s and '50s, making me laugh (and sometimes cry) with her memories, and for always believing that I could fly. On October 19, 2021, I let her go.